A SONG OF SIXPENCE

and

A POCKETFUL OF RYE

A SONG
OF SIXPENCE

and

A POCKETFUL
OF RYE

*

A. J. CRONIN

THE
COMPANION BOOK CLUB
LONDON

This edition is published by
The Hamlyn Publishing Group Ltd.
and is issued by arrangement with
William Heinemann Ltd.

*Made and printed in Great Britain
for the Companion Book Club
by Odhams (Watford) Ltd.*
SBN/S.600771318
SBN/D.600871312
3.71

CONTENTS

*

A SONG
OF SIXPENCE

ONE

EVERY EVENING at six o'clock a sense of expectancy filled
the house, brightening the long, vague and dreamy afternoon. As I went into the front room my mother, moving
about the kitchen preparing our supper, began to sing. It
was something about a miller's daughter who lay down and
died. She sang these sad Scottish songs in so lively a manner
and with such natural cheerfulness they sounded gay. I
stood on a hassock to look out of the window. Although I
was to go to school next week I still had need of the hassock.

The road to the village station was empty except for Mac-
intosh's dog, asleep in the shade of the sycamore tree outside
the smithy. Beyond the station with its beds of sweet william
and yellow calceolarias lay the wide sweep of deserted shore,
and beyond that the Clyde estuary, enlivened at present by
a white-funnelled paddle steamer, a Broomielaw boat,
going downstream. Presently a figure appeared, not the
expected one but still a friend—indeed my only friend,
Maggie, or as she was called most unjustly by the 'bad' boys,
Mad Maggie, a big awkward girl of thirteen who, festooned
with milk cans from Snoddie's farm, was now squeezing
through the bars of the shut gates of the level crossing. This
was a short cut so strictly forbidden me I watched reprovingly as she dragged up the road on the start of her evening
milk round. Passing our house, one of four little villas
primly in a row, she saw me at the window and, with a dull
clank of cans, waved an arm in greeting.

I had begun to wave back when there came a shrill
whistle. My eyes, diverted from Maggie, picked up a plume
of steam beneath which a dark maroon serpent snaked
slowly round the curve of the railway line. Painfully, as
though out of breath, it puffed to the single platform. In the
year 1900 only the slowest North British trains stopped at
Ardencaple village.

As sometimes happened, my father was the only passenger
to get off. He walked briskly, with the step of a man who
likes to get home, an alert figure, conveying, even at that
distance, an unmistakable and distinctive sense of style. He

was wearing his brown suit, with dark brown shoes, a brown bowler hat with a curled brim, and a short fawn coat. As he drew near, the dog looked up and, being unaware of the prejudices of the village, raised the dust with its tail. Then I saw, with increased anticipation, that Father was carrying a parcel. Quite often when visiting his customers in Winton he would bring home to Mother and me something for supper that rarely failed to excite us: perhaps a bunch of choice Colmar grapes, or a cut of Tay salmon, or even a jar of Canton green ginger, exotics which seemed to indicate that Father was himself not averse to having good things to eat and which, of course, went so far beyond the modest standards of our daily life that, unveiling them casually with one eyebrow critically raised, he secretly enjoyed our startled looks.

The door clicked open and Mother, plucking off her apron, ran to meet and hug him, an action I did not altogether approve but which unfailingly took place. Father took off his coat and put it on a hanger—he was always careful of his clothes—then came into the kitchen, lifted me up in a detached manner and set me down again. Mother put the soup on the table. It was Scotch broth, a dish Father particularly liked but of which, unless pressed, I would eat only the peas, arranging them first in a circle on the rim of my plate. There was boiled beef to follow. Against the native custom—and this was only one of our many failures to conform to the strict usages of the community in which we lived—we took our main meal at night, since Father, on the move all day, seldom had the opportunity for more than a sandwich. Meanwhile, with an air that I felt to be unusual, even slightly strained, he was slowly unwrapping his parcel.

'Well, Grace,' he said. 'It is all settled.'

Mother stopped ladling the broth. She had turned pale. 'No, Conor!'

He looked at her with a smile, affectionate yet ironical, and touched up the ends of his short blond moustache.

'I had the final meeting with Hagemann this afternoon. We've signed our agreement. He's taking the boat back to Holland tonight.'

'Oh, Con dear, you can't mean it.'

'See for yourself. There's the first sample. Before your eyes.'

He placed a round glass container on the table, sat down calmly, took the soup plate from her unresistant hand and picked up his spoon. I thought that Mother, unbelievably, was going to cry. She sat down weakly. Dimly aware that something terrible, a crisis, had occurred, disturbing the peace of my home, I could not take my eyes off that round glass bottle. It contained a yellowish powder and had a printed label with a red, blue and white flag. With a great effort Mother handed me my soup.

'But, Conor,' she said pleadingly. 'You're doing so well with Murchison's.'

'You mean I have done well for *them*.'

'Of course. At the same time, they are such sound people.'

'I have nothing against Murchison's, my dear Gracie, but I'm tired of wearing my boots out selling their flour. I've given them five good years of my life. Mind you, they've been fair with me. In fact old Murchison advised me to take the agency.'

'But, Conor . . . we are so comfortable now . . . and so safe.'

Father raised that single eyebrow, but not on this occasion to present Colmar grapes. This mysterious bottle must surely be a bombshell.

'We shall never get anywhere by remaining comfortable and safe. Now, do eat something like a good lass, and I'll give you the details later.' He leaned forward and patted her hand.

'I'm too upset.' Mother got up and placed the boiled beef on the table.

Unaware that I had not touched my broth, she removed my plate without scolding me. Father, with his invariable air of aplomb, carved the beef, calmly and elegantly. With his slight figure, his russet hair and warm complexion, his hazel eyes and even white teeth just showing beneath his curled moustache, he was a handsome man. I admired him intensely and was often spellbound by the unpredictable and daring audacities he would 'bring off' without turning a hair. But in the full meaning of the word I did not love him. I belonged entirely to my mother. Soft, timid, kept back by a chain of illnesses that began with mumps and ended with diphtheria—I could still taste the carbolic glycerine Dr Duthie had used to paint my throat—and forced by the remarkable circumstances of our life into ties with Mother and my home that were especially close and emotional, I fully merited that deplorable epithet, a mother's boy. Yet who would not have been with such a mother, at that time not more than twenty-four, rather short and soft in figure, with regular features, soft brown hair, eyes of a deep gentian blue, and in all her movements a kind of natural grace which, to my childish mind, seemed to explain her name. But above all, it was her look of sweetness that held me captive.

Now, with her chin cupped in her hand, she was listening to Father, who alone was doing justice to the beef.

'You must admit,' he was saying reasonably. 'The mustard, thank you dear . . . that I could not miss this chance. We are on the eve of a revolution in the baking industry. The old-fashioned barm method is on its way o-u-t, out.' When Father wished to be impressive he would often spell a word before he said it.

'But, Conor, the bread we get is perfectly good.'

Father, chewing with relish, shook his head.

'You don't know how often I've seen barm go sour. Bubbling out of the casks. And a whole batch of loaves completely spoiled. Ruined. After all, it's only distiller's scum. The new process will make cheaper and better bread. And it won't go wrong. Think of the opportunity, Grace, with my established connections. Why, I know every baker in the West. I'll be first in the field. And working for myself.'

Mother was being persuaded.

'You're quite sure of Mr Hagemann?'

Father nodded with his mouth full.

'He's straight as a die. I can import from him in Rotterdam on most favourable terms. Besides, he's advanced half the money to give me a start. Would he if he didn't believe in me?'

A faint gleam of reassurance appeared in Mother's eye succeeded by a remote look of expectancy. When supper was over she did not rise to clear the table. Nor did Father follow his usual habit of devoting half an hour to me—an elastic period often extended by my importunities—before I went to bed. Beyond the short stroll he occasionally took before retiring, Father never went out at night. After a long day spent in the society of men who were his friends he seemed perfectly content to be, as he put it, at his own fireside. Besides, there was no inducement for him to go out.

Though he had bare acquaintances, he had never sought, let alone made, a friend in the village. Ardencaple was for him, indeed for all of us, a hostile camp.

Our evening communion was partly educational—it was he who had taught me my letters, and he would instruct me to read out, for our mutual benefit, recondite facts from his favourite compendium, *Pears' Cyclopaedia*—but in the main, and especially since my illness, he had sought merely to entertain me. With an amazing fertility of imagination, he invented and related a whole series of fascinating adventures in which a young protagonist of precisely my age, small and rather delicate, but intrepid almost beyond belief, performed feats of outstanding bravery in tropic jungles or on desert islands amongst primitive tribes and man-eating savages, meanwhile interpolating from time to time side remarks to my mother which related usually to the natural appendages and accoutrements of the dark-skinned female members of the tribe and which, while I did not in the least understand their significance, made her laugh.

Tonight, however, as my parents continued to be absorbed in talk, I perceived that the prospect of my being regaled with a cannibal feast had faded and, meeting Father's eye when he paused in what he was saying, I suddenly demanded, in the tones of one wronged and neglected:

'What is in the bottle?'

He smiled with unusual benignancy.

'It is yeast, Laurence. To be specific, Hagemann's Royal Dutch Yeast.'

'Yeast?' I repeated, in bewilderment.

'Just so.' He nodded graciously. 'A living substance composed of innumerable living cells. Yes, a form of life itself, one might say, an organism that grows, buds, turns starch into sugar, sugar into alcohol and carbon dioxide gas, and so leavens our staff of life. Prepared,' Father went on, in his best vein, 'in mineral salt-sugar solution—as is my Royal Dutch Yeast—a modern technique far superior to the grain mash method, it offers a unique opportunity for introducing an entirely new process that will reorganize the Scottish baking industry.'

Father sounded as though he himself had discovered yeast and for long afterwards I believed he had. His exposition, obviously prepared, left me speechless. Mother, too, seemed

13

to find it overpowering or at least quite enough for me at present. She rose and, although the clock on the mantel-piece assured me it was well before my usual hour, suggested in a tone not to be disputed that I should go to bed.

This was ordinarily a lengthy process, prolonged by every pretext by which I sought to detain my mother, and complicated by all sorts of fetishes and rituals that I had built for my own protection and which, while unworthy of enumeration, may be imagined from my first action, which was to satisfy myself that a boa-constrictor was not concealed beneath my bed. Tonight, however, the advent of the yeast distracted me from all my ceremonies and shortened everything in a highly disagreeable manner.

Even when I was in bed and Mother had said good night, leaving my door ajar according to custom, this strange substance, mysterious invader of our home, kept fermenting in my mind. I could not get to sleep. As I lay with closed eyes I saw the yeast working in the flask, bubbling and frothing until it burst upwards in a swelling yellow cloud, overhanging our house, taking the form of the genie from the bottle in one of my father's stories. I stirred uneasily. Was this the beginning of a dream of some strange vision of the future?

Although they spoke in low voices, the resumed conversation of my parents came in snatches through the unshut door of my narrow bedroom. From time to time I heard impressive and disturbing phrases: 'away from this confounded village' . . . 'take up your music again' . . . 'he could go to Rockcliff, like Terence' . . . And finally just before I fell asleep I heard Father declare, in his most serious and decided tone:

'You wait, Gracie, we'll show your folks . . . and my lot too . . . that they can't go on treating us like this. One day they'll make it up to you. And soon.'

TWO

FOR WEEKS I had longed to go to school, an adventure skilfully built up for me in the most glowing terms by my father, and deferred only by my susceptibility to the commonest germs. But now that the day had arrived, my state of mind verged on panic. As Mother put the finishing touches to me, buttoning up my new blue serge trousers and pulling down my jersey, I begged her with tears in my eyes not to send me. She laughed and kissed me.

'You'll be all right with Maggie. See, here's your new satchel. Strap it on your shoulders like a real boy.'

The satchel, although empty, did help to brace me. I had begun to feel stronger when a knock at the back door made me jump.

Maggie was there, standing on the doorstep, with her usual expression, humble and lowering, her tangled locks falling over eyes which had that dull yet appealing look seen in young Highland cattle. She was the daughter of the village washerwoman, a known slattern whose husband had long since made his escape from her abusive tongue and who, while bewailing the lot of her deserted bairn, made a drudge of her. Dressed in an old cut-down tweed skirt my mother had given her, with a darn on the knee of one stocking, Maggie had few outward signs of grace. Self-acknowledged to be stupid, and with a heavy, depressed air that bespoke overwork and ill-usage at home, she was mercilessly teased with shouts of 'Daft Maggie' by the boys of the village, who nevertheless were wary of her, for she had a strong arm and a sure aim with a round pebble, gathered from the shore and always handy in her pocket. But to me she was both confidante and mentor. I truly trusted her, as did my mother, who liked Maggie and was good to her in many ways. Despite the numerous duties imposed upon her —and after school hours one rarely saw her without a bundle of laundry or her armour of milk cans which, after her round, she must scald and scour at the farm before her final task of feeding the hens—she had been during the long summer holidays a kind of nursemaid to me, taking me for walks in the afternoon during my periods of convalescence. Our favourite pilgrimage took us along the shore, passing on the way an isolated, sadly broken-down little cottage with a rotted green trellis, misnamed Rosebank, where, to my everlasting disgrace, it appeared that I had been born. How so momentous an event could have occurred in so deplorable an edifice I could not comprehend, yet presumably it had, for as we passed Rosebank, Maggie would launch into a fearsome yet compelling description, derived doubtless from her mother, of my

15

arrival in this world on a dark and dreary Sabbath night when it had rained torrents and the tide had risen so high that my father, desperately seeking Dr Duthie with his little black bag, had almost failed to reach the village.

'And to beat all,' Maggie turned her commiserating gaze upon me, 'ye came into the wurrld the wrong way round.'

'The wrong way! But how, Maggie?'

'Not head first. Feet first.'

'Was that bad, Maggie?' I demanded, petrified.

She nodded in sombre affirmation.

After this humiliating disclosure Maggie would revive me by taking me farther along the estuary to the Erskine Rocks, where, enjoining me not to tell my mother, who would have been shocked to hear that her spoiled darling was upsetting his stomach with such 'trash', we gathered fresh mussels which she roasted, nut-sweet, on a driftwood fire. The novelty of this repast alone delighted me, since I was, if anything overnourished; but for Maggie, sadly ill-fed, it was welcome sustenance, and by way of dessert, taking off her battered boots and the long black stockings, one or other of which despite the darns usually sported a hole, she would wade into the grey waters of the firth and, feeling in the muddy sand with her toes, uncover little fluted white cockles which she devoured like oysters, raw and quivering.

'But they're living, Maggie,' I protested, dismayed at the pain these innocent bivalves must suffer under her sharp teeth.

'They don't feel anything,' she assured me calmly. 'If you bite them quick. Now let's play shop.'

Maggie invented all sorts of games and was full of country skills. She could make a willow whistle, fashion intricately woven harvest plaits of a pattern that my fingers could never master, and magically unfold tight little paper boats that we sailed down the Gielston burn. She could also sing, and in a hoarse but tuneful voice would offer me current favourites like 'Goodbye, Dolly Gray' and 'The Honeysuckle and the Bee'.

But the game Maggie liked best undoubtedly was 'shop' and she never tired of it. When we had collected and set out on the shore our varied symbols, chips of shells, seeds of wild fennel, burdock tips and sea pinks, white sand, bladders of seaweed, marbled pebbles, each representing a different commodity, Maggie would assume the airs and responsibilities of the proprietress while I became the customer. This gave to Maggie, so poor and neglected, a sense of security, even of wealth. Looking round her shop with the pride of possession, counting her store of good things—tea, sugar, coffee, flour, butter, ham and of course black-striped peppermint balls—she could forget those days when she must stave off hunger with salt cockles, a raw turnip lifted from one of Snoddie's fields or even the skins from the dog-rose and hawthorn berries that we called 'hips and haws'.

We were happy together, and I felt her fondness for me until, glancing upwards suddenly during our game, I would find her eyes bent upon me with the wondering expression of one whose attention is drawn repeatedly to some incomprehensible singularity. I knew then what must come, for presently in a tone half puzzled, half commiserating she would soliloquize:

'When I look at you, Laurie, I still can't credit it. I mean, you're not much, but you don't seem any different from *us*. And your mother and father too, they're so nice you would never dream they were *that*.'

I hung my head. Maggie, in her blundering, good-natured way, had once again uncovered one of the hidden shames that seared my early years and which, without further pretence, must be confessed. I was, alas, a Roman Catholic. A boy bound hand and foot to the grinding chariot of the Pope, miserable acolyte of the Scarlet Woman, burner of candles and incense, potential kisser of the big toe of St Peter. Not only so, my parents and I were the sole adherents of that reviled religion, and worse, the only ones ever to have established themselves in the staunchly, exclusively true-blue Protestant village of Ardencaple. We were as conspicuously out of place in that tight little community as would have been a family of Zulus. Equally, we were outcasts.

Whatever the public attitude towards my father, which he delighted to provoke rather than to appease, I suffered nothing beyond that certain pitying or even sympathetic curiosity bestowed upon an oddity. Nevertheless, on this Monday morning when I faced the prospect of school, this had its part in lowering my morale. And when, after final admonitions from Mother, Maggie grasped my hand firmly and we set off up the road to the village, my mind was in a dither. A horse was being shoed in the smithy amidst an enticing fume of burnt hoof, yet I scarcely noticed it. The windows of the village store, against which I liked to press my nose, investigating the rich display of boiled sweets, peppermint oddfellows, slim jim and apple tarts, were passed unseen. It was a dolorous way, made more harrowing by Maggie's low-toned recital of the fearful punishments exacted by the schoolmaster Mr Rankin, whom she designated by the name Pin.

'He's a cripple,' she kept deploring, with a shake of her head. 'And a stickit minister. Nor more nor that! But he's a terror with the tause.'

Although we went slowly, only too soon did we reach the school.

This was a smallish old red-brick building with an open yard of beaten, stony earth in front, and here, but for Maggie, I should certainly have run away. In this playground a mimic battle was being waged. Boys darted about, struggled, shouted, kicked and fought; girls, flailing with ropes, skipped and shrieked; caps were torn from heads and sent skimming through the air, tackety boots slid and scraped, sparking living fire from the stones, the din was ear-splitting. And suddenly noticing me, the biggest of the 'bad' boys let out a wild and ribald yell: 'Look wha's here. *The wee Pope!*

This sudden elevation to the throne of the Vatican, far from sustaining me, produced in my innards a further apprehensive sinking. In a moment I should be surrounded by a crowd seeking to exact more from me than my apostolic blessing. But from this and other dangers, pressing through with her sharp elbows combatively extended, Maggie protected me until suddenly a clanging quelled the tumult, and the schoolmaster appeared, bell in hand, on the steps of the entrance.

Undoubtedly this was Pin, his right leg deformed and sadly shorter than the other, supported by a twelve-inch peg fixed to a queer little boot by an iron stirrup, the lower end capped with rubber. Surprisingly, he did not strike me as alarming. He was, in fact, though given to sudden explosions and choleric rappings on his desk with his knuckles, a mild, prosy, defeated little man of about fifty with steel-rimmed spectacles and a short pointed beard, seen always in a shiny black bobtailed suit, a celluloid dickey and a tucked-in black tie, who in his youth had studied for the ministry but, by reason of his deformity and a tendency to stammer, had failed repeatedly in trial sermons and become in the end a melancholy example of that supreme Scottish failure, the 'stickit minister' turned dominie.

However, it was not to him that I was delivered. Pushing away from the main turbulent stream, Maggie finally entrusted me to the assistant mistress in the lowest class, where with some twenty others, many younger than myself, I was given a slate and seated on one of the front benches. Already I felt better, since I had recognized our teacher—a warm-looking girl with soft brown eyes and an encouraging smile —as one of the two daughters of Mr Archibald Grant, who kept the store. Her younger sister Polly never failed to give me a butterscotch drop when I went to the store on errands for my mother.

'Now, children, I'm glad to see you back after the holidays and to welcome the new pupils,' Miss Grant began, and I thrilled, fancying that her smile dwelt on me. 'As Lady Meikle will be making her usual opening-day visit to the school this morning, I expect you all to be on your best behaviour. Now answer your names as I make out the register.'

When she called out 'Laurence Carroll' I imitated the others with a 'Present, miss', which, however, was so uncertain as to suggest that I doubted my own identity. Nevertheless it was accepted, and after we had all given our names and Miss Grant had entered them in the big book on her desk she set us to work. The class was at different stages. Soon one section was droning out the two-times table, another copying sums from the blackboard on their slates, while a third struggled with block letters of the alphabet. To me all this appeared such manifest child's play that my earlier apprehension began to fade and to be replaced by a tingling consciousness of my own worth. What infants, not to know a B from a D! And who, amongst these older boys, had dipped, like me, into the mysteries of *Pears' Cyclopaedia*, with the picture of the tramp on the frontispiece announcing that for five years he had used no other soap? Surrounded by such evidence of juvenile ignorance, I felt the power of my superior knowledge, the distinction of my new clothes; I wanted to display my talents, to shine.

The screech of the slate pencils had not long begun before the door was flung open and the command given.

'Rise, children.'

As we clattered to our feet Pin appeared and deferentially ushered into the classrom a stiff, self-important, overdressed little woman with a bust so swelling and aggressive as to give her, in conjunction with the tuft of feathers on her hat, a marked resemblance to a pouter pigeon. I gazed at her in awe.

Lady Meikle was the widow of a Winton corset manufacturer who, behind the blameless but intriguing slogan: 'Ladies, we use only the finest natural whalebone', plastered on the hoardings of every railway station—an advertisement that to me ranked in interest equally with 'The Pickwick, the Owl, and the Waverley Pen, they come as a boon and a blessing to men'—had advanced to considerable wealth, then, after a long term as provost of Levenford, to a knighthood, a distinction that had induced him to purchase and retire to a large property in the vicinity of Ardencaple. Here he had leisure to indulge his hobby of cultivating orchids and tropical plants while his spouse lost no time in assuming the duties and asserting the prerogatives of the lady of the manor, although with her down-to-earth ways and lapses into broad Scots idiom she was not, and freely admitted this to the manner born. Yet Lady Whalebone, as my father named her, was a decent woman, generous to Ardencaple—she had given the new village hall—and charitable to the entire county. She had moreover a characteristic grim sense of humour and a strong dash of sentiment, since besides giving her lamented husband a magnificent tombstone, replete with many awesome urns, she faithfully maintained and had indeed made famous the orchid collection he had instituted before his decease. Strange though it may appear, while I had never exchanged a word with so exalted a personage, I had good reason to be familiar with her estate in all its extent, with its woods and river, the avenue a mile long winding through the park between giant rhododendrons to the big house with its enormous adjacent conservatory.

'Be seated, bairns.' She swept forward. 'This room is unco' stuffy. Open a window.'

Miss Grant hurriedly complied while her ladyship, keeping a formidable eye upon us, conferred with Pin, who, bending forward, his deformed limb drawn back, half concealed behind the sound leg—a posture I soon saw to be habitual—made submissive murmurs of acquiescence. Then she addressed us, in the broadest Doric, beginning thus:

'Bairns, ye're a' young and fushionless, but I hope and pray that so far ye have come to nae harm or tummelt into evil ways. Now ye a' ken the interest I take in the village and in a' of *you*, for what ye are, or may be, so see ye pay heed to what I'm about to say.'

She continued in this fashion at considerable length, exhorting us to work diligently, to improve ourselves and to maintain always the highest standards of good behaviour and moral conduct, implying that it would go hard with us here and in the hereafter if we did not. Her address completed, she pursed her lips and favoured us with a dignified yet half-humorous smile in which might have been detected a trace of slyness.

'As yet ye ken nothing. Virgin soil, that's what ye are, virgin soil. But I am going to test your nat'ral intelligence to see if ye have any gumption or for that matter anything in your heads at a'. Miss Grant, a pencil.'

The pencil, yellow in colour, was immediately presented, and poising it before us for a moment, she threw it, with a dramatic gesture, to the floor. We held our breaths.

'Now,' she resumed impressively. 'Ye have no hands. None of ye have hands. *But I wish that pencil picked up.*'

Whatever prompted this extravagant experiment—perhaps she had been visiting one of her many charities, a home for paralytics in Ardfillan—the result was silence, dead silence. The class was stumped. Suddenly inspiration struck me. As in a daze, I got up, weak from my own boldness, tottered into the public gaze and, prostrating myself before the yellow pencil, snatched at it with my teeth. But the pencil was round and smooth. It escaped my feeble incisors, shot far ahead on the dusty and uneven floor. I followed, crawling face down, like a tracking Indian. Again I tried and again failed. The pursuit continued. Every eye remained riveted upon me. Now the pencil had discovered a crevice between the floor-boards. I nudged it forward with my chin, coaxed it to a favourable position, only to see it roll gently into a deeper crack beside the blackboard where the dust of chalk had already fallen. But my blood was up. Sticking out my tongue, I licked my quarry from its hold, then before it started to roll bit hard and true. The class gave a long sigh of applause as, whitened by chalk dust, my

nose skinned and raw, I staggered to my feet, with the
pencil impaled, clenched between my jaws.

'Well done!' cried Lady Whalebone, clapping her hands
enthusiastically, then placing one upon my head. 'Ye're a
verra clever wee laddie.'

I reddened all over, bursting with pride. To be commended thus by the lady of the manor before my teacher,
before the schoolmaster and, best of all, my classmates!
And on my first day at school. A very clever boy. What joy
to tell my mother.

Meanwhile, as Miss Grant dusted me off, her ladyship,
with the air of a phrenologist, still maintained a benevolent
hand upon my cranium.

'How old are ye?'

'Six years, m'am.'

'Ye're unco' small for six.'

'Yes, m'am.' I yearned to tell her of the illnesses, almost
fatal, that had dwarfed me, probably for life, but before I
could proceed she went on, encouragingly, a real patroness.

'Ye must sup your porridge, with plenty of milk. Not
skim, mind ye. And never turn up your nose at the staff of
life. Ye ken what I mean by the staff of life?'

'Oh, yes, ma'am.' Hot with triumph, conscious of my
superior knowledge, recollecting my father's use of the
same phrase in connection with the bottle, I gazed at her
brightly, answered confidently, loud and clear: 'Hagemann's Royal Dutch Yeast!'

A timid titter, swelling uncontrollably to a shout of
laughter, rose from the class. Utterly dismayed, I saw my
patroness's face alter, approbation supplanted by a heavy
frown. Her grip on my skull tightened.

'Are ye darin' to make fun of me, boy?'

'Oh no, m'am, no!'

She studied me narrowly for a long moment while my
insides seemed to liquefy. Then, repudiating me, she
removed her hand with, at the same time, a forward thrust
that impelled me forcibly towards my seat.

'Go! I see I was mistaken. Ye are nothing but a doited
clown.'

Humbled, disgraced for life, in fact once again an outcast,
I sat for the rest of the morning with bowed head.

On the way home, seeking the hand of my true protector,
blinking water from my eyes, I mourned:

'It's no use, Maggie. I'm no good at anything, just a doited clown.'

'Ay,' Maggie answered with despondent satire, apparently having had a bad morning in her own class. 'We're a braw pair.'

THREE

DESPITE Mother's misgivings, and the public humiliation it had caused me, the business of the Royal Dutch Yeast had made a most auspicious start. Undoubtedly the opportunity was there, and my father, naturally clever, with a sharp and far-seeing business eye, was the very man to seize it. His intimate knowledge of the baking trade, the connections he had established throughout the West of Scotland during his five years as a salesman for Murchison's, his attractive personality and easy manner, which he could attune exactly to the status of each customer and which made him generally popular, above all the aplomb with which he would fling off his jacket, tie on a white apron and actually demonstrate the new process in the bakehouse, all marked him for success.

Evidence of this was manifest after the first few months, in a family expedition to Winton when Father, having shown us with pride his new little office in the Caledonia Building, took us to a matinée of *Aladdin* at the Theatre Royal and afterwards to the famous Thistle Restaurant. Always an open-handed man, he was more than usually generous that Christmas. In addition to a new winter outfit which did not greatly interest me, I received a sledge of that superb variety, equipped with a steering-bar, known as a Flexible Flyer, while for Mother there arrived one December day from Winton in a big two-horse van something she must have longed for ever since her marriage, a gift whose unexpectedness, since Father characteristically had not breathed a word of its coming, doubled and redoubled Mother's joy. An upright piano. Not one of these yellowish cottage affairs with plush insets, such as we marched to in school, that twanged like an old banjo, but a brand-new, solid, ebony-black instrument, bearing the magic name Bluthner, with twin gilt candlesticks and shining ivory keys that on the merest touch emitted deep and vibrant chords.

Mother, still quite dazed, sat down on the revolving stool that had come with the piano and, while I stood at her shoulder, after running her hands up and down the keyboard with a discerning mobility that amazed me, remarking at the same time, 'Oh dear, Laurie, my fingers are all thumbs,' she paused for a moment to collect her thoughts, then began to play. So vivid is my recollection of this scene I remember even the piece she played. It was Chaminade's 'Danse d'Écharpes'. To say that I was stunned and spellbound is no exaggeration, not only by the delicious sounds that fell upon my eardrums, but because of the miracle that Mother, whom I had never before heard strike a note and who from loyalty to Father—unable until then to afford a piano—had never introduced the subject in my presence, should after these silent years suddenly produce this unsuspected and accomplished talent and enchant me with a sparkling stream of music. The two porters, having each received a shilling and already with their caps on, in the lobby, had been arrested on their way out. Now, with me, as Mother ended, they applauded spontaneously. She laughed joyfully but shook her head.

'Oh, no, Laurie, I'm so terribly rusty. But it will soon come back to me.'

Here, in this remark, was another enigma to add to those others, still unsolved, that complicated and disturbed my early years and that, when I pressed Mother for an explanation, caused her merely to smile and to make some evasive answer. Meanwhile nothing could detract from this new joy. Father was not musical and although sympathetic did not really care for the piano; this indeed—for I had begun to *know* Father—may in some degree have delayed its delivery. His idea of music was a stirring melodic mélange from a good brass band, and to this end he had provided himself with several pink Edison Bell phonograph cylinders of the famous *Besses o' the Barn*. But to Mother, particularly in our *apartheid* state, the beautiful Bluthner was both consolation and refinement. Every afternoon when she was 'dressed', after she had finished the day's housework and satisfied herself that all was shining and in perfect order, she would 'practise', leaning forward from time to time, since she was naturally a little short-sighted, to study a difficult passage, then, before resuming, brushing aside her soft brown hair which, waved in the middle, fell across her brow.

Often when I came home from school and always if the weather was wet, I would come silently into the front room and seat myself by the window to listen. I soon knew the names of the pieces I liked best: Chopin's 'Polonaise in E Flat', Liszt's 'Hungarian Rhapsody', followed by Schubert's 'Moments Musicaux', and my greatest favourite, to which perhaps the name contributed, Beethoven's 'Sonata in F Minor', which beyond all the others induced in me a precocious sadness, fostering visions wherein under a shining moon I saw myself leading lost causes in distant lands and reaping the soul-satisfying reward of a hero's lonely grave and from which, resurrecting myself, I would run into the kitchen to put the kettle on the range and make hot buttered toast for our tea.

That was a happy winter which nothing subsequently could destroy. Our little ship, sails set full to a favourable wind, rode the tide buoyantly on its safe though solitary course. Father was getting rich. At school I had been moved to a higher class and, although regretting Miss Grant, was agreeably surprised to find myself drawn to my new master. Pin, so unjustly condemned by Maggie—his outbursts were the result of a nervous affliction rather than ill-temper—might be a failure in the pulpit, but as a teacher he excelled. His education had naturally been superior to that of the average village dominie and he had that invaluable knack of putting things in an interesting way. Surprisingly, he seemed to become interested in me. A wry appreciation of our common inferior standing in the village may have appealed to him, or perhaps, though he never overtly made this evident, he had hopes of converting me in the manner of a brand plucked from the burning. Whether or not, I experienced more good than I deserved from this despised and rejected little man.

How swiftly those months slipped past! I barely realized that spring was on the way till Father, who had what he referred to as a 'bronchial tendency', caught a heavy cold in March due to his sardonic Irish disregard of the old Scots aphorism: 'Ne'er cast a clout till May goes out.' But he threw it off as the smithy sycamore began to bud and suddenly we were in the green days of April. A soft west wind was blowing, bearing on its wings the news of our increased prosperity. Was this, perhaps, the cause of that rare event, a surreptitious visit from my cousin Terence, a boy of sixteen, who from his earliest years had been blessed with a nose keenly receptive of the lightest airs of affluency?

Terence was a cool, long-legged, unusually good-looking fellow, endowed with more than his share of the Carroll charm. His home, which I had never seen, was in Lochbridge, only twelve miles away, where his father owned an establishment curiously named the Lomond Vaults. While I did not then comprehend the implications of that occult word 'Vaults' beyond its suggestion of subterranean depths, Terry's great distinction, enviable in my eyes, was that he attended the famous Rockcliff College in Dublin as a boarder. At present on his Easter holidays, he rolled up to the front gate on a shining new Rudge Whitworth bicycle. He was wearing well-creased grey flannel trousers, from which he negligently snapped off the clips, the blue Rockcliff blazer and a rakishly tilted straw hat banded with the school colours. An Olympian, straight from Parnassus—the Vaults?—he dazzled me.

Mother, ardently hospitable and long starved of visitors, was delighted to see Terence, although put out at being caught unprepared.

'My dear boy, if only you'd let me know you were coming, I'd have had such a nice lunch for you.' She looked at the clock, which showed twenty minutes to three. 'Tell me what I can get for you now.'

'As a matter of fact I've had my lunch, Aunt Grace.' I could see that term of kinship pleased my mother. 'Still I could do with a snack.'

'Just say what you'd like.'

'Well, I'm rather partial to a hard-boiled fresh egg, if you have some in the house.'

'Of course. How many would you like?'

'Should we say half a dozen, Aunt Grace?' Terence suggested carelessly.

Fifteen minutes later he was seated at the table gracefully making contact with six hard-boiled eggs and several slices of thickly buttered cottage loaf, while at the same time recounting to us, in an offhand manner and an accent tinged with the intonation of upper-class Dublin, his notable triumph of the past term, a win in the hundred-yard sprint at the school sports. Impossible not to admire, and we did, although Mother seemed to wilt slightly as for the third time Terence repeated:

'The way I left them in my final burst they might have been standing still.'

Indeed, it was she who suggested later on that Terence take me for a short walk, pending the return of my father. As we set off, up the road to the village, I put my hand in his and rapturously burst forth:

'Oh, Cousin Terry, how I would love to be at Rockcliff with you!'

Terence looked at me fixedly, then, producing a quill toothpick, began absently to work on his teeth.

'Don't mention it to your mater, who's a doat, but one of these eggs was a trifle off.'

He burped slightly to emphasize his point.

'Oh, I'm sorry, Terry. But did you hear what I said about Rockcliff?'

Terence shook his head indolently, but with a finality that chilled me.

'My poor little caper, you'd never stand the ferrula. Rockcliff would kill you stone-dead. Good God, what's that object over there?'

I spun round. It was Maggie, on one of her slavish errands, with a big bundle of laundry flapping on her head, uncouth, unkempt, and waving to me, waving wildly in friendly recognition. My skin contracted. To acknowledge Maggie before Terence? No, no, it was unthinkable. Guilty of the first of the two great acts of apostasy of my childhood, I turned away.

'God knows who it is,' I mumbled, in a feeble imitation of my cousin's manner, then walked on, leaving Maggie stricken, one arm frozen in mid-air.

At the head of the road Terence paused outside the grocery store. In the window, on a glass stand, lay one of Grant's special dessert apple tarts. Beyond, within the shop, bent over a book with her elbows on the counter and her back towards us, was Polly Grant. Her posture, which certainly presented us with a notably curvaceous view of the part usually sat upon, seemed to amuse Cousin Terence. He lounged in an athletic way against the window, his gaze wandering from the apple pastry to the unconscious Polly.

'That's not a bad-looking tart,' he commented.

'Oh, yes, Terry. Simply spiffing.'

'Very well rounded?'

'They're always round, Terry.'

To my surprise Terence laughed, and Polly, disturbed in her reading, stood up and swung towards us. Meeting my cousin's eye, she reddened and closed her book with a bang.

'We could do with something to sweeten our mouths, after the eggs,' Terence resumed. 'I daresay you have an account here.'

'Oh, we have. I often do messages for Mother and have them marked.'

'Then suppose you nip in for the pastry and have it charged.' He added airily: 'I'll square up for it later.'

Enthusiastically, I obeyed. Polly seemed unnaturally disturbed. She even forgot to give me my usual butterscotch drop.

'Who is that young fellow with you?' she inquired, with still heightened colour.

'My cousin Terence,' I answered proudly.

'Then tell him from me he has a pretty good cheek.'

Naturally I could not think of conveying such a message to my cousin, who, surveying the prospect as I came out with the tart, suggested that we should stroll across to a shady corner of the village green, known locally as the Common.

Here he settled himself comfortably with his back to a chestnut tree and undid the paper bag, releasing a delicious fragrance of crisp puff pastry.

'It's not so big when you see it close,' he remarked, inspecting the tart, which to my eye seemed much larger at near view. It was at least nine inches in diameter, oozing lovely juice and snowy with sifted sugar.

'Hmm,' said Terence. 'You wouldn't have a knife?'

'No, Terry. I'm not allowed one yet. For fear I should cut myself,' I apologized.

'Pity,' said Terence thoughtfully. 'We can't go tearing this apart or we'll have the innards all over us.'

A pause, during which Terence, frowning, seemed to ponder more deeply, while anticipation of those rich inner flavours made my teeth water.

'There's only one thing for it, man,' he declared at last, resolutely. 'We'll have to toss for it. You're a sport, aren't you?'

'If you are, I am, Terry.'

'Good, man!' He produced a penny gravely. 'Heads I win, tails you lose. I'll give you all the benefit. You make the call.'

'Tails, Terry,' I ventured timidly.

He uncovered the coin.

'And tails it is, more's the pity. Didn't you hear me say tails you lose? Well, better luck next time.'

In a way, although my eyes blinked, I was not too unhappy to have lost. Watching Terence eat the tart slowly and with every sign of relish, I enjoyed it vicariously, down to the last flaky crumb.

'Was it good, Terry?'

'Fair,' he decided critically. 'But too rich for your young blood.'

Without disturbing his reclining position, he eased a gunmetal cigarette case from his pocket, extracted a gold-tipped cigarette and, while I watched reverently, lit up.

'Wild Geranium,' he explained.

'Terry,' I said. 'It's so nice you being here. Why don't you come more often? And why can't I come to see you?'

'Ah,' he said, bringing smoke down his nose. 'Now you're getting into a bit of family history.'

I seized the opening eagerly.

'Tell me about it, Terry.'

He considered, half hesitated, as though about to consent, then made an airy gesture of negation.

'You're too young to be bothering about that sort of nonsense.'

'But I do bother, Terry. There's all sorts of things I don't understand. Especially why we never see any of our relations.'

He glanced at me sideways. Couldn't he sense my anxiety for news of the unknown members of my tribe?

'Don't any of your mother's folks come to see you either then?'

'No, Terry. At least only one of Mother's brothers. The one at the University, the youngest one, called Stephen. And then only once in a very long while.'

There was a pause.

'Well, man,' Terence said at last, pontifically. 'There's a certain situation, I will admit. And as you're bound to be told one of these days, there's no harm in giving you a slant on it now.'

He lay back, puffing at his cigarette, while I waited intently, then he suddenly began.

'First of all,' he spoke impressively, almost accusingly, 'if

29

it hadn't been for the Caledonian Railway Company you wouldn't be sitting here today. In fact you would never have existed.'

This unexpected statement staggered me. I gazed at him fearfully.

'You see,' he went on, 'every evening when Uncle Con came back from his work in Winton he had to change trains at Levenford to take the Caley local to Lochbridge, where he was living at that time. But for that he'd never even have set eyes on your mother.'

This contingency seemed so incredible that my alarm deepened. Pleasantly conscious of my riveted attention, Terry resumed with easy nonchalance.

'Usually Con would go into the waiting-room with the *Winton Herald*—for the Caley train was always late. But one of these evenings he found something, or rather someone, better to look at.'

'Mother!' I gasped.

'Not yet, man. Don't rush me. At the moment she's just Grace Wallace and sweet seventeen.' He frowned reprovingly. 'She came regularly, carrying a music case, to meet her brother, a schoolboy, coming back on the Caley train from the Drinton Academy.' He paused. 'Now Conor, your father to be, always had, if you'll excuse me, an eye for a pretty girl. Yet this was different. Although he wanted to speak he was afraid he'd offend her. But one evening he up and did. And at that moment, man,' Terry exclaimed sensationally, 'as they looked into each other's eyes, the damage was done!'

'What damage, Terry?' I whispered faintly.

'Her parents were dyed-in-the-wool Presbyterians, true blue, couldn't have been stricter, and she was the apple of her old man's eye, who, to make it worse, had a Scotch pedigree that went right back to the original William Wallace, if you ever heard of him. So here was a lovely girl, well thought of in the town, helped her mother in the house, sang like an angel in the church choir, never put a foot wrong.' Terry shook his head sorrowfully. 'When they found out she was going steady with an upstart Irish R.C., blood-brother to a publican and, God help us, a priest, hell's bells, man, did they raise the roof. Prayers and tears. For weeks there was the devil to pay while they tried every mortal thing to keep them apart. It couldn't be done, man. In the end, with never a word, and although Con hadn't a fiver to bless himself with, they just up and off to the registry office. She knew her folks would never speak to her again and Con knew he'd be the bad boy of his lot for not getting tied up in chapel, but never mind, they got spliced.'

'Oh, I'm glad they did, Terry,' I cried fervently, for I had followed his recital breathlessly.

Terry burst out laughing.

'At least they got you here on the right side of the blanket, caper.'

For a moment he sat studying me, as though trying to read my face, in which there was now only blankness. Perhaps what he had related did not altogether surprise me, I must have vaguely sensed something of my parents' situation. Yet suddenly an extraordinary depression fell upon me, intensified by the lively unconcern with which Terry treated a subject that affected me so deeply.

'So now you know.' He broke the silence. 'Only don't let on I told you.'

'I won't, Terry,' I said, numbly. I was less happy than I had hoped to be, and to cheer myself up I said:

'So I actually have two uncles?'

'It's three you have, on our side. There's my father, your Uncle Bernard in Lochbridge, and his reverence your Uncle Simon in Port Cregan, not to speak of your Uncle Leo in Winton, though nobody knows much about him.' He rose to his feet and hauled me up. 'Time we were getting back. I need a box of vestas, so I'll stop at the shop. Come on and I'll race you there.'

He set off springily, bent on showing me his style. I was not in the mood for running, yet now I felt strangely combative towards my incomparable cousin. I ran as hard as I could, so hard that Terry, glancing over his shoulder, was obliged to drop his clean-cut air in an effort to increase his pace. Perhaps the apple pie and the hard-boiled eggs incommoded him, possibly the report he had given of his prowess at the Rockcliff sports was coloured by a native talent for drawing the long-bow. When we reached Grant's store he had not shaken me off, I was exactly at his elbow. After we had regained our breath he looked at me for the first time with a shade of respect.

'You're fast, man. I couldn't have believed it. Of course, you know I wasn't going all out.'

While I waited outside he went into the shop and spent a very long time selecting his matches. Polly, who served him, did not seem at all displeased by his reappearance, or by his fastidious taste in vestas. As I watched through the window Terry appeared to be making her laugh a great deal. It was a way he had, careless and carefree. Could Terry really love anyone . . . let alone a poor little caper like me? I felt my throat tighten unaccountably.

My sadness persisted all the way home, deepened during the delicious chicken dinner Mother had prepared and which I could barely swallow. Father, in one of his best and most entertaining moods, showed a marked fondness for Terry, tipped him a sovereign, which Terry seemed to expect and which perhaps had been the purpose of his visit. Then, lighting his carbide bicycle lamp, my cousin swung himself on the machine and set off for Lochbridge.

When he was out of sight I went into the kitchen.

'Mother,' I said, coming close to her. 'I may not be much, but at least I am a sport.'

'Are you?' Mother said, without enthusiasm. 'I don't know that I want you to be a sport.'

'But it's a good kind of thing. Terry said I was one when we tossed for the apple pastry.'

'The apple pastry?' Mother turned in bewilderment, her hands covered with suds. 'Was that why you ate no dinner?'

'No, Mother. I didn't eat any of the pastry. Terry ate it all.'

'And where did this famous pastry come from?' Mother was now inspecting me very strangely.

'Why, Mother, it's the one I bought and charged to our account.'

'What! You charged it!'

Mother was stupefied. But Father, who had come back and had been listening, suddenly said:

'How did Terry toss?'

'He was quite fair, Father. He tossed heads I win, tails you lose.'

Father burst into a fit of laugher, so prolonged it brought on his bronchial cough.

'The young rascal.' He choked. 'He's a regular Carroll.'

'I don't think it's at all amusing,' Mother said frigidly. 'I'll talk to you seriously about it in the morning, Laurence. Now you'll go straight to bed.'

I undressed slowly, sadly. The afternoon, welcomed with such joy, was bitter in my mouth. A weight lay upon my mind, and upon my conscience too. Had I not openly rejected Maggie, dear Maggie, my friend and protector, yes, cut and repudiated her, and all for a cousin who thought no more of me than, well, than a box of Swan vestas? Above all, the mystery involving my parents which Terry had unveiled for me, the isolation in which we were compelled to live, pressed me down. I turned to my pillow and let the willing tears flow.

FOUR

AUTUMN CAME early that year. The leaves of my favourite tree, fringed with gold and scarlet, had begun to flutter down, weaving a royal carpet at the entrance to the smithy. Morning mists drifted in from the firth leaving dewy crystals on the feathery grasses of Snoddie's field. The soft air held a sense of change, and of something intangible that made me dream of far places, strange unvisited kingdoms where I still felt I might once have been in other long-forgotten days.

But today was Sunday, an actual day which, whenever I woke up and sniffed the revealing odour of frying bacon and eggs, brought always a more practical consideration. Father, from tradition and belief, was what I must call an affirmative Catholic, contumaciously so in the face of opposition, despite certain unorthodox reservations of his own, but as a performer he could only be classed as indifferent. If the sun shone on the seventh day and the weather promised fine he would hire farmer Snoddie's pony and trap and drive to St Patrick's, the nearest Catholic church, in Drinton, nine miles away. Mother, despite her Evangelical upbringing, amicably went with him. Such was her attachment to Father I am convinced she would have willingly accompanied him to a Hindu Temple had he professed that faith. I, of course, was taken along and, like Mother, held my breath at Father's amateur handling of the reins, a recklessness ill-disguised by a pretence of high expertise that deceived neither of us nor, for that matter, the pony. With a flick of its hooves as Father shaved the corners it would turn round and, craning its neck, stare at him with indignant wonder. A rare motor-car was now being seen on the roads, usually a red Argyle from the Lochbridge motor works, and as one sped past in a cloud of dust, missing us by a miracle, Mother, clutching her wide-brimmed hat, would exclaim chokingly:

'Oh, dear, these horrible machines.'

'No, Gracie,' Father replied coolly, tugging at the shying pony. 'They are wonderful inventions. Since I mean eventually to have one, don't run them down.'

'They may run us down,' Mother murmured in my ear.

But there were many Sundays when Father felt that God did not require him to expose his family to the hazards of the road, and, reading his face as he inspected the mellow grey sky and sniffed the soft west breeze that hinted rain, I knew this autumn morning to be one of them, that it would be for me another Sunday of high excitement, sharpened to a fine edge by alarm. And indeed, after breakfast, which he took in his dressing-gown, Father turned to Mother.

'Perhaps, my dear lass, you'd make a few sandwiches for the boy and me.' Father usually said 'my dear lass' when he wanted something done for him.

He went upstairs and presently came down wearing his usual get-up for our expeditions: a thick grey Norfolk knickerbocker suit, stout boots and knitted stockings, and a mackintosh cape, like a poncho, that fastened at the neck with a metal clasp.

We set off up the Station Road and through the village, where the bells of the parish kirk had begun to ring. In answer to this summons the *natives*—as my father insisted on naming them—universally in sober black and armed with their black Bibles, were moving towards the church in a slow, solemn, God-fearing stream.

'Black beetles!' came the disgusted ejaculation from beside me.

Father, I am sure, wilfully selected this precise moment so that as an R.C. outsider he could outrage the Scottish Sabbath convention. It was his way of defying the tight-lipped prejudice against us in the village. Nowadays, when an enlightened liberalism seeks to promote unity of the churches, it is difficult to conceive of the bitterness that existed then against Catholics, particularly against Irish

Catholics, in the West of Scotland. These descendants of unwanted famine refugees, many of whom had as yet failed to raise themselves above the level of the labouring class, were referred to as 'the dirty Irish' and were universally despised and execrated, both on account of their nationality and their religion, which was publicly referred to in such terms as: the Roman harlot, drinker of the cup of abomination, or the whore that sitteth upon the seven hills of sin. I myself had trembled as I spelled out the notice of a sermon to be preached in the village parish church: 'Rome, the seat of the beast, according to Rev. 18, 19.'

But Father's nature, unlike mine, was combative and it amused him to evoke shocked looks and pursed lips and to ignore contemptuously the general dour air of reprobation created by our appearance. Now, as always, he traversed the village with a springy, almost jaunty step, head in the air, manner aloof, a scornful smile curving his lips, which from time to time he rounded in an affected whistle. For me, trotting at his side and dreading disaster, the ordeal was racking, only slightly relieved by the hidden envious glances from other boys for whom Sunday was a penance, banefully filled by a two-hour sermon, a day of excruciating tedium, wherein the forgetful raising of the voice was a desecration, laughter a crime, and the passage of the one slow train known as the 'Sunday-breaker' which defiled the sanctity of the day, an instance, publicly proclaimed, of the evil that was bringing the world to perdition.

I began to breath more freely as we reached the last village landmark, Macintyre's sawmill, and came out to open country. Here, presently, we passed the entrance to the Meikle estate, a noble gateway with tall pillars each bearing a green bronze eagle flanked by twin lodges of cut stone built in the Scots baronial style. The avenue wound upwards between massed rhododendrons through the park, apparently to infinity. The sight of this privileged magnificence had already caused me a preliminary tremor which was intensified when Father, some two hundred paces farther down the country road, took a cautious look round and, motioning me to follow, plunged through a break in the hedgerow. We were now in the wooded, rigorously forbidden policies of Lady Whalebone. I quivered at the thought. Father, however, quite unperturbed, steered a familiar course under the beech trees—the beech nuts crack-

ling much too loudly under our boots—and brought us out
to a bracken-covered glen. He then circled a plantation of
young larch and entered a thicker wood, bushed with undergrowth and echoing with the sound of running water. This
was the Gielston River, strictly preserved, and noted for its
run of sea trout.

Arrived at the river-bank, immediately below the falls,
Father's next move was to remove a two-foot canvas case
from beneath his cape and to assemble therefrom the short
sections of a greenheart rod. The reel was fitted, the line
threaded and presently he had begun to cast into the creamy
spume at the head of the pool. As a boy, living near the
shores of Loch Lomond, he had passionately fished every
burn that fed the loch and now, as I watched intently,
allowed at intervals to take the rod, that same ardour was
communicated to me.

I wish I might boast of Father as one of the elect, a dry-fly
purist, or even simply a fly-fisher. He was not. He fished with
brandling worms dug for us at the farm by Maggie, and
which I disentangled, wriggling and rank, from the Van
Houten's cocoa tin I carried in my pocket. Father's object
was to catch fish and he held to the method that served him
well in his youth. Today, however, it seemed as if we should
have no luck.

'Not even a nibble.' Father was annoyed, he did not like
to be beaten. 'Yet the sea trout should be up. We'll leave
our line in the water and eat our lunch.'

Mother's sandwiches were always good, especially the
tomato ones. We sat down in a little clearing under a silver-
birch tree that diffused a soft silver-green light. The river
splashed and twinkled through the tall grasses and reeds.
The hum of the woods set a fearful privacy upon the place.
The sudden chatter of a jay made me start. Now, as on all
our expeditions, I was dreadfully scared that we should be
caught by the gamekeeper or, worse, by the owner, that
redoubtable little woman who had scorned me on my first
day at school and whom, in my mind, I had come to desig-
nate concisely and with odium as *her*. This was the terror
that salted my delight. Father, meanly, or perhaps to harden
me, would pretend sometimes to give the alarm: 'Hist!
There she is!' causing me to turn pale while he shook his
head disparagingly.

When our picnic was over Father lay back, hands behind

his head, hat tilted over his eyes. He had that slightly drugged look which suggested to me that he was about to take a nap, a suspicion confirmed when he murmured drowsily:

'Go and pick yourself some rasps.'

The raspberries grew wild everywhere in the wood. No need to go far, there was a great patch of them quite near. Once I was amongst the tall stiff canes, safely concealed, the spirit of adventure pricked my scalp. Transformed in a flash, no longer Terry's poor little caper, I became the hero of Father's evening stories. Picking the honey-sweet berries, staining my face and hands with the crimson juice, I sustained myself on desert islands, staved off hunger in untrodden jungles, quenched a burning thirst at desert oases whither I had been borne on the backs of camels.

Suddenly, a series of earsplitting splashes sent me running back to Father. He was standing on the bank, rigid with effort, his rod, gripped in both hands, curved in an incredible arc while a big fish tore madly about the pool, twisting and plunging, leaping into the air and restriking the surface with thunderous detonations.

For interminable minutes the struggle continued, while the pool boiled and I quivered in an anguish of suspense lest the prize should escape us. At last, slowly, the lovely fish came in, all spent and defeated, its silver made golden by the peaty water, and Father, with a quick but gentle pull, slid it on to the pebbled sloping bank.

'Oh, what a beauty!' I shouted.

'A fresh-run sea trout.' Father, too, was breathing with difficulty. 'At least five pounds.'

When we were calmer and had admired our trophy from every aspect, Father decided we had done enough for the day, since the sun had now broken through strongly. Really, he was dying to show the fish to Mother, who was often openly diverted by the size of our catch. He bent down, passed a stout cord through the trout's gills, then lifting the fish till it was suspended at waist level tied the cord securely round his middle.

'What the eye doesn't see, the heart won't grieve for,' he observed jocularly, putting on his cape. 'Let's be off, boy. No, not that way . . .'

Father, enchanted by his success, was clearly in his most exalted mood. Cordoned by the heavy fish beneath the hampering but necessary cape, I saw that he had decided against the long detour through the woods. Ignoring my alarmed protests, he declared that we would take the short cut through the fields after crossing the main avenue below the big house. I could only follow.

'Sunday afternoon.' He calmed me as we approached the shrubbery bordering the drive. 'There won't be a soul about.'

'But look!' I pointed to the lion standard above the house. 'The flag's up. *She's* there!'

'Probably having an after-dinner snooze.'

He had barely spoken when, emerging from behind a clump of rhododendrons, we almost collided with a short, plump figure in a light muslin dress who, from the shade of her lace-edged parasol, stared at us in shocked surprise. I almost fainted. It was *her*. I wanted to bolt, but my legs refused their function. Father, on the other hand, apart from an involuntary start and a momentary loss of his natural colour, was managing to conceal his discomposure. He removed his hat and bowed.

'Your ladyship.' He paused and gave a slight cough. I knew he was racking his brains as to how he could get us out of this frightful disaster. 'I trust you won't regard this as an intrusion. If I may explain . . .'

'Ye may,' came the reply in the broadest Scots, mingling suspicion with extreme displeasure. 'Whit's your *wull* in ma policies?'

'Gladly,' Father exclaimed, rather pointlessly, and coughed again. Then, by some sleight of hand and without disturbing the folds of his cape, he produced one of his business cards from his inside breast pocket. 'Madam, if I may introduce myself,' he said, politely yet winningly, pressing the card on the little woman. She took no notice of it whatsoever. 'The fact is that my partner, Mynheer Hagemann of Rotterdam . . . you see his name on my card . . . is by way of being something of a horticulturist. A Dutchman, you understand they are all gardeners there. When in conversation the other day I chanced to mention your famous collection of orchids he asked, indeed begged me, to seek an appointment for him. He expects to be in Winton some time next month. And so, if you could be so gracious . . .' He broke off.

Silence. Lady Whalebone's gaze, passing from one to the

other, had come to rest on me and in her eyes I saw a fateful recognition. Finally she put on her pince-nez, suspended from her neck by a fine gold chain, and studied the card.

'Hagemann's Royal Dutch Yeast.' Her eyes again sought mine. 'A close relation of the staff of life.'

'Yes, madam,' Father acknowledged with the modesty and assurance of one who has made his case good. Standing easily, almost playfully, he was quite unconscious of the mysterious yet steady drip, drip of water which was already forming a sizeable pool exactly between his feet. My heart sank. Had *she* seen it. And what in heaven's name would she make of it?

'So your partner is interested in orchids.' She meditated. 'I thocht the Dutch grew only tulips.'

'Certainly, tulips, m'am. Fields of them. But orchids also.'

The ghost of a smile playing around Lady Meikle's lips gave me hope. Alas, it was illusory.

'Come awa' then.' She spoke with decision. 'I'll show ye my collection and ye can tell your fancy Mynheer all about it.'

'But m'am, I only hoped for an appointment,' Father protested. 'We could not think of deranging *you on a Sunday.*'

'The better the day, my dear sir, the better the deed. Indeed, I insist. I'm rather interested to jalouse how both of the two of ye will react to my orchids.'

Father, for the first time, looked thoroughly taken aback, at a loss for words. But there was no escape. We were led by our cicerone up the avenue, along the terrace that fronted the imposing mansion and into the conservatory, a great high Victorian erection of glass and ornate white-painted ironwork that adjoined the far wing of the house. We entered this crystal palace through double glass doors that were closed carefully behind us and, greeted by a waft of humid air, were immediately in the tropics. Towering palms rose to the high roof mingling with giant ferns spreading enormous fronds far above my head, banana trees with bunched fingers of miniature fruits, strange twining creepers, spiky yuccas, great lily pads the size of tea-trays floating on a pool, masses of luscious greenery of which I could not even guess the names, and amongst all this, coloured wickedly, gleaming like brilliant jungle birds, the orchids.

In my normal state how ravished I would have been by this gorgeous materialization of so many of my dreams. Even now my anxiety was half forgotten. I gazed in wonder, dreamily following our guide as, in a manner which had turned discursive, even pleasant, she demonstrated her specimens to Father. It was hot, extremely hot. Already I was beginning to sweat. Deep banks of pipes ran everywhere, emitting a rising steamy vapour, and was it my over-strained fancy that wherever the access of calefaction became most intense Father was made to stop, examine, and listen? Looking at him directly for the first time since we entered I saw that he was suffering. Yes, suffering acutely, in his heavy woollen clothing. Great drops of perspiration were running down his face which, while not as yet matching the colour of the tomatoes in Mother's sandwiches, had taken on the hue of stewed rhubarb.

'Ye find it a trifle close, maybe. Will ye not remove your cape?'

'Thank you, m'am, thank you, no,' Father said hurriedly. 'I am not at all inconvenienced. I rather enjoy a warm air,'

'Then take a look at this verra special cattleya. There . . . ye'll get closer if ye bend forward over the pipes.'

Unlike the other orchids, which hitherto had been unremarkable for their odour, this cattleya seemed to emit a most distinctive smell. It smelled, in a word, as Father leaned over, of fish.

A fresh horror struck at me. Our trout, habituated to the chilly waters of the ocean, was not taking kindly to this equatorial pyrexia.

'Beautiful . . . extremely beautiful . . .' Father now scarcely knew what he was saying as, surreptitiously, he sluiced his drenched brow with a back-handed flick.

'My dear sir,' broke in our tormentor solicitously, 'ye'rt positively sweltering. I insist on ye taking off that heavy cape.'

'No,' Father gasped in a hollow tone. 'The fact is . . . we are really grateful but . . . an important engagement . . . already late . . . time getting on . . . we must be going . . .'

'Nonsense! I'll not hear o't. Ye havena' seen but the half of my treasures.'

And while our temperatures mounted and the torrid

emanations increased, this terrible little woman made us complete the slow suffocating circuit of the conservatory, forced us even, while she stood below, to climb the white-painted iron stair that spiralled to the roof where, intensified by its ascent, the killing heat produced a mirage in which the prospect we had been enjoined to view assumed the appearance of a deep green swelling sea with cool enticing waves in which Father, at least, would willingly have plunged.

At last she opened the double glassed doors. Then, as we stood weakly in the blessed fresh air she bestowed, first on me, then on Father, a grim yet somehow amiable smile.

'Don't fail to give my regards to your Dutch friend,' she said, almost with benevolence. '*And this once ye may keep the fish.*'

Father walked all the way down the avenue in total silence. I dared not look at him. How frightful must be his humiliation—the crushed abasement of a man whom I had hitherto believed capable of anything, of coming out top in the most embarrassing and alarming situations. Suddenly I gave a start. Father was laughing, yes, he had begun to laugh. I thought he would never stop. Turning to me with a look of complicity he clapped me companionably on the back.

'The old girl got the better of us, boy. And I'm hanged if I don't like her for it.'

With these few words he reinstated himself. My faith in him was restored. That was always Father's way—he had the knack of snatching victory from defeat. But just before we reached home he put a finger to his lips and lowered his left eyelid.

'All the same, we'll not say anything to your mother.'

FIVE

I HAD MADE my peace with Maggie, an act of amendment for which, afterwards, I had cause to bless my mother.

Consulting with her on the most appropriate means of atonement she suggested that I should spend my Saturday penny on whatever my betrayed friend liked best. I accordingly purchased, at Luckie Grant's, a ha'penny worth of

41

black-striped balls and the same amount of coloured transfers and carried these gifts to Maggie's home on the far side of the railway line.

She was seated by a dull fire in the dark little stone-floored kitchen that smelled of soapsuds. She had a sore throat and wore a woollen stocking fastened round her neck with a safety-pin. Perhaps because of this, she received me gently, so gently that I gave way to remorseful tears. For this weakness Maggie reproved me mildly in words I have never forgotten and which were so painfully true I must record them in Maggie's own native idiom.

'Och, Laurie, laddie, ye're a fearfu' greeter. Yer tear-bag is awfu' near ye e'en.'

Maggie's mother was out, to my great relief, for I could not bear her, not alone because she nagged Maggie, but because, calling me 'love', and other endearments which I knew to be false, she sought to pump me about my home with insidious questions such as did my mother get on with father, what had she paid for her new hat, and why did we eat fish on Friday?

All that afternoon Maggie and I sat together at the wooden table and stuck the coloured transfers on our hands and arms while sucking the black-striped balls. Cementing our restored amity I gave her a lucky medal which I said would cure her throat. Actually this was a little silver St Christopher medal of the size and shape of a sixpence, but as I dared not invoke the religious element, I made it out to be a charm. Maggie, who liked charms, was delighted and when we parted repeatedly assured me that we were friends again.

In spite of our mutual pledge I did not see much of Maggie that winter. My poor friend was never free. Nevertheless, as I sat at my homework I was pleasantly aware, listening with one ear to my parents' conversation, that good things were being prepared for Maggie and for her betterment.

As our circumstances improved, Father had been urging Mother to seek some help in the work of the house. He had never liked to see her scrubbing or sweeping although I must confess that he rarely offered his assistance in such undertakings. Mother, I truly believe, in spite of the apparent absurdity of the statement, enjoyed housework, and the deep satisfaction of creating a spotless, shining, well-ordered home. She was what the Scots term 'house proud' and I well remember how, on those days when she had washed the kitchen and scullery floors, I was made to take my shoes off and tread in my stockings on the spread newspapers. Hitherto she had demurred at Father's suggestions, but now twin circumstances induced a change of mind: the new piano demanded better care of her hands, and Maggie, now fourteen, was leaving school at the end of the month.

Mother had a tender heart. She was sorry for Maggie and had grown fond of her. She now made a suggestion to Father which he instantly approved and of which I became the instrument when Mother instructed me:

'Laurie dear, when you see Maggie tell her I'd like to speak to her mother.'

Next day when Maggie stopped at our house during the lunch hour to say that her mother would 'come round' on Saturday evening, Mother took the opportunity of sounding her out. Naturally, I was not present at the interview, but Maggie's expression, as she departed, was proud and happy. When I saw her at school that afternoon she had a new air, an important and entirely superior personality as, pausing only to beam a smile towards me, she confided to the other girls in her class that, freed of the tyranny of these everlasting milk cans, she was to be our maid, to have the small attic bedroom, a new dress and a good wage.

Next day was Saturday. In the afternoon, following her weekly custom, Mother put on her best dove-grey costume and, taking me by the hand, proceeded to the village in the open and friendly manner she invariably adopted on such occasions and which was of course completely the reverse of the attitude affected by her husband. Father's public attitude was really inexcusable. I believe he had been badly hurt in some way, unknown to me, during these early difficult days at Rosebank and he was not one who readily forgave an insult. Mother was different, amiably disposed towards all the world, willing to overlook a slight, eager to make friends, and she sought always to modify father's 'touchiness', to disarm prejudice and soften hostility. These Saturday excursions, although ostensibly for the practical purposes of shopping, envisaged this other objective and during our promenade, while holding herself in readiness to accept and return the few acknowledgements made to her, Mother, moving in a glowing ambience of good feeling, would maintain a lively conversation with me on all sorts of subjects, thus conveying to the village an impression of our strong social instincts.

On this particular afternoon she spent a very agreeable half-hour at Miss Todd's, the milliner's, choosing a dark dress and also a new pair of stockings and house shoes for Maggie. Thereafter she had a good gossipy talk with Polly Grant, who now never failed to ask after my cousin Terence, then emerging from the grocery, she actually received a bow from Mrs Duthie, elderly wife of the village doctor. Things were looking up for Mother. And this was not all. As we turned to go home, we encountered Pin Rankin, who pegged hard across the road to intercept us.

'Have you a moment, Mrs Carroll?'

Naturally Mother had as many moments as were desired. Pin, a bachelor, was always shy with women. He took a quick breath, which I knew to be the prelude to a longish speech delivered with the same involvement that, no doubt, had marred his sermons.

'You have a bright boy, m'am. Some of his compositions are outstanding. I read them to the class. But it's not that I wish to speak to you about. The fact is, Lady Meikle is organizing a charity concert for the Children's Home to be held in the village hall on the fifth of next month, and I wondered, *we* wondered if you would consent to perform a piano solo. I, we would be so pleased and grateful if you would favour us.'

I looked sharply at Mother. She had blushed deeply. She did not answer for a moment.

'Oh, do, Mother,' I cried. 'You know how beautifully you play.'

'Yes,' she said, in a low voice. 'I will play.'

On the way home Mother, ordinarily so discursive, remained completely silent. Yet from that silence I knew how deeply this recognition, so long delayed, had gratified her.

In the kitchen Father was brewing some herbal tea at the stove. His cold was apparently not quite gone and he had taken to dosing himself with a concoction of his own. Now, he looked seedy and in a mood that was far from propitious. When Mother disclosed her great news he stared at her. I could see that he was going to throw this precious invitation back in the teeth of the village.

'Naturally you told them to go to the devil.'

44

'No, Conor.' Mother shook her head firmly. 'It's a good thing. It means that they're taking to us at last.'

'They've only come to you because they need you.'

But Mother had known he would be difficult. She was determined to have her way. Countering all his arguments, she talked Father over. In the end, he became reconciled, in fact quite pulled up with the idea. Realizing that Lady Meikle was 'behind it' he was inclined, with the vanity of a reformed lady-killer to attribute the invitation to his influence upon her, the result of that memorable meeting.

'You see boy,' he gave me a conspirator's nod, 'she hasn't forgotten us.'

That jocular glance of Father's seemed to set a seal upon the new pattern of our life. We were getting on in the world. Father was prospering, Mother was to play at the concert, I had been praised by Pin for the little essays he set for the weekend homework and, to crown all, in the village people were actually beginning to like us. What a lucky boy I was, and how shining a future stretched before me.

That evening, as we were seated by the fire, variously engaged, the front door bell pealed. An unusual sound. Looking up from the pursuit of knowledge in *Pears' Cyclopaedia*, I wondered, in mild alarm, who had come to breach our little castle. But Mother, knitting placidly, merely said:

'That'll be Maggie's mother. Run, Laurie, and ask her to come in.'

I went to the door, and presently returned.

'She says she'd rather not come in.'

Mother looked surprised but, rolling up her knitting and spiking it with her needles, she immediately got up. I followed her halfway to the door. Already I surmised that something was wrong but nothing had prepared me for the violence or the virulence of the attack.

'You're not to have my Maggie.'

Mother seemed dumbfounded.

'If it's a question of a little more money . . . I'm quite willing . . .'

'Not all the money in the world will buy my Maggie.'

Was she drunk? No, peering into the darkness, I saw a face possessed, distorted by rage and spite. I shall not attempt to recreate the stupid and malicious abuse she

45

launched at Mother. When I first contemplated this story of my childhood I pledged myself to record no ill of anyone. But Maggie's mother was that unfortunate creature, a woman so envenomed by misfortune she sustained herself on hatred. Maggie had always been her drudge, the outlet for her rankling grudges, the living, ragged evidence of her own ill usage. She could not bear to think of her escaping to a happier and more comfortable life. Mother was trembling now under a fresh tirade in the midst of which, after the words 'you and your papist medals', I saw something thrown, a small silver disc, that hit the floor and rolled on its edge to my feet. The lucky charm I had given Maggie. As I picked it up I saw that Father had come silently forward, still holding the *Herald* which somehow increased his air of studied calm.

'My good woman.' He spoke moderately, without rancour, yet in a voice of ice. 'You have said enough. We are all fond of your daughter here. Anything we have done or proposed to do has been with the best intentions. But as you so obviously dislike and distrust us, we can only yield to your wishes. And now will you please withdraw.'

She was silenced. She had expected invective and was prepared for it, not for this dignified restraint. Before she could collect herself, Father quietly closed the door.

How I admired Father at that moment. Knowing him to be capable of the most inflammatory tempers, of truly majestic displays of contemptuous satire, he might well have reduced the incident to a vulgar brawl. But we ourselves were unduly silent for the rest of that evening. On Mother's account Father was obviously put out, the measure of which was that he lit a cigarette. He did not smoke—he hadn't the inclination, or perhaps he was vain of his beautiful teeth and did not want to discolour them—but in rare moments of stress he would resort to a Mitchell's Special No. 1. And now, puffing inexpertly, with one eye half closed against the smoke and the other directed at intervals reassuringly towards Mother, he sought to compose himself and her. Next day at school news of Maggie's predicament had reached the playground and obliquely, from the corner of my eye, I could not fail to note the ring of her tormentors. But Maggie, though downcast, was tough and could give back as good as she received. After class she waited and, taking my hand, walked down the road with me.

'Anyway, we're still friends, Laurie. And one of these days I *will* come and work for your mother.'

But Mother was still upset. She had not the heart to practise for the concert. However, on the evening of the last day of the month, after she had prepared supper, she went to the piano while waiting for Father's return. I was in my place at the window, yet so absent in my thoughts that the whistle of Father's train reached me from another world. Yet vaguely I had begun to be aware that he was a long time in coming from the station when I heard the familiar nightly click of the front door. Mother immediately broke off and went to meet him. As I turned away it was almost dusk outside. Suddenly, through the side window, I saw two men moving slowly up the road. Pressing close to the glass and rubbing away the mist of my breath I made out Jim, the station porter, and the signalman who worked the level-crossing gates. They were passing now very slowly, in single file, with bent heads, carrying something between them. Was it a long plank, covered with a blanket? At first I did not take it in, yet I received so sinister an impression from that sagging elongated thing and from the slow pace of the men who bore it that suddenly I was terribly afraid. I ran to tell Father. He was standing in the lobby with Mother. He had not taken off his hat or coat. His face was white with shock. In a voice I did not recognize he was saying to Mother:

'Her foot must have caught in the points, the train comes in so slow. But, Grace,' his voice broke, 'if you'd seen the poor thing we lifted up.'

Mother, with a terrible cry, covered her face with her hands.

Dumb with horror, I knew no immediate pain, only that Maggie had done with the milk cans for good.

SIX

HOW SAD and confused, above all how unforeseen, was the period that followed. Even now, disentangling it from memory, I still cannot view it without pain. Surely no one could have blamed Mother for Maggie's death. On that same night Father had gone back to the level crossing with a

lantern from the signal box and found, wedged in the switch
'points' of the rails, the torn-off heel of Maggie's boot. My
poor friend, trapped in this vice, had clearly made a frantic
effort to free herself. At the inquiry the procurator fiscal
had made it clear that if Maggie had wished to destroy herself she would not first have carefully inserted her foot in the
switch then tried to tear it loose. And I knew too from
Maggie's last hopeful remark to me that no such intention
had ever entered her mind. And yet, despite the evidence,
the certainty of accident was rejected by the village in favour
of the more awful alternative and Maggie, exalted by
tragedy became a martyr to our interference.

The theme was played with variations. Father, bitterly
reporting the latest gossip as we sat at dinner, did not spare
us. If we had not come between a devoted mother and her
only child, dangling false promises, arousing illusory hopes,
if only we had 'let the poor girl *be*' she would still be alive
and happy. And, of all people, what need had we of a
servant!

Mother, who had not stirred from the house for days, and
who now at our evening meal was barely touching her food,
pressed her hands together.

'We'll have to leave, Conor.'

'Leave?' Father stopped eating.

'Yes. Get away from this wretched Ardencaple. You've
always wanted to.'

'What!' Both Father's eyebrows shot up dangerously.
'Run away! Bolt like a rabbit! What do you think I am?
There's nothing wrong with Ardencaple *itself*. I like the
place and country here. Now especially, nothing would
make me leave. Besides . . .' He spoke slowly, with special
meaning. 'Don't forget you have an engagement at the
concert.'

'That!' Mother cried, all the softness in her nature
shrinking from the mere idea. 'I'm going to no concert,
never, never.'

'But you are, Grace.'

'No, no. I can't face it.'

'You must.'

'I'm not capable of it. I'd break down.'

'You won't.'

'But, Conor . . . to be up there, before them all, alone.'

'You won't be alone. I'll be with you. And so will

48

Laurence. Don't you see, lass,' he was looking at her grimly, 'if you don't go it'll be a clear admission of guilt. We are utterly blameless for poor Maggie's accident. So we *must* go, all of us, stand up for ourselves, and show that we don't give a tinker's curse for what they say.'

Already I was shaking at a prospect that had suddenly reached out chilly arms towards me. Yet while, like Mother, I sat dismayed, Father faced us with a calm, remote determination.

'You'll see,' he said, as though talking to himself. 'Yes, you will . . . will . . . see.'

On the afternoon of the concert Father came home by an earlier train. Under his arm he carried a long stiff cardboard box, the contents of which were revealed to me when, at half past six, Mother came slowly, almost unwillingly, downstairs looking lovely, but oh, so fearfully pale, and wearing a new blue silk dress, cut low in the neck and with a long pleated skirt.

'Yes,' Father said in a hard voice, after studying her critically. 'Exactly the colour of your eyes.'

'It's beautiful, Con,' Mother said faintly, 'and must have cost a ransom. But oh, I feel so nervous.'

'You won't lass,' Father said, in that same gritty tone. Then, to my amazement—for I had never seen such a thing in the house before and knew my father to be of a most temperate habit that rarely took him beyond a glass of beer with his customers—he produced a flat bottle distinctly labelled: *Martell's Three Star Brandy*. Carefully, as though measuring out a medicine, he poured a substantial draught into a glass, added a sudden generous splash, then held it out to Mother.

'No, Con, no.'

'Get it down,' Father said implacably. 'It'll put new heart in you.'

While Mother hesitated there came the clop-clop of horses' hooves and the rattle of a cab drawing up at our gate. Trembling at the sound, she feverishly snatched the glass and, while I watched wide-eyed, emptied it at a gulp that made her choke.

The darkness of the cab brought a temporary relief. I sat on the edge of the seat, stiff in my starched collar and Sunday suit. Father was wearing his best clothes too, and his moustache had been trimmed and curled so that the

49

points had a combative upward sweep. At least we were showing a brave front to whatever lay ahead. And suddenly, as the red glare from the smithy fire lit up the interior of the cab, I saw Mother reach out and press Father's hand.

'I'm not afraid now, Con. I feel all warm and strong. I know I can do my best.'

Father laughed softly, yes, to my shivering amazement the man actually laughed.

'Didn't I tell you, dearest lass?'

'Yes, Con darling.' Mother's voice held a strange note. 'Only . . . I feel I want you to kiss me.'

Was the woman mad too? To my shamed horror, unmindful of me and of the chasm that confronted us, they embraced each other closely, after which Mother gave a sustained, comforted sigh.

It was a minor relief to get her safely delivered at the performers' side door, then Father took my hand and we went round the building to the front entrance. The hall was full, already people were standing at the back, but at the front, immediately beneath the platform, places had been reserved for relatives of the performers. Towards there Father advanced, with his head high in the air, so high indeed, that while himself conspicuously visible, he need recognize nobody. However, despite this strategic posture, he had not failed to note the crowd, made up mostly of young men, at the back of the hall, for he hissed cryptically into my ear:

'Outsiders from Levenford . . . there'll be trouble.'

Our entry had been well timed. We had barely taken our seats when the proceedings were opened by Lady Meikle, who bustled on to the stage, made a short speech indicating the purpose of the concert and asked the audience to be receptive towards the artists.

'These good people,' she concluded, 'are giving their services free, for a most worthy cause. I want you to welcome them, every one, *without exception*.'

At these emphatic words Father turned to me with a meaning self-satisfied glance and murmured:

'That's for us, my boy. She distinctly caught my eye. You'll see, Mother'll be all right.'

Unfortunately, while her ladyship's request was greeted with restraint from the body of the hall, it met with exaggerated applause from the rear and as she went off someone exploded a paper bag. The loud bang was partly drowned by the hired accompanist who, by way of an overture, had begun to hammer out 'Land of Hope and Glory'.

After this the first vocalist appeared—a tall, thin young man draped in a borrowed outsize dress suit. Met with shouts of derisive recognition from the back, he began nervously to sing 'Thora'.

> Speak, speak, speak to me, Thora,
> Speak once again to me.

It was not a success. Indeed, the young man was loudly advised to gargle his throat, to have a bath, to take his suit back to the pawn, and finally, to go home to Thora and put her in a sack.

Next to come on was a violinist who, upset by frequent interruptions and urgings to put the cat out of pain, struggled through 'Träumerei'. By this time Father was moving restlessly in his seat. The chilly 'village' reception he had feared for Mother was nothing to what she might suffer from this rowdy mob, now recognizable as apprentices from the shipyard at Levenford who were known troublemakers. Father's feeling had been communicated to me, and as the disturbance continued my agitation increased so pitifully that actually my head began to quiver on my shoulders. I sat sweating and shivering for my poor dear mother who undoubtedly would burst into tears since, of all things, I knew she had chosen to play that difficult classical piece, Debussy's 'La Mer'. Nothing could have been more unsuitable, more likely to provoke abuse. Nothing worse.

But now she was there, actually on the stage. My spasm ceased, I was frozen. She seemed small on the wide platform and so ridiculously young and pretty that my fear deepened. What a tender morsel to be thrown to the lions! A storm of whistles had greeted her and now a voice shouted something that made Father bristle. He was sitting erect with his most steely look. For a moment I dared not look at Mother but when I forced my eyes upwards I saw that she had seated herself at the piano and, half turned, had actually waved a friendly greeting towards the back of the hall. Good heavens! What had come over her? She did not look like my mother at all but, disregarding the whistles and the catcalls, she was smiling now at her tormentors. Suddenly, as I shrank

51

down in my seat, waiting for the first feeble whimper of 'La Mer' to destroy her, her hands descended hard on the keyboard, startling me with the stirring strains of one of Sousa's *Besses o' the Barn* marches: a favourite of Father's entitled 'Washington Post'.

Was I dreaming? Apparently not, for when this ended, without pausing, without acknowledging the rattle of applause, before even someone yelled, 'Give us another,' Mother dashed intrepidly into another rousing tune, the famous Pipe Band favourite of the Highland Infantry, 'Cock o' the North'. If the first number had pleased the Levenford contingent this completely won them. Before she was halfway through she had them singing:

> *Piper Finlater, Piper Finlater,*
> *Played the Cock o' the North!*

While the last verse still vibrated against the roof more applause burst out, stamping of heavy boots, and repeated shouts of ' 'core, 'core'. And now Mother was in full cry. Scarcely hesitating she broke into what I can only call a medley, or rather an improvisation—since she played many of them by ear—of the old Scottish airs: 'Ye Banks and Braes', 'Green Grow the Rashes, O', 'Over the Sea to Skye', and ending with the local favourite, 'The Bonnie Banks of Loch Lomond'. The effect was tremendous, even those most unresponsive in the body of the hall, whom I had thought to be our enemies, were conquered, beating time now, nodding and humming, swept away by this brilliant melodic surge of sentiment and national spirit.

I was glowing with pride, my palms hot with clapping in homage to this wonderful mother whose undreamed-of cleverness and skill had saved the day for all of us.

And they wanted more. Even when Mother rose from the piano they would not let her go. Someone unseen in the wings must have signed to her to yield. What would she play now? The answer came quickly and it seemed that her eyes had sought us out. She struck the first chords of Moore's 'Far from the Land', a tribute, not to her old loyalties, but to the new. And she was singing it, too, calmly and confidently, as though she were sitting at the piano at home. I scarcely breathed as her voice rose, clear and sweet, in the perfect attentive stillness of the hall.

52

Father, leaning back, twirling his moustache, and with a strange rapt smile, had kept his gaze riveted on Mother as though he could scarcely believe his eyes. And when at last after a final curtsy, she left the stage, he rose abruptly and, demonstrating in every action that the event of the evening was over, he took me by the collar, steered me down the aisle and out of the hall.

We had not long to wait for Mother. She came hurrying down the steps of the upper entrance wearing her coat, with a fringed white shawl round her head, and ran straight towards us. Father gave her such a hug it lifted her off her feet.

'Gracie, Gracie . . .' he murmured in her ear, 'I knew you had it in you.'

'Oh, Mother!' I was hopping with delight. 'You were splendid.'

Mother gave a little gasp.

'It was an awful hash of sentiment but I fancied it was the only thing, and I think they liked it.'

'They loved it, Mother,' I shouted.

'Couldn't have been better,' Father purred.

'I didn't want to go on so long, but Lady Meikle made me.'

'Ah,' said Father, with a satisfied click of his tongue. 'I knew the Whalebone would be on our side. But what made you think to do it in the first place? Did she give you the idea?'

'No.'

'Who, then?'

Mother gave him a sly glance.

'It must have been your Mr Martell.'

Shouts of delirious laughter from all three of us. What joy, what bliss! What a triumph for the Carrolls.

'Oh, we mustn't, Con,' Mother said suddenly. 'Think of poor Maggie. You know, all the time I was playing, somehow at the back of my mind I felt I was doing it for her.'

We walked back together under the shining moon, Mother and Father arm in arm, talking, talking as though they would never stop, but I did not feel jealous or that I was at all excluded, for Mother with her free hand had found mine and snuggled it into the pocket of her coat. There she held it cosily, all the way home.

How bright the moon was, how clear and high. And our

star, the Carroll lucky star, was rising too, yes, rising again, clear and high, to join the galaxy above.

SEVEN

THE NEXT DAY was Sunday and, perhaps in a spirit of thanksgiving, we went to Mass at Drinton, coming home to a late and rather special lunch of roast duck followed by the trifle, with crystallized cherries and whipped cream, that Mother made so well. In the dwindling winter afternoon, after Father had had a nap, Mother suggested a stroll along the shore. The golden aura of yesterday still lingered about her and, in addition, a kind of happy languor which, from the dreamy reminiscent glances she directed towards him, I somehow associated with the attentions of Father. Already I had begun to sense the strong physical attraction that existed between my parents which in the beginning, over-coming every conceivable obstacle, had brought them to-gether almost from different worlds and which now en-dured in a close responsive union. In later years, when I came to read the records of other childhoods so often marred by constant parental strife, by conjugal incompatibility and mutual hatred, I became more fully aware that in their marriage my mother and father were uniquely fortunate. Although there were sudden minor storms, provoked by Father's quick temper, they never lasted more than a few hours and ended in spontaneous reconciliation. And always between them, even in their silences, there existed a mutual understanding that made my home a safe, warm place in an often threatening world.

This feeling was palpably in the air as, having been to Geddes Point, in the direction opposite to Rosebank, which for reasons I dimly glimpsed Mother always shunned, we were returning slowly through a soft mist gathering on the dead, deserted estuary. The air was so still that the sob of the tide came like the faint echo from some distant sea-shell. Mother idled in front, accompanied by Darkie, the Snodgrass farm cat, which often attached itself to her on these excursions. Father and I had fallen some paces be-hind, competing in a game of 'skiffers' and being cautioned, though indulgently, by Mother for our shouts as we counted

the skiffs when the flat stones, smoothly polished by endless
tides, went skimming and leaping over the calm grey
water.

Suddenly, as he threw, Father gave a short wincing cough,
straightened, and put his handkerchief to his face. I looked
up in surprise, then, with the air of making an announcement, called out importantly:

'Father's nose is bleeding!'

Mother turned round. I saw her expression change. I saw
too that the handkerchief was covering Father's mouth.
Mother came near.

'Conor, it's your cough.'

'It's nothing.' He had moved the handkerchief and was
staring almost stupidly at a small scarlet stain. 'Only a spot.
I must just have strained myself.'

'But you coughed,' she persisted, in concern. 'You must sit
down and rest.'

'It's nothing. Just a stitch in my side.' By way of evidence
he produced a very slight artificial cough. 'See, it's all
gone.'

Mother made no answer. Her lips came together in a
manner more determined than submissive, and as we
resumed our way, though she glanced at Father from time
to time, there was no languor in her eyes, and her silence
persisted until we reached our house.

This cough of Father's, appearing intermittently, particularly in damp weather, and dismissed in his off-hand style
as 'a touch of bronchitis' or even, with a sort of possessive
pride as though it were an attribute peculiar to him, as 'my
bronchial tendency' and alleviated by herbal remedies of
his own, had come to be accepted in the family, despite
occasional protests by Mother, as a natural phenomenon. I
thought nothing of it, and its relation to that absurdly small
spot of crimson which Father had himself made light of
seemed so improbable or at least so unimportant that immediately we got home I went off whistling to the farm with
Darkie to fetch the milk, an evening task that had now
devolved on me.

In the byre the milking was still in progress and for
perhaps twenty minutes, while the hot milk squirted and
frothed into the pail, I waited, amused by the antics of the
cat as it caught and lapped the driblets that splashed to the
stone flags. Sauntering up the road with my jug of milk I

was totally unprepared for the sight of Dr Duthie's gig standing outside our house, a shock heightened by the fact that the gig lamps were already lit and, magnified by the misty dusk, seeming to typify the personality of the village doctor, were glaring at me like two enormous eyes.

This Dr Duthie was a formidable figure, and not to me alone. A fierce old red-faced man, past seventy, dressed invariably in corduroy breeches, shiny brown leggings and a baggy velveteen jacket, he stamped in and out of sick-rooms like a Highland bull, discharging his diagnosis in a voice comparable to the Erskine foghorn, so forcibly indeed that when he had attended me I was often hit by a spray of saliva upon my cheek. By all the canons of romantic fiction this rough exterior should have harboured a heart of gold. It did not. The doctor was coarse and often brutal with his patients. Caring nothing for public opinion, he was generally admitted to be 'a hard nut to crack'. He had a farm in the back country where he reared saddle-back pigs and was often heard to declare that he preferred them to his patients. If he had a weakness, beyond the bottle of whisky he drank daily and which served him as an *elixir vitae*—for he seemed to grow more potent with every dram—it was for a pretty woman. He squeezed the dairy maids at all the farms he visited while they giggled and pretended to protest, bumping them against the steading wall with his knee. While his manner towards her was less amorous, since he had the wit to know where to stop, I always felt that he had a soft spot for my mother.

Of course, I dared not enter my home while this ogre was in possession. I had suffered enough at his hands. Creeping into the shadow of the wall I peered cautiously into the lighted parlour. Father lay on the sofa, stripped to the waist, while Dr Duthie, with his ear on a short wooden tube, bent over him. Never had I seen my audacious parent at such disadvantage, so subdued, dominated, almost possessed. The sight was unbearable and, turning away, I slid down and sat with my back to the wall, supporting the warm jug of milk between my knees.

A longish interval elapsed before the front door opened and Dr Duthie and my mother appeared on the threshold, both figures clearly visible against the lighted lobby. I crouched lower as the doctor's voice boomed out:

'Send to the surgery for the medicine. I'll let ye have the

56

cod liver oil and malt as weel. But mind, woman,' he pressed Mother's arm, giving point to his words by a series of reproving yet caressing shakes as though trying to turn her towards him, 'the main thing is to get him out of here. Didn't I tell you at Rosebank to keep away from the shore? It does nobody good to spend their lives on damp mud and silt. Forbye, river fogs are fair poison for a man with his chest.'

I did not properly interpret this pronouncement, I was too fully occupied in watching Dr Duthie safely off the premises and into his gig. Nor, when I went into the house, was Mother disposed to elaborate upon it. Her mood was not communicative and, relieving me of the milk jug, she quietly set about preparing our tea.

For two days Father remained at home, restively and with a very ill grace, then went back to work. And although I did notice the conferences, yes, and arguments, that began, and were continued, between my parents, if I gave any thought to them at all, I assumed them to be connected with the business of the yeast. Everything seemed to have returned to a happy normality. Father, energetic as ever, soon, in typical fashion, discarded his bottle of medicine and consigned the jar of cod liver oil and malt to the dustbin. I was quite unprepared when one April afternoon, as I came rushing in from school, Mother, wearing all her best clothes and with the air of having returned from a journey, took me aside.

'Laurence, we are leaving this house next month and moving to Ardfillan.' Quickly, reassuringly, seeing my look of consternation: 'To such a nice place, dear. Really a move for the better.'

This sudden prospect of change, always alarming to a child, quite disconcerted me. All at once Ardencaple had never seemed more attractive. I was now altogether at home in school where I had moved up two classes. I liked Pin, and had become friendly with a few of the boys. Last Saturday I had caught two speckled trout in the Gielston burn. And we were to leave all this when everything was going so well for us.

Mother must have read this in my face, for she put her arms round me, smiling at me confidingly, in such a manner that I knew all this to be her doing and that she was deeply pleased with it.

'Ardfillan is a lovely town, dear. And our new flat is high up on the hill and not far from the moors. I'm sure you'll like it.'

EIGHT

THE REMOVAL was accomplished with surprising ease and, as Mother had promised, our new home proved to be a great advance upon the little villa we had relinquished. Like the town of Ardfillan, it quite overcame me with its splendours. Reaching uphill from an expanse of estuary so wide as to be almost open sea. Ardfillan was a fashionable place, a select resort with a discreet pier, promenade, and bandstand, yet, at the same time, a residential town favoured by wealthy Winton businessmen who utilized the fast train service to the city, and by others, of equal or greater affluence, who had retired. Big houses, pretentiously styled and surrounded by large enclosed gardens, studded the hillside, making the most of a choice view of the Gareloch and the Kyles of Bute yet in no way intruding upon the wide sweep of heather moor that reached up behind to Glen Fruin and on to the shores of Loch Lomond. There were many superior shops, a private circulating library, and two of the most exclusive schools in Scotland, one Beechfield for boys, the other St Anne's for girls. I soon discerned, too, a particular well-bred manner of speech, an accent rather, that stamped and distinguished this society, was indeed obligatory for admission to its membership. There existed, in short, an air of 'tone' which Mother immediately liked, which Father ignored and which at first intimidated me.

Prince Albert Terrace enjoyed a good situation well up the hill amongst some excellent neighbouring mansions, and although slightly dimmed, still maintained much of an earlier elegance. Built of finely cut stone, in a semi-Georgian, part-Victorian style with elaborate double entrance porticoes and wide bay windows, it consisted of a number of large luxurious maisonettes with separate, roomy flats above. These maisonettes had finely proportioned high-ceilinged rooms, an attractive ornamental garden in front and the privacy of a long walled-in lawn behind. Naturally we could not aspire to such grandeur, but in the storey above, in flat number seven, all freshly papered and painted, we had ample accommodation, and here we faced a future that seemed favourable, especially to my father who, responding to the change of scene and the briskness of the air, which he inhaled deeply in breathing exercises morning and evening at the open window, was full of sanguine expectation. Yet I was troubled by something altogether new in my mother's expression, when she paused in her arrangement of the house, a subtle harassment which, when aware that I was looking at her, she would banish with a smile.

In Ardfillan there was no excuse for Sunday self-indulgence. We had in the lower town the double advantage of St Mary's Church and its parochial school in Clay Street. Moreover the first person to call upon us one afternoon, and to win us utterly by his frank gaiety and unselfconscious charm, was the young parish priest, Father Macdonald, a Highlander from Inverness-shire who had studied at the excellent Blair's College in Aberdeen. Angus Macdonald was the kind of man whom, as my father put it, even the staunchest Orangeman must have liked. Mother, still a little scared of priests, whom she had never seen at close quarters, could not believe her eyes, when after tea, he got up and, to my unrestrained delight, demonstrated the Highland Fling. In due course, under his tactful persuasion, certain technical adjustments, which I scarcely understood, were made in my parents' marriage which reconciled them to ecclesiastical orthodoxy. Moreover, without in any way deploring the inadequacy of my own religious knowledge, which was extreme, he suggested that, at least for the present, I should attend the parish school. So to St Mary's, the following week, I was sent.

I am obliged to confess that while gratified by my advancement to the third class where my teacher, Sister Margaret Mary, seemed prepared to make much of me, I missed my old friend Pin and was not, on the whole, entranced by my new school. To get to Clay Street I had a long walk by a back road that led downhill to the poorest part of the lower town, which was in effect the working-class district of Ardfillan. Here in a narrow street, with a tenement building opposite, were the precincts of St Mary's—church, school, and presbytery, all of raw red-brick construction, practical, but starkly indicative of restricted means. So too, amongst the schoolchildren, did this sad note of poverty prevail. They came almost entirely from the poor, immediate neighbourhood of the church, many of them children of despised Irish 'tatie howkers' who had come to work in the Clydeside potato fields, and some, alas, in a very ragged state. They played odd games which I did not understand, the makeshift games of the underprivileged, using clay marbles, tin-cans, chalk-marked walls, balls made of paper and cloth tied together with odd pieces of string. The truth is that Ardfillan Catholics who had the means sent their children to other schools, to Levenford Academy or to the Jesuit College in Winton, though never, of course, to Beechfield, an establishment which remained supremely and exclusively patrician. And so, despite the goodness I found there, the general effect of St Mary's was depressive. A feeling of social inferiority was immediately implied and communicated to me, a sort of spiritual wound, deriving from my religion. When I tried to convey something of this to Mother, who had other more serious preoccupations, she would try to comfort me.

'It's for your good, dear, and it won't be for long. You must just put up with it for the time being.'

Lack of companionship was my greatest cross. I use this phrase since I was by this time learning the idiom of the saints. Whatever their moral excellence, Mother could not bring herself to allow me to be friendly with boys who, as Father put it, had no backside to their trousers. And so, feeling myself neither fish nor fowl, I mooned around during my leisure hours in boredom and solitude.

My sole recourse, though it served merely to increase my discontent, was to wander across the hill to the beautiful green playing-fields of Beechfield School. Peering well concealed behind the surrounding hawthorn hedge, I watched the games in progress with a burning, envious longing. Here was everything that I craved, twin white goalposts flanking well-marked green pitches on which the players, many as small as I, in their varying fascinating house colours ranging from scarlet to vivid blue, thudded balls about, ran, passed, tackled and scrummed, in a manner to be expected of boys who would go to Fettes, Glenalmond, Loretto, or even, as some did, to the best English public schools. When I could bear it no longer I turned moodily for home, kicking imaginary goals so wildly that I stubbed my toes against the kerb, thus causing Mother to complain that I was ruining my new boots.

One Saturday, when at a particularly loose end, I was attempting to amuse myself by taking pot-shots at imaginary targets in the road outside the front garden of No. 7. Suddenly one of the stones flew sideways out of my hand and, describing a lethal parabola, crashed through the front window of the maisonette above which we lived. The icy splintering of falling glass horrified me. I dashed upstairs to Mother.

'You must go at once and apologize. The lady's name is Miss Greville. Say that you will pay for it. Come and I'll give your face a quick wipe.' She called after me as I went out: 'Mind now, your best manners.'

Agitatedly, I pressed the bell of Miss Greville's front door. Out of the corner of one eye I could see the big jagged hole in the window. An elderly maid in a neat cap and uniform admitted me. She had grey hair and, I thought, a discouraging expression.

'Wait here,' she told me, when I had explained the nature of my visit.

As I stood in the hall, I was struck by the remarkable sight of two crossed oars on the wall, both cut down in size, and with the blades painted bright blue. Other unusual objects were catching my eye, notably a pair of foils, but now the maid had returned and was showing me into the front room where Miss Greville, standing by the fatal window, turned to take a good look at me. I, in turn, looked at her.

She was a tall, solid woman of, I guessed, about forty-five, full-bosomed and exceedingly erect. She had a pale, full face, its fullness exaggerated by her light-coloured hair puffed out at the sides under pads, and by her tight, stiffly starched collar fastened with a stud. Her dress was simple, even severe: a grey trailing skirt and white blouse over which dangled the thin chain of her pince-nez. She looked what she was, unalterably a gentlewoman, and also what she had been, a schoolmistress. I had heard my mother say that she had taught, at one time, in St Anne's Girls' School. She would have been to me at that moment a formidable figure but for a certain absence of manner, an air that detached her from the more sordid realities of life amongst which I was one.

'Please, miss, I have broken your window.'

'So it appears.' She spoke in a high, clear voice, her accent not of Ardfillan, but rather what the local accent unsuccessfully affected. 'At least it was honourable of you to come of your own free will.'

I accepted the unworthy compliment in silence.

'How did it happen?'

'I was throwing, please, miss.'

'Young Carroll . . . I assume you are young Carroll . . . do not address me as though I were the girl in a teashop. You may call me Miss Greville, at least until our intimacy develops. What were you throwing?'

'Stones, Miss . . . Greville.'

'Stones! Good heavens, what a depraved habit. I shouldn't mind you breaking my window with a ball. But stones! Why?'

'If you want to know,' I answered, beginning to warm up, 'it's because I've a pretty good aim. I can hit any post on the other side of the road you like.'

'You can?' she exclaimed, with a show of interest.

'Shall I show you?'

'No, not with stones.' She paused. 'Don't you ever throw a ball?'

'No, Miss Greville. I haven't got one.'

She studied me, almost with pity, then, telling me to sit down, she went out. While she was gone, I sat on the edge of a stool and looked about me. The big room baffled yet awed me. Strange pieces of furniture, the like of which I had never seen, not dark and shiny with french polish like our best mahogany suite from the Emporium, but mostly of a faded, honey colour, the chairs with seats worked in coloured threads, an inlaid cabinet revealing china patterned in yellow and gold, the carpet a soft grey with a central design of faded pink. Flowers were in the window space and also in a great blue bowl on the piano which, bearing no resemblance to ours, was long and flat.

My vision had travelled to the mantelpiece on which stood a considerable number of small silver cups, when Miss Greville came back.

'You may have this.' As I stood up she handed me a ball. 'It has a history, which probably wouldn't interest you. It belonged to my brother.'

'The one with the oars?' I asked, feeling myself inspired.

'No, no. Not the wet bob. The other younger one.' She smiled absently, and though not unkind, it was to my regret unmistakably a smile of dismissal. I had not wished to come but now, strangely, I did not want to go. These mysterious references to wet and presumably dry Bobs intrigued me. I made an effort to prolong the conversation.

'Doesn't your young brother want the ball himself?'

'He doesn't want anything now,' she rejoined impersonally. 'He was killed two years ago at Spion Kop.'

'Oh, Miss Greville,' I exclaimed in a burst of sympathy. 'He gave his life for his King and country.'

She considered me with inexpressible repugnance.

'Don't be a sentimental little prig, or our acquaintance, hitherto brief and uneventful, will cease forthwith.' And she rang the bell for me to be shown out.

My mother, although distressed that I had forgotten to offer payment for the window, evinced both interest and pleasure when I gave her an account of my visit, from which I tactfully suppressed the final passage. Ever since our arrival she had been politely curious about our neighbour. But the ball, on inspection, seemed rather profitless. Hard, covered in leather, with a sewn seam, it did not bounce and was in every way unsympathetic to my usual practices. That evening I showed it to Father.

'It's a cricket ball,' he explained. 'And it's been played with.'

'She told Laurence it had a history,' Mother interposed interestedly.

'No doubt.' Father gave her his ironic smile. 'According to the house agent, she's full of history. They were very grand people at one time. A big estate near Cheltenham. But her papa went through most of it, and she took up teaching. First at Cheltenham College, then at St Anne's. But she's given it up now.'

'I wonder why?' Mother meditated.

Father's smile deepened.

'I am led to believe,' he murmured in his best manner, 'that in certain of her manifestations she is inclined to be a trifle pec-ul-iar.'

He gave to the word an intonation it had in a popular song of the day which began 'Oh, isn't she pec-ul-iar?'

'Nonsense,' Mother exclaimed defensively. 'That's just idle gossip. She seems a perfect lady to me, and she was exceedingly kind to Laurie. I mean to bow and thank her next time we meet.'

In this way, through the broken window, our momentous acquaintance with Miss Greville was begun.

NINE

THE ACKNOWLEDGEMENT, correct in every way and even reserved, that Mother made towards Miss Greville some days later met with an agreeable response. Our neighbour, living alone and with, apparently, a restricted circle of friends, seemed disposed to an acquaintanceship. She called and left her card. Ten days later Mother returned the call and was given afternoon tea, an entertainment from which she returned flushed with pleasure and teeming with exciting news.

Miss Amelia Greville, she reported to Father and me at supper, was charming, and very much, Mother stressed the words, a lady. Her furniture and silver, which had come from the family home near Cheltenham, were lovely, in fact everything in the house was in exquisite taste. She was artistic, fond of music, played the 'cello, and hoped to arrange duets with Mother. An enthusiastic botanist, she had displayed a wonderful album of pressed wild flowers. She often had gone climbing in Switzerland. Her parents were dead. She had two brothers who had been educated at Eton, the surviving one now farming in Kenya. She attended St Jude's, a church notably High Anglican, and was therefore well disposed towards Catholics. She was most . . . Suddenly meeting Father's eye, bent on her with more than usual ironic indulgence, Mother had broken off.

'Yes,' she blushed slightly, 'she was nice to me. But quite apart from that, I like her. And you know, Con, I have missed having a woman friend, especially with you away all day.'

'Then I'm glad you've found one,' Father said generously, 'only don't . . . well, don't push too hard, lass.'

I did not in the least agree with Father. Miss Greville had deeply impressed me. Indeed I had fallen into the habit, when I returned from my ragged school, of hanging around the front garden in the hope, which so far had proved illusory, of attracting her attention. Now, thinking of those fascinating blue oars, I said rather wistfully:

'It must be nice to have had a brother at a school like Eton even if you didn't go there yourself.'

Father laughed, as if he found something in my remark, or my manner of making it, to amuse him.

'Don't worry, my boy. St Mary's is only a stopgap. Things are going to turn up trumps for you pretty soon.'

He was in excellent spirits these days. The change of air undoubtedly suited him. He enjoyed the express, luxurious train service between Winton and Ardfillan for which he had a first-class season ticket. He was rising in the world, an unmistakable promise of prosperity was implied in his words, his manner, his elegant, well-groomed person. He seemed quite recovered from his strange mishap on the Ardencaple shore and did not fail to remind us that his own efforts were mainly responsible for this happy result. When we left Ardencaple Dr Duthie had given him a note of introduction to a colleague in Ardfillan. This was Dr Ewen, a thin, stooping, soft-stepping, elderly little man with hollow cheeks and a tuft of grey beard always carefully trimmed to a point. With his silent approach, almost on tiptoe, his manner maintained a gravity unvaryingly professional, and he was known to be clever.

At first sight Father disliked him. 'He has a graveyard face,' he reported to Mother and thereafter, although periodic examinations had been advised, he reduced his visits to the doctor's house to a minimum, and had recently allowed them to lapse altogether. Mother half suspected that some sort of disagreement had occurred, that Father had, as she put it, 'fallen out' with Dr Ewen. On the other hand, on principle, he had never liked doctors; his amused and sceptical distrust of the profession had long been a feature of our household. 'Burnt sugar and water,' he would scoff with a shake of his head, indulgent towards our gullibility, as he watched Mother—who had a steady belief in tonics and administered them to me regularly—measuring out a tablespoonful of my Parrish's Chemical Food.

He believed in nature and in the natural restorative powers of the body. Thus while conforming to the rules of hygiene imposed by Dr Duthie—whose strong words, which had probably shaken him when they were delivered, still retained some force—he followed confidently a health régime of his own. He had evolved an elaborate system of breathing exercises, and a diet rich in butter and cream supported—though he was always a temperate drinker—by Guinness's stout. He slept between blankets with the window open, wore woollen underwear next the skin, and red rubber soles to his shoes.

So all was going well with Father, and with us. Yet gradually it dawned on me that Mother was not altogether satisfied with Father's interpretation of his own condition. How was this made evident? Perhaps in her extra solicitude towards him, yet more probably by those moments of abstraction when she would pause suddenly in her work as though a sudden anxiety had dispossessed her happiness, and a play of shadows and reflections would flit across her face, imperceptible almost, yet revealing to one who translated everything, even her most obscure expressions, with complete and intuitive fidelity.

One evening, as I sat at the table doing my homework, Mother, who was knitting by the fire, said reflectively and with a casual air, that did not deceive me:

'Conor, dear, isn't it about time you were looking in on Dr Ewen again?'

Father, reading his *Evening Times* in the easy chair, did not appear to have heard. Then slowly he lowered the paper, looked fixedly at Mother over the top edge.

'I beg your pardon?'

Nerving herself now, Mother repeated her remark, which undoubtedly Father had heard. He studied her.

'Is there any apparent reason why I should go to see your Dr Ewen?'

'No, Conor. Still, you were advised to have an examination once in a while. And you haven't been to see him for ages.'

'True,' said Father, in his most sententious tones. 'However, as I can't stand the man and always felt worse after I'd been to him than before I went, I decided, reasonably and sensibly, to stay away. In plainer language, I have no faith in him.'

'That's rather odd. He's very highly regarded in the town and has a first-class practice.'

'Yes, he caters for the idle rich and panders to them accordingly. He may have a practice but he's not *practical*.'

'How can you say such a thing?'

'Because I found him so.' Father spoke heatedly. 'If you can believe it, he actually wanted me to knock off work for three months and take a long sea voyage to Madeira. Sea voyage indeed! That may be all right for the old ladies he looks after but it's no use to me.'

He broke off, looking as though he had said too much, and attempted to resume his paper. But Mother forestalled him.

'Yes,' she said equably, still knitting and revealing nothing of the shock she had received, 'I admit Ewen is fussy. Still, there are other doctors. And I do think you ought to find one you can like.'

'But why?'

'Well . . . to find out how you're getting on. After all, you haven't quite got rid of your cough.'

Father was frowning at her uneasily.

'It's nothing, I've told you a dozen times I've always had that tendency.'

'Still . . .' Persuasively, Mother lowered her knitting and leaned forward. 'Isn't there a doctor you know of in Winton who could occasionally look you over?'

There was a silence. I waited, my eyes on my book, expectant of an indignant outburst, or at least a dignified and magniloquent refusal. Instead, Father yielded, though half grudgingly:

'Well, lass, if it pleases you . . . there's a chap near my office. Medical Officer for the Caledonia Insurance Company, I run into him occasionally. Since you're so insistent, I might drop in one day and see him for you.'

Ignoring the onus Father had skilfully put upon her, Mother gave a soft sigh of relief which, though suppressed, was still audible.

'Then go, Conor. Why not go tomorrow?'

Father, having resumed his paper, apparently took no notice.

On the following evening when he returned Mother met him at the door in the usual way. As they came in together I noticed nothing wrong in Father's expression except that he seemed tired. But often, when he had been unusually busy, he looked tired. During dinner, which was nicer than usual, with the beef stew Father liked, he ate with a good appetite. No reference was made to the conversation of the day before. When I had finished I moved to my seat by the window with a book. Only then did I hear Mother say, in a low voice:

'Well?'

Father did not immediately answer. When he did, his voice was calm, rather thoughtful.

'Yes, I went. Dr Macmillan. A very decent sort. It appears that you were right, Grace. Apparently one of my lungs is slightly affected.'

'Affected? But with what?'

'With . . . well . . .' Father did not want to say it, but he had to. 'A bit of a touch of T.B.'

'Oh, Con . . . is it serious?'

'Now don't get alarmed. After all, it's nothing unusual. A common complaint. Lots of people get it. And they get over it.'

I heard Mother's breath go out in a long troubled sigh. Then she reached slowly across the table and pressed Father's hand.

'At least now we know where we stand. You'll give up now and really get well. Go to a sanatorium or take a sea voyage, like Dr Ewen advised.'

'Yes, I'll go. It's to be a sanatorium apparently. I'll go like a shot. I promise you. But not quite yet.'

'Conor! You must go at once.'

'No.'

'You must.'

'It's impossible, Grace. Simply can't be done. Every penny we've got is in the yeast. I've even borrowed from the bank. And all my plans are just coming to a head.'

'What does money matter at a time like this?'

'It's not the money. I'm doing well. But the business is young, you know it's a one-man affair, and there's something extra special come up with the U.D.L. that I *have* to be there for, I simply can't leave, with the next few months going to be so critical.'

'Oh, Con . . . Con . . . I don't know what you're talking about with your U.D.L. It's you, and your health, that come first.'

'Now, Grace, we must be sensible. For your sake and the boy's, as well as my own. U.D.L. is United Distillers Limited, one of the biggest companies in the country, and they're definitely, yes positively interested in my yeast. I'm sure I can bring off an amalgamation in a matter of three, per-

68

haps only two months. Such a short time, lass. After that I'll be free to take a six, even nine months' rest to get well. In the meantime, I can work shorter hours, take an extra day off once in a while. I'll be careful, extra careful in every way. I've thought it all over in the train coming home. I'll do everything you say except throw away all I've worked and sweated and hoped for. It would be madness just when I'm in sight of the chance of a lifetime.'

In their intensity of feeling they had both forgotten me. I stole a fearful glance at Mother. Tears were beginning to bud beneath her eyes. I knew that she was beaten and that Father would have his way.

Yet for once my sympathies were with him. At that moment, and all through the period that followed, I never for a moment doubted my father. My confidence in his astuteness, judgement, and general aplomb, confirmed by scores of instances in which I had seen him carry off a difficult situation without turning a hair, remained absolute and unshakable. Even in his few failures, he had somehow managed to remove the implication of defeat by a final attitude of amused or careless indifference. His two phrases 'leave it to me' and 'I know what I'm doing', uttered calmly and confidently, had become for me the touchstones of triumphant achievement.

Mother no longer sang as she went about her work. I failed to understand her constant air of stress. In her worried state she had been driven to confide in Miss Greville and to seek relief in our neighbour's sympathetic response. Yet as the days slipped past, all was going according to plan. Father certainly did not look ill. His colour, always ruddy, remained good, his eye was bright and he had suffered no loss of appetite. As he had promised, while never affecting the attitudes of invalidism, he was taking care of himself, avoiding the worst of the weather, and taking things easy during long weekends. If he still coughed, expectorating surreptitiously into the little flask he now carried for that purpose, then in only a short time, a matter of weeks, he would go away—Switzerland, suggested by Miss Greville, was now definitely agreed upon—and be quickly cured. Meanwhile he was persisting with his own herbal remedies, periodically he called upon Mother to massage his chest with olive oil and one evening he came back from the city with a strange appliance, which he introduced to us confidently as a medicated inhaler. This consisted of a metal canister with a spirit lamp beneath and a length of rubber tubing fitted with a mouthpiece above. Water and a special mixture of herbs, supplied with the apparatus, went into the canister, the lamp was lit and when the hot medicated steam hissed out Father faithfully breathed in. And all this, and the rest, was carried out with a sanguine assurance of recovery that would have been comic if, in the light of what followed, it had not proved to be so tragic.

In later years, when I came to analyse this obstinate folly, the reasons were not far to seek. Father was an ambitious man who constantly took risks. He knew the danger of delaying his cure but, since his business had reached a crucial stage, which if successfully passed would elevate him to a position of real importance, associated, as was later revealed, with his mention of the U.D.L.—letters which, to my youthful mind, assumed a cabalistic significance— he was prepared, in his own phrase, 'to chance it', for all our sakes. There was courage here, yet beyond this natural hardi- hood the superabundant optimism of his Irish tempera- ment betrayed him into the belief that his gamble must come off. But above all, his conduct could most truly be explained by a strange and characteristic manifestation of the actual malady itself and which, years later, I came to recognize as the *spes phthisica*, a false and persistent hope, engendered in the nervous system by the toxins of the disease, the false illusion of ultimate cure and complete recovery.

Father had this to a marked extent and, inevitably, com- municated it in varying degree to Mother and me. We were quite unprepared for the calamity that followed.

The month was March, as far as I remember the second week, and it must have been towards two o'clock in the morning that I awakened. Through persistent mists of sleep I had the dim and unreasoning sensation that Mother was calling me. Suddenly, as I was about to turn over, I heard her voice, very loud, and charged with such a fearful urgency that I immediately sat up.

'Laurence! Laurence! Come here!'

I got out of bed. My room was dark but when I opened the door the lights in the hall were on. The door of Father's bedroom was half open and from within Mother called again. The dread of some terrible disaster held me back,

70

but I went forward and into the room. It is a moment I have never forgotten.

Father lay on his side with his head over the edge of the bed. He was coughing, coughing and coughing, as though he would never stop, and from his lips a bubbling scarlet stream gushed out. His face was the colour of clay. Mother knelt by the side of the bed. One hand held Father's head, the other with difficulty supported the big white basin from the washstand. The basin was half full of that scarlet froth which, all at once, sick with horror, I knew to be blood. There was blood everywhere, on the sheets of the disordered bed, spattered on Mother's nightdress, even on her hands and face. Without changing her position or taking her eyes from Father, Mother spoke to me, in that same strained note of anguished command.

'Laurie! Run for Dr Ewen. Go now. Immediately. Hurry, for pity's sake.'

I turned and ran, ran from sheer shock. Without stopping to put on my jersey and trousers, a sensible act that would have delayed me not more than half a minute, I ran straight out of the house into the street in nothing but my night-shirt. Barefooted I scudded along the pavement of the Terrace, my heart already beating against my ribs. The darkness made my speed seem beyond all human speed. I knew that never before had I run so fast. At the end of Prince Albert Road I swung into Colquhoun Crescent, then downhill to Victoria Street where, ahead of me, halfway to the Esplanade, I saw the red lamp outside Dr Ewen's house. A square, ornamental lamp embossed with the town arms— he had once been Provost of Ardfillan. Not a soul was in sight. The empty silence was broken only by my gasping breaths as I ran and ran, into the doctor's driveway at last, not caring for the hurt of the gravel on my feet, and up the steps of his front porch. I pressed the night bell long and hard, heard it buzz loudly within the house. For some painful moments of suspense nothing stirred, then as I pressed again a light went on upstairs. Presently the door was unlocked. The doctor stood there in his dressing-gown.

I guessed that he would be angry at being disturbed since, from my parents' conversation, I knew him to be a difficult man. Worse still, had not Father quarrelled with him, cast him off and ceased to be his patient? Before he could speak I gasped:

'Please, Dr Ewen, come to 7 Prince Albert Terrace at once. Father is bleeding terribly.'

Yes, he had meant to show annoyance, even anger, that exasperation experienced by a doctor knocked up in the middle of the night after a hard day's work. But instead he compressed his lips and stared at me in a kind of wonder.

'Please do come, sir. You know my father, Carroll is the name. Never mind anything else. Just come.'

He still stared at me.

'*You* come,' he said. 'Out the cold.'

I followed him inside.

'Is your father coughing much?'

'Oh yes, sir, very much.'

He muttered something under his breath.

I sat in the hall while he went upstairs. Above the hall-stand a stag's head mounted on the wall stared down at me with glassy implacable eyes. I heard the slow pendulum beat of a clock from another room.

The doctor was not long in dressing. When he came down he was carrying a pair of carpet slippers and a tartan travelling-rug. He tossed these to me.

'Cover yourself.'

He watched while I draped myself in the plaid. I did not feel cold but my teeth were chattering. The slippers were old but they fitted not badly—Dr Ewen was a little man— and I could shuffle along in them. He picked up his black bag from the hallstand. We set off.

On the way uphill, though he kept glancing at me from time to time, he said not a word. But as we drew near the Terrace he unexpectedly exclaimed:

'You seem not a bad sort of boy. Don't *you* ever be a fool.'

I did not grasp his meaning. With my mission accomplished I felt limp and spent and could only dread this return to the nightmare disruption of my home. I had not closed the door of our flat when I rushed out. It remained open. We entered. I dared not look, but as Dr Ewen went into Father's room and was greeted by Mother's cry of relief, my head, by a kind of reflex, came round. Mother was still kneeling by the bed, still supporting Father, but the basin, already fixed in my consciousness as the atrocious frothing symbol of unforgettable horror, the basin had gone.

I slipped into my own room, discarded the plaid and

shoes, and crept into bed. For a long time I lay shaken by occasional tremors, listening to the movements about the house, interspersed with the muted voices of my mother and Dr Ewen. How long the doctor was staying! I wished with all my heart that Mother would come to see me before I fell asleep, to take me in her arms and tell me that all was well. Above all, to praise me for my splendid, breathless run. But she did not come.

TEN

THE LITTLE paddle steamer splashed gaily through the sunlit waves. She was the red-funnelled *Lucy Ashton*, plying across the firth between Ardfillan and Port Cregan. On deck, the passengers were promenading, sniffing the sparkling air, or sitting in groups, laughing, talking, listening to the lively music of a four-piece German band. Below, in the deserted, plush-upholstered saloon, smelling of stale smoke, Miss O'Riordan and I sat alone, in silence. Since, until that day, I had never set eyes on her, I ventured an appraising sidelong glance from time to time, although hampered by the roughened edge of the stiff collar that went with my best suit. She was a reddish fair woman of about forty-five with full watery eyes, pointed features and a tendency to pale freckles. Her expression, manner and general appearance all seemed to convey a sense of pious resignation to a life of sacrifice and suffering. I had begun to wonder why it should be my fate always to be in the charge of women and, in particular, such a holy woman as this, when she broke the silence.

'Your father being so ill, dear, I didn't think you ought to be up there with that band. Besides I'm a poor sort of sailor.' She paused. 'We might put up a prayer to pass the time. Have you a rosary?'

'No, Miss O'Riordan. I did have one, but it broke.'

'You should be more careful of a sacred object, dear. I'll give you a new one when we get to the presbytery. His reverence will bless it for you.'

'Thank you, Miss O'Riordan.'

I perceived, with some dismay, that my Uncle Simon's housekeeper was even holier than I had feared. Beyond this

73

the motion of the boat seemed so little to agree with her that eventually I was constrained to inquire:

'Are you ill, Miss O'Riordan?'

'Ill, dear?' She leaned forward, half-closing her eyes and pressing a hand into the small of her back. 'The good God knows I'm never well.'

As she did not speak again I had leisure to brood rather dejectedly on the changes in my life. Was I actually going to stay with a priest? Yes, I was. Father's desperate illness had induced a reconciliation with his brothers, of whom the youngest, Simon Carroll, had considerately proposed that it would greatly relieve my mother in her self-imposed duties as nurse if I should spend at least several weeks with him. Although when he came to visit Father I had liked Uncle Simon very much, looking across at Miss O'Riordan, whose lips were moving in silent prayer, I had begun to feel that the prospect was forbidding, when a bump and a creak indicated that we were alongside Port Cregan Pier.

However, as we disembarked Port Cregan seemed to me a nice sort of place with interesting shops and lots of movement on the front. Like Ardfillan, across the firth, it was built on a hill, and on top of the hill, which Miss O'Riordan, a hand to the favoured spot in her back, climbed with extreme slowness, stood the church and rectory, both small but pleasingly built of cut grey limestone. We entered a darkish hall panelled in oak, smelling of candlegrease and floor polish, then Miss O'Riordan, having first regained her breath by a prolonged series of gasps, inquired in a discreet whisper if I wished to 'go', meaning, I assumed, to the lavatory. On my replying in the negative she led me to the sitting-room at the side of the house. This was a large room opening on to the garden and well lit by a bay window with an exciting view of the harbour. As we came in, Uncle Simon had been sitting at the roll-top desk against the far wall. Now he got up, came forward and took my hand.

As he smiled, I saw immediately that he was shy, and I knew that I should like him more than before. He did not speak but, still holding my hand, looked inquiringly at Miss O'Riordan who gave him a long and detailed report on our journey. While she talked I had a chance to re-examine my uncle. Of the four Carroll brothers two were fair, two dark. Simon, the youngest, at that time not more than twenty-six, was a dark one, black-haired and blue-eyed, so tall that he stooped slightly as though to avoid hitting things like chandeliers with his head, and boyishly, almost alarmingly, thin in his long soutane.

'And Conor?' he asked in an undertone, when she had finished.

She did not answer, but with a meaningful glance that passed over my head, silently compressed her lips, imperceptibly shook her head and left the room.

'Miss O'Riordan will be bringing up our tea. I expect the sea air has given you an appetite,' my uncle said cheerfully. He put me into one of the two old and rather battered leather chairs on either side of the fireplace, and went and stood at his desk. 'Just let me finish what I was doing. I'll be with you in a minute.'

I felt instinctively that he was giving us both time to settle down. Certainly these were strange surroundings for me. Beyond the chairs and the roll-top desk, on which stood a large blue and white statue of the Madonna, there was little furniture and less comfort in the room. The drab curtains were shabby, and the carpet, like the chairs, was badly worn, as though trodden by many feet over many years. On the mantelpiece a biretta and a long row of pennies arranged in little piles caught my eye. On one wall a black and ivory crucifix hung. But what startled me was a large engraving on another wall of a long-bearded, half-naked, hairy old man, perched on top of a high stone pillar.

'Do you like him?' Uncle had risen and was watching me with a faint smile.

'Who is he?'

'One of my favourite saints.'

'But whatever is he doing up there?'

'Nothing much.' Uncle was really smiling now. 'Just being a peculiar person, and a saint.'

At this point, with an air of supreme effort, Miss O'Riordan brought in a black japanned tray on which the tea things and a large plate of thick slices of bread and butter were set out. Although accustomed to much better fare, I barely noticed the absence of cake. My mind was so filled with this amazing old man on the pillar that when the housekeeper had gone I broke out:

'How high was he up, Uncle, and how long?'

'Thirty-six cubits high, on top of a mountain too. And he stayed up for thirty years.'

It was so truly astounding I choked on my first slice of bread and butter.

'Thirty years! But how did he get his food?'

'By lowering a basket. Of course he fasted a lot.'

'Why didn't he fall off when he was asleep? I know I would have.'

'Well, he was a very miraculous old man. And probably he didn't sleep much. Perhaps his hair-shirt kept him awake.'

'Good gracious, Uncle. A hair-shirt!'

He smiled.

'I can't see why he did it,' I said at last.

'Well, Laurence.' I felt a throb of pleasure as he used my first name. "Simeon lived long ago, in wild mountainous country, amongst savage tribes. As you may imagine, great crowds came to see him. He preached to them, often for hours on end, healed the sick, became a sort of judge, worked miracles, and in this way made an immense number of conversions to Christianity.'

There was a silence.

'Is that why you have him in your room?'

He shook his head.

'When I was at college in Spain I got to know of him. And as his name was like mine I felt rather flattered. So you see it's just vanity on my part after all.'

I gazed warmly at my uncle, enchanted by our conversation which, instead of the expected references to my father that might have made me blubber, had raised me up to rare historical and intellectual heights.

'I wish I might see a miracle, Uncle,' I said thoughtfully.

'They're happening every day, if we only look for them. Now tuck into your bread and butter. It's Mrs Vitello's day off and we won't get much more before breakfast tomorrow.'

I wanted to stay with this newly discovered uncle for further talk about pillars, but he told me he must go to the church to hear confessions, adding however, and so whetting my expectation, that he would be free after Mass tomorrow to show me something interesting. And so, when Miss O'Riordan came for the tray she claimed me. After she had again satisfied herself that I did not want to 'go', we went down a short flight of stairs to the kitchen. Here she produced a bottle with a label depicting a huge cod with its mouth wide open.

'I'm putting you on Purdy's Emulsion, dear. A tablespoonful three times a day. It's wonderful for the chest.'

She slowly decanted the creamy fluid which, though well disguised, tasted of cod liver oil.

'Now,' she said, when I had gulped it down, 'let's look what you've on.' Prodding my shirt open with a forefinger she gave an exclamation of distress. 'What! No flannel, dear? You should have flannel next the skin. God knows we don't want you to go the way of your poor father. I'll see to it for you before you're a day older.'

She then released me, telling me to go into the garden and play, but not to catch cold or spoil my clothes. I went out. The garden was a square of green, bordered by a shrubbery in which a little grotto had been made with a large statue of Our Lady wearing a coronet of stars and standing upon a pediment of sea-shells. A narrow concrete path traversed the grass, giving access to the side door of the church. I longed to go there to look for my uncle but held back, aware that he would be in his little grilled box.

I hung about with my hands in my pockets, thinking of a great many interesting things about the man on the pillar, and wishing that I had witnessed the many miracles he had performed. What a splendid sight—a miracle—and they could be seen, too, if one looked out for them. I thought also that, although the fading light made me long for my mother, I might do very well here with Uncle Simon, if only Miss O'Riordan would let me alone.

Alas, as the town clock struck six, she appeared at the back door of the refectory, and beckoned me in.

She had made porridge for my supper and a plateful, with its attendant glass of milk, steamed on the kitchen table. As she sat down opposite to watch me sup she may have observed in my expression a flicker of discontent. She said:

'We never turn up our noses at good food, dear. We live very plain here.'

'Plain, Miss O'Riordan?'

'Yes, plain, dear. The church is fair loaded with debt. And your uncle, poor soul, is fair killing himself to pay it off.'

77

'But how could the church get in debt?'

'It was the rebuilding of it, dear. Fifteen years ago, when I first came here. I won't mention names, but a certain reverend gentleman had ideas that went more than a trifle beyond his station.'

'But don't the people pay, Miss O'Riordan?'

'Pay, dear?' she exclaimed with a scorn that lashed nameless congregations. 'Have you seen the coppers on your uncle's mantelshelf? That's how they pay. Pennies and halfpennies and, God save us, sometimes farthings too, the brutes. Why, with the debt redemption and the interest, and what he does for charity, there's scarcely enough for the poor man to put a decent shirt on his back. But he's a clever one, and a good one, and with God's help, and mine, he'll do it.'

These startling revelations, while depressive, had enabled me to finish my porridge without noticing that there was no salt in it. Later, I discovered that she was a firm advocate of a saltless diet being, as she put it, easier on the kidneys. We rose from the table.

'I have your rosary now, dear,' Miss O'Riordan confided, in an intimate tone. 'We'll just say five decades in your room before I put you to bed.'

Upstairs, we knelt down in the bare bedroom that seemed to exhale the austerity of the many missionaries it had harboured, going and coming between the port of Cregan and the interior of Africa.

'We'll take the five sorrowful mysteries,' Miss O'Riordan whispered. 'And remember. Our intention is for your poor father.'

She began: 'First sorrowful mystery: the agony of Our Lord in the Garden': and first moving my lips noiselessly I finally joined in. Despite our intention I did not think about my father. I was sorry for him. I deplored his pitiable state. But that fearful midnight scene which kept recurring in grotesque forms throughout my dreams had made him taboo during the daytime when my will, such as it was, could exercise command. Instead I thought about Mother, and as I was then, and have been since, a visual, her face rose vividly before me. I saw her look of strain and sadness, mingling with tenderness and sweetness when she said goodbye to me that morning. I thought on no other agony but hers. And suddenly, though she had begged me to be

78

brave, while I continued to pray mechanically, a flood of tears defiled my cheeks. I did not care that my companion's eyes were glued upon me—this, indeed, increased the flow. At last we finished. Miss O'Riordan got slowly to her feet, still viewing me and with—could it be?—a new interest and respect.

'Before God, dear,' she said solemnly, 'you pray well. Such piety! I will certainly tell his reverence. Never have I seen a child so touched to the heart over his beads.'

I reddened guiltily. But in an odd way, I felt comforted.

'Look, dear,' she went on persuasively, when I had undressed. 'Here's a little something I've run up for you. It'll keep your poor lungs nice and cosy.'

She produced a sort of chest protector made of red flannel and fastened it on with tapes round my neck and back. I found it hot and uncomfortable but was now so worn down by her ministrations I had not the strength to resist. This is my hair-shirt, I thought sadly, and Miss O'Riordan is my pillar.

When I had closed my eyes in simulated sleep, but still keeping a faint chink through which I could warily observe her, she stood for a few moments looking down at me. Then she made the sign of the cross over my bed and turned out the gas-light. Suddenly, in the darkness I felt the press of lips on my forehead, not the soft warm lips to which I was used, but dry, stiff, strangely unaccustomed lips. Still, a kiss—and from Miss O'Riordan. I heard the door quietly close behind her.

Poor Miss O'Riordan, I must never permit myself to record anything really unkind of you. What harder thing is there in all the world than to be a frustrated, lonely self-martyred, hypochondriacal spinster housekeeper of forty-five, with only a daily Italian cleaning woman for help, in a struggling parish rectory? Nothing, unless perhaps to be the priest.

ELEVEN

MY STAY at St. Joseph's was to prove longer than I had foreseen and although, unlike his housekeeper, my uncle did not at the outset overwhelm me with attentions, I soon sensed that he welcomed my presence in the rectory and that my companionship, absurd though this may seem, relieved that special and very human loneliness enforced by his vocation, the more so since he could not fail to observe that I was beginning to be attached to him. This was not difficult. Simple goodness, so different from Miss O'Riordan's religiosity, is always attractive and, for all his self-imposed discipline, there was a softness in his nature, a fine sensibility, that must have won any child.

He was, like my father, naturally clever, with the same inborn distinction, an attribute which, I was soon to discover, had not been bestowed by heaven on their two brothers Bernard and Leo. At an early age he had been sent to the Scots College at Valladolid in Old Castile where, during seven formative years, he had lived and studied with outstanding brilliance. Spain had educated, moulded him, imbued him with its traditions and culture. He loved Spain, and deeply admired its people—I well remember one of his phrases, 'the nobility of the men, the grace and purity of the women'. In his dark clothes, with his thick black hair, dark eyes and sallow skin, his clerical cape drooping from his shoulders, he had indeed a Spanish look which rather consciously he sought to emphasize by many little mannerisms. And how often, in a nostalgic way, did he speak to me of— the happiness of his life at Valladolid, the lovely city of Cervantes and Columbus that was saved from the Moors by Sancho de Leon, evoking not only the dramas of history, but more personal images of sun-splashed cloisters, a white-walled study facing on distant ochre mountains, and of the College gardens, scented with orange trees, leading to a special arbour of vines under which he took the midday siesta, and from which the small honey-sweet grapes fell, as he put it, almost into one's mouth. To be transported to a raw, run-down Scottish parish, amidst uncouth accents and the din of nearby shipyards, seemed to me a sad dismissal from Eden.

But Uncle Simon did not mind. He was completely at home in his parish, knew all the children, and most of the old women, by their first names, and seemed actually to enjoy the many parochial duties and demands, in my view dull and fatiguing, which, from six o'clock in the morning when he rose to prepare for his early Mass, complicated a day often extending until late at night. Because I enjoyed his society and missed him when he was away it annoyed me that he should place himself at the disposal of everyone, especially since in addition to his normal routine, he now devoted a half-day every week to crossing to Ardfillan to see my father, visits from which he returned with a fictitious cheerfulness that did not deceive me.

Nor did I approve his readiness to respond to every distressful story. I sensed that he was being imposed upon, a view vigorously shared by Miss O'Riordan, who was especially critical of what she called the Beggars' Procession. Every Wednesday afternoon a string of needy petitioners presented themselves with unfailing regularity at the kitchen door, to be rewarded with their established perquisites. Watching from the open window of the kitchen with Mrs Vitello, the daily woman, while Miss O'Riordan dealt with the queue, I suspected that not a few were impostors and of these, one especially seemed the worst, an old crone with a shifty eye named Sarah Mooney who hobbled on a crutch, dragging one leg, with many wails and groans, and who never was satisfied that her 'peck' of tea and canister of sugar contained full measure. In my suspicion I was fully supported by Miss O'Riordan, and time and again I heard her protest to my uncle against Sarah's depredations on the larder.

Uncle Simon, however, despite the handicap of youth, had a way with his difficult housekeeper who through long tenure had come to believe herself the keystone of the parish. He let her have her head in many directions, tolerated her foibles, did not interfere in the management of the house, and above all, endured her atrocious cookery without complaint. Of Miss O'Riordan's culinary skill I may say that never before or since have I known anyone inflict more harm on a simple mutton chop or an inoffensive joint of beef. But unlike me, Uncle had apparently slight regard for what he ate, his only indulgence being a large cup of black coffee after the one o'clock dinner, with which he smoked a thin, curved cigar with a quill at the end selected from a box sent to him by a colleague in Spain.

By this forbearance in matters which he considered of small account, he not only earned Miss O'Riordan's regard but was able to assert himself without interference in all that pertained to his ecclesiastical office. Quietly and with firmness he interposed on my behalf, and while he could not defeat all her ministrations—notably those directed

81

against my bowel, for she purged me relentlessly, nor must I omit the large camphor cross which for hygienic reasons she hung round my neck and which, impregnating my skin, made me smell like an animated mothball—he negatived her untimely religious plans for me, too ambitious steps to saintliness that would have compelled me to make my first confession, take the order of the Brown Scapular, and learn by rote the Latin responses so that I might serve my uncle's Mass within the brief compass of my visit. If she had had her way I believe this devoted woman would have had me ordained, tonsured, perhaps even canonized before she had done with me. But Uncle Simon would not have it. He had both the sense and the sensibility to realize the psychological shock I had sustained, and to see me as a nervous, highly strung and physically undeveloped child, often tormented by nightmares that awakened me in a cold sweat and which, since they were centred always on grotesque variations of my father's haemorrhage, I referred to as my 'red dreams'. How grateful I was for the time he somehow managed to devote to me. In the evenings we played draughts, a game I already knew. He taught me the rudiments of chess, and engaged me without his queen. Our conversations were always interesting since he never laughed at my naïveties, and I recall that we touched on further notable eccentricities amongst the saints, while on another occasion we had a very reassuring talk on the subject of hell. On several Mondays, his least occupied day, he hired a row boat and took me out to that part of the firth known as the Tail of the Bank. But our greatest diversion was the entertainment he had hinted at when we first met.

One morning, when he had said his office immediately after breakfast, he led me up to the attic and there amidst the lumber of years stood a model locomotive, covered in dust, but a real working model, so big, so full of magnificent potential that I jumped at the sight of it.

'I've no idea how it ever came here,' Uncle meditated. 'The remnant from a jumble sale perhaps. And I don't believe it works very well. But we might have a shot at it.'

We took it down to the garden, placed it on the concrete path outside the back door. I ran into the kitchen to Miss O'Riordan for dusters. Cleaned, revealing gleaming driving wheels, double cylinders and pistons, and a shiny green tender, it was an engine to thrill the heart.

'Look!' I exclaimed, pointing to the bronze letters on the casing of the driving box: 'The Flying Scotsman.'

It was actually a scale model of that famous locomotive. What joy to fill the boiler with water, to charge the little firebox from the bottle of methylated spirit Uncle had thoughtfully provided, to light—with matches obtained over Miss O'Riordan's protests—the well-trimmed wick and then to stand back, holding one's breath, expectant of immediate action. Alas, when all this was done the Flying Scotsman refused to fly. The water boiled, promising steam floated from the funnel, even the tiny whistle emitted its shrill and fascinating note, but for all its inner agitation, and mine, the beautiful machine remained indifferent and inert.

'Oh, Uncle, we must get it to go!' In my eagerness I scarcely noticed that I had used Miss O'Riordan's classic phrase.

He seemed to be of the same mind. He removed his coat and knelt down with me on the bare concrete. Together we oiled the engine with the oiler from his bicycle kit. We examined in detail all its working parts. Vainly we unscrewed nuts and retightened them. Lying flat now, with dirty smears of oil on his face, Uncle was blowing hard on the spirit flame with a view to intensifying the heat when Miss O'Riordan suddenly appeared.

'Your reverence!' Her hands and eyes went up in horror. 'In your shirt-sleeves. And such a state. And Mr and Mrs Lafferty waiting for you in the church with the poor unbaptized innocent infant, a good half-hour.'

He got up, with an apologetic smile to Miss O'Riordan, looking rather like a guilty schoolboy. But as he hurried off he gave me an encouraging glance.

'We're not beaten yet, Laurence. We'll try again.'

We did try again. We tried repeatedly, and always without success. The reluctant engine became, for us, an absorbing hobby. We discussed it daily, in unmechanical terms, determined not to be beaten.

On Wednesday of the following week we had just had dinner, Uncle's coffee had been brought in, he had selected and lit his thin cigar. He always smoked this in a dreamy manner with half-closed lids as though transporting himself back to his beloved Valladolid. How surprised and saddened I should have been had I known that within a few months he would in fact be transferred back to that city to become a member of the College staff. But this afternoon I did not know nor, I am sure, did he. Mellowed by the coffee and cigar, there was a quizzical look in his eye.

'The Flying Scotsman?'

'Yes, Uncle,' I shouted.

We brought the engine out from the toolshed. While Miss O'Riordan watched disapprovingly from the kitchen window, making remarks under her breath to Mrs Vitello, we fed it oil, spirit and water, saw it boil furiously to bursting point. And all without effect. It simply would not 'go'.

With our heads over the straining machine Uncle said, in a voice wherein, at last, I detected a note of pessimism:

'It must be blocked somewhere. Try giving it a shake.'

I gave it a despairing shake, a hard, a violent shake, and finally, in a temper, I kicked it. Immediately there was a sharp explosion. The boiler, from its internal parts, shot out a blob of viscous matter. Steam hissed from an unsuspected valve. The wheels spun violently and the Flying Scotsman shot away from us like an arrow.

'Hurrah!' I yelled. 'It's going. Look, Miss O'Riordan, look!'

Straight down the concrete path it sped, gathering momentum with every thrust of its powerful pistons, wheels racing, steam flying, its firebox sparking like a comet's tail. A glorious, stupendous sight!

'Oh, heavens,' suddenly exclaimed my uncle.

I followed his eyes. Sarah Mooney had come out of the church and, with her head down and her bad leg dragging, was hobbling towards us on her crutch.

'Look out, Sarah!' shouted Uncle Simon.

Sarah, absorbed by the prospect of tea, did not hear, and the engine, bearing down with an accuracy almost inspired, struck her crutch fair and square. The crutch flew into the air in a perfect arc and broke with a resounding crash. Mrs Mooney sat down on the concrete, while the engine, emitting billows of steam, spun over on its side and lay panting hoarsely on the grass. For a moment Sarah sat stupefied, enveloped in a heavenly cloud, then with a screech she scrambled to her feet and ran, ran like a hare, to the safety of the church.

'Well, thank God she isn't hurt.' Uncle turned to Miss O'Riordan, who had now joined us.

'But Uncle Simon,' I clutched his arm, finding my voice at last, 'didn't you see? She ran. No crutch. Actually ran. It's a miracle.'

He looked at me thoughtfully, but before he could answer Miss O'Riordan, who for once was looking pleased, interposed.

'If she's not back tomorrow with two crutches that *will* be a miracle.'

Uncle still said nothing, but he was smiling now. I think he had enjoyed Sarah Mooney's twenty-yard dash.

The Flying Scotsman, after its brief moment, never was the same again, and without any attempt at repair, was retired to the attic. Indeed, from that day on, the whole complexion of my stay at the rectory changed. I was told nothing, but from Miss O'Riordan's expression and my uncle's manner, which became serious and more concealed, the news from Ardfillan was obviously much worse. Simon began to cross the firth more often, returning with a sad face which he tried, not always with success, to lighten when I appeared. In the kitchen, too, I would break in on muted conversations between Miss O'Riordan and Mrs Vitello, to be greeted with excessive and too obvious endearments, but not before I had heard the two ominous, often repeated words, 'galloping consumption', words which immediately and vividly created in my mind's eye a vision of my father, pale as on that unforgettable night, galloping madly to destruction on a great white horse.

I never understood or sought to explain to myself why the horse should be white, but I knew then, knew absolutely, and with a strange apathy, that my father would soon die. Had I not sensed, unconsciously, on that night of blood that he would not recover? I hung about the house, feeling neglected, hearing with impatience the whispers of 'another haemorrhage', resentful of the gravity and preoccupation of the others, chilled by the loss of the warmth that had enveloped me.

One evening, some ten days later, I had coaxed, perhaps tormented my uncle into a game of draughts. We were at the board and he had permitted me to crown a man when I heard a door bell ring, a sound I disliked since it usually was the prelude to a sick call. But when Miss O'Riordan

85

entered, she had a telegram in her hand. My uncle read it, turned pale, and said:

'I must go to the church, Laurie.'

Miss O'Riordan went out of the room with him, leaving me alone. Not a word to me. Yet I had known instantly. I did not cry. Instead a dullness, a kind of heavy dreariness descended on me. I looked at the draughtboard, regretting the untimely ending of the game where, with my crowned man, I held a winning position. I counted the piles of pennies on the mantelshelf, twelve pennies in each pile, studied again my friend, the old man on the pillar, then went down to the kitchen.

Miss O'Riordan was weeping and, with many fervent ejaculations, saying her beads.

'I have a headache, dear,' she explained, concealing the rosary under her apron.

I felt like saying: 'Why tell a lie, Miss O'Riordan?'

But I gave no sign of grief until the following morning when Miss O'Riordan, deputed for the occasion, led me to the window of the sitting-room, put an arm about my shoulders and while we both gazed distantly to the harbour where a Clan Line ship was in process of unloading, proceeded by a series of low-toned graduated remarks, to break the news gently. Then, because I felt I must, that it was expected of me, I burst dutifully into tears. But they were quickly dried, so quickly that Miss O'Riordan was able to remark several times in the course of the day, and with a complacent air of self-achievement: 'He took it well!'

In the afternoon, having dressed herself 'for the town', she took me into Port Cregan and bought me a ready-made black suit which, being chosen, as she put it, for my growth, was a shameful misfit. The jacket hung on me like a sack, the wide trousers, unlike my own neat shorts, sagged halfway down my calves, giving the impression of a man's long trousers, amputated well below the knee. Determined to make me a walking example of grief the good Miss O'Riordan completed the outfit with a black bowler hat that extinguished me, a black tie, a crape band for my arm and black gloves.

Next morning, in this hideous panoply of death that made me look like a miniature mute, I said goodbye to Miss O'Riordan who, in embracing me, calling me 'her poor lamb', bathed me with her incomprehensible tears.

But perhaps she foresaw better than I what lay ahead of me. Then, accompanying my uncle, I departed in a cab for the Ardfillan boat.

We sat on deck where the same German quartet discoursed the same lively Viennese waltz tunes. My heart lifted up at the music to which some children were skipping around. I wanted to jump up and join them, but sombrely conscious of my attire which, in fact, had drawn upon me much sympathetic attention, I dared not.

TWELVE

THE FUNERAL took place privately in Lochbridge where, in the local cemetery, a family plot had been honourably provided by my father's humble yet eminently worthy parents. It was in this industrial town that Laurence and Mary Carroll, driven from their Irish croft by the great potato famine, had settled to lead out their lives in pious obscurity, here my father had lodged in bachelor rooms before his marriage, and here too was Uncle Bernard's establishment, the Lomond Vaults, now revealed, to my surprise and chagrin, as a rambling, run-down public house, above which my uncle and his wife resided with my two cousins, Terence and Nora.

The afternoon was grey and drizzling as the cortège set out from the church. But I was not there to view it. To my immense relief Mother had ruled that I must not attend the burial. On the previous day, over my frantic protests, I had been induced by Uncle Bernard to take what he called 'a last farewell' of my father in his coffin. This was my introduction to death, and I had been frozen by the sight of Father, so young, so handsome, a perfect waxen image of himself, stretched in the sumptuous, embossed, richly cushioned shell that Uncle Bernard himself, with extravagant sentimentality and against Mother's wishes, had ordered. Prepared immaculately for the grave, hair brushed, moustache clipped, Father was groomed, as he himself would have ironically phrased it, 'to a hair'. Then, as Uncle Bernard, oozing tears, lifted one of those flaccid, clay-cold hands and placed it in mine, tightening my skin with horror, I noticed at the same instant on the dead chin, cleanshaven by the undertaker only the day before, a faint reddish beard beginning to sprout. With a shriek I tore myself free and dashed so wildly from the room that I cut my head on the jamb of the door. So now, with a bandage round my brow, but freed from the further terrors at the graveside, I waited with my new cousin Nora in the backyard of the Lomond Vaults.

The yard lay between the railway line and rear premises of the red-brick Vaults, a strange, unbelievable yard, enclosed by broken wooden palings, a no-man's-land, littered with lumber, with wooden cases, with stacks of empty and broken bottles and their rain-sodden straw casings. A heap of coke blocked the cellar door, in one corner there was a dilapidated poultry hut before which hens scraped, pecked and cackled, in another a range of dog kennels that seemed held together by a tangle of rusted wire. And all this existed in such a state of wild disorder, contrasting with the spotless order of my own home, with all that I had known or seen before, it actually became invested with a fearful and attractive charm.

Something of this must have shown in my face as I glanced around, for Nora favoured me with a mischievous, inquiring smile.

'It's not very tidy, is it, man?'

'Not very,' I agreed tactfully.

'That's how things are here. We're always in a mess.' She added carelessly: 'The whole property's condemned.'

'Condemned?' The word had a sinister sound.

'Ordered to be pulled down. By the town council. If it doesn't fall down first.'

At that moment a Caledonian train roared past, perhaps the very train that my poor father had taken in his youth, and in the thunder of its passage, as though bearing out Nora's words, the entire yard rattled, boxes fell off the top of the pile, the hens scuttled for shelter, while the house itself, quivering and vibrating throughout its aged structure, loosed a small piece of mortar that fell exactly at my feet.

I gazed at her apprehensively.

'But what will you do then, Nora? When it's pulled down?'

'We'll just go bankrupt, I suppose, like we nearly did before.'

Was she joking? No, apparently she was serious, yet she did not seem to mind a bit, and with complete unconcern was smiling at me again. I liked her smile, so full of a careless ease that was beyond me. Indeed, although I had known my cousin only a few hours, I was inclined to like all of her, especially her thin, delicate, vivid face which, despite the bereavement in the family, was bright and full of fun. Her skin had a creamy colour, her eyes were almost black with long curling lashes and her hair, which she kept tossing about, was a glossy black also. Although almost three years older than me, she was small, still about my height, and very skinny, with thin elbows and legs. She had been dressed for the occasion in a smart new braided black voile dress with fetching pleats which, contradicting her protestations of financial insolvency, had a most expensive look.

'That's Terry's dog. The Joker.'

As though anxious to stir up our lagging conversation she had resumed her air of cicerone, pointing to a long, lean, mouse-coloured hound with melancholy eyes and a thin curved rat-like tail that silently materialized in an elongated manner from the recesses of the kennel, a dog of a species I had never seen before and which bore absolutely no resemblance to the aristocratic canines that I had hitherto observed being carefully walked out in the privileged Ardfillan thoroughfares.

'Is it a mongrel' I inquired.

'God, no. Don't you know a whippet when you see one? The Joker's a valuable animal that cost a mint of money. And has made a mint for Terry. You'll not beat Terry at the races, dog, horse, or man.'

My expression of total incomprehension must have made her want to give me up. Yet although she shook her head she was not easily defeated. She chose however a simpler gambit.

'Well,' she commented, breaking the silence, 'they'll soon be back. But not Uncle Simon. He can't get out of his appointment with the Bish.'

Not to be behind her, I nodded agreement, although I had not the faintest idea what she meant or who the Bish might be. Before leaving for the cemetery Uncle Simon had talked privately with my mother, but I had no idea of the nature of their conversation.

'Naturally the old Bish is against it,' she went on, 'but

he'll have to give in. You understand it's a great honour for Simon.'

'Oh, yes,' I lied. This little wretch seemed to have the inside track on everything. Only a fearful curiosity made me ask:

'Who is the Bish, Nora?'

She stared at me.

'The Bishop, man, old Mick Macauley in Winton. Don't you know that they want Simon back to teach at the College in Spain?'

I gazed at her in shocked dismay. So Uncle Simon would be leaving us, just when I had become so fond of him. And Mother had been counting on him too.

'Uncle Leo will be coming back though,' I said, after a pause, anxious not to lose the stabilizing presence of this other uncle whom I had never seen until today.

'Oh, yes,' she said indifferently. 'Leo'll be back, he has to wait for his train. He's a queer one.'

'Queer?'

And deep . . . You'll see for yourself. Terry calls him a cold-blooded bastard.'

This unmentionable word uttered with such casual aplomb she might still have been referring to the Bishop, shook me to my heels. But I persisted.

'What does he do, Nora?'

'He has a warehouse in Winton. Sells cloth wholesale. But Uncle Conor used to laugh and say that no one ever knew what Leo was up to.'

Since the day before I had been in a highly agitated state and this unexpected reference to my father, alive and laughing, brought a sudden rush of tears to my eyes. She frowned at me protestingly.

'God, don't start that again, just when I was beginning to take to you. Here, come on and I'll show you the hens.'

Grasping my arm she dragged me forcibly into the hen house, bent on distracting me at all costs.

'See, there they are. Chookey, chookey, chookey. We had a dozen but two died. That one's broody, I have to chase it off the nest. Get off, there, you old devil. And here's an egg, a brown one too, we'll take it up and I'll boil it for your tea.'

She held up the smooth, brown, slightly speckled egg enticingly. But it was no use. The startling change from daylight to the dim mysterious interior of the hen house, redolent of straw and other more acrid odours, had increased my woe.

'Will you stop it, man, for the love of God?'

Holding the egg, she pushed me against the wall of the hen house, and with one arm firmly round my neck and the other braced above me against the wall, she began to butt me hard with her head. The brush of her hair against my cheek, the warmth of her nearness, the determined encirclement of her arms, all this was strangely soothing. When, at last, rather short of breath, she paused, I felt a sharp regret that her restorative treatment had not continued longer. I had begun to smile wanly when suddenly I became conscious of a sticky coagulation on the top of my skull that was now running down the back of my neck.

'Oh, God, the egg's broke,' she exclaimed. 'Quick, give us your hanky. There now, never mind, never mind, it's a grand shampoo, nothing better for the hair.'

What could I do but submit to her ministrations as she mopped me up?

'Anyway, that's knocked the water out of you,' she declared, examining me critically. 'But you could still do with a sup of something on the way up.'

Docilely, I permitted her to lead me across the yard to the back door, then along a narrow passage into the saloon bar. While I gazed with a neophyte's wonder at the ivory beer pulls, the rows of bottles on the shelves, the sawdust thickly strewn on the floor, making round islands of the brass spittoons, she remarked:

'Out of respect we're closed till the evening.'

She advanced calmly to a small china barrel on the counter emblazoned with the words RUBY PORT. Turning the little nickel tap she expertly drew off two full glasses of the wine.

'Here,' she said. 'Put this down. But don't tell. It'll stiffen you up.'

I was now clay in her hands. While she sipped her portion, I 'put mine down'. Then I followed her up the back stairs to the parlour, a big room full of good but knocked-about furniture and, in its own way, almost as untidy as the yard. Above the fireplace, before which some towels hung drying, was a large coloured photograph of Pope Leo XIII, with some strips of yellowish palm stuck in at the top, and at the bottom a pink notice for the June Ayr Races. A treadle harmonium with broken keys stood at the far end of the room, and in an adjoining corner were some odd shoes, a split bag of dog biscuits, some battered prayer books, and a pair of old striped braces. It seemed inconceivable that Uncle Bernard should be so different from my father, who hated slovenliness and in his own person, and in all that applied to hygiene, was almost excessively fastidious.

As I entered, feeling perceptive and extremely light on my feet, Mother was busy helping Bernard's wife, whom I now knew as Aunt Teresa, to set the long mahogany table for tea. Mother's activity and resolved air of cheerfulness astounded me. True, she was much thinner, but when I returned from Port Cregan I had expected to find her prostrate with an inconsolable grief. I had failed to realize that, whatever reaction the future might bring, for the present she had no sorrow left. Worn out by months of nursing, knowing that my father must die, she could only feel relief to see his suffering end.

'How nice your breath smells, dearest,' she said, kissing me. She had kissed me a great deal since my return. 'Have you been sucking sweets?'

'No, Mother,' I said virtuously.

At that moment Aunt Teresa wandered in with a platter on which lay a huge red boiled ham.

'Didn't I hear the cab?' she said, smiling and nodding to me. 'If so, we may as well dish up.'

Nora's mother was a gentle wavering little woman who seemed wrapped in an air of abstracted wonder. Her bosoms, swelling visibly under a rich black satin blouse, gave me the odd notion—was it promoted by the port?— that for comfort she had removed her stays or perhaps forgotten to put them on. Her face, naturally pale but faintly flushed now from the stove, had a dreamy remoteness as though years of these condemned Vaults and the disorder that reigned there had in the end exalted her to a supernatural plane where she drifted peacefully, isolated and immune.

'There they are now,' Nora confirmed. 'On the stairs.'

Almost as she spoke the door opened and my two uncles entered. Bernard came first, a heavy, round-shouldered, flabby figure, half bald, with a full, sagging face and pouches under his eyes which, although he could not have been more than forty-five, made him look much older. Since already I had observed in him an emotionalism so acute that he seemed unable to contain it, I was not surprised to see his black-bordered handkerchief still in his hand as he approached my mother and laid a consoling arm upon her shoulders.

'My poor girl, the hand of the Lord has been laid upon us. But you must be brave, it's over now, he's at rest under the sod, with his own kith and kin, and we can only bow our heads to the will of the Almighty. God's will be done. But I tell you, it fair broke my heart as they lowered him down, Conor my own brother, so young, and well favoured, with most of his days and his future before him. And to leave you and the boy, ah, that must have been the bitterest cut of all. But God help me, I'll see that you don't want, neither of the two of you. I swore it at the grave, and by your leave I'll swear it again. Now dear, you must keep your strength up, so sit down and we'll have a bite. When we've had our tea we'll go into everything and see what's to be done for you.'

Bernard's affirmation, delivered almost in one breath with lyrical intensity, and which my mother listened to with averted head, touched me deeply. I glanced expectantly at Uncle Leo, but to my surprise and disappointment he remained silent. This uncle, a few years younger than Bernard, was tall and extremely thin, with a long pale cleanshaven expressionless face, topped by a plastering of smooth black hair. Unlike the others he gave no evidence of mourning, being dressed in a plain navy-blue suit, so tight fitting and shiny with use that he seemed to have grown into it.

While Bernard was speaking his features remained completely blank except for a slight, yet most peculiar twitching of the corners of his lips which, but for the fact that his personality seemed so reserved, repressed and distant, might have been the vestige of a sarcastic smile.

At this moment my cousin Terence came bustling in, looking smarter, more handsome than ever, quite a man of the world in fact, and when Bernard had said grace we all sat down.

The lavishness of the repast provided me with a further indication of Bernard's generosity, all the more commendable in the face of his own financial difficulties. As Aunt

Teresa kept drifting in and out, absently bringing fresh hot supplies from the kitchen, sausages, white puddings, a boiled fowl—never had I seen such quantities of food— Bernard repeatedly pressed us to eat and, considering his grief, sustained himself with remarkable fortitude. Mother had not much appetite nor, indeed, had I. The ruby port was taking its toll and my head felt as if it were stuffed with cottonwool, an extraordinary yet not unpleasant aerial sensation that made me forget my earlier miseries. Most curious of all, however, were the table manners and gastronomic proclivities of Uncle Leo, who at the outset of the feast had resolutely reversed his plate to preclude all possibility of the funeral meats being placed upon it and, avoiding like the plague Aunt Teresa's steaming dishes, contented himself with a glass of milk, a plain wheaten scone, masticated with extreme thoroughness, and four tablets taken from a little bottle which he extracted from his waistcoat pocket.

'And now, my dear Grace,' Bernard gazed at Mother with admiring sympathy, 'if it's agreeable to you, should we have our little family chat about your future. From what I can gather, our poor Con didn't leave you with too much of the ready—if I may put it that way without offence.'

'Almost everything we had went into Conor's business,' Mother answered quietly. 'And to very good purpose. He had paid off every penny he owed, both to Hagemann and the bank. He was his own master.'

Uncle Leo, who had so far said nothing, had a strange way of not looking directly at anyone. Now his gaze travelled well over Mother's head as he asked despondently:

'Was he insured?'

'No. I believe he tried eventually, but was refused a policy.'

'What exactly is in the bank?' Leo persisted, still viewing the ceiling.

'A matter of two hundred pounds.' Mother flushed as she answered. 'And of course there's the doctor's bill and the funeral expenses.'

Bernard raised a restraining, benevolent hand.

'Not a word more about that, dear. As I told you before, I'll take care of the funeral, every penny of it. And we'll throw in the doctor's bill as well.'

'Even if that's done, two hundred won't take you far,' Leo said gloomily. 'In my opinion the first thing you'll have to do is sell some of your furniture and get out of that big expensive flat.'

'I have already arranged to do so.'

I wanted to cheer Mother for that calm, composed answer, and such was my elevated state, I would probably have done so had not Leo immediately resumed.

'Next, you must try to sell the agency.'

Mother shook her head.

'No.'

'Why not? It must be worth something . . . if we can find a buyer. Even if the U.D.L. have cooled off they'll make some sort of offer.'

'I don't want a buyer.'

I reached under the table and found her hand. It was cold and trembling slightly. But she went on firmly:

'Conor made the business. It was all his idea, and a wonderful one too. Apart from my loyalty to him, I'm not going to see it thrown away. It's essentially single-handed work. I believe I can do it. And I'm going to try. I'm going to carry on the agency.'

There was a silence, then Bernard thumped the table enthusiastically with his fist.

'And you'll do it, too. You'll have sympathy on your side. You'll get orders for that alone, not to speak of your pretty face. By God, you're a brave little woman. But what about the boy? You'll be in Winton all day. Shall I send him to Rockcliff for you, like I did my Terry?'

'He'll go later, perhaps,' Mother said. 'I can't part with him now. I've arranged with a neighbour, the lady downstairs, to rent three rooms in her house. She'll keep an eye on Laurence when he's not at school.'

So we were going to Miss Greville! Following on Mother's previous announcement, for which I had been equally unprepared, this news gave me a real start in which apprehension and excitement had an equal part. While Bernard continued to praise Mother with the most optimistic prognostications of her success, I tried to foresee the possibilities inherent in our new lodging and, although I failed, somehow sensed they would be profound. The discussion between Mother and my uncles went on, but I had now passed beyond the stage of coherent attention, although from time to time I was vaguely conscious of the note of pessimistic protest in Uncle Leo's voice.

'Well,' he declared finally. 'If your mind is made up, there's nothing more to be done.'

In the pause that followed Uncle Bernard made a special sort of sign to Terence who nodded and got to his feet.

'He'll open up below,' Bernard explained with a sigh. 'Life must go on.'

'I'll feed the dog first,' Terry said. 'Get his dinner, Nora. Like to come?' he added, with a glance that casually took in me.

We descended to the yard by an outside stair I had not noticed before. Repulsing the Joker's frantic leapings and quiverings with the words: 'Down, brute,' Terence dusted off a convenient box and seated himself judicially.

'Well, caper, here we are again.'

'Yes, Terence.'

'And not under the best of circumstances.'

'No, Terence.'

A pause while he looked me up and down.

'As a matter of interest, who slapped these duds on you?'

'Miss O'Riordan.'

'I thought as much.' He shook his head in slow disparage-ment. 'You know, caper, if you don't watch out women'll be the ruin of you. You've got to learn to stand up for yourself, and not let them run you, or you'll be under their thumb for the rest of your life.'

Terence's homily was not altogether comprehensible but as it seemed to manifest some interest in my welfare I took it as a compliment to my bereaved state. He seemed indeed to be on the point of offering me further sage advice; however, at this point Nora appeared with a plate on which lay a thick outsize slice of prime raw steak.

'You'd better hurry, Terry. There's a crowd outside with their tongues hanging out.'

'Ah, let them wait, it'll strengthen their thirst. I want to show caper the Joker.' Holding off the hound whose whip-like tail lashings had now become intense, he took the plate from Nora, placed it on the ground and in a solemn tone of warning said: 'Friday.'

The Joker, already launching himself on the steak, was stopped by what had every appearance of a lethal electric shock. Curved in an acute parabola over the plate, saliva drooling from his jaws, he fixed one intense imploring eye on Terence.

'You see,' remarked Terence, lighting a cigarette in a manner so leisurely as to exacerbate the Joker's anguish. 'That's a good Catholic dog. He'll not touch flesh meat on days of abstinence.'

'But today isn't Friday, Terrry,' I objected.

'For the Joker,' Terence said, 'my word is good enough. Yes, man, for that dog I'm as infallible as the Pope. In a minute I'm going to tell him it's Saturday.'

I was deeply impressed until a thought struck me.

'But how do you manage in Lent, Terry? Practically every day's a fast day then.'

'In Lent,' Terence appeared to reflect. 'In Lent we get him a dispensation. Yes, man, that's a very holy dog. Strange too, when you consider I bought him from a Jewish gentleman by the name of K. Q. Fink. I had a bit of trouble getting him out of his Kosher habits but in the end, thank God, we converted him. And has it paid off, man! Now he's just full of piety. You ought to see him play lame just before I match him in a race.'

Where this remarkable dialogue would have led us is impossible to determine. Certainly it appeared to cause Nora a series of suppressed internal spasms. But it was interrupted by a violent banging on some outer door and a voice shouting:

'Open up, will ye, for the love of God. We're all parched out here.'

At this Terence lounged to his feet and released the Joker with truly apostolic gesture and intonation.

'There's proof for you, caper,' he remarked as he went out. 'The Joker never fails me.'

In three swift snaps the steak had gone.

A somewhat hollow silence followed this remarkable demonstration. It was broken by my mother calling me from the head of the stair. Apparently we had been pressed to stay the night with Uncle Bernard but to my disappointment, since I harboured an extraordinary inclination to resume my acquaintance with Nora in the hen house, Mother had declined. And now, as it was past four o'clock, she said we must leave for our train.

While she was getting her coat and hat Leo, who had not spoken to me once, had not even appeared aware of my existence, came slowly towards me. While his tall, sad, enigmatic presence loomed above me, he produced from his shiny trouser pocket a short handful of silver amongst which, after a diligent search, he found a threepenny bit.

'Here, boy,' he said. 'Don't waste it. It's hard-earned money. And always remember this. Your best friend is your own bank book.'

So far I had not been at all favourably impressed by Uncle Leo but now, discovering him to be so poor—a suspicion I had already entertained—yet willing to spare me this coin, albeit the smallest in the realm, and as I now observed, thin, darkish in colour and slightly bent, all of which made me dubious of its negotiability, I felt a twinge of sympathetic pity and thanked him profusely.

'It seems Bernard has you in hand,' he said impassively, though his lips were twitching again. 'There's no end that he means to do for you. I've a poor sort of business myself, but if ever you should need a job or want to learn a trade, come to me. I've told your mother.'

Without saying goodbye he turned and went off.

Nora and Terence, now released from duty by his father, came with us to the station. How pleased I was when Nora took my hand, swinging it as we walked along. I reddened with gratification when Terry asked me if I could still run fast.

It was good to be in the open again with a fresh breeze to blow away all the strange and conflicting impressions so summarily forced upon me. Mother's step seemed lighter too, as though she had not been at ease in Bernard's house, and that while she had supported it with calm and fortitude the day had been for her a fearful ordeal.

Seated together in the corner of a third-class compartment she did not speak. Gazing intently into her face I felt sadness descend upon her. What were her thoughts? Of my father no doubt, and perhaps of how blessedly different he had been, as was Simon too, from those other brothers. Or did she think of the strangeness of her life, contrasting her up-bringing and early background, both so proper and correct, with all that she had experienced and endured today? I could not guess. Then, all that mattered was that she held me close to her as the train rumbled past the Lomond Vaults and, gathering speed, bore us through a pale serene sunset towards the darkening valley of the Fruin beyond.

THIRTEEN

IN THE SECOND WEEK of April Mother and I moved down to Miss Greville's house—a memorable transition, not in domicile alone, but also in our lives. The accommodation so graciously offered was pleasing and, everything considered, well suited to our needs. At the back of the first floor of the spacious maisonette we had two nice rooms, not large but well lit and cheerful since both overlooked the lawn, and an adjoining smaller room, actually a deep alcove which Miss Greville, by installing a gas cooker and a porcelain sink, had converted to a small but practicable kitchen. A bathroom, too, was conveniently near on the half-landing.

Care had undoubtedly been taken and thought expended to make us comfortable and while I had no exact knowledge of the sum Mother paid in rent it must of necessity have been disproportionately modest, representing, in my view, Miss Greville's wish to help us rather than any sordid desire for gain.

Here, then, in this miniature lodging, our new life began. Every morning Mother rose at seven o'clock and made our breakfast. Usually I had a cereal called grapenuts, then we each had a boiled egg and hot buttered toast. I drank a glass of milk while Mother had several cups of very strong tea. She confided in me that she could never do without her morning tea. It seemed to brisken and fortify her, although she still looked sad. She had not yet lost the pinched look that startled me when I returned from Port Cregan.

After breakfast she washed the dishes and I dried them, then, while I finished dressing, she put on her new business suit, a costume of dark grey material, and how relieved I was to see her out of that sinister funeral black, which she had wisely decided would be prejudicial to her work. At quarter past eight we left the house together, Mother resolutely to take the eight-forty train for Winton, I reluctantly, to go to school. I need hardly add that I was still attending St Mary's—our position at the moment was too uncertain to justify any change to a better school.

Nevertheless, if that cherished dream seemed deferred, I was amply compensated by a new and striking departure from my dull routine. Since my poor mother was away all day, did not in fact get home until six o'clock at night, and made the best of some kind of lunch at one or other of the city tea rooms, Miss Greville had suggested, had indeed insisted, that I take my mid-day meal with her. Lunch with Miss Greville became then the fascination and, at least in the beginning, the bane of my existence.

On the first day, when I arrived breathless at half past twelve, having hurried all the way back from school for fear of being late, she was waiting for me in the dining-room, standing erect with her thumb in her waistband. She glanced at the curious bronze and porcelain clock on the mantelpiece.

'Good. You are punctual. Go and wash your hands. And brush your hair.'

When I returned, she indicated my place. We sat down. The food, served by Campbell, the silent elderly maid who behaved as though I did not exist, was delicious, hot, and startlingly strange. The table appointments, among which twin silver pheasants were outstanding, no less than the arrangement of the heavy silver cutlery, embarrassed and intimidated me. I dropped my stiff napkin and had to grope under my chair. When I had retrieved it Miss Greville addressed me pleasantly.

'We are going to have our first little talk, Carroll. You observe that I call you simply Carroll. As you are now the only Carroll in this vicinity you have no claim to be known as *young* Carroll.'

To a boy endearingly denoted Laurie, and only on the strictest occasions referred to as Laurence, I could only regard this repeated use of my second name a brutal assault on my feelings.

'To resume. When we go to table you must in future withdraw my chair and see that I am properly seated before *you* seat yourself. Do you understand?'

'Yes, Miss Greville, ' I said, abjectly.

'Again, during our lunches, which I trust will always be agreeable to you, we must cultivate the art of conversation. We shall talk of current events, of sport if you wish, of natural history, books, music and of people. The first person to be discussed, Carroll, is you.'

I turned hot all over.

'To begin, I assume that you have no desire to become a confirmed brooder. You know, of course, what that is?'

'Some kind of a hen,' I faltered.

'Apt, Carroll, if erroneous. A creature perpetually wallowing in self-pity. Would you wish to be like that?'

'No, Miss Greville.'

'Then you must stop being sorry for yourself. Fond though I am of your mother I regard you as suffering from an excess of maternal leniency. I therefore propose to introduce you to the Spartan ideal. Doubtless you know of the Greek city of Sparta, where weak children were simply exposed and left to perish? Or better still, simply thrown over the cliff.'

'Oh, no,' I gasped.

'I,' said Miss Greville coldly, 'have seen the actual cliff. Now, Carroll, do you want to be thrown over the cliff or to live like a real Greek boy?'

'And how *did* he live?' I tried to express contempt.

'From the day he went to school at the age of seven he spent a considerable part of each day exercising under trained supervision, in the palaestra. He wrestled, ran, punched a ball filled with fig seeds, rode bareback, learned to throw missiles and ward them off, his interest being kept alive by innumerable competitions for boys of different ages. But enough of history. For the present it will suffice to suggest to you the virtue of a cold bath every morning, of strenuous exercises, of endurance tests that harden the body and summon up the blood. The uncomfortable truth is, Carroll, that I find you a soft, spoiled, spineless, and abnormally solitary boy.'

Outraged beyond belief, I felt my eyes fill with water.

'If you weep, Carroll,' she said firmly, 'I shall, from this instant, utterly disown you.'

Repressively, I bit my lip hard. Cruelly maligned though I was, I did not, strangely, wish to be disowned. Besides, indignation was beginning to seethe in me. The phrase 'abnormally solitary' stuck in my throat.

'Perhaps you will tell me,' I said carefully, so as not to break down, 'how a boy in my position can help it. Who can he not be solitary with?'

'With me. I am going to take you in hand.' Miss Greville regarded me calmly. 'Do you know anything of botany?'

'No, I don't,' I answered sulkily.

'Then tomorrow, as it is Saturday, you shall begin to learn. Be ready at nine sharp. And now you must have another cutlet. Only, remember that your fork is not a shovel. The prongs are to be utilized. Do not scoop. Impale.'

Having thus reduced me, Miss Greville now appeared to withdraw into herself. With a faint, peculiar smile on her lips, her mood seemed focused on the invisible. Her eye, however, remained on the clock. When it struck one she rose and, taking the cup of coffee that had been served her, advance to the window. Spellbound, I watched her take her stand behind the long lace curtain where, partly concealed, she slowly sipped her coffee. Suddenly the cup was arrested, her smile deepened, remained. At last she turned and with a satisfied, almost a gay expression, put down her cup.

'You may go now, Carroll,' she said pleasantly. 'And don't forget. Tomorrow morning at nine.'

That afternoon in school, instead of attending to Sister Margaret Mary who was endeavouring to instruct us in the principles of compound fractions, I brooded darkly, almost heroically, on the insults I had received, and in the evening, when Mother returned from Winton, I informed her that I wished to be no party to the plans Miss Greville had conceived for me.

'I think you should go, dear,' Mother said soothingly. 'I'm quite sure Miss Greville means well by you.'

Thus it became apparent that Mother was in league with my detractor.

Next morning, between apprehension and expectation, I kept my appointment. Miss Greville presented a somewhat singular figure. She was wearing an oatmeal Harris tweed skirt much shorter than I thought proper, revealing muscular calves encased by a strong pair of weather-beaten high-laced brown boots. Her green Tyrolean hat, turned up at one side and perched on her head, sported a bushy ornament indistinguishable from a shaving-brush, and over her shoulder was rakishly slung a curious black japanned container.

'*That*,' she explained, reading my expression, 'is a vasculum. And *this* is our lunch. You may carry it.'

Handing over a bulging knapsack as weather-beaten as her boots, she helped me to strap it on my back, then we strode off at a cracking pace along the Terrace and into Sinclair Road which led straight up the hill, Miss Greville using a curious spiked walking-stick covered with little silver badges. I wanted to ask what they were, but so furious was her assault upon the slope, I thought it wiser to save my breath. Besides, I was horribly conscious of the odd glances directed towards us by the passers-by, looks of amused recognition which my companion disdainfully ignored.

Up we went, without a word exchanged between us. Soon we had passed the last big villas that were widely spaced in their extensive grounds among the first of the big pine trees. Civilization now lay behind us. We were totally in the pine woods.

Sweat had started to run into my eyes, my breath made a sharp whistling tune, and when I saw that even this remote wood was not far enough, that she meant to take me to the high moors, I almost wilted. But I would not give in. Whatever puny spirit I possessed had been ignited by this abominable yet absorbing woman. I meant to show her that I was not the sort of boy to be chucked off-hand over that Spartan cliff.

With a dry throat and a pumping heart I kept on, sometimes at a half-trot, refusing to lag behind, and when at last we broke out of the woods on to that great wide expanse of moorland that ran on and on for many miles, free and undefiled across Glen Fruin to the shores of the Loch, I was still, though completely blown, at her side.

Here, mercifully, she drew up, looked at me, then took her watch out of her waistband.

'One hour and twenty minutes,' she announced. 'Not altogether bad. We'll do better as you progress. Are you fagged?'

'Not in the least,' I lied.

Inspecting me closely, for the first time, she actually smiled.

'Then we'll start on the real business of the day.' She spoke with animation. 'It's been an open winter and with luck we should find some interesting things for your collection.'

Without enthusiasm, I followed her as, with bent head, she stalked off slowly into the heather.

'You know, I'm sure, the commoner heath flowers. The ericas, not yet out, the yellow gorse, the broom and the cotton grass— these white tufts blowing in the wind.' She paused. 'But have you seen this?'

'No, I haven't,' I said sourly.

Kneeling down she had parted the grass and exposed a delicate little plant with pointed green leaves and starry, bright golden-yellow flowers.

'The bog asphodel. *Narthecium ossifragum*. One of the *Liliaceae*.'

Quite against my wishes and inclination, I was impressed, not only by her manifest erudition, but by the sudden uncovering of this hidden, sparkling and wholly unsuspected flower.

'Shall we dig it up?'

'Decidedly not. But we'll take one raceme for pressing.' And she snipped off a single stem which, rather to my surprise since I had decided not to co-operate, I accepted and tucked away in the vasculum.

We proceeded for some minutes without incident, then she stopped again.

'Here is something rather striking. The round-leafed sundew. *Drosera rotundifolia*.'

As I gazed questioningly at the graceful little rosette, she went on.

'Each leaf, as you see, bears several rows of crimson hairs, terminating in rounded heads, like a sea-anemone's tentacles. Indeed they serve a similar purpose. They secrete a clear sticky fluid which entraps small insects crawling over the leaf. Their efforts to free themselves irritate the hairs which bend over the insect so that it is secured, digested and assimilated by the plant.'

'I say!' I exclaimed, in a tone of wonder. 'A fly-eating plant!'

'Precisely. We shall dig this one up—I have no love for the sun-dews—plant it in peat moss and you may observe it in action at home.'

'May I really, Miss Greville?'

'Why not?'

She allowed me to wield the trowel taken from the vasculum and, when the plant was safely stowed, made a gesture of liberation.

'Now that you're launched, Carroll, you may go off on your own. Call me if you find anything that looks exciting.'

I started off, with a willingness I would not have believed possible, eager to demonstrate my tracker's skill. To my chagrin, although Miss Greville seemed to be having success, my untrained eyes found nothing. But at last, suddenly, I stumbled on a splendid bloom, starting up from amongst the withered grass, big as a hyacinth and of a deep glowing purple.

'Quick, Miss Greville,' I shouted. 'Please come quickly.'
She came.

'Do look, Miss Greville. Isn't it a beauty?'
She made a generous gesture of assent.

'The *Orchis maculata*. Tubers palmate, bracts, green, three-nerved. A first-rate specimen. I congratulate you, Carroll. If only we can find its neighbour, the *morio*, we may count ourselves fortunate.'

I blushed with pride, watching as she carefully snipped two flowers from the spiky stem and, with some other specimens she had collected, permitted me to stow them away.

We were now in a grassy saucer of the moor, probably an old sheep dip, sheltered on one side by a marbled ridge of rock. She glanced upwards. The pale sun was now directly overhead.

'Does this strike you as a suitable spot for lunch, Carroll?'
I immediately approved the terrain.

'Then see what Campbell has given us.'
I unpacked the knapsack, reverently handling the damp napkin-wrapped packages, noting with enthusiasm that several home-made sausage rolls were included. Finally, tucked in beside the flask of coffee, a splendid bottle of Comrie's lemonade was revealed.

This foresight touched me so acutely that involuntarily I exclaimed.

'Oh, Miss Greville, you are terribly kind.'
'Campbell,' she replied calmly.
'But Campbell does not like me.'
'Campbell does not show her feelings.'
'But Miss Greville, Campbell does not answer when I speak to her.'

'Campbell is not naturally predisposed to conversation. Besides, she is rather deaf.'

With Campbell disposed of, we began lunch. As this exceeded my expectation I ate a great deal, an indulgence made possible by the fact that Miss Greville herself appeared rather indifferent towards the sausage rolls. She had removed her hat, and, sitting erect with closed eyes and that faint withdrawn smile, had surrendered herself to the spirits of the moor. From time to time, while eating steadily, I gazed at her with awe. The wind was singing in the heather, overhead curlews were circling and calling against the blue sky. No other sound but the faint hum of an early bee.

'May I tell you something, Miss Greville?' I ventured, taking up the last egg-and-cress sandwich. 'I think I am going to like doing botany very much.'

Imperturbably, she inclined her head.

'Then we shall do some more presently. We still have to find an *Orchis morio* to match your *maculata*.'

After we had rested for a while we started off again, not deeper into the moor, but across, towards the road. Charged with botanical ardour, I surpassed myself. We found the *morio* orchid, and specimens of bog myrtle, yellow pimpernel and St John's wort, for all of which Miss Greville knew the Latin names. She also showed me a lapwing's nest with four eggs, and a bed of whortleberry shrubs that in a few weeks would yield us fruit.

The afternoon was fading into an umbered haze as at last we struck the road. But now, though long, it was all downhill. My legs were tired but my chest felt full of fresh air. This inflation and an intoxicating sense of achievement supported me during an unexpected encounter—which otherwise might have unnerved me—with Mr Lesly, the vicar of St Jude's, Miss Greville's church. Although I felt myself automatically suspect by all clergymen of denominations other than my own, this was a pleasant man to whom, when questioned, I identified myself as a Papist in a manner Miss Greville subsequently commended.

'Mr Lesly is exceptionally gifted. Broad-minded too.' She continued in the same strain of praise.' And of course, Carroll, we Catholics at St Jude's are in many respects in accord with you Romans, although naturally celibacy is not imposed on our clergy.'

After that we were soon home. With effusive thanks I parted from Miss Greville and dashed upstairs with the vasculum.

'I've had such a time, Mother. I found a rare orchid. We got a plant that actually eats flies, and all sorts of other specimens. Miss Greville's going to show me how to mount them, and to cut sections too, for her microscope.'

She was seated at the table, adding figures on a sheet of paper. As she raised her head, her expression remained so preoccupied that I called out:

'Mother, what's wrong? Didn't you hear me?'

She recovered herself immediately.

'Yes, dear, of course I did.'

Drawing me towards her she held me tight. 'And what fine red cheeks it's given you. Now sit beside me, very close, and tell me all about it.'

FOURTEEN

DURING that spring and summer I spent entrancing hours of happiness and well-being on the moors, sometimes with Miss Greville, more often alone. My passion for natural history had at least the merit of improving my health. Or perhaps this was due to the light dumbbells Miss Greville had placed in my room and those morning cold baths which, though Mother demurred, I now persistently endured under the admonitions of my patroness who, with compelling instances of the austerities endured by runners training for Olympia, continued to fire me with the Greek ideal.

'You have not been endowed with too remarkable an anatomy, Carroll. You must make the most of it.'

While no visible muscular bulges appeared, and it was mortifying when Miss Greville sought vainly for the first sign of my biceps, nevertheless, I did at last begin to grow. And beyond this, I became absurdly expert in moorland lore. I knew, and had found, practically every wild flower between Ardfillan and Glen Fruin, could spot the subtle difference between a Cinquefoil and a Tormentil and, when I wanted to show off, could even cut and stain sections to demonstrate to Mother on Miss Greville's ancient Zeiss microscope.

My solitary wanderings through the heather had failed to afford me my greatest wish, the congenial companionship of someone my own age, but they had brought me, incredibly, the friendship of that spectre of my early childhood, a gamekeeper. After a painful introduction when, observing my figure against the horizon, keeper John Mackenzie had come striding in pursuit to charge me with 'herrying' grouse eggs, the contents of my vasculum had partially reassured him, and the botanical jargon which I gabbled in excuse probably convinced him that he was dealing with an oddity. On subsequent occasions, watching through his stalker's telescope, he must have assured himself of my innocence and took occasion to meet up with me, to sound me out and, when later on he found me useful in locating outlying nests for him, to have a companionable chat. As keeper for Glen Fruin his task was to provide a maximum of birds for the twelfth of August. I think in the end I earned his respect for he took trouble to tell me many interesting things about his work, which provided me with stimulating topics for my lunchtime conversations with Miss Greville.

'Do you know something, Miss Greville?' I would begin, having sampled with relish my first spoonful of a red soup which was apparently called *borscht*.

'I know a great many things, Carroll, to which of these do you refer?'

'Grouse, Miss Greville.'

'Yes,' she replied meditatively. 'I am fairly familiar with that bird, both on and off the table. My poor father shot a great many of them on the Yorkshire moors.'

'But do you know, Miss Greville, that when the young bird flies only five days after hatching it couldn't exist without two things?'

'The young green shoots of the heather?' she suggested.

'And?'

She shook her head.

'Midges!' I exclaimed.

She looked up from her soup.

'Good heavens, Carroll. You startle me.'

'I thought I would,' I said triumphantly. 'That's one of the reasons the old rooty heather must be burned off, and the damp patches kept on the moor as a breeding ground for the protein-rich insects.' I was rather proud of that word 'protein'—Mr Mackenzie was quite a learned man. 'Water is needed too, Miss Greville. The hen bird drinks a lot when she's sitting. Of course the sheep are Mr Mackenzie's greatest curse, he's always counting them.'

'Does he sleep badly?' she inquired, blandly.

'Oh, not that, Miss Greville. The sheep grazing on the moor. Only a certain number are supposed to be allowed and they eat the young heather day and night. They're worse than the hooded crows. They never lose their appetite.'

She at last allowed herself to smile.

'Well, I'm glad you haven't lost yours. Have some more soup.'

In these adventures, I should have been happy all through the long school holidays but for the change, that suddenly became apparent to me, in my mother. Because I loved and trusted her best in the world, I had always taken her for granted, and I had imagined that she had 'got over' Father's death. Nor could I guess what deprivation she endured beyond the loss of Father's companionship and support. Absorbed in my own pursuits, I had barely noticed her lost look when she returned from Winton in the evening, or how at times she would sit, her gaze detached, a finger pressed against her cheek, her lips moving slightly, as though she were talking to herself.

'Come, Grace,' Miss Greville would remonstrate, making a sudden appearance upstairs. 'This melancholy moping won't do at all. You must come down to me. Miss Gilbraith and Alice Charteris have called and we're going to have music.'

'I'm rather tired,' Mother would say, 'and don't really feel like it. You'll manage very well without me.'

'Nonsense, dear Grace. We all want you. And it will do you a world of good.'

These friends of Miss Greville's were mistresses at St Anne's, desirable in every way, and when she yielded to persuasion, these musical evenings did take Mother out of herself.

Yet there were responsibilities of which I realized nothing, that could not be relieved by a Haydn quartet. To me it seemed simple and natural that Mother should have taken over Father's business. Everything was settled, going well, and would continue as before. Not a breath of financial stress was in the air.

One evening the post brought a letter for Mother, an event unusual enough for me to wait expectantly while she opened and read it. Suddenly I heard her gasp, saw her press a hand to her forehead.

'Oh, dear,' she exclaimed, in a pained voice. 'This is too bad.'

'What is, Mother?'

Overcome, she sat down, holding the letter.

'Your Uncle Bernard has sent me the bill.' Mother was almost incoherent, but I saw that she must speak to me. 'Before your father died he told me he wanted, yes, insisted on a simple burial. But Uncle Bernard would not have it. He took all the responsibility. So we had all these unnecessary, hateful, expensive trappings. And now the unpaid bill, that I thought was settled long ago, has come to me, with the threat of a summons.'

'Is it much?'

'Terribly much.'

I felt myself go hot all over with indignation.

'He must pay it. He promised he would. I heard him say so.'

Mother was reading the letter again.

'He says he can't. That they've condemned his property, that he owes other people, that he's very hard pressed.'

'What a beastly thing to do. Mother, he must be a . . . a perfect cad.' This was a word I had learned from Miss Greville, and was in this case entirely misapplied. My Uncle Bernard was a soft, muddled, impracticable, self-indulgent man, always in debt and skirting the edge of disaster yet somehow managing to live well and to do well for his children. Morever, like others of his sort, he was full of good intentions. His fulsome promises and extravagant ideas of doing good were genuine. Not only did he believe at the time that he would fulfil them but often, by a sort of hallucination, became firmly convinced that he had done so. Perhaps Mother felt this, for she sighed.

'He meant well, I suppose, and I dare say he hasn't the money. He says he may have to go bankrupt. His affairs are in a bad way.'

'He always seems to be going bankrupt, Mother.' I was still unforgiving. 'And doing very nicely out of it, with lots of good food and fine clothes, and all sorts of comforts, like we saw at the funeral.'

'Some people live like that, dear. Anyway, it is my responsibity, I'll settle it at once.' Mother spoke slowly, and she added, to herself: 'My poor Conor, there will be no mean squabble over your grave.'

Bernard's letter must have made Mother feel very much alone. Uncle Simon was cloistered in Spain. We never by any chance heard a word from Leo. It was natural for her to seek encouragement elsewhere. Although she never once wrote to her home, she could get in touch with Stephen, her youngest brother, at the Winton University Union. Such a letter was sent: I posted it for Mother.

Stephen came on a Saturday afternoon and was exactly as I remembered him on his rare visits to Ardencaple—a pale, quiet and thoughtful young man, with well-cut, regular features and a fine intellectual forehead inclined to furrow in a studious frown, not saying much, but so glad to see Mother, holding her hand for a long time and looking questioningly into her eyes. Only to see them like this was to be made aware of the affection that existed between them.

A good high tea with cold ham and potato salad had been prepared, and when we had finished Mother gave me money and said I might go to the town for a box of Eman's toffee. I knew they wanted to talk so I did not hurry, but when I got back they were still talking, with their heads bent over a pile of papers on the table.

"You really mustn't worry, Grace,' Stephen was saying. 'Things are going quite well.' He had a pencil in one hand and with the other was ruffling his black hair, sending little sprays of dandruff on to his jacket collar. 'When everything is paid off, including the defaulted bill, you'll still have one hundred and fifty pounds in the bank.'

'It's little enough. With Laurence's education to think of.'

'But you have your job. Hagemann's been very fair in guaranteeing deliveries on the same terms as before. The business, as I see it, is extremely easy to run. And your orders have more or less kept up.'

'They only give them because they're sorry for me. And because they liked Conor so well.'

'They'll like you too.'

Mother shook her head, yet not so despondently as before.

'I can't go in and be hail-fellow-well-met with them over a bottle of beer, like poor Con.'

The idea of Mother with a bottle of beer was so comic I gave a shout of laughter which made them both look up, and in a moment Mother smiled back at me. She gathered up the papers.

'Did you know that your clever young uncle has taken his degree with honours and won another special research bursary at the University? You'll do that too, won't you, dear?'

I had no doubt that I would do it.

Stephen stood up, looked at his watch, a plain five-shilling Ingersoll like mine, and said it was time for his train. Then with a guarded look at me he said, in an undertone, to Mother:

'I don't want to press you again, Grace. But won't you reconsider Father's offer?'

'What's the use?' Mother said. 'Am I to go back and pretend that I'm sorry, that I made a terrible mistake, but now I'll be good and make up for it?'

'I think I could promise you'd be welcome. You'd have a comfortable home again, your own folks around you.'

'But on their terms? I couldn't bring myself to accept them.'

'Is that one point as important to you as all that?'

Mother, looking down, seemed to be debating some question with herself.

'Oddly enough it is. And certainly it is for . . . you know whom. What in all the world would he think of a mother who suddenly recanted and said, now you've got to forget all you've been brought up to and knuckle under and become something else? Besides being cruel, it would be an act of horrible disloyalty to . . . to the dead.' Mother shook her head. 'What's done is done. I don't regret it. And there's no going back on it.'

There was a longish silence. Then Stephen said:

'I believe you're right, Grace. I respect you for it.'

This conversation which I did not understand had nevertheless made me feel extremely uncomfortable. I was glad when Stephen asked me to walk with him to the train.

On our way to the station he encouraged me to stick in at my lessons. He had heard that I was clever and for any boy who hadn't a father behind him hard work was the road to success. He told me he was going to have a shot at the Indian Civil Service, not necessarily to go to India, for if he got a high enough place in the examination he would be kept at home. But he was modestly pessimistic about his chances.

Finally, just before the train pulled away, he said to me, in his cautious way:

'Don't worry your mother, Laurence, for things you don't actually need. She has enough to look after at present. And she's making quite a few sacrifices for you.'

I promised faithfully to be considerate, prudent and vigilant. Yes, in all possible ways, to cherish Mother. Did I not love her with all my heart? Alas, my promises were easily made, and soon I was careless of them. Now that the weather had finally broken and winter was drawing near, a new passion had begun to absorb me.

FIFTEEN

MISS GREVILLE had an extensive library, inherited from her father, to which I had free access. It was, I imagine, a typical English country-house library of the period, well bound, full of things both good and bad, and with a sporting flavour. During that cold, wet and sleety winter—climatic conditions normally found at that season in such latitudes—I read with ever-increasing voracity.

In the recollections of those who, like myself, have ventured into descriptions of their early years, nothing has bored me more than those long, tedious, and particularized listings of the books the author has read and which led, in the end, to the formation of a literary taste that was demonstrably excellent. For this reason I refrain from presenting a catalogue and state simply that I read everything.

But the manner of my reading may be worthy of note if only because it was so bad. Lying flat on my face in a secluded and therefore dark corner of the room with my nose pressed close to the volume, I read at a great pace, a technique of speed that increased with habit. Not only did I skip mercilessly, I acquired the unholy knack of getting the sense of a page by the almost express absorption, through my flickering vision, of certain key words and phrases. I vividly remember racing through *The Scarlet Letter* in the space of a short forenoon, getting Hester Prynne with child —by obscure processes entirely beyond me—and burying her, all between breakfast and lunch, a performance of malassimilation that even the most expert professional critic might envy.

Whatever the mental results of these endeavours, and my imagination seethed with hectic visions amidst which I strayed as in a trance, the physical effects were soon apparent. My eyes stung and reddened, I had headaches, developed a permanent crick in my neck and tossed my bed into disorder when asleep. Yet I persisted, would not, or rather could not give up, so firmly was I in the grip of the drug.

One Saturday in March when the first pale fingers of spring sunshine were feeling their way into the room, I looked up mistily from my prone position on the floor. Miss Greville was observing me with distaste.

'This won't do, Carroll.'

'What won't do, Miss Greville?'

'This bookworm business. Don't you see that the sun is out? Where is my Spartan youth?'

'Yes, but this is so awfully good, Miss Greville. Mr Jorrocks has just taken a terrible toss in the bog.'

She relented slightly.

'Yes, Jorrocks is good, isn't he? And James Pigg. Still, there's a limit, Carroll.'

She went out. Relieved, I rejoined Mr Jorrocks in his chase for his horse.

However, in the afternoon, just as I was again nicely settled, she returned.

'You still have that ball I gave you?'

'Yes.' I had in fact never used it. 'In a drawer in my room.'

'Get it,' she commanded.

With great unwillingness I obeyed, submitted while she led me to the garden.

Three cricket stumps had been pitched at the far end of the lawn while a fourth, against which a bat reclined, stood at the house end. Advancing, Miss Greville picked up the bat and flourished it.

'This is now yours, Carroll. See you keep it well oiled. Mind now, only pure linseed oil.'

When I had accepted the bat she removed her long cardigan and with a businesslike air rolled back the sleeves of her blouse, unexpectedly revealing arms as muscular as her calves. She then silently extended her palm, upon which I placed the ball, an action that afterwards supported my claim to have begun my cricketing career with a ball used at Lord's in the Eton and Harrow match.

Meanwhile. however, I had been motioned to my stance at the batsman's wicket. Although my knowledge of the game was rudimentary, I knew I had a good eye, and the bat felt extremely comfortable in my hands. As Miss Greville's grand manner had put my back up and I had resented being taken from Surtees, I resolved to hit her out of the garden and, if possible, since she would be responsible, through a window.

'Play,' she called, and with a short, fierce run, bowling underhand, launched the ball towards me.

I took a vicious swing, missed, and found my wicket in ruins.

'That was a sneak,' I protested.

'A yorker, ass.'

My humiliations during the next fifteen minutes were acute. She had been brought up on cricket, had played with her brothers as a girl, had attempted even to introduce the game at St Anne's, an unapproved act that may in part have contributed to her resignation from that prim establishment. She bowled leg breaks, off breaks, lobs, more yorkers at which, enraged, I swiped crookedly and in vain. Only when, in this manner, she had convinced me of the necessity of a straight bat did my instruction begin and with such good effect as to enable me after a further quarter of an hour to experience the delight of striking the ball sweetly with the bulge of the bat and driving it hard beyond her to the back door steps.

One of the qualities of this remarkable and, alas, unfortunate woman was her ability to communicate her enthusiasms to me. I fell madly in love with the game of cricket and played endless games with Miss Greville, a willing victim, throughout that mild dry spring. She had introduced me to the *Captain* magazine wherein, with envious rapture, I studied photographs of public-school elevens, exclusive, immaculate Olympian groups in white flannels, gay blazers and striped or quartered cricketing caps. Gone now were my expeditions to the moors, my ambition to excel in natural history. I wanted to be a famous cricketer, like George Gunn of Notts., whose name was on my bat and whose scores I followed with a passionate interest in Miss Greville's *Winton Herald*, sharing his triumph whenever he scored a century, bitterly downcast when he made a duck.

One afternoon in early June, after I had made a particularly handsome square cut that buried the ball in the currant bushes, Miss Greville looked reflective and, although she made no remark, I observed her that evening in conversation with my mother, who seemed pleased. Afterwards Mother said to me:

'Hurry back after school tomorrow, Miss Greville wants you.'

Next day, in expectation of our usual game on the lawn, I got home in good time. Miss Greville was waiting on me, but she was dressed, though sportingly, for the street, and her bicycle, with my bat strapped on the carrier, stood at the gate.

'Hop on the back step when I get going,' she told me.

Miss Greville's bicycle was a Dursley-Petersen, a first-class and expensive machine but one with its unusually high seat and unorthodox frame so distinctly original in design as to compel attention on the road. With Miss Greville aloft, in her Tyrolean hat, pedalling hard and myself hanging on by the back step, we were soon afforded evidence of presenting a unique combination to the public gaze. But these amused stares were easily ignored when at the west, superior end of the town I discovered that she was taking me to Willow Park, the ground of the Ardfillan Cricket Club.

Miss Greville swung through the open gate into the select, immaculately mown enclosure. We dismounted at the neat white pavilion. With appalling disrespect Miss Greville leaned the Dursley-Petersen against the flagstaff. In the middle of the green oval a man in yellowish-white flannels and an old sweater was slowly pushing a roller. Cupping her hands to her mouth Miss Greville shouted:

'Heston!'

He came over, hastening and touching his peaked blue cap when he recognized my companion.

'How are you, Heston?' She held out her hand.

'Pretty spry, thank you, m'am. Haven't seen much of you lately. Not since you had me over to St. Anne's.'

He was a brown, thick-set, close-cropped, tight-lipped little man, just short of middle age, whose skin seemed made of tough leather. He combined, as I well knew, the duties of professional and groundsman to the Ardfillan Club.

'You're still doing a bit of coaching, Heston?'

'Oh yes,' he admitted. 'Quite a few of the Beechfield boys come round. Especially in the holidays.'

'I want you to take on this boy. Give him three or four nets a week and send the bill to me.'

He looked at me, and under his doubting eyes I felt my chin quiver.

'He's small, Miss Greville.'

'You are not large yourself, Heston.'

He gave a faint, dry, self-contained, rather sad smile which as I afterwards discovered was his nearest approach to a laugh. No, never once did I see Heston laugh.

'All right,' he said, in an off-hand manner. 'We'll have a look at him. Now, if you like.'

We went into the pavilion, where he tossed me a pair of boy's pads. On the inside, printed in ink, I saw the name Scott-Hamilton and beneath, Beechfield School.

'Put these on. Or one of them. No, not the right leg.'

I buckled a pad on my left leg, so nervous I could scarcely fasten the straps. The pad was too big for me, it felt difficult and flapped as I walked to the practice ground. Miss Greville was already there, behind the net.

Heston began by tossing me some ridiculously easy balls, clearly indicating his opinion of my ability. The first was a soft full pitch. I attempted feebly to block it, missed completely and it hit the off stump.

'Don't be an ass, Carroll,' said Miss Greville encouragingly.

I stiffened my shaking knees, determined not to be an ass. More than anything I had ever longed for in my life, I wanted to have the entry to that cricket ground and I knew that if I made a fool of myself with Heston I should be returned to the nursery of the back garden.

I began to hit out at everything. For five minutes Heston continued to bowl at an easy pace, then he increased his run and bowled faster, so fast indeed that I flinched away from the crease. Now it was not a question of hitting, although I made one good hard square cut off a short ball, but of keeping my wicket intact. At the end of the half-hour Heston had knocked out my stumps only three times and I saw with satisfaction that he was sweating.

I know that I had done well and fully expected praise or at least congratulations. But although Heston had a private talk with Miss Greville, whom he seemed to regard with favour, to me he said no more than:

'We'll have to teach you not to run away from the fast stuff.'

But this indication, grudging though it was, that I could continue with him was enough to raise me to the heights. On the way home the Dursley-Petersen seemed to soar. Arrived, I rushed upstairs.

'Mother, Heston's taken me. Not counting the full toss he only bowled me twice.' I considered myself justified in subtracting one I had played on to my wicket.

She had just come in and, still in her outdoor clothes, was beginning to make our tea. She looked even more pleased than I had expected. Amongst her other anxieties she had been worrying about the summer holidays and what she should do with me during the long two months of the school vacation, a situation complicated by the certainty in her mind that we could not afford to go away for a change of air.

'So you can go to Willow Park in the holidays?'

'Yes,' I said boastfully, and with unutterable selfishness 'You'll not see much of me, Mother. I mean to go there every day.'

SIXTEEN

THE SUMMER was unusually fine. The long, sunny days diffused a golden light. In the boundary wood of the cricket field honeysuckle flourished, twining wild over bush and hedgerow, and whenever I drew near to Willow Park the scent intoxicated me with the promise of the afternoon.

By some further quite unrecognized personal economies Mother had bought me in Ardfillan a second-hand Raleigh bicycle that gave the impression of being almost new. From Winton one evening she brought and unwrapped a parcel containing white flannels, a navy blazer and a blue and white cricket belt with a silvered snake clasp. Alone in my bedroom I tried on this rigout and studied myself carefully in the looking-glass—Miss Greville had instructed me never to say 'mirror'. I decided that my general aspect was that of a cricketer, and although hitherto I had entertained grave doubts of my own appearance, often wondering how two such handsome parents could have had so insignificant a child, regretting especially the green colour of my eyes even to the point of discovering in *Pears' Cyclopaedia* that this almost invariably was the unhappy fate of offspring of blue and brown-eyed parentage—despite all this I was rather taken with this unusual reflection of myself. Did my eyes look a trifle less green, picking up the shade of the blazer and tending rather towards blue? Perhaps not, but I had grown a bit in a straight sort of way, my hair was a soft russet brown, and I had at least inherited my father's fresh complexion and sound white teeth.

Was it this new look that falsely established my status at Willow Park, that select preserve of affluence and snobbery? More likely my sponsorship saved me from being regarded, and possibly discarded, as an interloper. Despite her eccentricities Miss Greville had a definite status in the town. Amongst the members of the club I passed as a visitor, staying with her, perhaps her nephew, for the holidays. The keenness with which I fielded and made catches won an approval that sanctioned this view.

With the Beechfield boys my situation was more critical. Many of these boys, whose parents were stationed with the army in India or elsewhere in what was then proudly referred to as the Empire, remained at the school during the holidays, and there were others living in Ardfillan, notably the boy called Scott-Hamilton, whose pad I had worn, and his younger brother, who came often to the ground for a scratch game. At first their attitude was stony, but one day, after I had held a particularly hot return, Scott-Hamilton, a strong tall boy of thirteen who was captain of the Beechfield eleven and like myself, a cricket maniac, lounged over with his brother.

'Would you care to join us in a game? You're here for the holidays with your aunt, aren't you?'

'Yes.'

'By the way, what school are you at?'

This was a question I had long anticipated and to which, with premeditated cunning, I had prepared the answer, knowing that if in effect I had admitted to attending my unspeakable little school in Clay Street I would be damned and cast off on the spot.

'I have a tutor,' I lied calmly, yet excusing myself with the thought that after all, Miss Greville, if not my aunt, was a sort of tutor.

'Oh, I say,' said Scott-Hamilton in a tone of sympathy. 'Have you been ill?'

'Chest.' I tapped my ribs in an offhand manner.

'Hard cheese!' murmured the younger brother.

'Anyhow, it hasn't jolly well interfered with your cricket,' said Scott-Hamilton. 'Let's pick sides.'

I breathed again. It had come off. I was accepted.

Heston, of course, could have given me away. But beyond the fact that I often came down in the mornings to help him with the roller, mark the crease, or put up a new net, Heston was on my side of the fence. The sense of equality between the amateur and the professional that developed half a century later was then not even dreamed of, and Heston's position was that of a paid servant who must inveterately 'sir' his masters and be subject to their command and abuse: 'Heston, blanco my boots, will you?' or, 'Heston, give me half a dozen on the off side.' 'Damn it, Heston, where the devil have you hidden my sweater?' But Heston, if he suffered, was imperturbable, the most impassive man I had ever known. He had just failed to get his Hampshire county cap and, coming north to coach, had married the very pretty young waitress who served the teas at Willow Park. They had a baby girl, he was provided with a cottage and a garden, his home life was happy. Beneath that unconcerned exterior, I felt that he thoroughly despised the snobbery and 'side' of his employers, some of whom, at least the newly rich, had all the affectations of the parvenu.

All that summer I played cricket with the Beechfield boys, in whose companionship the sweet sound of bat on ball became sweeter still. At last I had friends, the kind of boys I had always wanted as my intimates. The sun burned me a deep Indian red, real muscles appeared on my arms and legs, I had never felt or played better. Most delicious of all, an achievement beyond my wildest dreams, was the patronage, verging on friendship, with which the elder Scott-Hamilton, my senior by three years, had come to favour me. Friendship existed on my side, a longing for affection and companionship, but it was never returned in kind. He had a code of casual, superior, slightly bored indifference that must never be infringed. His favourite epithet of disparagement was the word 'toad'. Demonstrativeness or gaucherie of any kind was met by: 'Don't be a toad, toad.' He repeatedly enjoined all of us not to be toads.

Inevitably, there were dangerous moments, but I carried everything before me. Miss Greville, who from the first failed to esteem my cricketing belt with the snake clasp, had suggested a more stylish support for my trousers, and to this end she gave me an old tie of her brother's—after his death a great many of his belongings had been returned to her.

'I say,' commented the younger Scott-Hamilton, who was more impressionable than his brother, 'Carroll's sporting an old E. tie.'

I then elaborated further, ignoring Spion Kop but bringing in Kenya, creating relations, all with a fertility of imagination and an offhand use of Beechfield slang that quite startled me. Was I a snob? No. I was elevated far above myself. But most of these boys boasted, arrogantly and quite naturally. Douglas bragging of his father's steam yacht, a yellow-funnelled monster that lay in the Gareloch, and young Colquhoun never failing to remind us that his parents kept fifteen servants in Bengal. I had nothing to boast of, so instead of exaggerating, I invented. But all that I said and did was defensive, the fervent, ridiculous and pathetic expression of a lifelong longing for social acceptance and equality.

I could not bear to think that autumn would bring the cessation of my joys, yet as the season drew to a close that sting was palliated by the thought of the final game, the traditional annual fixture between the boys coached by Heston and the second eleven of the club. Scott Hamilton had picked our side: ten Beechfield boys and myself. True, I was last man on the list, but that did not seem to matter. I was in the eleven. From now on, as the afternoons drew in to early dusk, our practice at the nets became intensive. Although his attitude was casual, verging between boredom and a kind of sleepy indifference, I knew that Scott, as I now called him wanted desperately to win this match. Not only was this his last year at Beechfield before going to Fettes, he had a special animus, amounting to a vendetta, against one of the Beechfield masters, Cunningham by name, a 'complete outsider', according to Scott, with no chin and buck teeth, who was captain of the club eleven.

SEVENTEEN .

THE MORNING of the match was crisp and sunny with only a faint autumnal haze, which gave promise of a fine still day. It was of course a single-innings game, and was due to start at eleven o'clock. To my sorrow, Miss Greville was debarred from seeing me perform by an engagement at the vicarage where Mr Lesly, with extremely bad taste, had chosen this particular day for St Jude's annual garden party. Yet, in a way, I felt slightly relieved at this enforced absence of my 'aunt', since there was always the horrid possibility that one or other of her more outspoken observations might expose the true nature of our relationship. It was enough that I carried her good wishes with me as, at ten o'clock, I set out for the club ground.

Now the game of cricket is presumably not a matter of passionate interest for every reader of this book, nevertheless this particular match was an exciting one, and since its upshot proved even more memorable, I must briefly describe it.

A coin was spun in front of the pavilion and Cunningham, having won the toss, elected to bat first. Our opponents, with a jocularity that we found offensive, were prepared to treat us lightly. They began by offering catches in the deep field which to their surprise we accepted. When they settled down to be serious it was a different matter. But our bowling was steady. Douglas, son of the yachtsman, had a particularly deceptive off break, and our fielding, of the swift dash and one-handed-pick-up variety, kept the score down, besides bringing frequent bursts of hand clapping from the spectators. Although Cunningham, unfortunately, carried his bat for fifty-seven, which included eleven boundary hits, they were all out just after one o'clock for a hundred and thirty-nine.

Mrs Heston had provided an excellent buffet lunch which was taken standing up, people moving about with plates of chicken salad and cold veal pie, in a general air of heartiness. All my running had made me extremely hot so that I did not feel up to eating much which, in view of the excellent fare, was rather a pity. But I had a ham sandwich and several glasses of lemon squash. As I went up for my final squash Mrs Heston, who must have known of me from her husband, said in my ear:

'I do wish you a good knock, Laurence.'

After the luncheon interval it was our turn to bat. Scott, a first-class batsman and good all-rounder, had bowled without change at one end. Now, with Bethune, he went in to open our innings. How I admired him as he walked elegantly to the wicket and calmly took centre. He played the first over confidently, scoring two off the last ball.

Seated on the pavilion veranda with the others, applauding that strong, clean, cover drive, I felt a rising hope—despite Mrs Heston's good wishes—that I should not have to go in. Although in my usual fashion I had built extravagantly on a spectacular performance, now that deeds might be demanded of me, the prospect of that lonely walk to the wicket had begun to intimidate me. Thus far, while I had made no catches, I had fielded extremely well. My reputation might rest on that with safety. Bethune, having taken middle and leg, was now set to receive an over from Cunningham who, taking an alarmingly long run, delivered his first ball. Fast and well pitched up, it knocked out Bethune's middle stump. One out, and only two on the scoreboard—it was a shock.

When Bethune returned, to averted glances, while I entered a painful nought in my scoring card—which I have retained to this day—Colquhoun followed. Next to Scott he was our soundest bat, one who could be relied upon to stay. Unfortunately, on this occasion, he remained for a bare ten minutes and a stodgy nine. The next batsman's effort was equally short and even more uneventful. He contributed three. A chill air of despondency had now settled on the veranda bench. My agitation was increasing by the minute. Once the rot started the sorrowful procession continued and was held up only by Hailey, our wicketkeeper, who made a solid ten, all singles, before being caught and bowled by Cunningham. A final, momentary respite was provided by Douglas, the spin bowler who, hitting out at everything, scored fourteen including three wild but valuable boundaries that sailed over second slip's head.

When Douglas left, out to a catch at long leg the score, aided by some kindly extras, stood at no more than ninety-two for eight wickets, of which Scott-Hamilton had made forty-six. And I now shivered as the younger Scott-Hamilton, who immediately preceded me on the batting order, went swaggering out to the pitch in a manner that made me envy his cheek. There was a good deal of the clown in Harry, he liked to raise a laugh even if against himself. On this occasion he succeeded. After taking guard in exaggerated fashion he walked up and down patting imaginary imperfections in the bone-dry pitch. Having succeeded in amusing the spectators, who as the afternoon wore on had grown in number, he took guard again and faced the bowler. The ball was a slow leg break. Harry turned to pull it to leg, missed his footing and sat down on his wicket. The result was an enormous shout of laughter in which, irresistibly, even the fielders joined. So in this atmosphere of hilarity I would have to go in. My pads were already on. With a frightful hollow in my stomach I put my bat under my arm and stumbled down the wooden steps of the pavilion into that wide green arena.

Scott came to meet me halfway to the wicket. Pale with anger and disappointment he greeted me with a string of scarifying bad words.

'The bowling is absolute blank, blank tosh. These blank, blank toads have simply got themselves out. Just keep your blank end up and let me do the scoring.'

These profane injunctions did little to fortify me. I was so wretchedly nervous when I went to the wicket that I forgot to take guard. The game had degenerated into farce and in the interests of cricket must be terminated at once by my dismissal. The first ball shaved my wicket, the second hit me a sad crack on the elbow. It was then the end of the over.

While the field changed, Heston, who was umpiring at my end, strolled towards me, hands in the pockets of his long white coat.

'Straight bat,' he said mildly. 'Don't run away from them.'

In the events that followed Scott-Hamilton was the hero, I merely the accessory to the fact. It is enough to report simply and briefly that, with incredible good fortune, I stayed there for more than three-quarters of an hour, surviving by the skin of my teeth, while Scott hit up another thirty-one runs. His score was seventy-seven, my total no more than a miserable seventeen, but beyond keeping my wicket intact I had one moment of glory when, off what proved to be the last ball of the match, I ventured on a square cut that somehow sped past cover point then trickled to the boundary. I did not realize that it was the winning hit until I saw Scott waiting for me to walk to the pavilion.

In the pavilion, as we took off our pads, he brushed off all congratulations.

'I never believed I would have the misfortune to know such blank collection of blankety toads. You, Harry, were the toadiest of the lot. Lucky there was one toad,' he announced, 'who wasn't altogether toadish.' Then turning to me: 'You'll come home to tea with me, won't you, Carroll?'

The invitation went to my head like wine. This was the final accolade, an honour and an intimacy I had never hoped to attain. My powers in the game had already raised me well above myself. Now I floated, disembodied, an elected member of the élite.

When we had changed we set out, Scott, Harry and I,

sauntering towards their house, which stood quite near, in a secluded position behind the wood. On the way over we discussed the match, Harry with his usual sense of fun, Scott mockingly amused at Mr Cunningham's discomfiture. To me the master had not appeared at all upset at the defeat of his side, rather the contrary, and apart from his unfortunate teeth he seemed a genuinely nice sort of man. He had clapped me heartily on the back and said 'Well played' as we came off the field. But it was enough that for reasons of his own Scott detested him. Strolling along easily in my new-found arrogance I derided the unhappy Cunningham, inventing comic names for him, of which one, 'Rabbit Teeth', won approval. Scott said that it would *stick*.

The grounds of the house were imposingly large. We went along an avenue of chestnut trees that revealed a paddock on one side and distantly on the other the fruit and vegetable garden, where two men were working, and beyond which I made out an inviting row of glasshouses. A shrubbery and a rock garden appeared next before finally we came to the house, a half-timbered mansion draped in virginia creeper, fronting a wide stretch of lawn flanked by twin herbaceous borders.

A woman, tall, thin, with greying hair and a distinguished look, was crossing the lawn as we approached. She was wearing gardening gloves and carried a trug in which lay a profusion of full-blown roses.

'Mother,' Scott said, 'this is Carroll. I've asked him to tea.'

She smiled pleasantly, viewing us all, not with the outgiving affection my own mother would have shown, but with a certain aristocratic, faintly amused contraction of her brows which, to my shame, I now preferred.

'How did the match go?'

'We won, naturally,' Scott said offhandedly.

'Behold the two heroes, Mother. I made a duck.'

'Oh, you wretch, Harry. Never mind, you'll have tea with me when I've finished cutting.' Turning to go, she said: 'Then you may tell me all about it.'

Scott led the way into the house, through the hall and along a passage at the back to a green baize-covered service door.

'Let's have a drink,' he said, pushing open the door. 'You won't mind coming in here?'

Gaily, in a free and easy manner, I followed them to the

kitchen which was large, white-tiled and well lit. At the window a smartly dressed maid was polishing silver while a stout cook, with her back to us, was at the stove bending over the oven.

'We'd like some ginger beer, Bridgie.'

'Take it then,' said the cook, over her shoulder. 'But leave these pancakes be, Master Harry, they're for the mistress's tea.'

Harry, who knew his way about, had supplied us with glasses of stone ginger beer, when the cook swung round and straightened, exposing to us a full red amiable face set with a pair of button black eyes. I stiffened, choked on my ginger beer. I recognized her instantly. Bridget O'Halloran, staunch devotee of St Mary's and leading member of the Guild of St Teresa. Did she know me? Idiotic, futile question.

Had she not sat beside me in church, walked in the same procession, even passed me occasionally on her afternoon off as she went to the church and I emerged from school? If this damning evidence was not enough, her stare of wondering surprise that plainly said 'What is *he* doing here, where he doesn't belong, with Master Scott and Master Harry?' would surely have convinced me. And now her expression had changed. I saw that she distrusted and resented my upstart appearance in a society so far above me, a sphere where as an old and privileged servant she had the right to feel at home. I was an offence against the sound established order that she believed in as firmly as she did the Communion of Saints.

She placed herself in a conversational attitude, one hand on her hip.

'You have a new friend, Master Scott?'

'Decidedly,' he agreed, drinking deeply.

'That's nice He'll be at the Beechfield with you?'

'No, Bridgie,' Harry interposed. 'For your private information, he has a weak chest and doesn't go to school at present.'

'Indeed now, that's interesting. And where does he get his education like?'

'He has a tutor.'

'A tutor is it?'

Disregarding Master Harry, who was now helping himself to pancakes, she fixed me with a chilly, penetrating stare.

Yet her tone was persuasive as, in a meditative manner, she queried:

'But surely . . . haven't I seen you in Clay Street with a school satchel?'

I affected an incredulous smile. It was a feeble effort.

'Of course not.'

'Strange,' she pursued. 'I could have sworn it was you. Down by St Mary's School?'

I was pale. The smile had stiffened on my lips. Ineffectually I tried an edging movement towards the door.

'I don't know what you're talking about.'

'You're sure it wasn't you?'

'I'm dead positive,' I said violently. 'What the dickens would I be doing down there?'

She considered me for a long moment, then said slowly: 'And the cock crowed thrice.'

Master Harry went into a fit of laughter.

'Silly Bridgie. And the cock crowed. Cock-a-doodle-do.'

But Scott-Hamilton, unsmiling, was looking at me very curiously.

'Shut up, Harry. Let's clear out.'

Tea in the drawing-room where, basking in glory, I had hoped to shine, was a torment. Despite Mrs Scott-Hamilton's puzzled efforts, conversation flagged and died. As soon as I could, I said that I must go

'Must you?' said Scott, getting up immediately. 'Pity you have to leave,' he said with cold politeness, having escorted me to the front door.

'I have to meet someone,' I said.

He raised his eyebrows with a faint, contemptuous smile. 'The tutor?' These were his parting words.

I went out of the house and along the avenue, past the two gardeners, the peach house, and the twin tennis courts. Sick with shame and blind with rage I saw nothing. All the hot bitterness of my burning heart was directed against Scott, against all the Scott-Hamiltons, against Beechfield, the cricket club, the entire world, most of all against myself. I loathed and despised myself with a searing and corroding violence that, while it must end in abysmal misery, kept me striding instinctively, in some such manner as the murderer is compelled to return to the scene of his crime, towards St Mary's. Had Bridget's final word stung so fiercely as to stir in my perfidious soul emotions of compunction and contrition that could be assuaged only by a solitary visit to the church? If so, I did not reach that haven of penitence. Beyond the Victoria Library at the junction of the main road and Clay Street a game was in progress, a low, common vulgar game of 'kick the can' played in the public thoroughfare by a ragged scattering of my schoolfellows. My eye dilated. Here, I thought, are my compeers. Welcomed by acclamation, unmindful of my patrician clothes, I flung myself into the game, running, sliding, kicking, falling in the gutter, shouting and sweating, revelling in the awareness that I was shedding the spurious veneer with which for the past two months I had encased myself.

In the midst of one hectic mêlée I heard a shrill exclamation of dismay. I looked up. An elderly lady in a spotted veil and feather boa, with a bundle of library books under her arm, was gazing at me in horror. She was Miss Galbraith, one of Miss Greville's tea-party friends who played the violin and painted nicely in watercolours, and to whom, not long before, I had made my bow.

'Laurence! What are you doing! With these dreadful little ragamuffins!'

'Playing.'

'Oh, no, no, not with these frightful young hooligans. You must go home at once.'

'I won't.'

'Do come away with me, dear.' She took my arm. 'You must.'

'No,' I shouted, breaking free. 'I won't come away. These are my friends. You can go to h—l.'

The game proceeded until dusk. I did not give up until I felt myself completely purged. Then, pledging myself to more games when school took up next week, I set out for home, with a tear in the knee of my flannel trousers, exhausted, dirty, and sad, but for the moment at peace.

EIGHTEEN

OH, THE DREARINESS of that ensuing winter when, under perpetually weeping skies, I passed, with lowered head, a shadow of myself, to and from St Mary's School, travelling by the unfrequented back road, avoiding all that pertained to Beechfield in such a manner as my peasant ancestors

had shunned the famine-stricken, typhus-ridden town of
Bandon. Unhappily this alternative route presented me, on
occasions, with a painful reminder of my fallen state since
it was unpredictably the choice of the St Anne's junior
'crocodile', thus confronting me at a turn of the road with
a double line of young girls, swinging along in their
fetching green uniforms, aristocratic, arrogant, yes, all of
them arrogant to the point of insolence, and to whom I
must yield the pavement by stepping humbly into the
gutter. As I stood there, an ignored obscenity, one in particular held my eye, a captivating little blonde with long
double flaxen pigtails that swung with her dashing step.
She it was who, by her fascinations, confirmed my outcast
state. By chance I even learned her name. As she swept past
with her indubitably snub nose in the air and never a side
glance, her partner in the parade remarked, in the high,
affected Ardfillan voice: 'Oh, I say, Ada, how absolutely
jolly!' Resuming my way, Ada became the touchstone of
the unattainable, the token of my miseries, the central figure
in fantasies which I created, not only by day but more often
at night, in bed, before I fell asleep. Then Ada, dear Ada,
watched rapturously, in company with Heston and George
Gunn, while I carried my bat for a century at Lord's. Permu-
tations and combinations of my Ada complex transported
me, the brilliance, the mutual admiration in our exchanges
dazzled me. How often did she lean towards me and
exclaim: 'Oh, I say, Laurie, how absolutely jolly!' And on
what flights was I borne by her daily letters!

Dearest Laurie,

*How can I thank you enough for the exquisite orchids.
And how splendid your being so friendly with Lady Meikle
that she allowed you to pick them in her beautiful big conservatory. I will keep them as a constant reminder of your
thoughtfulness.*

*Please don't imagine I didn't see you when I passed the
other day. I had to pretend not to.*

*Have you been to the moor lately? It would be nice if we
could meet there one day. But of course we are kept in very
strictly at St Anne's. That's why it is so jolly to be able to
write you.*

Affectionately yours,
Ada

I wrote these letters after my homework and dropped them into the letter-box so that I should find them when I set out for school next morning. On my way to Clay Street I read them with a beatific smile fixed upon my lips, which, alas, slowly faded as cold reality dissolved a dream, springing not from any seductiveness Ada might offer, but only from a yearning for her esteem.

Fortunately, after some weeks I began to be bored with Ada. Perhaps she was tired of me, for her letters noticeably cooled off and eventually ceased. But it is truer to say that she was supplanted by a humbler being, possibly more worthy of my affection. I had fallen in love with Amoeba Proteus.

The chance discovery of an elementary textbook of zoology of Miss Greville's entitled *Pond Life* had sent me, idly at first, in pursuit of the protozoa. But it was a chase which, to my salvation, soon became a passion, supplanting my botanical researches of the past year, convincing me that I must become a scientist.

As spring came in I returned from my moorland expeditions not with a packed vasculum but with scum-filled jars that teemed with fascinating life and which, once my eye was glued to the tube of Miss Greville's Zeiss, gave me the entry to an unknown world peopled with amazing microscopic creatures whose elaborate activities, from the swallowing of diatoms and formation of food vacuoles to the halving of chromosomes and division of the nucleus in the final act of partition, filled me with wonder, an emotion that intensified as, passing from these primary cells, I came upon rarer and wilder inhabitants of this subaqueous jungle, the solitary volvox, the whirling rotifer, the shapely polystomella. And what joy when, one March evening, a glorious paramecium, with all its cilia waving, swam majestically through the green algae into my field of vision.

This was the interest that truly sustained me during a period of dullness and uncertainty when I felt that I was getting nowhere. I realized that St Mary's could take me no further and that I was soon due to leave. Yet I dared not ask my mother what the future held for me. In her face now there was a reserve that forbade my question, an expression that I did not wish to read yet which instinctively I recognized as an omen contrary to all my hopes.

At first, through sympathy for her, and the general

regard for Father, she had done well enough with the agency. But gradually the decline had set in, competition increased, and more and more she came back with a thinning order book and a set, harassed expression, the presage to increasing economies that dispelled the blessed ambience of security in which I had hitherto lived.

As the months went on it became more and more apparent how painfully short we were of money. Particularly in our diet was this stringency noticeable, for although worse was in store for me, Mother now concentrated on the cheapest and most nourishing foods, such things as baked beans, boiled salt codfish and cottage pie, which I accepted with an added sense of grievance, since it must now be revealed that those sustaining lunches with which Miss Greville had regaled my pampered stomach had practically ceased.

This, indeed, touched another of our problems, a mysterious enigma, surrounding my benefactress, that passed my present understanding. Miss Greville, caught up in new and unforeseen activities, was seldom in for lunch. When I came back from school at the midday recess, hoping against hope, I would be met in the hall by Campbell who, with a grim smile that made my heart sink, would remark: 'Lunch is not being served today, Master Carroll.' She gave always to the word 'Master' an imperceptible sardonic inflection that, intensifying my sense of deprivation, wounded me deeply as, my nostrils dilating to the good smells of Campbell's own lunch coming from the kitchen, I slowly went upstairs where, on the alcove table, I would find a pencilled note left by Mother: *Soup in the pot on the stove for you to heat, dear. And some cold rice pudding in the cupboard.*

What, I asked myself repeatedly, was happening to Miss Greville? Towards Mother and myself she was more forthcoming, more gaily affectionate, than ever. Yet it seemed as though in this effusiveness Mother found something oppressive. At first she had been pleased to be invited to those little tea parties, and even to play and sing there. But now, returning tired and dispirited from Winton, she was apparently in no mood for such festivities, and only once during the previous six months when Miss Greville had entertained her few St Anne's friends to a musical evening had she attended, with reluctance, and then because she felt it an obligation to play, or at least to accompany Miss

Greville's performance on the 'cello. After this event she had returned depressed and with a disinclination for further social intercourse. It was difficult to escape the conclusion that the more Miss Greville offered intimacy, the more my mother had withdrawn from it, not obtrusively, but rather with discretion, as though anxious to moderate these approaches. I particularly noticed this reserve in Mother's manner on Sundays when Miss Greville, sumptuously dressed for church in a high-waisted cream costume, an enormous exuberant hat on top of her chignon, a parasol in her white-gloved hands, and exuding a faint smell of Parma violets, came upstairs to be approved.

'Does this suit me? Will I *do*, Grace? Am I fit to be seen?'

Envisaging that full, richly moulded figure, Mother repressively replied:

'You will certainly be seen.'

'I believe so.' Miss Greville smiled confidently. 'And why not, dear Grace?'

Of course Miss Greville had always been an assiduous churchgoer, and her penchant for remarkable attire was no secret to me, yet in these over-elaborate Sunday toilettes there must surely be some meaning which so far had escaped me. Nevertheless I, as opposed to Mother, welcomed every sign and symptom, no matter how displayed, of Miss Greville's partiality. Not only did I admire her intensely— 'look up to her' is perhaps the better phrase—I knew all too well what she had done for me. And I dared to hope that she would do more. Indeed, her interest in me now seemed the only chance of bringing me what I most desired.

This thought was in my mind when one March day, as still occasionally happened, I was lucky enough to find Miss Greville at home. Lunch was being served. Rejoicing that I need not, for once, face up to cold rice pudding, I washed and brushed my hair with unusual care before entering the dining-room. She greeted me with a bright appraising smile. If sadness reigned in our part of the house, here surely the reverse held sway. Miss Greville, during these past deadly months, had been consistently animated.

'You are presentable, Carroll,' she remarked approvingly, as I placed her chair. 'Indeed, extremely so. Rather a different person from that scrubby little window-breaker of . . . how long ago?'

'Four years, Miss Greville.'

I do not recall how our conversation developed after that promising opening. I do not doubt that it was interesting, since this remarkable woman had an extraordinary gift of stimulating and often bizarre talk and had even taught me to respond in a civilized manner and, apparently, with intelligence. Today, however, I was at first too busily engaged with some excellent roast beef to give her my complete attention. But of the ending of that lunch my memory is exact, my recollection unforgettably clear. She had proceeded to the window with her cup of coffee according to invariable habit, and after remaining rather longer than usual returned to the table in a mood which I rightly judged to be communicative.

'You are remarkably discreet, Carroll,' she began, looking at me intently, yet amiably.

'Am I, Miss Greville?'

'And, thanks to me, well mannered. So often, during our moments of agreeable intimacy, you have observed me go to the window, yet never once have you chosen to inquire why.'

'That would not have been polite.' Falling into her mood I mouthed this appalling answer like a well-behaved little prig. For that roast beef, with my eye on a second helping, I would have made myself a triple prig.

'But you've been curious?' she pressed, unwilling to dismiss the subject. 'Admit the soft impeachment.'

Scarcely knowing whether it would be to my advantage to admit or deny I eventually inclined my head soberly.

'I *was* curious, Miss Greville.'

'But you didn't guess?'

'I imagined you were waiting for a friend, who passed here regularly every day.'

'Well done, Carroll!'

She seemed so pleased at my deduction that my inveterate wish to shine drove me to continue.

'And whoever it was would naturally see you there.'

She smiled.

'It would be rather pointless if there were not an exchange of glances. The human eye, Carroll, as a means of communication is more expressive than the tongue. More subtle too, and truer The tongue can lie, the eye, never. More beef?'

'Please, Miss Greville.

While I partook of another juicy slice she kept playing absently with her long chain necklace of ivory beads, that odd little smile coming and going on her lips.

'You know Mr Lesly, of course. Our vicar at St Jude's.'

'Why, certainly, Miss Greville. I often see him in the street. And you remember he stopped and spoke to us that first day we were coming back from Glen Fruin. The day we found the *morio*.'

'Of course. You liked him?'

'He seemed an awfully nice young man.'

'Not nice, Carroll. Not that deplorable word. Charming, if you wish, intelligent, sympathetic, handsome. And not so young. He is coming to tea next Saturday. I want your mother to meet him.'

A considerable silence ensued. When I finished rolling my napkin and hopefully putting it in its silver ring for possible future use, she was gazing at me benignantly.

'What age are you, Carroll?'

'Thirteen, Miss Greville.'

'As I was saying, you have improved. I regard you, in a manner of speaking, as my own creation. And I wish you to understand this. Whatever changes may be effected in the immediate future I mean to do something for you.'

All at once my heart came into my mouth. Did I interpret her meaning correctly or was I merely carried away by my own expectations? Surely asking how old I was had been significant. She had often said that fourteen was the proper age to . . . I did not dare ask, yet the longing in my soul made me falter out the words:

'In the way, perhaps, of sending me to a decent school, Miss Greville?'

She made a spirited gesture of acquiescence.

'What else, Carroll? A very good school.' Then quickly, seeing an idiotic wildness in my eye: 'No, not *there*, Carroll. You would not, I fear, be altogether comfortable in that establishment. You must go to one of your own persuasion.'

'Rockcliff . . . perhaps . . . Miss Greville?'

'Why should we send you to Ireland? If you insist on the Jesuits, you'll do better in Yorkshire at Amplehurst, which is not a bad little institution in its own way.'

Amplehurst! Beyond question the best Catholic public school. Stricken dumb, I gazed at her with glistening eyes.

That afternoon I could not be still, could not think of returning to imprison my bounding spirits in my malodorous Clay Street classroom. I simply played truant, put on an old pair of shorts and a jersey and went out for a long run in the rain. I liked to run and believed, with some justification, that I could run fast. Miss Greville had encouraged me to take these cross-country chases and, like the morning cold bath which I shiveringly endured, they had become not the expression of my devotion alone, but of the authority she exerted upon me in forming a régime, quite foreign to my nature, that I had now come to enjoy. As I flashed along the sodden by-ways, leaping the puddles as though each were a Becher's Book, I wished, though vainly, that I might encounter Scott-Hamilton to convey to him in that brief moment of transit the brilliant changes in my fortunes.

Mother was annoyed with me when I got back. She had returned by an earlier train and was at the stove making our supper.

'Oh, Mother, not beans again!' I protested.

She looked at me coldly.

'Where on earth have you been? And soaking wet, too.'

'Don't be cross,' I told her expansively. 'I'll go and change. Then, Mother dear, I have some rather interesting news for you.'

A few minutes later, when we were seated at our narrow table in the alcove, I related, with impressment, my conversation with Miss Greville. Mother, gazing over her cup, from time to time taking sips of tea, heard me in silence. But when, finally, or perhaps as a kind of postscript, I conveyed Miss Greville's invitation to her for Saturday, she gave a short disturbed exclamation.

'Mr Lesly is to be there?'

'Of course. Why are you so surprised? Don't you know that Miss Greville and he are great friends? Why, every day at lunch they smile at each other through the window.'

Mother made to speak, but checked herself and was silent. But her expression remained decidedly odd. This, and the manner in which she had received my announcement, offended me. I did not offer to wash the dishes and instead went into my own room.

What could be wrong between Miss Greville and Mr Lesly? It was painfully evident that Mother was upset by the idea of this invitation and had no wish to accept it.

Naturally, I was not blind to Miss Greville's oddities. These, especially in the early stages of our relationship, had fascinated me. Her unusual personality awed and stimulated me so that I had come to regard her as a brilliant eccentric, and for this reason was prepared to accept her unconventional behaviour. But having her vicar to tea was not unconventional. Why, then, all this fuss? I should not have been at all surprised if she had asked someone like Buffalo Bill, or Harry Lauder, rather than the estimable Mr Lesly, the more so since, despite my pretence of ignorance, I had sensed that she valued him.

Nevertheless, when Saturday came a vague uneasiness creeping over my skin made me want to be out of the way that afternoon. It was fine, a good day for another run, I told myself, especially since the Harriers were out in a paper chase to Stair Head. These Harriers, made up of young men who were clerks, apprentices, shop assistants and the like, were now, more properly, my friends, and in the previous autumn I had established myself amongst them by winning the Junior Steeplechase open to boys under fourteen. After Mother had made me a scrambled egg on toast I slipped out of the house in my shorts and jersey. I was late. The meet had started at the edge of the Darvie Woods and soon I was amongst the pines following the paper trail that had been laid down. The excitement of picking up the track, losing it, then striking it again soon absorbed me. A thrill of pride shot through me as I overtook some of the club stragglers, and with my chin up and elbows pressed in, ignoring the stitch in my side, left them floundering behind. Yet the very merit of my speed proved my undoing. When, still trotting and spotted with mud, as the afternoon drew to a close, I swung into Prince Albert Terrace, I saw that I had misjudged my time. The door of No. 7 was open, revealing Miss Greville and my mother with Mr Lesly in the very act of leaving. He was a handsome, measured kind of man with an exact middle parting of his hair, who looked rather like an actor. But now he appeared flushed and terribly uncomfortable as he hurriedly shook hands, and he almost stumbled as he came down the porch steps. Contrary to his usual civil habit, he did not recognize me. Perhaps he did not see me. If ever a man seemed anxious to expedite his departure it was the Vicar of St Jude's.

I went into the house. Mother and Miss Greville were

in the hall and, as I slipped past hurriedly, for somehow the situation appeared to have got out of control, Mother, in a low tone of remonstration, said something which I did not hear but to which Miss Greville replied, with a burst of joyful animation:

'It's not what was said, dearest Grace. Did you not see how he looked at me!'

Mother was a long time coming upstairs. When she came she sat down heavily at the table and put a hand to her brow. She alarmed me. I had been sweating and now I began to shiver.

'Mother, what's wrong?'

She raised her head slowly and looked at me.

'It will never end for us, Laurie. Never, never. Miss Greville is going out of her mind.'

NINETEEN

HOW STRANGE were the months that followed, for me so unreal as to maintain me in a perpetual daze, and for my mother so charged with an ever-growing anxiety, the extent of which I did not realize till later, that her nerves were worn to shreds, causing her to start and turn pale whenever some unusual sound would reach us from the main part of the house. Even now I can scarcely bring myself to re-create the pitiful disintegration of a mind that I had always regarded as cultured and superior, the more so since that mental dissolution shaped itself ostensibly in the pattern of farce, the spinster's infatuation for the young clergyman, subject for the music-hall stage, for vulgar laughter provoked by a cheap comedian with baggy trousers and a red nose. For us, it was far from funny but a reality with which we lived and suffered. That Miss Greville, of all people, should be the central figure, the victim, of such a spectacle—I could not believe it.

Yet, although of course I could not know this, Miss Greville's condition was one now well recognized in psychiatric medicine and not at all uncommon in women of her age and condition who have slight paranoid tendencies. In such subjects at the involutional period a flood of libidinal impulses, hitherto repressed, or sublimated, or dealt with by other mechanisms of defence, is released with specific imbalance of hormones and resultant delusions which are frequently centred upon a favourite physician or clergyman. This absolute and utter certainty that they are beloved and to be married is explained by the almost cryptic indications, yet in a supremely reasonable way.

This to me was the most perplexing feature of Miss Greville's behaviour, the rational manner in which she gave effect to her delusion. Her preparations for marriage were proper and well considered. The additions she made to her wardrobe, no longer exuberant, exhibited a severity which, as she informed my mother, befitted the clerical status of her future husband. The plans she outlined for doing up the vicarage could not have been bettered, and the materials she had already bought for new curtains were all in quiet good taste. Her activities in all directions were endless, she seemed always on the move, going to and coming from the town, and when she found time to sit down she would take up sewing, or start cutting out and shaping patterns, with commendable industry.

Most baffling of all was the manner in which she received every attempt to dissuade her. At first my mother had been diffident, tactful and discreet in her approach, but as time went on and all her efforts failed she had come to speak in the strongest terms and to use outright and forceful arguments which no one could reject. Miss Greville rejected them. With her calm and confident smile she would listen, amused almost by Mother's intensity, then, with a shake of her head, would dismiss the most irrefutable logic: 'You don't understand, Grace. There are reasons for everything. *I know.*'

These two final words, absolute conviction of inner knowledge, were unassailable to reason. Mother was at her wits' end. From whom could she seek advice? Those acquaintances at St Anne's, familiar with Miss Greville's previous foibles, were disinclined to take Mother seriously and advised against action on the grounds that this new manifestation would pass. In any case, from their position with the school, it was apparent that they had no wish to be drawn into the affair. Campbell, with whom Mother tried to take council, was not helpful. This deaf, taciturn woman had from the beginning resented our presence in the house. She considered that she had prior rights on her employer and was not prepared to divulge the address of Miss Greville's brother in Kenya when Mother proposed writing to him. The difficulty presented by any course of action seemed insuperable, since the first sign of interference on our part would undoubtedly precipitate a scandal in the town. There was nothing to be done but wait. And so there ensued a period of suspense during which Mother often exclaimed, in a tone of gathering foreboding: 'How will it end?'

I must confess that the bizarre aspect of the situation with its suggestion of further awfulness had a morbid excitement for me, stimulated by the changes developing in Miss Greville's personality and physical appearance. Phrases of unprecedented frankness startled and embarrased me. Her bust and hips were fuller and she had a new way of standing with her legs apart, and what I took to be her stomach but was undoubtedly her pelvis, thrust forward. The fascination of these transformations was, however, dulled by persistent intrusions of a most depressing thought. If Miss Greville did not resume her normal state, if she continued to deteriorate, how could she fulfil her promise to send me to school? What of my giddy aspirations then? They would never be realized. Never. My heart sank at the dismal prospect. I would be lost.

It may be imagined then how anxiously I studied Miss Greville on the occasions when we were together. These were diminishing, since in the evenings Mother kept me closely by her side. Nevertheless, lack of opportunity did not debar me from hoping and fearing, nor my spirits from rising and falling, like a barometer. In the main, I was optimistic. This can't go on, I told myself, it must pass. Nothing will come of it. And if we can last it out for another six months all will be well. Alas, I was deluding myself. Other factors were already operating, contingencies I had not even contemplated. All my thoughts and efforts had been concentrated on Miss Greville. I had forgotten about Mr Lesly.

It was a wet Saturday afternoon and Mother was reading the *Ardfillan Herald* which always appeared at the weekend.

Suddenly I heard her exclaim, in a startled voice:

'Merciful heavens!'

She had changed colour, yet she did not put down the

Herald, but went on reading almost desperately. Then she let the newspaper slip from her hands and lay back in her chair staring unseeingly at me. This could only mean disaster. Already my scalp was beginning to creep as I put that too familiar question.

'What's wrong, Mother?'

She did not answer, did not apparently discover me within the remote field of her vision. Her lips were moving not, experience told me, in prayer but because, silently, she was talking to herself. I was about to repeat my question more pressingly when, as though breaking through the sound barrier, these words escaped her.

'She's bound to see it . . . or to hear of it.'

'Mother.' I had to shake her arm. 'What has happened?'

She had to find me before she answered.

'Mr Lesly is going to be married.' She paused. 'On the fifteenth of next month.'

As though unable to continue, she handed me the paper. A paragraph in the Social and Personal column was headed: *Popular Vicar to Wed.* And beneath in small type: *Nuptials announced of Mr H. A. Lesly and Miss Georgina Douglas.* Reading on, I was not long in discovering that Miss Georgina was none other than the sister of the spin bowler, my late cricketing acquaintance in whose conversation that twin-funnelled steam yacht had largely testified to parental wealth. Hurriedly I skimmed through the rest of the paragraph: a long-standing attachment . . . sudden decision on the part of the happy couple . . . welcomed by their numerous friends and wellwishers.

'But this is wonderful,' I cried. 'It settles everything.'

Mother eyed me silently.

'Don't you see, Mother, when Miss Greville sees he's going to marry someone else she'll know he can't marry her.'

'That will be a great help to her, poor creature.'

Mother's pale, sad smile disconcerted me.

'You mean, she won't . . .'

'I don't mean anything,' Mother said firmly, with an air of terminating the conversation. 'But I don't want you to go down to her for a bit. Not till we see how things work out.'

All that evening Mother and I kept very quiet. The house was quiet too. On the following morning we went out to the ten o'clock Mass. Occasionally on Sunday we had an invitation from Miss Greville to have midday dinner with her. Today, when we returned from church, there was no invitation, and Miss Greville had not gone to St Jude's.

The house was still quiet. I forgot what Mother made for our lunch because, for once, I certainly did not notice what I was eating. Afterwards Mother lay down for an hour, while I did my week-end homework. At four o'clock I made the tea. We were now so under the spell of this perpetual stillness that we were talking almost in whispers. I took the tea things to the sink, glancing at Mother while I washed and dried them. I could see that she was terribly on edge, she kept walking up and down our little corridor, but softly, in her indoor slippers, listening all the time with her head to one side.

It was getting dark now and it had begun to rain again. Suddenly, as I was about to light the gas, there came a knock at our door.

Visibly, Mother started. I looked at her, with questioning alarm.

'Shall I open it?'

She shook her head and, moving to the door, threw it open.

Campbell stood there, a sudden apparition, her thin, black angular figure ominous in the dusk. But her expression was as withdrawn, as impassive as ever. Her hands were folded in front of her starched apron.

'Madam would like to see you,' she said formally.

'Yes,' Mother said slowly. 'I'll come.'

'Madam wishes to see you both,' Campbell said, in the same manner as before.

There was a pause.

'I don't think—' Mother began, turning towards me.

'It's all right, Mother,' I interrupted. 'I'll go with you.'

Nothing heroic prompted this declaration. My heart was beating fast and my knees were uncertain, but I did not wish to be left out of this. I felt indeed that Miss Greville, facing a crisis in her life might well be impelled to a vital declaration upon my future.

Mother hesitated. I sensed that she wanted to question Campbell, to glean some information as to the present state of affairs. But Campbell was not one to be questioned. Already she had begun to move off. We followed her. Outside Miss Greville's bedroom she paused and, always correct, opened the door for us.

It was a large room with a double window opening on to the front terrace, but now the lined silk curtains were drawn and the gas lamps lit. I had never been in this room before and would have been curious to examine its furnishings had not my attention been immediately riveted to Miss Greville. She was sitting at a long sofa table, not fully dressed, but wrapped in a fringed bathrobe, and writing so industriously that as we entered she did not look up. Four letters had apparently been written—instinctively I counted the stamped envelopes that lay on the table—and now she was busy on a fifth. She seemed calm, indeed perfectly composed, and although her hair was in some disorder, the normality of her appearance gave me a quick glow of reassurance.

'There!' she exclaimed at last, putting down her pen. 'Do forgive me for keeping you.'

She folded the letter, tucked it in an envelope which she then sealed, addressed and stamped. Gathering all the letters together she made a neat pile in front of her and sat up, erect and competent.

'Well, Grace,' she remarked mildly, 'I suppose you have seen the paragraph in the *Herald*.'

There was no point in denying this and Mother did not do so. I could feel her relaxing with relief at Miss Greville's reasonable attitude. Not a sign of frenzy, hysterics or delirium.

'I thought at first that I should ignore it,' Miss Greville went on, 'since it is, at best, a clumsy device. But on considering the matter more fully I have decided that action is necessary.'

Mother had gone rigid again.

'You realize, of course, that *he*, poor man, had no part in this. The whole scandalous affair is an intrigue, instigated by that woman with the connivance of the editor of the *Herald* and, in all probability, the provost of the town.'

Brushing aside Mother's attempted protest she continued, as moderately as before, but with a new note of gravity.

'So I have written these letters . . . which you will be good enough to post for me, Carroll.' She held them out and I found myself accepting them. 'One is to Mr Lesly, another to his Bishop, the third to the editor of the *Herald* and the fourth to the town clerk. The final letter is to that woman.'

She paused, glanced significantly towards her dressing-table. I felt Mother start. The foils had been brought up from downstairs and their end buttons removed. 'Yes, Grace, I have challenged her to a duel.'

'Oh, no,' Mother cried. 'You simply mustn't do that.'

'Even if I must not, I will.' Miss Greville smiled, and in its vacuity, its total blankness, I knew it was the smile of an utterly demented woman, even before she added: "Naturally, dear Grace, I am relying on you to be my second.'

I don't know how we got out of that room. The moment we escaped Mother went straight downstairs to the telephone and rang Dr Ewen. He came in about half an hour. By that time, overcome by a sense of utter desolation, feeling like an idiot myself, I had retired to my burrow in the kitchen alcove. There I remained during the doctor's visit, emerging only as I heard signs of his departure. As I looked down over the banisters of the stairs into the hall below I heard him say to Mother:

'She will have to be certified and removed at once.'

TWENTY

THREE MONTHS LATER, sitting opposite Mother in the Winton train, I examined her covertly, trying to read her face. What I saw there gave me a sinking in my inside, I sensed that desperate measures were in prospect for us. Several times, in the hope of discovering the secrets that sealed her brow, I had made an effort to draw her into conversation and presently I tried again, using the visit we were now making to Castleton Asylum as an opening gambit.

'Do you think Miss Greville will be better?'

'I hope so, dear. We shall soon know,' she answered, and lapsed again into silence.

Defeated, I turned and looked out of the window, blind to the fleeting vista of the river shipyards, seeing instead the sequence of events that had brought us beyond the edge of disaster.

Not long after Miss Greville's removal her brother had arrived—tall, lean and bronzed, with a commanding manner and an appearance formidably correct. He had immediately taken charge and, after visiting his sister, and several interviews with her doctors, had terminated the lease of the maisonette and ordered the removal of the furniture to a depository. Towards Mother he was at first polite, then coldly polite, and finally merely cold. Campbell had his ear, he relied on her, the old family servant, and Campbell had never liked us. We had come solely on Miss Greville's invitation, and Mother, even when we were living from hand to mouth, had never failed to pay her rent, yet we were made to appear as interlopers. In the end, just three weeks ago, a lawyer's letter had arrived curtly giving us a month in which to vacate our apartment.

True, with Miss Greville gone, and with the main part of the house dismantled, there was nothing to keep us at No. 7. But as the period of our notice began to run out, the uncertainty of our future increased. While maintaining a disturbing reticence, Mother was unnaturally active, not at the agency, where her work seemed almost to have ceased, but in sudden sorties to unknown destinations. Never before had I known her write so many letters: to Uncle Simon in Spain, to her brother Stephen who now had an appointment in the Civil Service in London, to Uncle Leo in Winton, and others to people I had never heard of in places as distant as Liverpool, Nottingham and Cardiff.

A sudden blackout of the landscape, as the train roared into the low-level tunnel, indicated our approach to the Central Station. In a few minutes we were making our way up from the smoky platform, sunk in the very depths of the city, to Union Street and the yellow tram.

It was a long, slow ride to Castleton—in those days, although the Corporation trams ranged far and wide, their speed was not excessive. But the day was sunny, and as we left the drab core of Winton, passed through the scattered suburbs, and emerged to the pleasant open countryside beyond, my spirits, always responsive to a prevailing green, lightened considerably. Castleton, still untouched, was a pretty little village. At the Asylum entrance, where the tram conductor put us off, two massively ornate gates were flanked by twin lodges set in the high surrounding stone wall. I felt a strange emotion, half anticipation, half dread, as I pulled the wrought-iron handle of the big jangling bell.

Mother had a pass which she showed to the lodge keeper,

and when it had been carefully scrutinized, he went to a wall telephone, whirred a little handle, and spoke.

'It's very hard to get in, Mother,' I whispered.

'But harder to get out,' she answered sombrely.

Eventually the keeper came back, smiled and nodded, the gates were unlocked.

As we entered and began to walk up the broad sanded avenue that wound between tall beech trees towards the castellated mansion on the hill, I gave an exclamation of wonder at the extent and beauty of the estate. On one side a broad orchard of apple and pear trees was in full flourish, through which I made out a model farm with barns and haystacks, while on the other a rising stretch of parkland, studded with specimen chestnut trees, gave way at the far end to the more formal garden that fronted the house. We passed a croquet lawn, a row of tennis courts, a trellised shelter set between double herbaceous borders blooming with pink tulips.

There seemed nothing to offend the eye until suddenly, on the skyline, I made out a long dark procession of plodding figures, some grotesquely bent, others gesturing, all exercising slowly, like a string of prisoners, with a nurse in front and another behind.

At the main entrance we were now expected and admitted by a sister in dark blue uniform. Using a key, which was chained to her belt, with the dexterity of long practice, she took us through a series of doors, all without handles, along a wide thickly carpeted corridor embellished with ornate gilt furnishings and set at intervals with other heavy doors, all shut, then into a small end ante-room where she paused and, looking at me without enthusiasm, spoke in an undertone to Mother, who turned to me.

'Sister thinks you had better wait here, Laurence.'

Although I wanted to see Miss Greville, at least the real Miss Greville, restored to herself, I was not sorry to be left behind. This progress by key, locking us in, away from the bright outer world, the strange sounds, mumblings and shufflings, muted by heavy doors, the atmosphere, tainted by the commode, of discreet morbidity, even the black convoluted ornate furniture of the reception room in which I now sat—it was Buhl, a variety I had never seen before— all conspired to send a shiver down my spine, a sensation heightened by a sudden shriek, instantly suppressed, that made me jump from the spindly velvet-upholstered chair in which I had cautiously placed myself.

Mother was a long time in coming back, but at last she reappeared. In that instant through the open doorway I caught a sudden fleeting glimpse of a narrow corridor leading to another room, the door of which the sister was in the process of closing, and there, framed in that narrow aperture, was a strange, flaccid face, the hair cropped to the skull, the eyes staring yet vacant, meeting mine in a frightening exchange, without a shadow of recognition. The shock of that unknown, unearthly face still vibrated along my nerves as Mother took my arm. I could not speak. I knew that I had seen my good friend Miss Greville, and that I would not see her again.

Outside, Mother drew a long deep breath of the fresh spring air and, having thanked the sister and said goodbye, began to walk down the drive, still holding my arm. When we reached the trellised summer-house she said:

'Let me sit here, Laurie. Just for a little while.'

We went into the summer-house. Although I knew, I had to ask.

'How is she, Mother?'

'Hopeless, quite hopeless.'

'What was she doing?'

'Drawing up petitions, all day long, petitions that no one will ever see. And writing letters that will never be posted.' She added, after a pause, as though to herself: 'Now at least I know where we stand.'

She rested her head on her hand and sat silent. I watched her uneasily.

'If we stay here too long we may not get out.'

She looked at me and smiled. I was amazed. Her expression had altogether changed, a transformation that seemed to wipe out that fixed distress, the disquiet and indecision not only of today but of all these past troubled weeks. She stood up and to my further surprise, for I knew how hard up we were, very cheerfully declared:

'Let's go, darling, and have a real, slap-up tea.'

Outside the gates, in Castleton village, there was an excellent tea room above the local baker's shop. Here Mother ordered tea and all the things I liked, hot buttered toast and a new-laid boiled egg, fresh wheaten scones, honey, and a plate of cream cakes. While she sipped the hot tea she kept pressing me to eat so that, under this repeated prompting, I ate all the cream cakes. She had watched me with a hovering smile but now, glancing round to assure herself that we were still alone in the room, she turned to me seriously.

'Laurence,' she said, 'your mother is a failure.'

A silence followed during which I felt extremely uncomfortable. Yet there had been no misery in her voice, merely a firmness that sounded almost defiant as she resumed.

'The agency is finished. It was a wonderful idea of your father's and now it's gone. The mistake I made was not to sell it and realize something as your Uncle Leo suggested.' As she paused to take a sip of tea, I had a sudden, fleeting vision of Mother and me singing for our supper in a wet Winton street. 'I'm not going to weary you with my difficulties over the past years. I've always tried to keep them away from you. But you must have guessed them. It was no work for a woman, at least not for me. Sympathy doesn't last for ever. It's not a business asset. So all I have to tell you, and I must tell you, for you're a big boy now, we have nothing left, nothing but our furniture, for which I've an offer of forty pounds.'

My lavish meal may have given me courage to withstand this shock. Perhaps that was why Mother had fortified me. I felt nothing more than a queer blankness which drew from me, involuntarily, the only possible response.

'So what are we going to do?'

'You are going to your Uncle Leo, and I am going to Wales.'

This, being quite incomprehensible, was much worse. My expression must have warned Mother. She leaned forward, drew her fingers softly across my cheek and began persuasively, undramatically, to explain how extreme was our situation and how, after considering every expedient, this was the only way she could resolve it. I must leave school, at least for the time being. Uncle Leo had promised to take me and teach me his business so that at the worst, I should at least have something to fall back on. Her own case was more difficult. She had no qualifications for business, music was her only asset, and even so she had no teacher's diploma, and now would never get one. Yet Uncle Simon, writing from Spain, had managed to obtain a place for her as music mistress at St Monica's Convent, a girls' school in Monmouthshire. Here, in her off-duty, during the next

147

twelve months she would have the advantage of attending special classes in Cardiff. She was going to take an intensive course and pass the examination to become a public-health visitor. Four of these appointments, a new departure open to women, were to be made in Winton and, through the intervention of a friend of Stephen's on the City Council, she had been promised one of them if she could take her training and get her certificate within a year. She would then be sure of a regular salary in a position for which she felt herself fitted. We would be together again, and if I did not wish to remain with Leo, she would be able to send me to a tutorial college to renew my studies, so that later on I could sit the bursary examination for the University.

Finishing on a high note of encouragement Mother looked at me entreatingly, while I tried to recover myself sufficiently to grasp the implications of this staggering proposal. I did not like it. Yet, through all the confusion of my mind, I could not fail to see how hard and painfully she must have tried, enduring all sorts of rebuffs, to put this plan together as a last resort. This, in part, tempered by resentment, as I said:

'Why can't I go with you to Wales?'

'It's not possible, dear.' Mother forced a placating little laugh. 'Not in the convent. You'll be better off with Leo.'

The possibilities of being with Leo in a real business had already flashed intriguingly across my mind, but I would not admit this, saying instead,

'Uncle Leo is a queer fish, Mother.'

'Yes, he's perhaps a trifle odd in some ways. But I'm inclined to trust him, if only because he doesn't promise us the earth.'

'Wouldn't Uncle Bernard help us?'

'Never,' Mother said shortly. 'And I would never ask him.'

She was right. Bernard, with the best intentions and tears in his eyes, *would* promise us the earth and completely forget about us next day.

A silence followed during which I examined our predicament, looking for an escape hatch through which we might both get out of it.

'Mother,' I said at last, though hesitantly, for this was a forbidden subject, though I had to broach it. 'Wouldn't it be possible for you . . . I mean didn't you have a long letter from Stephen last week . . . couldn't we go to your parents, your own family . . . ?'

I broke off, stopped in my tracks by the sudden colour that rushed into Mother's face and then as quickly receded, leaving her paler than before.

'Yes, Laurence, I had the chance to go back . . . but on conditions I could never accept.'

I had a great curiosity to know what these conditions were but I did not dare ask. Instead, rather dismally, I began to reflect on our coming separation, which made me ask:

'When is all this going to happen?'

She took a quick breath and exclaimed spiritedly:

'Not until we've had a jolly good holiday together.'

I stared at her in stupefaction. Had misfortune turned her brain? And now she was smiling at me, with that same challenging, almost reckless expression, carefree too, as though a load had fallen from her shoulders.

'Yes, I mean it, Laurie. We'll go to the Highlands. We both deserve a holiday and need it. I'm taking the offer for the furniture and we'll spend every penny of the forty pounds on ourselves. After that we'll be all set up and fit for anything.'

Before I could say a word she took up the little bell from the table and summoned the waitress by ringing it like mad.

TWENTY-ONE

AS WE CAME OUT of the railway station Fort William lay under a raw mist that blanketed Ben Nevis and dripped from the slate roofs of the town. Looking about me while Mother arranged with a porter to deliver our luggage by hand-cart in the afternoon, I became afflicted by a strange, sinking premonition that this Highland resort boded ill for me.

Ardshiel, the boarding establishment of our choice, stood half-way up the hill, a small, square, red sandstone house set behind a prodigious monkey-puzzle tree, in a neat garden overlooking the loch. Mother had favoured it because it was kept by two sisters, maiden ladies who advertised its virtues, and their gentility, in one telling word—*select*. Indeed, Mother's judgement seemed justified by our rooms which, though small and on the top floor, she pronounced to be of an exemplary cleanliness. No sooner had she concluded her examination, which began with the bed-linen and ended with the water in the ewer, than the gong boomed startlingly for lunch.

We went downstairs. Not more than ten people were seated at a long mahogany table in a bay-windowed room cosily furnished in worn red plush. At the head of the table a tall angular woman in black rose to greet us, explaining that she was Miss Kincaid. She then introduced us to the other guests, and to her younger sister, Miss Ailie Kincaid, who sat at the foot of the board. Seating herself again, she bowed her head, said grace devoutly and began to carve the joint. This I soon found to be the standard procedure, while Miss Ailie, at the other end, dispensed the vegetables, and later, the semolina pudding and prunes.

Despite its plainness the food was good and hot, a welcome discovery corroborated by Mother's quick communicative glance. I already liked the smaller, softer Miss Ailie, and although I was rather wary of Miss Kincaid—a totally unjustified prejudice—I saw nothing wrong with the other guests. All were decent Scots, middle-aged or elderly people and all, with two exceptions, women. Of the males, seated beside me on my right was a short, thick-set, red-faced man whom I had heard addressed as Baillie Nicol. He had a salmon fly, which I recognized as a Jock Scott, stuck in his lapel. And next to Miss Kincaid a little ghost-like old man with white hair had flitted in noiselessly in felt-soled slippers. During the meal he remained completely silent, keeping his eyes upon his plate and having considerable difficulty in controlling his false teeth. It took me some time to discover that he was Miss Kincaid's father, and stone deaf, but in the meantime I was inclined to regard him as something of a phenomenon.

Another curiosity which took my eye was a china pig with a slot in its back that stood in the centre of the table.

'Are you wondering about our wee porker?' Miss Ailie was smiling to me. 'You see, we like everyone to be served properly while the meals are hot. And that means punctuality. So the rule is that if one comes late one must put a penny in the pig. Naturally, it's all for a good cause—our cottage hospital.'

I looked across the table at a vacant chair.

'That person will have to pay up?'

'Oh, no,' she laughed. 'That's Mr Sommen's place. He's gone off to Ballater for the day. To the Highland Games.'

'I never knew anyone so taken on with the Highlands as Mr Sommen.' A stout lady opposite took up the conversation. 'For an Englishman, I mean. He fair dotes on the tartan.'

'I hope it's fine for him at Ballater,' rejoined Miss Ailie, glancing out at the weather.' He was so looking forward to the step-dancing and the reels.'

'Had he the wee plaid on him when he left this morning?'

'He had indeed. And very braw he looked in it.' Miss Ailie sighed. 'Such a nice gentleman. What manners!'

'Aye, you don't often see the like. And forbye, the life and soul of our little party.'

At this point my Baillie neighbour cleared his throat noisily, as though something had gone the wrong way, and changed the conversation. Doubtless he had seen me coveting his Jock Scott, for he turned abruptly and asked me if I liked to fish. He told me he came every year to spin for salmon in the Spean, and when he promised to show me a pool where I might catch brown trout, my spirits improved further. I nodded to Mother, indicating that after all Fort William was not a bad sort of place. She and I would certainly go together to the pool and she could knit and watch me while I fished. I gave no thought to the absent Mr Sommen, or if I did it was in the vague yet optimistic expectation that he too, being the man he was, would contribute further to the satisfactions of our holiday.

At five o'clock that evening, while the others were finishing tea, I had gone to the front door to unravel a gut cast my new fishing friend had given me and which I had already succeeded in tangling, when an open carriage rolled up to the porch and a man sprang out briskly, paid the coachman with an added, 'That's for yourself, chappie,' then bounded up the steps towards me. He was of a neat medium figure with a pale, glossy skin, large dark eyes, and a narrow black moustache that curved thinly and stylishly, like an extra eyebrow, across his upper lip. He had on a sporty check suit, a rakish balmoral with the ribbons sweeping across one shoulder, and over the other a short tartan plaid pinned by a silver dagger studded with a large cairngorm.

'Well, well, well, young fellow-me-lad.' He greeted me genially. 'You a new arrival?'

'Yes, sir.'

'With your parents?'

'My mother, sir.'

'Pater still turning the wheels of industry?'

'My father's dead, sir.'

'Oh, sorry, old chap.' He was immediately contrite. 'Fearfully sorry I dropped a brick. No idea. Not the foggiest. Come and have some tea.'

I told him I'd already had my tea.

'Then come and have another go of cake. Can do? Good. Fill the aching void.' With an arm companionably round my shoulders he steered me into the drawing-room where, sweeping off his balmoral, he bowed elegantly from the waist.

'Am I too late for the cup that cheers but not inebriates, ladies? If so, just say the word and I'll apologize, depart, put sixpence in the pig, abscond, in other words, buzz off, anything to make amends.'

When several voices reassured him he advanced, accepted a cup from Miss Ailie and having implemented his promise, with a wink, by back-handing me a thick slice of cake from the tray, took his stand by the fireplace.

'Well, ladies, I suppose yours truly was never missed, that absence did not make the heart grow fonder, and you haven't the slightest interest in his adventures at the Games, even though he did brush shoulders with none other than Royalty?'

'But we have, Mr Sommen. Do tell us.'

As I ate my cherry cake I gazed at him in wide-eyed admiration. He was so much at ease, so fluent, never at a loss, so amusingly at home with everyone and above all so dashingly good-looking, with his pale skin, small neat features, stylish little moustache and dark engaging eyes. When he concluded his racy description of his doings during the day I was especially struck by his manner when, taking advantage of the pause, Miss Ailie introduced him to Mother. All the jocularity vanished from his expression, he was immediately serious, correct, respectful. He bowed again, talked with her for a few moments and, with a companionable glance that lightly comprehended me, wished her a top-hole stay at Ardshiel. Then, as a kind of afterthought, he added:

'After supper we have little musical evenings here, just by way of entertaining ourselves, if you care for that sort of thing?'

Mother admitted that she was fond of music.

'Perhaps,' he ventured, 'perhaps you play a little . . . or sing, yourself?'

To my chagrin, Mother said that she would really prefer to listen. So acute was my disappointment I forgot my shyness and exclaimed:

'Oh no, sir, Mother plays the piano awfully well. She played once at a concert before hundreds of people. And she sings too.'

He looked at me with such pleased approval that I reddened with gratification. Removing his gaze in a well-bred manner from Mother, who had blushed too, he said quietly:

'Well spoken, old chap. Perhaps between us we may be able to persuade your mater to oblige the company. And now, if you'll excuse me, I must be off for my tub. Nothing like a tub after a day in the open. Au revoir then, till we meet again.'

Mother was cross with me as we went upstairs.

'I hope your tartan friend isn't going to be a nuisance, with his little musical evenings. He is rather a gusher, isn't he?'

Nevertheless, I noticed that she put on her best dress, red with a lace collar, which she had sponged and pressed before we left Ardfillan, and extremely nice she looked in it.

When the gong boomed us down for supper Mr Sommen was already in the dining-room standing rather absently in a welcoming position with his hands behind his back, wearing a snowy-white shirt set off by a black bow tie, well-creased black trousers and a poplin tartan jacket. I thought he looked terribly smart, and so did the others. The jacket, which was apparently new, evoked murmurs of approval. Assiduously placing chairs for the ladies, he modestly admitted he had bought it at Ballater after the Games.

Only one of our company seemed openly at odds with this general adulation and when we had begun on some excellent tomato soup, with the kind of lentils in it that I liked, Baillie Nicol, after darting several caustic glances from beneath his bushy eyebrows at the new garment, suddenly remarked:

'Ye know, of course, sir, that the tartan ye have on is the Mackenzie.'

'Is it, by gosh? Delighted to hear it.'

'And the plaid ye wear is the Macgregor. While that strip

on your balmoral is the Royal Stuart. It looks as though before you've done ye'll be a regular one-man "Gathering o' the Clans".'

'Well, good luck to them,' Sommen said airily. 'I like gatherings and from what I saw of these Highland lasses at their eightsome reels I jolly well like the clans.'

'But apart from the fact that it's almost illegal to sport a tartan ye're not entitled to, what's your object, man?'

'When in Rome do as the jolly old Romans.' Sommen laughed with perfect good nature, not a bit discomfited. 'That's my motto when I travel. Last summer I took in Switzerland. When I stepped off the last mountain you couldn't have told me from William Tell. Not bad that, eh? Told, tell!'

The Baillie persisted, inquisitively.

'Ye must have a grand business to be able to get away so much.'

Sommen inclined his head, answered with a sudden note of gravity.

'Yes, sir, my family are perhaps the oldest tobacco merchants in the city of London. We are cigarette manufacturers, sir. May I show you our product?' He took out a morocco-leather cigarette-case and pressed it open, revealing a row of long, flat, elegant-looking cigarettes. As it was passed from hand to hand I saw stamped in blue on each, 'C. R. Sommen. Special No. 1.'

'May I offer you one, sir?'

'Thank you, no,' the Baillie growled, thoroughly put out by this demonstration of solid worth. 'I have my pipe.'

After these exchanges in which the cigarette-maker had clearly had the better of it, supper proceeded with renewed amiability. When Miss Kincaid formally gave the signal to rise we went into the drawing-room, or as Miss Ailie named it, the 'best parlour'. Here the curtains had been drawn against the evening chill and a cosy fire of peat was glowing on the hearth, emitting its aromatic moorland scent. While coffee and shortbread biscuits were handed round, Sommen advanced to the piano and, standing over the keyboard, played 'Chopsticks' with one finger.

'Excuse my humble overture, ladies and gentlemen. We are now exceeding fortunate to have a real genuine topnotch pianist in our midst and with her kind permission I'm going to ask her to start the ball rolling.'

He came forward and crooking his arm in invitation, exclaimed amidst appreciative laughter:

'Madam, may I have the honour of escorting you to the instrument?'

Now I must confess that by this time I was beginning to be considerably bored by our new friend. His attentions to Mother at supper had been rather too marked and now this cheap gallantry seemed to confirm her own worst fears. I glanced at her sympathetically but, to my surprise, she did not snub him. Instead she rose, yielding without protest, indeed rather gracefully, to this unwelcome foolery.

She played a Chopin prelude then dashed into 'Danse d'Echarpes' with great brio and finished to sustained applause.

I saw that for once Sommen was quite taken aback, as though, unexpectedly, he found himself in an element totally foreign to him.

'I say,' he said, almost with deference, 'that 'ad real class.' Then, recovering himself from that fearful missing aspirate: 'Absolutely topping. Good enough for the Albert Hall.'

'Nonsense.' Mother laughed, and went on rather as if poking fun at him. 'Now it's your turn. Let's hear you sing. If you can? I'll play your accompaniment.'

After much turning over of music, the song 'The Mermaid' was selected. To my disappointment, he had not a bad voice, a light tenor, and he put great dramatic feeling into the words:

> *And down he went like a streak of light,*
> *So quickly down went he,*
> *Until he came to a mermaid*
> *At the bottom of the deep blue sea.*

The effect of this double display of talent upon the company was so pronounced that, to my annoyance, there arose a general demand for a duet. Surely now Mother would refuse, draw the line, put her foot down firmly. But no, still in the same lively, challenging way, almost, one might have thought, with enjoyment, she had already selected 'The Tarpaulin Jacket', the first line of which, 'A tall stalwart Lancer lay dying', gave me such a thrill of anticipation that I had come to regard the ballad as my own special property. They began. I wished I might have stopped up my ears. At least I kept my eyes on the ceiling and refrained from joining in the prolonged hand-clapping.

By this time the singing, talking and laughter, the growing sense of camaraderie, above all the patter and too pressing urbanities of this bogus clansman had, in a manner I scarcely realized, made me extremely hot under my collar. I decided that it had gone far enough and should be terminated. Seizing a rare moment of silence I called out:

'I think I'll go upstairs now, Mother,' imagining, naturally, that she would come with me.

Instead, still bent over the music with Sommen, without even turning round, she replied:

'Yes, do, dear. It's past your bedtime. I'll be up soon.'

As I was already on my feet there was nothing for it but that I must go. And she did not come soon but late, much later than I had hoped. Still, the desire to express my conflicting emotions had served to keep me awake. I sat up in bed.

'You were right after all, Mother. It *was* a nuisance, wasn't it?'

She smiled at me. Her eyes seemed bright and there was colour in her cheeks.

'Oh, I don't know, dear. In a way it was really rather fun and goodness knows neither of us have had much of that lately.'

'But Mother, it was all so . . . so cheap and nasty.'

'Was it as bad as all that?'

'*He* was, anyhow, the cigarette-maker.'

'Well, perhaps he is rather officious, dear, but I think he means well, so we mustn't be too critical. Let's just remember we're here for the one holiday we've had in four years and try to make the most of it.'

This was not the kind of response I expected from my mother. Turning on my side I gave her a brusque good night.

However, next morning my sense of injury had gone and after breakfast, carrying my fishing-rod and a picnic lunch, I set out with Baillie Nicol for the Spean. Mother, seeing us off from the porch, promised to join me in almost an hour. The pool the Baillie showed me was not far upriver, a deep brown tarn among pine trees, fed by a rushing waterfall and contained by ledges. Having seen me settled he went off upstream to his own beat, having finally averred with a pessimistic survey of the clear blue sky that it was not an anglers' day.

Certainly I didn't look like having much luck. In the space of two hours I caught a three-inch parr, which of course I unhooked carefully and returned. As nothing seemed to be taking, I began more and more to look for the appearance of Mother. What on earth was keeping her? Could my Ingersoll be wrong? No, from the sun, directly overhead, it must now be noon. My neck was stiff from craning towards the path through the wood and the roar of the waterfall had made my head swim. I reeled in, retreated to the pines and ate my share of the lunch. Still not a sign of her. Angrily, after only a moment's hesitation, I ate her lunch as well. She would not deserve it when she did come.

With nothing else to do, I resumed my fishing, but in so spiritless a manner I permitted an eel to take my hook unnoticed and to digest my bait so thoroughly that it had to be destroyed, in a slimy mess, before I could recover my tackle. After that, as the afternoon was well advanced, I decided to give up.

I had trudged to the end of the wood and was on the road that led uphill from the river, when an approaching figure became visible against the skyline. It was she.

Immediately I threw off my despondency, set my expression to an injured and resentful coldness. Ignoring her too cheerful greeting, I said accusingly:

'You didn't come.'

'I'm so sorry, dear.' She smiled, breathlessly. 'Our plans somehow seemed to get upset.'

Apparently, though I gave her no marks for that futile and belated effort, she'd been hurrying.

'You see, there was such an interesting expedition arranged to Banavie. Somehow I was persuaded to go along.'

'Who persuaded you?'

'Why . . . Miss Baird.'

Had she hesitated before answering me? Miss Baird was the stout woman who liked Sommen.

'So you and she went off all by yourselves.'

'Good gracious, no, dear.' She made the idea seem ridiculous. 'Two women, all alone! Your friend Mr Sommen went with us. In fact he organized the trip and took care of everything most handsomely.'

That evening at supper I studied him, viewing him after the manner of Scott-Hamilton with a critical, appraising eye. What a clown he was, or rather, what a cad, monopolizing the conversation—keeping things going I suppose he would have called it—and showing off in every direction. Why, at this moment, as Miss Kincaid, having sliced the boiled ham, seemed to be having trouble carving one of the chickens, and with a reproachful glance at Miss Ailie, had murmured that the carver was not sharp, he had the colossal cheek to interfere. I could scarcely believe my eyes when this bounder leaned over, with a 'Permit me, madam', and taking the knife from her hand began to carve the bird. I longed for him to make some horrible gaffe that would draw down on him the laughter and contempt of everyone. I hoped the chicken would squirt off the platter to the floor or, better still, bounce up and hit him in the eye. But no, with unsuspected skill and a dexterity I believed impossible, he had it sliced and sectioned perfectly. This was too much for me and apparently for Baillie Nicol too. He kept muttering under his breath and glowering at our enemy. I was glad to accept his invitation to a game of draughts in the smoking-room; I felt I would do anything to avoid the entertainment in the parlour.

The Baillie was not of a talkative disposition, but as we set out our men on the chequered board, he fixed his gaze on me and said:

'You seem a decent sort of boy, and your mother looks to me a sweet little woman. If I were you, I would just drop a word in her ear against the counter-jumper of a cockney. I may be wrong, but, for my part, I wouldn't trust him as far as I could throw him.'

The warning alarmed me. And as the next few days passed, there was no longer the least possibility of doubt. This man, this Englishman, this tartaned Sommen, was—I sought a phrase that would not wound me too deeply—'making up' to my mother. Despite the deceptive mildness of these two words they sent a hot flush over me. And it deepened at the thought of Mother's response. At first she had merely seemed flattered: a natural reaction which I had persuaded myself was pardonable in a woman whose life had lately been so dull and hard. But gradually she had warmed to these hateful attentions and now, in her glance, her gesture, in her whole being, she could not conceal from me, nor from others in the boarding-house whom I had heard whispering, the change that had come over her. She looked younger and prettier, with a strange attractiveness that exuded and bloomed upon her skin. She had a new liveliness, an unnatural vivacity, a sense of letting herself go that I had never known before. Worst of all was her change towards me: that excessive solicitude and open show of tenderness, which I felt to be propitiating, even insincere, since most of the time, to be free of my questioning eye, she kept avoiding me, or pushing me off to fish, so that she could go off with *him*.

At the start of the second week, as I sat at the Spean pool, I decided I wouldn't put up with it. I would not be cast off. Burning with indignation, I reeled in my neglected line, from which the worm had long ago been devoured, and set off for Ardshiel.

Mother was on the porch, but not as though expecting me.

'Any luck?' she exclaimed with specious brightness.

'No.'

'Never mind, dear. I'm sure you'll catch something when you try again this afternoon.'

I didn't answer. My mind was made up. I ate my lunch with apparent calm. Immediately the meal ended I excused myself, got up, and disappeared. I had not returned to the river. I was in the shrubbery at the edge of the garden.

They did not keep me waiting long. My heart gave a big, extra thump as they emerged, Sommen in his idiotic tartan get-up, Mother wearing her brown tweed costume and a new gay scarf which she certainly had not bought and which therefore he must have given her. Together, yet discreetly separated, they sauntered down the hill towards the town. Gazing from between the laurel branches I allowed them a fair start, then, with a casual air, though my pulse was throbbing like mad, I cut round the side of the garden and went after them.

The bitter excitement of the chase made me want to run, but I knew I must keep a safe distance behind them. Out of sight of the boarding-house, they had drawn closer to each other. They reached the town and turned the corner into the main street. Trying not to hurry, I followed. It was market day and the town was busy. For a minute I couldn't pick them out, then I saw them on the opposite side of the street looking into the window of a shop that

sold Gosse china and other tourist souvenirs. He was gab-
bing, as usual, and pointing in a persuasive manner, but
Mother shook her head lightly and they moved off. A rush
of traffic held me back, but when I crossed the street, out
of the corner of my eye I saw them veer right into the
Mealmarket, a narrow wynd leading to the old part of the
town.

Now I increased my pace and swung into the Mealmarket.
They were not in sight. With a catch of anxiety I pressed
on, moving in and out of the stalls that crowded the narrow
wynd, seeking everywhere, like a hound at fault. Minutes
passed, five, ten. Not a sign of them. Had I lost them? And
then, as I came out of the far end of the Mealmarket into
the cobbled square that faced the open loch, my eye was
caught by a rowboat moving easily on the sunlit water only
a few hundred yards offshore.

I took a long breath. Now I had them, and I could wait.
Slowly, without removing my gaze, I walked down to the
stone jetty from which the boats were hired and took up
my stand behind one of the bollards.

He was at the oars, alternatively sculling and drifting,
while Mother sat facing him in the stern. When he leaned
forward to make a stroke the intimacy of their positions
stung me. I choked with jealous rage, invoking all the
powers of light and darkness to work a miracle that would
make this dandy, this bogus Clansman, this cigarette-maker,
catch a crab and somersault backwards into the water,
where, strangled by the strings of his balmoral and shouting
vainly to me for aid, he would sink in all his finery to the
bottom of the loch which I knew to be fabulously deep.

At last they came ashore. Instinctively I crouched low,
hiding under the edge of the pier. Now, although I could
not see, I could hear. I heard the bump of the boat against
the jetty, his step ashore and then his voice as he assisted
her to land.

'Dear Grace, give me your hand.'

The words made me wince.

Now I heard footsteps on the stones above and judged it
safe to raise my head. Mother had taken his arm and was
smiling up at him as they moved off. I folded my arms and
in that dramatic attitude, with the frozen immobility of
the betrayed, watched them go.

When I returned to Ardshiel I revealed nothing of the

treachery I had witnessed, merely maintaining an attitude of stoic coldness. All that evening I confronted Mother with my silence and hostility. She had now begun to look at me reproachfully. and after supper tried to induce me to come with her to the drawing-room on the pretext that there were to be parlour games. Games, indeed! I resisted, saying that I was tired, and went upstairs to bed where, as I lay awake, the misery of the afternoon was re-created by their intermingled voices ascending in another hateful duet. When she came up, quite late, I closed my eyes and pretended sleep.

Next morning came clear and sunny. Mother, eager for reconciliation and with the faintest hint of guilt in her manner, was all sweetness and light. After breakfast she came out to join me in the garden where already I had taken up a strategic position by the gate.

'Darling,' she smiled placatingly—ah, I thought, the Judas smile! 'Mr Sommen has suggested taking us for a drive this afternoon. Along the coast to visit Onich Castle. But I daresay you can't be bothered with sightseeing.'

'Why not?' I inquired.

'Well . . . you're such a fisherman I thought you'd surely want to go to your pool again.'

'Considering that I've gone to my pool for the past week and caught nothing, doesn't it occur to you that I might prefer to go sightseeing? Especially,' I added, with heavy emphasis, 'as there will probably be plenty to see.'

She flushed slightly and was silent.

'Then you'd . . . you'd really like to come?'

'Yes,' I said, not looking at her. 'I definitely and positively would.'

The carriage arrived at two o'clock. The cigarette-maker who, while we waited in the porch, had been jocular with me in his best 'old chap' manner, through which I detected a strain of unease, now gave me a hand up beside the coachman before taking his place with Mother behind. We set off with a slow clip-clop of hooves. I could not observe the pair at my back but at least I was with them and I swore that this time they would not get away. Never again would Mother have the chance to be alone with all that charm.

Partially reassured, I almost enjoyed the drive. The sun shone, the sky was a duck-egg blue, the little waves lapped along the shore. It was good to be seated so high, and the coachman was friendly, pointing out places of interest with his whip. If only this interloper had not been with us. His intrusion was a profanation of our existence.

Too soon we arrived at the clachan of Onich and drew up at the little harbour where a few small blistered fishing-smacks lay moored against the pier. In the foreground, high up on a cliff, was the castle. As I climbed off my perch the cigarette-maker assisted Mother to alight.

'I say,' he suddenly exclaimed, looking down, 'what a spiffing day for a cruise!'

Two fisherboys in rubber boots and blue jerseys were hoisting a lug sail.

'Would you like it, young fellow-me-lad?' he said, turning to me. 'Don't you think it a good idea?'

I thought it an excellent idea. How better could I keep them under my eagle eye? I nodded stiffly.

'Come on then,' he cried gaily, leaping down and speaking to the boys. When I followed he helped me aboard solici-tously, then, still on the pier, and before I knew what he was about or could collect my scattered wits, he had pushed the boat off, the sail caught the wind and I was out of the harbour and away while Mother, with a despicable pretence of affection, took out her handkerchief and waved to me from the shore.

I turned wildly to the bigger of the two boys.

'Go back. Go back to the pier.'

He shook his head. The 'gentlemans' had hired him 'py the 'oor'. He let out more sail and the boat took an un-balancing heave. Weak with rage and distress I collapsed in the thwarts. Yesterday they had been in the boat and I on shore. Now precisely, the positions were reversed. This was the final treachery. They had begun to walk arm-in-arm along the cliff towards the castle. Yes, I had always thought him a cad, and now I knew him to be a cheat as well. As for Mother's . . . duplicity . . . oh, dear, the wind was making my eyes water.

For more than the specified time we tacked monotonously up and down outside the harbour. My captors had prac-tically no English but they had the Gaelic and in this, to me, outlandish tongue they conversed continuously in low derisive voices, gazing from me to the castle, then back again to me. Although I could not understand a word of their ghastly lingo I sweated with shame, fully aware that they were discussing me, my correct attire, my pallid looks which, because of the movement of the boat, betrayed that I was on the verge of nausea, above all—and this was the hardest to bear—the obvious beastly reason why I had been shanghaied by the *gentlemans*.

At last there came a hail from the beach. The despicable couple had reappeared, and with a final sadistic tack into the wind to prolong my misery, I was returned to the harbour.

'Have a good time, old chap?'

'Yes, thank you.' I met his ingratiating gaze with the prim unsmiling politeness I had resolved to assume.

Mother, who seemed flushed and agitated, was looking at me nervously yet with an earnestness that told me her one desire was to make up with me.

'I don't think you'd have liked the castle, dear.'

'I don't think I should.'

'It was very old.'

'It looks old.'

'And damp.'

'I thought it might be.'

'You weren't too cold on the water?'

'Not at all, thank you.'

'Were the boys nice?'

'Delightful.'

There was an awkward pause before our unnatural dialogue could be resumed.

'Well,' exclaimed Sommen, with an effort at heartiness, 'it's about time we were off. I'll go and dig the cabby out of the pub.'

On the way up from the pier Mother tried to take my arm but I pretended to stumble and kept away from her.

We got into the carriage and drove off. Up on the box again I decided that neither of them were quite themselves. Something undoubtedly had happened. Even now they were unusually silent. Was this an omen favourable to me? I longed to turn round but pride forbade me, though I kept my ears well cocked. And still they weren't speaking, no, not a word. They've quarrelled, I thought, with a surge of joy. I could resist no longer. Cautiously moving my head I squinted over my shoulder. The cigarette-maker, leaning towards Mother, with an arm round her waist, was kissing her. Oh, God, my own mother spooning in the open, in full public view, with that cad . . . I nearly fell off the box.

When we got back to the boarding-house I removed myself in silence and went directly to my room. I was seated on the edge of my bed staring at the faded roses on the wallpaper when I heard the handle of the door turn and hesitantly, almost timidly, Mother came in. She sat down beside me and put an arm round my shoulders. From her manner, her apologetic caress, I thought for one wild moment that she had repented and was going to ask my forgiveness for the injury she had done, not to me alone, but to our love. Instead she said:

'Laurence, dear. Charley . . . Mr Sommen has asked me to marry him.'

I did not answer for some time. Shock had silenced me. I felt a fearful burning in my heart that made me want to cry out, abjectly: 'Don't, Mother, I beg of you, for pity's sake. You know we have always been together, how much we mean to one another. Don't, please don't let anyone come between us.'

But the vision of that hateful public embrace choked back the words. It hardened me.

'And will you?' I said coldly.

'I think I should, dear.'

'Why?' My tone was slightly contemptuous. 'Are you what's called in love with him?'

'I like him, dear. And I think he is in love with me. Of course, he's a queer sort of chap, not altogether what you might call a . . . well, the sort of person you're used to, but he's generous and kind. He's so gay too, and that's good for me. He's got a good heart. Besides, it would be so much better for our future, yours as well as mine. It's been hard for me, trying to keep things going, alone. This way, we wouldn't have to separate, you needn't go to Uncle Leo. We could be together, in London. Charley, Mr Sommen, says there are all sorts of good schools for you there. He likes you, dear.'

'I don't want him to like me. I hate him.' I disengaged myself from her arm, and although my breast was torn with wounded love, I stared at her cruelly. 'He's an utter bounder, an absolute outsider, a common masher. What's come over you, a woman of your refinement! Baillie Nicol says he's nothing but a counter-jumping cockney. I suppose you know that the whole boarding-house is talking about the

164

way you're behaving, and how silly you are, running after a man younger than yourself, and all heated up about it.'

'Laurence!'

'And what do you really know about him beyond the fact that he's got a cigarette factory and flings his money around like a would-be lord? Two weeks ago you didn't even know he existed. And what have you told him about us? Is he aware that we're practically in the poorhouse?'

'I won't have you speak to me like that.' She had drawn back to the end of the bed and was facing me with a look of pained anger. 'Mr Sommen would never dream of asking me about our circumstances.'

'Well, he as good as asked me,' I sneered. 'Not long after we came he tried to pump me about Father's business. I bragged, of course, and said Father had built up the finest yeast agency in Scotland. So he probably thinks the sweet, soft little widow is rolling. And that's why he's swarming all over you.' My voice broke suddenly. 'I saw him in the carriage, the vulgar cad.'

Provoked beyond endurance, Mother gave a little moan and struck me a ringing box on the ear that almost knocked me off the bed. We stared at each other in a terrible silence. I could not remember that she had ever hit me before.

'You're a wicked boy,' she gasped. 'A wicked, wicked boy. Trying to spoil the one little bit of happiness I've had since your father died. And in spite of all you say, and all the fibs you tell, I'll do exactly as I please.'

I stood up. Through the singing in my head I shouted:

'Go ahead and do it, then. I'm only warning you. You'll be sorry.'

I walked straight out of the house, my ear burning and hurting like mad, and although I hated the place now, somehow I found myself at the pool. I sat down on a rock, and clamped my head between my fists. This woman, sole possessor of my heart, whom I had loved exclusively from the moment I first opened my infant eyes, or perhaps when she first offered me her breast, had betrayed me. My immediate impulse was to desert her, to inquire the road to Winton of the first amiable stranger and set out by forced marches for Uncle Leo who, after all, expected me. Yet there was a flaw in this course of action that held me back. I wanted justice, and more, I wanted revenge. Revenge on Mother and on this . . . this mountebank—the word consoled me slightly—who had supplanted me. If only there was someone to whom I could turn for help. I racked my brains, dismissing one after another the Carroll relations, all uninterested, inept. I even considered the possibilities of Baillie Nicol. And then I thought of Stephen—safe, sure, reliable Stephen could always be depended on. And Stephen, now established at the Ministry of Labour, was in London.

The possibilities of my idea sent a shiver down my spine. I bounded to my feet. Hurrying back to Ardshiel I begged some notepaper from Miss Ailie, then locked myself in my room. Stretched out on the floor I took a pencil and dashed off a letter to Stephen. Within half an hour I had posted it in the town. I even remembered to send it express.

When all this had been accomplished, a sudden calm descended upon me, perhaps the realization that, whatever the outcome, I had displayed determination and resource. In the days that followed I maintained a steady reserve. Although I watched 'them' secretly at meal-times, I assumed indifference, and when they went off on their excursions I no longer shadowed them, I could afford to wait. On several occasions Mother attempted to reopen the matter, and to break down the barrier I had erected, but always without success. I refused to allow myself to be cajoled.

Yet I was anxious, beneath these pretences, and as time drew on with no word or apparent sign of action from Stephen, my nervousness increased. Ardshiel, being some distance from the centre of the town, was served by only one delivery of mail and every afternoon towards three o'clock I hung about the porch, waiting for the postman. At last, one wet afternoon, a letter was handed to me. Yes, it was stamped with the London postmark. Feverishly, I locked myself in the downstairs lavatory and tore it open.

Dear Laurence,

It was extremely awkward for me to take time off but, as I judged your letter important, I have done so.

The telephone directory revealed five Sommens, of whom one was listed as Tobacconist & Newsagent, at 1026a, The Mile End Road, E.C. I thereupon took a bus to that unsalubrious quarter—not quite a slum, but almost. The shop proved to be a small drab affair, newspapers, including racing sheets, on one side, cigarettes on the other. I entered and bought—guess what?—the News of the World! I was

*served by an elderly arthritic dame in a worn spencer,
buttoned up to the neck. In the back shop a girl—dark,
untidy hair, wearing a grubby overall—was rolling
cigarettes on a small hand machine. Emerging, I entered
the nearest pub—very near, three doors down, where
information was readily forthcoming.*

*The father is dead, the business, negligible and declining,
kept going, barely, by the widow. There are three daughters,
one of whom is the cigarette maker. Father had some connections for this brand, now practically nil. Debts were mentioned. Mother, girls and the son all live above the shop.*

*The son, your man, takes no part in the business, is
described as a good sort, generous, would do anything for a
pal, but flash, a fancy dresser, and soft. Bit of a singer and
performs at 'smokers'. Likes to bet, which he does with
occasional success, and when he pulls something off, takes
a holiday in style. His job—he is a waiter at the Metro-
politan Sporting Club in the West End.*

*I trust this information will quash the incipient romance.
Give my love to your mother and tell her please not to be
foolish.*

> Yours,
> Stephen.

A thrill of fearful joy electrified me. Holding my breath
I stared at the damning words—a waiter at the Metro-
politan—then, unbolting the door, I rushed towards the
staircase. I could not wait an instant before avenging myself
for all I had suffered by delivering this fatal blow, not only
to my mother's hopes, but to her pride.

During the past two days of rain Mother had drawn more
within herself, resting and reading in her room after lunch.
I knew that she was there now. A cruel, an unholy triumph
intoxicated me, sent the blood rushing to my head as I
knocked at her door, with the letter in my hand.

'Come in.'

She was not reading, but standing at the window, wearing
that look of abstraction, a kind of meditative sadness, which,
in later years, came over her more and more. She half
turned, ventured a smile.

'Mother . . .' I went forward. Her expression, tender and,
for some reason, forgiving, unnerved me. Not only that,
before I could prevent her she actually took my hand and

pressed it against her cheek. Yet I was not to be deterred by such sentimental tricks. I was trembling now and sweating all over, but I made myself go on. 'There's something I have to show you . . .'

'Yes, Laurie, dear.'

Still holding my hand she was again looking out and down. Instinctively my gaze followed hers. A station cab stood at the front door and luggage was being heaped upon its roof. Then, hurriedly, bent as if to avoid the splashing rain, a figure. familiar though untartaned, emerged from the porch and dived into the cab. The door slammed, the cabby mounted the box and drove off.

There was a mortal silence in that little bedroom.

'He's gone?' I stammered.

She nodded slowly and turned to me.

'I've sent him away.'

'Why?'

'There was your father, Laurence. And now there's you. I suddenly discovered there wasn't room for anyone else.'

Something in my throat tied itself into a knot so that I could not speak or swallow. I stared at her, then in my free hand I crushed the letter to shapeless pulp and blindly flung myself upon her breast.

TWENTY-TWO

THE HABITAT of my Uncle Leo was a four-storey warehouse somewhat peculiarly named Templar's Hall and situated in that unsalubrious district of Winton known as the Gorbie-law. The building, which occupied one corner of two mean, narrow cobbled streets, was old and in poor repair with the side windows plastered over and painted a dingy black, but as it stood in the centre of the city, adjacent to Argyle Street and convenient for the docks, it presumably had for my uncle advantages of a commercial nature. As a residence it had less to offer. The top floor, consisting of a long dark passage with a great many rooms opening off on either side, served as the living quarters. However, as I had arrived late the night before I had as yet no idea of the nature of these rooms, only that my own, furnished with an iron bed, a washstand and a burst cane chair, was at the far end of

168

the corridor, and the kitchen, where a sort of general servant to my uncle, Annie Tobin, had given me bread and cheese for my supper, at the other.

I had slept intermittently, disturbed by the clanging of the Argyle Street trams and by an unmanly heartache for my mother, whom I had seen off at the Central Station on the previous afternoon. The prospect of a separation for at least a year—despite Mother's assertion that it would quickly pass—had made it a difficult parting. But the morning brought the promise of new experiences. I got up, washed and dressed, then, opening my door, moved circumspectly in search of breakfast.

Mrs Tobin stood at the kitchen stove. She was a shapeless woman of about fifty-five with a bright-red face, pitted by acne, small deep-set eyes and wild grey hair that seemed to be standing on end. An old brown wrapper was tied about her middle. Scuffed carpet slippers adorned her feet.

Apart from her blowsy appearance, her strong Irish accent and familiar manners had already offended me and I had quite decided that I should not like Mrs Tobin at all.

'Is my uncle not up yet?'

She turned and considered me good-naturedly.

'He's up and out a good hour ago.'

'Has he gone to Mass?' I inquired, conceiving no other reason for so early an excursion.

Mrs Tobin burst out laughing. When she laughed her stomach shook and her blue eyes dissolved completely in folds of inflamed red skin. Good heavens, I thought, she seems to be enjoying some kind of joke.

'My dear lad,' she replied at last, 'that fellow hasn't seen the inside of a church for more nor thirty year. He's a black atheist, none other. But you'll soon get used to his comings and goings, though God Himself wouldn't know what he's up to, or after. A gombeen man, no less. Are you wanting your breakfast?'

'Please,' I said coldly, determined to repress all familiarity.

'Then you shall have it, my lad,' she replied agreeably.

'Where is the dining-room?'

'Just here, dear, none other. Kitchen, drawing-room, dining-room combined. So take a seat and be easy.'

As with some reluctance I sat down, she removed a china bowl from the shelf, half-filled it with a yellowish mealy powder and stirred in boiling water from the kettle on the stove. The result was a sort of muddy-brown porridge which did not smell at all well and which, with a cup of bluish milk and a spoon, she placed before me.

'What's this?'

'Just a kind of stirabout, only made with pease meal. Your uncle favours it, and gets it wholesale by the hunderweight bag.'

I picked up my spoon and took a mouthful.

'You don't fancy it, dear,' she said sympathetically, studying my face. 'Still, as there isn't much else, if I were you I'd sup it up.'

'It would taste better with a lump of butter in it,' I said demandingly, with a grimace.

'Butter, dear?' Her twinkling eyes began to disappear again. 'You'll not get as much butter from Leo as you could put on the end of a bumbee's arse.'

Naturally, as far as I was concerned, this vulgarity was the end of Mrs Tobin.

Nevertheless, anxious not to offend my uncle, since it was his choice, I supped the stirabout up, meanwhile reflecting gloomily on all my mother's appetizing breakfasts, not to speak of the delicious luncheons provided me by Miss Greville.

When I had made my way to the bottom of the bowl Mrs Tobin remarked:

'If you're not full, I'll give you a cut off my loaf.'

'Your loaf!' I exclaimed, exploding with indignation.

'Well, yes, lad. I do buy myself a few things now and then, just by way of what might call an extra.'

Her tone was so mild and with that constant hint of laughter lying behind, ready to spring up and make light of any difficulties, I felt obliged to hold back my resentment. Besides, cradling the loaf in the crook of her arm, she was sawing off a thick slice of sweet-smelling fresh bread and spreading it generously with dripping.

I accepted it in silence. After the stirabout it tasted like real food. I was still chewing when steps sounded on the stairs and my uncle came into the room.

Although it was more than four years since I had first encountered Leo at my father's funeral, I now found not the slightest change in him. He presented to the world the same tall thin figure, almost emaciated, in the tight shiny navy-blue suit, the same long, smooth, pale, expressionless, self-contained, unreadable face. Leo was an ageless man who remained fixed permanently, as by an effort of will, in the same changeless mould, and when he died, some thirty years later—worth, incidentally, three-quarters of a million sterling—I felt convinced, although I was then four thousand miles away, that he had expired inscrutably in precisely the same form, and was buried in the identical blue suit.

Meanwhile, putting a hand on my shoulder, he had made me welcome, pleasantly enough, although with a deprecating shake of his head he seemed to take exception to my slice of bread.

'That bleached white flour rots the coating of the bowel, Laurence. But I see you've had your pease meal. That's the stuff that'll really stick to your ribs. You'll soon get used to our ways. We're careful what we put in our stomachs here. Now if you've finished I'll take you downstairs.'

We descended by the stone staircase to the first floor, then, selecting a key from the shiny bunch secured to his braces by a thin chain, he opened a door and led me into the stock-room. This was a long hall which ran the entire length of the building, and so high—it contained both the first and second stories—as to produce a faint echo when we spoke. In this lofty and extremely dusty repository a double row of trestle-tables was laid out, leaving a passage in the middle which was covered by a strip of frayed red drugget, while on the tables bales of cloth were piled and strewn in some disarray.

'Now,' said Uncle Leo, in a confidential manner, so plausible it would have deceived the entire College of Cardinals, 'you'll begin to learn your trade.'

After testing my knowledge of linear measure he presented me with an inch tape, which I assumed had got into the establishment by mistake since as he draped it professionally over my shoulders I saw on the reverse side, in plain black letters, 'Property of Morris Shapiro Tailor'. He then began to take me round the tables, stopping at each to instruct me in the goods displayed. First the saxonys, then the cheviots, next the angolas, the broadcloths, the tweeds—Donegal, Harris, Shetland. To each bale a ticket was attached on which was marked the price, not in figures but in letters, and glancing down at me obliquely with a deepening of his confidence and flattering implications of my fidelity, Uncle Leo entrusted me with the secret of his code. It was simple, a reversal of the alphabet in which Z stood for zero, Y for one, X for two, and so on back to Q which represented nine.

All this would have impressed me more but for the unworthy suspicion that those materials, which my uncle spoke of and indeed caressed with a proprietary touch as though they were rare and precious fabrics, seemed rather more shop-soiled, ill used and exhausted than I, even as an untrained neophyte, would have expected—seemed, in brief, scarcely to merit the high-sounding titles and rich encomiums bestowed upon them. Indeed, while I hesitated to mention the fact, my eye had more than once been attracted by other tickets, unrelated to Uncle's code, but crudely stamped in red with such devices as: *Bankrupt Stock, Sale, Job Lot*, and finally a fearfully incriminating tag on which was scrawled in blue pencil: *Knocked down to Pinchpenny C. at 50% off*.

When our circuit had been completed Leo drew up at the last trestle.

'You understand, Laurence, that in the ordinary way I would expect a premium from an apprentice. And a handsome one at that. But blood is thicker than water. We'll let you off the premium. You'll have your board and lodging, and over and above I'm going to give you sixpence a week for your pocket.'

Mother had told me that Uncle had promised to pay me wages, but this seemed very little. Still, I managed to say:

'Thank you, Uncle Leo.'

Perhaps he noticed the hesitation in my tone for he went on quickly:

'What's more, if you need anything, and I think you need a suit,' he paused, with an air of serious liberality, 'I'll give you it.' I looked at him gratefully, I undoubtedly had need of a suit. In the past few months I had shot up, and out of my present garments so that my trouser ends were well above my ankles and the sleeves of my jacket failed to cover my wrists.

But before I could express my thanks Leo went on:

'Now here's a lovely piece of stuff.'

The cloth he displayed, with a professional toss that unwrapped the bolt and spread it hurtfully before my eyes, was a strong pepper-and-salt check, of a pattern so vivid I would have judged it suitable only for gentlemen of the most pronounced sporting tastes.

'Isn't it a trifle loud, Uncle?'

'Loud!' He dismissed the idea. 'This is a classic, Laurence, and the only piece of it I have. As for wear, it stands by itself. It'll last a lifetime. I'll get Shapiro up to measure you this afternoon.'

I was quite overcome, but whether by his generosity or by the design of the material I scarcely knew. While I remained silent he drew a large silver watch from his waistcoat pocket and thoughtfully consulted it, an action which, as I soon discovered, was the usual prelude to his sudden and mysterious departures.

'I have to go now,' he said. 'If anyone comes in call down Mrs Tobin or just say I'll be back soon. Meanwhile, I'll give you some work to keep you busy. Come into the office.'

I followed him through a door I had not previously observed, into a small room furnished with a flat desk, a single chair and a large green safe. The bare floor-boards were cluttered with a great many packages and cardboard boxes, some open and disclosing to my gaze a varied assortment of attractively labelled tins, bottles and jars. Hustling through some papers on the desk he found a magazine which had the title *The Health Food Bulletin*. Turning the pages he indicated a number of advertisements, each of which he had marked with a cross.

'You write a pretty fair hand, I hope?'

When I had assured him on this point the instructions he then gave me, though astounding, were precise. Thus, five minutes later, when he had departed, I found myself seated at the desk, pen in hand, inditing a letter, the first of a series, which ran as follow:

Mr Leo Carroll presents his compliments to the Ocean Seaweed Food Company and requests them to forward to his business office at the above address, liberal free samples of their product Sargossa as advertised in The Health Food Bulletin, for his personal use and possible future commercial orders.

When I had finished the letters, all addressed to patent-food companies, it was almost noon and no customers had as yet appeared. I went through the warehouse and opened the door to satisfy myself that a queue had not formed outside. It had not. Then, as I turned, I saw pinned on a panel of the door a cryptic notice which read *Call again. Back at two. Leo.*

The realization that my uncle had so little faith in me caused my spirits to droop. I went back and stared through one of the front windows. Masked by the grime on the panes the narrow street nevertheless revealed itself mercilessly: mean little shops, a public house, a short string of hucksters' barrows, and at the far end, the familiar three brass balls of the pawnbroker. I could not comprehend why my uncle should have chosen to live in such a locality or to own so vast and dilapidated a building in order to carry on his business in so small a part of it. How could I guess, in those early days, his astute precognition that changes in the city planning would raise the value of this property to fantastic heights?

A sudden laugh from behind disturbed my brooding and made me spin round.

'The sight of you there with the inch tape on you!'

Forgetting that I had made up my mind not to like her, I felt surprisingly relieved to see Mrs Tobin.

'I thought I'd see how you were getting on. Anyhow it's time for your dinner.' She added: 'Such as it is.'

She locked the outer door and we went upstairs to the kitchen where I was not long in perceiving that my dinner was to be derived from a large pot of boiled potatoes and a wedge of Dunlop cheese. However, before this was served Mrs Tobin set a frying-pan on the stove and, almost from nowhere, by a kind of legerdemain, shot into it two fat sausages which immediately began to sizzle and to emit a seductive aroma that brought the water to my teeth. While she tended them she kept watching me with a broad, suggestive smile until I could no longer contain myself.

'Yours, Mrs Tobin?' I queried.

'Mine,' she agreed, and lifting the pan from the stove she forked one of the sausages on to my plate and placed the other on her own.

'This looks awfully good, Mrs Tobin.'

'Annacker's,' she replied succinctly.

I was hungry. Despite Uncle's assurances, the stirabout had not stuck long to my ribs. Several minutes elapsed before I added:

'And these potatoes are beautifully floury.'

174

'I have the knack of the spuds, dear, like most of the Irish. And don't call me Mrs Tobin, just Annie.'

'Does my uncle not come in to dinner?' I inquired, with my mouth full of hot sausage and mash.

She shook her head.

'In the first place he hardly eats what would feed a sparrow. In the second, except when he's messing about here in the evening with his patent foods and what not, he takes his meals in the Vegetarian Restaurant in Union Street.'

'Good gracious. Is he really a vegetarian, Mrs Tobin, I mean, Annie?'

'He'll not put meat in his mouth. Sure if it was raining pork chops he'd only use the fat to grease his boots. Fornent which, he doesn't smoke. And as for liquor, and this is the quarest of all, he's never had a drink in his life. Leo's a quare fellow, dear, and *deep*. He never lets his right hand know what his left hand's doing. But you'll soon get to know him,' she added slyly, 'if you haven't already.'

'It does seem to me,' I spoke interestedly, anxious to pursue the subject, 'that my uncle is not very well off.'

If I had made the wittiest joke of the century the effect on Mrs Tobin could not have been more pronounced. She literally rocked with laughter. When finally she had composed herself she wiped her eyes and said:

'What makes you think that, dear?'

'Well,' I reasoned, reddening with embarrassment, 'Uncle doesn't seem to live very well here. I mean, the food isn't too plentiful. And, as a matter of fact, this morning not a single person came to the showroom to buy cloth.'

'Oh, they'll come, dear, they'll come,' she said mildly. 'In the afternoon when himself is there. And even if they didn't what's the odds?'

'The odds, Mrs Tobin, Annie?'

'That little bit of a shop down there isn't but a fraction of Leo's interests. He has property all over the city. If you'd walked like me up and down the tenements at Anderson Cross collecting his rents you'd know to your sorrow just how much he has. And that's not the big thing.'

'What big thing, Annie?' I gasped.

'Whisky!' she proclaimed, enjoying the effect of that omnipotent word. 'Whisky in bond. Barrels and barrels of the stuff, all sealed by the revenue, maturin' and maturin' and gettin' dearer and dearer all the time. You'll know about that too, my lad, when we come to the next bottling day.'

I looked at her dazedly, all my notions of Leo whirling around in a haze of amazed uncertainty. What was I to make of this uncle of mine who was so outrageously rich yet starved himself, and me, on pease-meal stirabout? I didn't dare pursue the matter for fear of further revelations.

When dinner was over and Mrs. Tobin had refused my subdued offer to help her wash the dishes, I went pensively down to the shop to ensure being there when Leo returned.

He arrived punctually at two, seemed pleased to find me on duty and even went so far as to congratulate me in restrained terms on the manner in which I had written his letters. He then took off his jacket and put on a waistcoat with black alpaca sleeves, then, still wearing his bowler hat, which indeed he rarely removed, indoors or out, went into his office, where for some time he was busy, alone, working over some stiff-backed ledgers. But these were restored to the safe as his customers began to arrive. What surprised me was the number of poor women, some even draped in shawls —sure emblem of the slums—who came in looking for what they described as 'remnants', and which I soon discovered to be end pieces of the material just short of an adequate length. A few of these were apparently tenants of my uncle, for they addressed him as 'Leo' but despite this familiarity and the cajoleries, usually prefaced by the exclamation: 'Ah, Leo, for the love of God . . .', he remained unfailingly polite, merely pointing to one of a number of cards prominently displayed on the trestles and marked *This house does NOT extend credit.*

It could however be said for Leo that when they did buy he courteously presented them with a pattern from *Weldon's Home Dressmaker* on the back of which was stamped 'Free Sample'. But in the main his customers were cheap, single-handed tailors in a small way of business, some of them foreign, and many of Jewish persuasion. Mr Morris Shapiro, entrusted with the honour of making my suit, and who came into the warehouse towards the end of the afternoon, was unquestionably in this category. A frail, cadaverous, ill-looking little man, pale-faced, with enormous dark shadowy eyes and a plastered streak of black hair across his yellowish skull, his manner towards Leo, expressed in fluttering gestures, was painfully ingratiating.

Nevertheless he seemed to betray some misgivings when he was confronted by the chosen material. He looked at it, fingered it, looked a me, then at Leo.

'The young gentleman likes it?'

Too shy to speak, I permitted Leo to incline his head without a rebuttal.

'Not a trifle flash?'

'No.'

Mr Shapiro hesitated, then picking a single strand from the web of the material, he struck a match on the box he took from his pocket, lit the strand and brought the charred end to his nose. He then looked up at Leo again.

'Short on wool,' he said.

'Perhaps,' Leo said, turning away with extreme coldness. 'But it will wear.'

'And make up lovely,' Mr Shapiro agreed hastily. 'It will hang a treat.'

When he had measured me, he bundled up the material and tucked it under his arm. Then, as he hurried off, he took a cautious side glance, cupped his head and literally hissed in my ear:

'He's been trying for years to get rid of it.'

Although Leo could not possibly have heard, I sensed that for some reason unknown to me the incident had upset him. He paced up and down, glancing at me from time to time, as though about to refer to it. But, in the end, he did not.

When I asked if I should light the gas, as it was getting dark, he shook his head. Inspecting his watch, thus again signalizing his immediate departure, he came forward and put his hand on my shoulder.

'You're my nephew, boy, you know I mean to do the right thing by you. You've done well for your first day and we'll see how you get on. But always remember that money is hard to come by here.' He gave me an approving pat. 'Now I have to go out to see a man. It's time to close up.'

He locked the door with the key from his bunch and went quickly down the stairs while I went slowly up to Mrs Tobin. It had been for me a strange, unprecedented day and my head was spinning from it.

177

TWENTY-THREE

DURING the weeks that followed it became evident that my uncle meant to keep me fully occupied, and as we were frequently together in these endeavours I had ample opportunity to observe this truly extraordinary man.

In the morning, on his instructions, I wrote most, though not all, of his letters. There was of course no typewriter in the office, recording machines were not at all to Leo's taste. Moreover, despite the diversities of Uncle's business, his correspondence was relatively modest, since the major portion of his affairs was conducted by word of mouth. Nor when he wrote did he trouble the penny post. I was sent to deliver his missives. When not engaged on such forenoon errands I remained on duty in the showroom draped in the inch tape and with a pencil behind my ear. I was now allowed to sell to the odd customer who came in at that hour, provided ready money was produced on the spot. But the expeditions which I took in Leo's company were the most revealing of all.

Why did he take me? While using me to his best advantage I believe that a residual spark of conscience, faint survival of his early upbringing or perhaps a reluctant sense of obligation to my mother, induced him to try to give me some grounding in a commercial career or the 'art' of business as he practised it. Thus, while so far he had excluded me from the rent collecting, managed by Annie and himself, he permitted me to accompany him to all the auctions he attended, and to the bonded warehouse at the docks.

At the right price Leo would buy anything, not bankrupt or salvaged stock of cloth alone, but any article whatsoever on which, immediately or in due course, he knew instinctively that he could make a profit. Standing beside him in the crowded, raucous auction marts that opened off Argyle Street I would gaze in wonder at his pale impassive face as with an almost imperceptible blink of his eyelids he increased by sixpence his bid for some incongruous object which if portable I must carry back to join the jumble in the storage rooms upstairs. These rooms, on both sides of the upper corridor, were so choked to the ceilings it was difficult to open a door without being crowned by an outrush of piled-up furniture.

The auctions eventually proved wearisome to me, but I

was never bored by our visits to what Leo referred to simply as 'the excise'. To enter our door in this building, which was officially sealed, two keys were necessary, one from Uncle's bunch, the other kept by the revenue officer. The array of barrels revealed in the dim light of the frosted windows confounded me at first, not only from the number and size of these deep-bellied receptacles, but because I had naturally expected Uncle's whisky to be stored in bottles —a view which he soon dispelled by explaining that the spirit would never mature unless contained in sherry or seasoned casks.

Here, then, was Leo's main business, his capital, his source of future profits. He bought whisky, bought at the right time, stored it free of excise duty, and as it ripened watched its value steadily increase. He was not only a shrewd buyer but a thoroughly expert blender. How often I watched, fascinated, as he took half Highland and Lowland malts, a 'taste' of Islay, and mixed these with a patent still whisky the name of which he refused to divulge. Then, taking a measured sip, he would sample the blend by rolling it round his mouth and tongue, gargling almost in his throat, and finally, with a nod of approval and a hoarse expectoration, blow the whole swill out. As Annie had told me, he never let a drop down his gullet.

Even in those early days, Leo undoubtedly possessed unique and amazing foresight. He anticipated the danger of currency depreciation and placed his trust in property and whisky. Yet, as I became aware of his present and potential wealth, I couldn't help asking myself what on earth he got out of it. His life was a model of the dullest, most stringent and most utterly miserable austerity. Then it dawned on me that for Leo the supreme enjoyment, the pinnacle of inner delight, lay in the secret knowledge of his own worth, *under this pretence of penury*. I have said that he never smiled. Yet sometimes when in conversation during some business deal he would emit a typical phrase, such as 'I'm a poor man' or 'I couldn't afford it' or 'you could buy and sell me'. I would observe a twitch, that faint transient convulsion of the lips, as though with immense difficulty he was suppressing delicious gusts of internal laughter. Strangely, although I saw or surmised all this, and despite the exactions and deceptions he imposed upon me, I could not dislike him. Instead, as I gazed at his pale, peaked face, I felt an unaccountable rush of sympathy, and was disposed to pity him. This precisely was the emotion he sought to inspire, the triumph of all his guile, for it established and confirmed the character he had created and within which the real Leo Carroll lived.

While life with Leo was not too onerous, my main problem centred on food. Uncle himself, apart from the patent pabula towards which his faddism directed him, seemed to exist almost without sustenance. He took his breakfast alone very early before I was up, his lunch was enwrapped in equal mystery and when he came in late at night he would go to the stove and, still wearing his bowler hat and with a look of abstraction, stand silently concocting himself one or other of his messes: Gluten Groats, Arrowroot, or Sandfood Rusks and stirabout.

Certainly, he kept us on preposterously short commons, and as I was growing rapidly, I almost constantly felt hungry. I should have fared badly but for Mrs Tobin who had an undetermined arrangement for board wages with Leo which, while lapsing periodically through Uncle's protests that he was short of ready cash, were eventually forthcoming when she threatened to give notice. This pittance enabled her to supplement the bare necessities of our diet by what she called 'her extras', all of which she shared unhesitatingly with me. Indeed more often than not when it came to a matter of division it was I who received the larger portion.

Nor was it solely through my stomach that my first impressions of Annie were reversed. When my new suit arrived, its atrocious pattern threatened to condemn me to endless misery and shame. But one Saturday night, after a week of anguish during which I felt myself the object of every laugh and stare in the city of Winton, Mrs Tobin removed the offensive garments, dyed them a dark, inconspicuous brown, dried and pressed them, and by Monday morning presented me with an outfit that was at least respectable.

Annie was without exception the most obliging, cheerful person I had ever known, seldom put out, a fount of amiability, always ready to laugh off her troubles and mine. To her most things, even my uncle's incomparable stinginess, seemed good for a laugh, and although she would explain this to me with the most devastating clichés, such as 'life's a queer business, dear, we've got to face it with a smile' or 'laugh and the world laughs with you, weep and you weep alone', these were merely the expressions of an untaught mind. Nothing could detract from a nature that exuded generosity, honourable decency, and in which there was not a single streak of malice. When she told fortunes— she greatly liked to 'read the tea-cups'—she always predicted favourable happenings, never ill tidings. In all our association I did not once hear her make a mean or uncharitable remark. Even Leo, who surely merited her worst reproaches, she dismissed with a commiserating laugh. 'You can't help but be sorry for the poor man. Faith, he's harder on himself than he is on us.'

She was a widow with four surviving children, all sons. Three were in the British Army—she never said 'the army', invariably prefacing the qualification as though her boys were in the service of a foreign power—two in India, one in Singapore, and the fourth had emigrated, but without success, to Canada. Although she seldom heard from them and then only briefly, she would sometimes speak of them to me, recalling some incident of the past with a reminiscent smile. On the mantelpiece of the kitchen, beside the glass bowl in which she affectionately maintained a rather senile goldfish, was an old postcard with a moonlit view of the Taj Mahal on which was written: 'Dear Mother, I hope this finds you well as it leaves me. Your loving son, Daniel.' When it caught her eye she would smile at me and begin: 'Danny was always a good boy though a trifle wild at times. I'll never forget the day he fell off the pier at Dunoon . . .'

But mainly, during our long evening conversations, she had most to say about her husband. She called him 'Da'. I must confess that I had slight interest in these family reminiscences, but as I had become extremely fond of Mrs Tobin I made myself listen with every appearance of sympathetic interest. Usually they went like this:

'Da was a good man, dear. Intelligent too. But he never had a trade. He'd get a job for a couple of weeks then be knocked off. He was too much of a gentleman, in his own way, for the labouring. He bought a horse and lorry, but the horse fell down on us. Yes, dear, it died on him. Still if he'd got paid for what he did, we'd of been well away. But making money wasn't in him. It wasn't his line. Oh, he was popular. When he died the whole street turned out. A lovely funeral.'

Annie herself was deservedly popular among the group of Irish expatriates in the district who congregated, usually on Tuesday nights, at a public house kept by one of their number and named, with nationalistic spirit, 'The Shamrock'. Not infrequently these were festive occasions for me. When Annie had a few extra coins in her purse or when she had backed a winner, since she was not above having threepence or even as much as a shilling on a horse, she would put on a man's cloth cap which she secured carefully with long hatpins and take me first to Bonelli's fish and chip shop for a fried-fish supper, then, although I was still under the legal age, smuggle me in with her to the snug of 'The Shamrock'. Her entry was invariably greeted with shouts of welcome and when she had ordered a Guinness for herself—she never drank more than one—and a ginger ale for me, there would be cries of 'Give us a song, Annie.' After an exchange of chaff and without the least self-consciousness she would oblige with 'The Minstrel Boy' or 'Tara's Halls', followed, as an encore, by a great favourite which I think was called 'The Wearing o' the Green'.

> *Oh, Paddy dear and did you hear*
> *The news that's goin' round,*
> *The shamrock is forbid by law*
> *To grow on Irish ground.*

Then a chorus, in which with tremendous feeling everyone joined:

> *The dear little shamrock,*
> *The sweet little shamrock,*
> *The dear little, swe-eet little, shamrock of Ireland.*

Despite these pleasures, or perhaps because of them, I could not blind myself to the fact that circumstances had reduced me to a submerged level of existence. For all practical purposes I now lived and worked in the slums of Winton. The change was alarming, the locality deadly. Back-to-back tenements surrounded us, interspersed with narrow streets and mean alleys in which one saw exhibited every sign and symptom of poverty and misery—the shawled women, idle men, and worst of all, the ragged, rickety, deformed children. Perpetually noisy, dirty and choked with traffic, Argyle Street seemed to me a running sore. Saturday night on its crowded flaring pavements was saturnalia : drunks rolling around, lying in the gutter, or being frog-marched to the police station, sailors on leave from the docks looking for trouble, factions of the rival football 'brake' clubs fighting it out with fists and knives after the match, while with a clash of cymbals, a thump of the drum and a blare of brass that heightened the pandemonium, the Salvation Army paraded up and down, pausing from time to time to sing a hymn, preach the terrors of damnation, and pass the tambourine.

In all my daily contacts, human and inhuman, there was nothing to improve or stimulate my mind. When, driven by the afternoon vacuum in my stomach, I slunk into Bonelli's for a penny plate of chips only to be met by a rush of broken English from the back shop: 'Chipapotata no ready. Green pea ready. You wanna green pea?' I felt bitterly that my star had waned since those days of happiness and promise when Miss Greville, discoursing on the *Orchis maculata* in an ambience of Eton, paused to address me across the impeccable table: 'Another cutlet, Carroll?'

I knew now that my mother couldn't have had the faintest precognition of what lay in store for me. Those earnest conversations with Leo, while she anxiously studied his sad, pale, plausible face, must have induced in her an entirely false impression of the prospects he could offer me. Yet I could not bring myself to write and reveal the truth. This would alter nothing of my situation, and from her frequent letters, Mother had trouble enough fulfilling her teaching obligations at the school in time to take the train journey to Cardiff to attend her all-important night classes, which, she had confided to me, were proving harder than she had foreseen, with many technicalities she found difficult to understand.

Nevertheless, as I felt myself slipping into a kind of bog, stifled by the prevailing smoke and grime, I tried to brace myself by striving again for that elusive Greek ideal which I had pursued in the past, a physical adequacy which was so far not reflected in my attenuated form. The solitary bath in Leo's establishment served at present as a repository for an accumulation of useless household rubbish, old door handles, bent nails, broken picture frames, bashed cardboard boxes and the like, which Uncle had not allowed to be thrown out; but aided by Annie I cleared away this debris. Although the enamel was chipped and rusted the antique tub held water, and thereafter, every morning when I got up, I did fifteen minutes of body-building exercises, then took a cold dip. In the evenings, which had begun to lengthen, I returned with joy to my old love. It cost only a halfpenny fare to take the yellow tram from Argyle Street to Kelvingrove Park on the western outskirts of the city, but as I often lacked that coin I did not mind walking all the way along Sandimount Street and Western Road, since I was wearing my old gym shoes which made me feel light and full of springiness. At the Park, which extended in a series of tree-lined avenues and curving drives beneath the University, I would pause to gather myself, then begin to run, through the gathering twilight, on the circuit I had mapped out for myself. Except for an odd couple spooning on a bench, few people were about at this time. The sense of freedom and inexplicable delight which I experienced in this swift transit through the cool air, still luminous with the fading sunset, afforded me an escape from all my woes which, as though blown away by the wind of my speed, fluttered and fell behind me.

After I had spent myself I would sit and rest looking up at the University, the old noble building outlined dark and towering against the western sky. The chances that I should ever study there were now depressingly remote, yet when my breath came back, impelled by an ineradicable longing, I climbed the hill and wandered round the precincts. Passing through the deserted cloisters I read the names above the lecture rooms, drawn always to the Department of Biology where, lingering outside the locked door, I sniffed the aromatic odours of carbofuchsine and Canada balsam. Then indeed, turning away to return to the city, I felt that I had fallen on evil days and that my life had sunk to a dull and profitless routine.

TWENTY-FOUR

ONE AFTERNOON as I walked up Union Street rather slowly, returning from yet another of Leo's commissions, a young man, bareheaded, and of extreme elegance, came out of the Criterion Hotel accompanied by a stylish but rather over-

dressed woman somewhat older than himself. I knew him
instantly, and as his eye met mine in mutual recognition I
instinctively called out 'Terence.'

He did not appear to hear me. Avoiding my glance, continuing to address his companion in the liveliest manner, he
passed me as though I did not exist while, cut and humiliated, I stood staring like a fool. A few paces up the street,
opposite the entrance to the hotel grill, an open red Argyle
car upholstered in padded red leather was waiting with a
chauffeur in attendance. Towards this rich vehicle Terence
escorted his lady friend, saw her seated with every sign of
solicitude, then after a vivacious and tender farewell,
watched her driven off.

As he turned I stirred myself and began to move hurriedly
away, confronted suddenly by the recollection of that
moment eight years ago when in Terry's company I had
repudiated Maggie. Now she was avenged. At that moment,
however, a piercing whistle, such as might be used to summon a cabby, made me spin round. Terence was coming
towards me in a leisurely fashion, handsomer, more charming than ever, not a hair out of place and immaculately got
up in striped trousers and a dark jacket, a regular fashion
plate.

As he looked me up and down I quivered slightly.
In the face of such sartorial, mannered perfection it was
impossible not to blush for my own inadequacy.

'Well, well, well. What a long drink of water you've
turned into,' Terence said slowly. 'What are you doing up
here, man?'

The total absence of communication that now existed
between my mother and Lochbridge had left him in ignorance of our present situation. When I explained he emitted
another whistle, but in a low and meditative key.

'So you're working for that skinflint. I never pass him in
the street but I want to spit in his eye. Why didn't you come
to me, man? I always liked your mother. A nice little woman.
I'd have straightened you both out in no time. No time
at all.'

'Why . . . what are you in, Terry?'

'The hotel business. Learning it on the inside. I'm the
receptionist here at the Cri.'

Deeply impressed, I looked from Terence to the pillared
marble portico and through the wide glassed doors to the

vista of rich carpeting and gilt chairs in the foyer beyond. The Criterion was a new hotel with a sophisticated Continental atmosphere, not large but exclusive. In Winton it touched the heights of fashionable opulence.

'I suppose Leo feeds you well,' Terence said suddenly, examining me sideways with a satiric eye. 'Or could you do with a bit of a snack?' Before I could answer he went on, 'Well, then, you nip round to the back of the building and I'll let you in at the other entrance.'

The service entrance was easily found and Terence, already at the door, admitted me to a long passage which led into the hotel kitchen, an enormous lofty chamber, dazzling the eye with its display of shining metal and gleaming white tiles. A young man in a white apron and puffed cap was reading a newspaper.

'Tony,' Terence said, 'I've just discovered a long-lost starving relative. Can you knock up something for him?'

Tony lowered his newspaper. He did not look particularly pleased.

'Three o'clock in the afternoon. And me the only one on duty.'

'That's why we're here.'

When Terence smiled no one could withstand him for long. Tony put down his paper and got up.

'What does he want?'

'Something with beef in it. And plenty.'

It was a relief to find the staff dining-room, into which Terence now led me, completely empty. Here, after a surprisingly short interval, Tony brought me a large helping of what looked like stew.

'That suit you?'

'Oh yes, thank you.'

As I began to eat Terence took a chair opposite me and lit a cigarette.

'Heavens, kid,' he said, after a few minutes, 'you've got a swallow. You must be famished.'

'Not really, Terry. It's just that this is the most delicious meat I've ever tasted.'

'It ought to be. It's Bœuf à la Bordelaise. As a matter of fact, my friend, Miss Josey Gilhooley, had some for her lunch today in the grill.'

When he said this in so conscious a manner I felt some response was expected of me. I could not well say that she was pretty, since even in my brief glimpse of her I had been struck by the prominence of her nose. So I said:

'She's very smart, Terry.'

He nodded complacently, with a gratified proprietary air.

'Was that her car?'

'Her old man's. Gilhooley the builder. They're rolling. For your own information, kid, and strictly on the q.t., Josey and I are as good as engaged. At least, it's not official yet but she's practically my fiancée.'

'I always thought you liked Polly Grant,' I said, unthinkingly.

The nearest possible approach to a flush passed over Terence's face, confirming those early rumours of his frequent visits to Ardencaple.

'That was just a flash in the pan. This is the real thing.' He added after a pause: 'Don't you ever go out with the girls yourself?'

The idea was so preposterous I merely shook my head.

'What!' exclaimed Terence, 'you haven't got a girl yet?'

I felt myself redden. I had no wish to enlighten Terence on my longings in that direction defeated by an abysmal shyness—a state of inner conflict only maintained in balance by the discipline I inflicted on myself.

'I'm not interested in girls,' I lied, bravely.

'Then what in God's name do you do with yourself?'

'I'm kept busy all day,' I said, defensively. 'And at nights I go out to the Park and run.'

'You do?' For the first time Terence seemed interested. 'I remember you were pretty fair.' He seemed to make a joke of this, then considered me thoughtfully. 'Have you done any serious running—at sports and such like?'

'Oh, yes, I went out often with the Ardencaple Harriers, and won the under-fourteen steeplechase two years in succession.'

'You did.' He regarded me even more thoughtfully. 'One of these nights I might come out and clock you. I still keep up with the track, although I've too much on my mind to go in for it myself.'

'I remember you telling us how you won the hundred yards at Rockcliff.'

He looked pleased.

'Sure. I left them like they were standing still. I was the

champion there, man, or near enough to it. A pity you never managed to Rockcliff.'

I acquiesced sadly, adding under my breath: 'I'd still give anything to go.'

'Well, who knows?' he said encouragingly. 'It's not too late. There's ways and means. As I mentioned before, I have connections. Gilhooley is a big man. A strong Catholic, too, and Irish as you make them. Don't give up too easy. Why, speaking off-hand, it just occurs to me that the Bursar there now, a fellow called Phelan . . . or is it Feeney, was a pal of mine. He took the collar. I might write to him, he'd do anything for me. Or even the Principal, they remember me there, I can tell you.'

Terence's expansive attitude quite lifted me up. My eyes glowed as I murmured my gratitude.

'Say nothing of it.' He pushed back his chair and got to his feet. 'I must get back to the reception now. We've some important guests coming in this afternoon. But keep in touch with me. I want to time you on the mile. If it works out it might do you some good. Don't forget now.'

'I won't, Terry. I'll come to the service door.'

'That'll be easier for you,' he approved. 'By the way, did you know that Nora was in town?'

'No, Terry.'

'Well, she is, and doing famously for herself.'

'In what way?'

'She's junior assistant to Miss Donohue, the buyer in Earle's. The Donohues are good friends of ours, old Donohue and my old man were pretty close at one time, so it was all fixed up nicely for Nora to train under her. You know what a buyer is, don't you?'

I did, more or less. And as Earle's was the leading establishment in Winton for women's fashions I knew also that Miss Donohue's position must be a good one.

'Nora's always asking about you,' Terence went on. 'Why don't you look her up? She lives with Miss D. I'll give you the address. It's in Park Crescent.'

He took a gold-cased pencil from his waistcoat pocket and wrote it down.

I could not thank him enough. Indeed, when he had shown me out by the back door, I went on my way rejoicing in the fortunate chance that had reintroduced me to my own people. I had been so long without proper human companionship that the prospect of friendship with Terence and Nora excited me. And more: the subject of Rockcliff had been raised. What might Terry, or Terry's friends, do for me? The name Gilhooley, linked to that splendid car, to say nothing of the dashing daughter to whom Terence was affianced and soon would probably marry, suggested possibilities which, while as yet undetermined, seemed almost unlimited.

TWENTY-FIVE

FOR SEVERAL DAYS I waited hopefully in the expectation that Nora would get in touch with me. I was reluctant to take the initiative and Terence must surely have spoken to her of our meeting. But as no word came from her, on the following Saturday when I was free I wandered in a desultory fashion towards Park Crescent. The afternoon, I remember clearly, was mild, still, and sunny, full of a delicious promise of spring.

Park Crescent was situated in a favoured residential district on the west side of the city. It stood high, a quarter circle of tall Georgian houses, now converted to flats, overlooking Kelvingrove Park. Already discouraged by the superior atmosphere of this locality, which contrasted markedly with the crudities of Argyle Street and Templar's Hall, I barely paused outside No. 9 and did not arrest my self-conscious transit until I was fifty yards farther down the Crescent. Here, with the air of a disinterested observer, I leaned over the railings and surveyed the Park beneath me. Should I or should I not advance boldly and ring the bell? The spears were breaking on the chestnut trees, yellow forsythia was already in bloom, perambulators were circling on the broad path where I took my evening run. Nora could not possibly wish to see me. Yet I had liked her when we last met and now I wanted her as a friend. Half-turning, I perceived that the street maintained a total emptiness. At least I should be unobserved if I were rejected and thrown out. Bracing myself, I turned back. mounted the portico steps of No. 9 and went into the long entrance hall. From a variety of doors, peering in the semi-darkness, I selected one on which was tacked a visiting-card with the name: Miss Fidelma Donohue. I straightened my tie and, reminding myself that I was fairly presentable in my soberly dyed brown suit, pressed the bell.

The door was smartly opened by a short, tight, bustling little woman dressed for the street in a stylish hat and coat who, in a well-corseted attitude, her head thrown back, appraised me with a hard, bright, competent eye and inquired:

'Well, young man?'

'Is Miss Nora Carroll in?' I murmured. 'I'm her cousin, Laurence Carroll.'

She relaxed immediately, her expression altered, she smiled a welcome. At ease, she had a full, rather humorous mouth, richly embellished with a gleaming double set of false teeth.

'Come in. Why haven't we seen you before? And why didn't you give us word you were coming?'

As I entered she put a hand on my shoulder and continued to look me up and down.

'Yes, you're a regular Carroll. I knew your father well, poor lad. So now you're making your fortune with your Uncle Leo.' Without giving me time to deny this suggestion she went on, impelling me towards a half-open door. 'Nora's in there. Hurry in now and get acquainted, for as bad luck would have it, we've both got to go out. But don't forget to come again.'

I saw that, like a fool, I had come at the wrong time and was prepared to apologize and retire. But, under her propulsion, I entered the room she indicated, a small feminine bedroom, done up with flowered chintz curtains and chair covers of the same material.

My cousin was seated before the looking-glass of her dressing-table. She turned, and we gazed at each other. Although I knew she must be my cousin I scarcely recognized in this alarmingly attractive girl the skinny child who had butted me at my father's funeral. For there was no doubt about it—Nora was a beauty. Not only so, but untouchably smart, wearing an embroidered silk blouse, dark green pleated skirt, and a necklace of speckled green beads, exactly the kind of girl for whom, with a lowered glance, I hurriedly stepped off pavements, lest my contaminating presence should offend her. Yet she was smiling to me, and her dark eyes, with their thick fringe of long curling lashes that seemed darker against her fresh delicate complexion, sparkled with pleasure and mischief.

'Oh, Laurence, what a fine tall boy you've grown into!
But oh, dear, I can't help thinking how I treated you in the
hen house. Do you remember the egg?'

'Of course, Nora.'

'Anyhow, it's done wonders for your hair. You've lots of
it, and such a nice chestnut shade. But oh, dear, I did bang
you against that wall.'

She came forward, put her arms round me and gave me a
full long kiss.

'There!' she said. 'That makes up for it. After all, aren't
we cousins?'

At that soft warm pressure I felt a kind of shock as though
something within me had given way.

'Oh, Nora,' I said faintly, 'it's a treat to see you again. I've
wanted to.'

'Then why didn't you before now, you silly fellow? No,
no, it's really my fault. We're an awful family, the way we
don't keep up with one another. Of course Simon's in Spain,
and Leo is impossible, but we shouldn't have lost touch with
you. We'll have to make up for it now. Stuck all those
months with Leo can't have been any fun.'

'No, not much, Nora. But then I'm not much of a one for
fun.'

'We'll have to go into that, And into all that's been happening to you.' She had taken up her hat from the dressing-
table. It was a little chip straw with a single rose on the brim.
'But not now, dear Laurence. It's a great shame, but Miss
Donohue and I have an engagement that just can't be
put off.'

'I'll clear out at once,' I said hurriedly.

'Oh, dear, aren't we touchy!' She finished putting on the
hat at the mirror and swung round. 'Now tell me, is that
becoming? Be careful, it's a model borrowed from the showroom.' She burst out laughing. 'Oh, Laurie, you are a funny
chap, but if I'm any judge, a nice one. Now listen, we're all
going, Miss D., Terence and I, and some others, to the second
house of the Alhambra on Saturday night, and you're coming
with us unless,' she looked at me mockingly, 'it will make
you even more miserable!'

'Oh, no, it won't, Nora.'

'Then meet us at the stalls entrance at nine o'clock. We'll
have the tickets.'

I left the house walking on air in a trance of happiness

which, as I turned instinctively into the Park, was succeeded by a surge of restless exaltation. How kindly Nora had received me, how naturally and affectionately I had been accepted, invited to another meeting, made to feel that I was wanted. No one had ever kissed me like that . . . never, never in my life. The soft warmth of those lips pulsed and persisted in my guileless blood, and in a slow, delicious expansion I felt my heart go out towards my cousin. Sudden recollection of my absurd fancy for Ada, with whom I had not even been privileged to exchange a word, made me blush. That had been mere childish play. This was the real thing. I was grown up now. I understood life. And as I hacked along at a pace that made me sweat, I began to picture a future in which Nora and I would constantly be together. I no longer felt alone and Winton had ceased to be a wilderness.

Suddenly, as I came along the river walk, sharply intruding upon this blissful reverie, a static object, peculiar yet strangely evocative, caught my downward abstracted eye. Surely, in the remote past, I had been familiar with that short ebon stump, terminating in the angle iron that affixed it to the thick-soled surgical boot. I stopped instinctively and raised my head. Seated alone, on the park bench, a little shrunken man in a black bobtail suit, celluloid dickey and string black tie was regarding me with a benevolent half smile.

'Laurence Carroll,' he said.

That he should recognize me, in my present state and after an interval of seven years, struck me with such force I dropped out of my dream and responded involuntarily:

'Pin Rankin!' And then, hurriedly apologizing: 'Oh, I'm sorry, sir. I was so surprised you knew me it just slipped out.'

'I'd have known you anywhere, Laurence,' he said amiably, making a sign that I should sit beside him. 'As a matter of fact, despite your elongation, you haven't really changed one iota.'

Dubious as to whether this was complimentary or disparaging, I accepted his invitation and sat down. He continued to inspect me.

'Were you walking for pleasure or for profit?'

I had a wild and frantic desire to reveal myself, to tell him about Nora and of the splendour that had gloriously changed my life. Fortunately I was now sufficiently sane to restrain the impulse.

'Actually for neither reason, sir. I was on my way back to Argyle Street.'

'Why Argyle Street, of all places?'

'That's where I work.'

'Work? In what capacity?'

'Well, sir, I'm a sort of apprentice in a wholesale warehouse.'

'You mean that you have left school?' When I nodded he looked at me quizzically and murmured: 'Then we are in the same boat.'

'Have you retired, sir?' I asked tactfully.

'In a manner of speaking,' he said. 'I have, in fact, been pensioned off. But I am still active, thank God, in a personal and particularly interesting way. I am compiling the Annals of Ardencaple parish, Laurence. I have access to all the records in the University Library, and as I now occupy a quiet, decent room in Hillside Street quite near, I have every facility for what one might well term a labour of love.'

He was still the same mild, prosy little man, characteristically making the best of his present situation, which did not strike me as particularly entrancing, and with my mind too overcharged to allow me to appreciate our meeting properly, I had begun to seek some means of escape when he said:

'Now tell me about yourself.'

With some reluctance I set off on a bare outline of the events since my father's death, of which he had heard. But he would not permit this brevity and kept drawing me out, pressing for more information, interspersing my answers with barely suppressed exclamations of interest and regret, until he had squeezed me dry of my entire history.

When I had done, having eventually warmed to my subject, I looked for some expression of sympathy by way of reward. Instead, with his head cocked at a sharp angle, he began to tug at his little pointed grey beard. Finally, in an absent manner, he said:

'And your poor mother was such a douce, happy little body.' Then, before I could recover from the shock of this remark which, from Pin, seemed almost indecent, he glanced at me then away again in a manner which made me feel he was bringing himself to say something unpleasant. 'I'm bitterly disappointed in you, Laurence. I thought you were a bright boy. I never imagined I'd find you clerking in a city warehouse.'

193

'But how could I help myself?' I protested.

'In a dozen different ways. Most of all by showing some gumption. You want to go up there, don't you?' He cocked the little beard upwards, not of course suggesting that heaven was my destination, but in the more immediate direction of the University which, from our position by the river, towered on the hill above us.

'I've wanted to go in for science, or even medicine, for long enough,' I answered shortly. 'I've wanted a lot of things I never got.'

'Then why don't you try a little harder? There are scores of University bursaries, especially in classics, open to clever boys. You are clever, aren't you?'

'I don't know. I hope I am.'

'Then let's see, right away, how we stand.' He spoke with enthusiasm and, while I gazed wonderingly, fumbled in the inside pocket of his braided jacket and produced a thin, black, worn morocco booklet, rather like my prayer book.

'This is my New Testament, Laurence,' he said briskly. 'Just open it at random and construe.'

I opened at random then, after a blank pause, attempted a feeble joke.

'This is Greek to me, sir. I don't know a word of it.'

'What, no Greek? Oh, dear, that's a blow!' He paused, frowning at me. 'Then how are you in Latin?'

'I've gone through *Selections from Ovid,* and all of a book called *Pro Patria,* and, well, I sort of started a bit of Virgil.'

'Started a bit of Virgil,' he repeated, making a clicking noise with his dentures which appeared to express the ultimate in dissatisfaction.

Again there was a silence. Then he said:

'Define the fifth proposition of the third book of Euclid.'

Hot with embarrassment, I faltered: 'Afraid I haven't been taken beyond the second book.'

Even then he did not give up. There, on that park bench, while the perambulators rolled past and a park attendant watched suspiciously as though we were conspiring to pillage his flower-beds, Pin put me through a comprehensive examination and when it was over he gave out a kind of hollow groan.

'Who has been teaching you? Or ruining you?' He tugged at the straggle of beard as though trying to uproot it. 'You are utterly and completely uneducated.'

194

'No, I'm not,' I said angrily. 'I know lots of things about botany and zoology, perhaps more than you do, sir. I'll bet you can't tell the difference between the four different species of Erica, or how the chromosomes fission in an amoeba's nucleus.'

He considered me with a wan, compassionate smile.

'My poor boy, these are precisely the subjects you would take, and doubtless excel in, *after* your admission to a scientific curriculum. But to gain that admission you require knowledge of a totally different kind, a standard textbook proficiency, which you simply have not got.'

There was nothing I could say to this. Suddenly I looked up.

'Couldn't you . . . I mean, as we're both in Winton . . . couldn't you coach me, sir . . . ?'

At once, and with fatal certainty, he shook his head.

'Impossible, Laurence. You're so far behind you need at least two years' hard and constant study. I'll not be here more than six months. On your side and mine it would be hopeless.'

A long and dull unhappy silence followed this extinction of my one sustaining hope, always at the back of my mind, that I would somehow break through my difficulties to a brilliant, scintillating career.

'It's a great pity, Laurence. You were such a promising pupil. Don't you remember those little sagas you produced for me when I set the week-end essays? They were uncommonly good. You had such a unaccountable sense of words. I used to read them to the class.' He paused suddenly, reflectively, looking at me in a manner which struck me as odd. He murmured a word, to himself, which came to me indistinctly. It sounded like *elison*. Was it a final benediction? Then, rather undecidedly, he said: 'I suppose there's no harm in our keeping in touch. Have you a pencil? Take down my address. Two-twelve Hillside Street. You might come and see me one evening next week. And now I mustn't keep you. I'll walk down with you to the tram stop.'

I answered sulkily. 'I don't take the tram.'

'But I have to, Laurence,' he said mildly.

We walked together to the Park gates. His progress, conspicuously slow and more ungainly than before, attracted curious and often vulgar stares. On the inclines he was audibly short of breath. In a bad, sullen mood it did not please me to be publicly identified with him, to be an adjunct to this freakish, hobbling progress. He had not helped me in the least, but had merely cast me down. When, at last, he hoisted himself to the step of the tram and called, 'Mind now. Come early next week,' I barely answered before abruptly turning away.

At least he had not robbed me of all my future. I still had Nora. And as I went on towards Argyle Street I began to think of her again.

TWENTY-SIX

THE SECOND 'HOUSE' of the Alhambra opened at nine o'clock, but on Saturday night, as could be expected, I arrived outside the entrance to the stalls well before that hour. I was in fact so early that outrush of the audience from the first performance almost swept me off my feet. Thereafter, a cold wind blowing fog from the river made standing a chilly business. With an eye on the Central Station clock I paced up and down, warming myself, less with this activity than with the prospect of seeing Nora. But time was going on. Ten, five, three minutes to nine . . . now the curtain must be going up. I began to worry. Had I mistaken the date, or come to the wrong door? Fifteen minutes late, as I was on the point of leaving, they arrived.

The party was larger than I had expected: Terence and Miss Josephine Gilhooley, Nora, Miss Donohue, and a hard-looking young man in an expensive suit who turned out to be Miss Donohue's brother. They were all in a mood of combined and well-established gaiety which induced the belief that they had probably had dinner together. The suspicion that I had been excluded from this prior event was confirmed by the effusiveness with which, by way of compensation, they greeted me.

'I do hope you haven't caught cold, dear,' Miss Donohue exclaimed, clutching my arm.

'Just had to step in and see a dog about a man,' Terence explained. 'Josey, this is Laurence.'

'Pleased to meet you, I'm sure. I always say that any friend of my friend's is a friend of mine, only they ought to have told me about you sooner.' Miss Gilhooley, who was wearing a rich-looking fur coat and swathes of mauve tulle round her head and neck, joined in the attempt to make amends. She pressed my hand, leaving on my palm an imprint of perfume that persisted throughout the evening, and added: 'I hear you're a great runner. You look it too. I always say you can tell by the look.'

'We think he might be good,' Terence said judiciously. 'Martin and I mean to give him a try-out one of these days.'

So far Nora had not spoken. Now, though still silent, she smiled to me, a smile of recognition and acknowledgement, with, I thought, a hint of intimacy that more than made up for all my waiting. Better still, as we went into the theatre she said quickly in my ear, explaining everything:

'It was Miss Gilhooley's party, Laurence. So I couldn't very well invite you to the Criterion. But next time you'll be sure to come.'

Unfortunately, in the disturbance created as we crushed our way into the centre of the stalls, I lost my place so that Terence, in the lead, sat with Miss Gilhooley, then came Martin with Nora, while I, at the end, was left with Miss Donohue. This arrangement did not at all suit me. In my disappointment, I looked along the row hoping for a commiserating glance from Nora, but with her usual animation she was talking to Donohue. On the stage a juggler was tossing balls in the air.

'The opening turns are never much good, dear,' Miss Donohue whispered in my ear. 'But just wait till you see Hetty King.' She had unwrapped a large box of chocolates and having offered me my choice placed the box conveniently open on her lap. 'Help yourself when you feel like it, dear.'

These repeated endearments from Miss Donohue, in which I detected a note of compassion, were making me feel like an orphan charity boy at a free treat. A man in a small bowler hat, with a red-painted nose, was now singing a song at which everyone seemed to be laughing but me.

'He's a scream, isn't he, dear?' Miss Donohue giggled.

I forced my stiff features into a concurring smile, taking, at the same time, another glance along the row. Miss Gilhooley, lying back almost in hysterics and showing all her gold-filled teeth, was clutching at Terence for support.

Then, with an inward sinking, I perceived that Martin was holding Nora's hand. At first sight I had not liked Donohue, who had not spoken to me, merely favoured me with a cold hard look, and that impression was now strongly reinforced. He was too good-looking, in a raffish, morose, dangerous way. With his prominent cheekbones and slightly flattened nose he had the appearance of a boxer.

'Look, dear, the Simultaneous Brothers.'

Obliged to give some attention to the miming of these integrated twin-like figures, in flannels, striped blazers and straw hats, I nevertheless could not remove my troubled gaze from that other pair. The unnatural position thus maintained, with one eye on the stage and the other along the row, at last attracted the attenion of Miss Donohue, who asked in an undertone:

'Have you twisted your neck, dear, you seem to have a crick in it? Or don't tell me you have a squint?'

With an effort I returned my eyes to their normal focus and hastily reassured her that I didn't need glasses.

The fall of the curtain for the interval saved me. Terence and Donohue immediately rose to go out to the bar and, as Miss Gilhooley stretched across the intervening space to talk to Nora, I turned to Miss Donohue with rare determination.

'I haven't had the pleasure of meeting your brother before, Miss Donohue,' I remarked, conversationally, with a painful attempt at subtlety. 'Does he live in Winton?'

'Well, part of the time, dear. But then he travels round the country a lot.'

'On business, Miss Donohue?'

'Naturally, dear. He's a commission agent.'

'Do you mean a commercial traveller, Miss Donohue?'

She studied me commiseratingly.

'You are green, aren't you, dear? Still, I like you for it, you're a very sweet boy. No, dear. Martin's a bookmaker. Not making books to read, you understand. Taking bets. A bookie, if you've heard the word. He has a stand at most of the race meetings and is in the way of building up a fine connection. Have a chocolate, dear, one of these, I don't like the caramel centres, they get in my dentures.'

'It seemed to me, Miss Donohue, that he and Nora are pretty good friends.'

'You might put it rather stronger than that, dear,' she

said, giving me a queer look. 'There's what you might call an understanding there.'

'An understanding, Miss Donohue?' I forced the words out from between my teeth.

'They're not exactly engaged, Nora's too young yet, only seventeen you know, and I want to bring her on for a year or so, at Earle's, so she can have her own business when she settles down. But take it from me, dear, already it's a settled case.'

That there was no engagement might have afforded me some solace but, while I did not precisely understand its meaning, the word 'case' had a fatal sound, made worse by the fact that it was settled. I gazed at Miss Donohue in silent misery as she went on.

'Nora's a lovely girl. A trifle wild maybe, it's the Irish in her, too full of mischief. But a dear girl, I'm very fond of her.'

'I'm sure we all are, Miss Donohue,' I croaked, in a vain effort to save face.

The rest of the show was dust and ashes in my mouth. Even Hetty King failed to stir me despite Miss Donohue's impressive whisper that her hit number 'Oh, You Beautiful Doll' was King Edward's favourite song.

As the final curtain fell and the orchestra bashed off a few bars of 'God Save the King', I had a melancholy sensation of relief. In the general scurry Terence and Donohue hurried to the bar for a last quick drink, while the two ladies, with a conscious air, retired to Cloaks. At last I was alone with Nora, waiting in the emptying foyer. She came close to me, so that her eyes looked straight into mine. They were serious yet her mouth, so mobile, so warm when it had pressed against my cheek, had a humorous twist.

'You haven't enjoyed yourself,' she said accusingly, yet with a note of sympathy, as if to indicate that she understood me. Indeed, when defensively I protested that I had, she shook her head. 'No. You thought it was pretty crude, and perhaps it was. This isn't at all the kind of thing you like.'

I felt, then, in sudden desperation, that I must unburden myself.

'I would have liked it, Nora, if I'd been sitting with you.'

'Then why weren't you?' She widened her eyes. Her breath, as she stood close to me, was warm and sweet. 'It would have been nice.'

'I thought you wanted to sit with Martin.'

'Martin!' she exclaimed. 'I get enough of him. He's much too pressing. I was wanting you to be beside me.'

My heart gave an enormous, joyful bound. Freed of my load of misery, I felt the blood run into my face.

'But, Laurence,' she was looking at me provokingly, 'Terry says you don't care much about girls.'

'I care about you, Nora. If you want to know, I've never cared about anyone the way I do you. I like you very much.'

She smiled and I thought she would go on teasing me. But after a moment her expression changed, a soft look came into her blue-black eyes.

'Well, I like you too,' she said. 'I really mean it. And I want to see a lot of you, show you around a bit, take you out of yourself. It's a hard world, Laurence, and if you'll forgive me, I think you could do with a little more experience of it. You've got to learn to mix with people and to have a bit of fun now and then. Am I offending you by saying all this?'

'No, you're not, Nora.'

The others were approaching, and she went on rather quickly.

'Then I tell you what. Next Sunday Mart and Terry are going to be away. So you come up to Park Crescent and we'll do exactly what you want.'

'Oh, Nora,' I breathed. 'How perfectly wonderful. Shall I come in the morning?'

I thought she was going to laugh. Her lips twitched and her eyes, under those curling lashes, screwed up into sparkling black slits.

'Come when you're ready,' she said. 'But not too early or you'll find me in bed.'

I was alive again, quite ready to smile when the others reappeared and pretend gaily that I'd had a wonderful time, to exchange hearty goodbyes and thank Miss Gilhooley when she said she wanted me to come to her next party, all of which was a performance completely foreign to my nature but which I now accomplished because I knew that Nora truly cared for me.

When at last I left them, I walked on air all the way back to Templar's Hall and the clanging of the trams made music in my ears.

TWENTY-SEVEN

APART FROM my mother's regular weekly letters, I had nothing to expect from the mail. The postcard which arrived by the morning delivery on the following Wednesday and was handed to me at breakfast by Mrs Tobin was therefore a surprising event. It came from Pin, and it said briefly:

Why have you not come to see me? I shall expect you Wednesday or Thursday of this week without fail.

Now, I had already given Pin up. His appraisal of my ability, or lack of it, had left a sore spot on my mind, and I had no wish to be catechized and dismissed again. If my prospects were as bad as he made out he could clearly be no possible use to me. I would not go to him. Any action to improve my situation must await the return of my mother.

Nevertheless, as the day wore on, I kept pulling the card out of my pocket and staring at it. After all, it was a rarity. And I began to ask myself if some sense of urgency might not be detected in the message. Then, after all, I did owe an obligation to my old teacher. In the end, with characteristic inconsistency, at seven o'clock that evening I stood knocking at the door of 212 Hillside Street.

It was a boarding-house, of a noticeably modest class, a fact which I deduced from the smell of boiled cabbage in the bare little hall and the cracked linoleum on the stairs leading to Pin's lodging, a bed-sitting-room on the second floor back. He was there, reading at the window, but obviously expecting me, and he received me without reproach. Over his shoulder I saw immediately that he had provided for me, obviously from his own purse. A bottle of lemonade and a plate of sweet biscuits had been set out on the round table by the window.

'Laurence,' he began, when he had seated me. 'I had a thought the other day which might or might not be a happy one. Since then I have made it my business to pursue it.'

'Yes, sir,' I said dutifully.

'First of all, let me offer you some refreshment.'

He poured the lemonade and pushed the biscuits hospitably towards me.

'Won't you have some yourself, sir?'

He smiled and shook his head, then after watching me for a few minutes, he said, with a certain impressiveness:

'Laurence, I want to talk to you about the Ellison.'

'The Ellison,' I repeated blankly.

He nodded, and pressing his fingertips together, so that his hands formed an inverted V, he leaned towards me.

'As you probably know, there are all sorts of foundations, trusts, scholarships and the like endowed to the University. Some of them are unusual, and while perfectly acceptable to the Senate you might even call them peculiar—in as much as they reflect the character of the donor.' He paused, holding me so tightly with his eye that I forgot to finish the biscuits. 'Now John Ellison was an odd sort of man, Laurence—a Forfar grain miller in a modest way of business, not particularly literate, but a perfervid Scots nationalist with a passion for Scottish history. I'm led to believe that he went every year to Bannockburn on the anniversary of the battle. At any rate, when he died, at the age of eighty-three, he left all his estate to found a scholarship, thirty pounds a year for five years, open to students bent on entering the University, for the best commemorative essay on a Scottish historical character, the subject to be set unseen by the Professor of Divinity, the essay to be written in the space of two hours in the University Hall on the last day of the first week of August. That's just about three months from now.'

Again he paused, then said mildly, but with a certain impressiveness: 'Laurence, how would you like to spend those three months cramming Scots history, and sit the Ellison at the end of it?'

I gazed at him stupidly. My reaction, beyond the initial surprise, was mainly one of instinctive rejection. The idea was so utterly unexpected, the basis of the scholarship so preposterous, verging even on the absurd, and my competence for the undertaking so manifestly questionable, I shrank away from it, like a rabbit bolting for its hole. I knew that I could not do it, that it was all quite beyond me, and I immediately set about arranging my refusal, logically, and in terms least likely to hurt Pin.

'It's kind of you to bother about me, sir. But when you speak of time you forget I have a job already, that keeps me occupied most of the day.'

'I was speaking of your spare time, Laurence. In the

evenings and possibly the nights at your disposal you could, with my help, steep yourself in history.'

'But where would I get the books?'

'With my present facilities at the University Library I could borrow all the books you need, and more. Rare books, splendid, interesting books.' He added pointedly: 'And you know how you used to love to read.'

That stung me—it was months since I had nourished my faculties on anything more substantial than Mrs Tobin's weekly copy of *Tit-bits*.

'In any case,' I said, 'you have no guarantee that I could do the essay, beyond those early compositions, which were only childish efforts. And you've already informed me that I'm only half educated.'

'Nevertheless, you're clever, Laurence,' he countered dryly. 'Besides, I doubt if literary ability is the main criterion in question. The judges will be looking for national spirit.'

'National spirit!' I protested. 'I'm half Irish!'

'That gives you the imagination to transpose yourself and become more Scottish than the Scots.'

This gentle yet insidious pressure was getting me down.

'No, I really don't feel up to it, sir. I'm too young to go to the University. I'd rather wait till my mother comes back. Her course finishes in September. When she gets her appointment in Winton she means to take rooms, or a small flat. Then I may be able to go to school again.'

'You're not too young for the University. You'd be past sixteen if you entered in the autumn. And that's too old to think of school, at least the kind available to you.' He went on accusingly: 'As for your mother, wouldn't it be a great thing if you were able to tell her that you'd tried the Ellison, perhaps even,' he paused, 'that you had won it? In that event, what a joy, what a relief for her. You starting the University with more than enough to keep you there. Thirty pounds a year guaranteed for five solid years. Think of that, Laurence. And don't forget, I'd help you.'

Whether deliberately or not, he was pulling out all the sentimental stops, evoking tenderness for my mother and contempt for myself, playing so unfairly on my emotions that an angry flush came into my cheeks and I could find nothing to say.

He glanced away, tugging at his beard, appearing not to

notice my humiliation, but not before, in a subdued tone, he sounded the last outrageous, unpardonable chord.

'I suppose you can imagine what it would mean to a useless old man like me if I coached you through to win the Ellison.'

Was he play-acting, descending to these base ends to win me over? Pin was a scholar, a classicist, and a man of culture, yet in his veins there flowed a strong infusion of kailyard sentiment. I believe now that he meant and felt every word he said. Then, it was enough for me to know that I was defeated. And he knew it too. Rising spryly, he hopped— being at ease in his slippers and divested of the stump— towards a cupboard in the wall.

'You can't drink that now, it's gone flat. I thought you'd manage another bottle. I have it in the press.' He produced fresh lemonade and decanted it into a clean tumbler. 'There's more biscuits too if you want them.'

I wanted neither biscuits nor lemonade, feeling that, having elevated me to manhood, he was now treating me as a child. But I accepted them to gain time to collect myself, and disposed of them in downcast silence. No one could have been less elated at the prospect of our enterprise than I. He must have sensed this, for he addressed me in a different, authoritative manner.

'Now pay attention. You will come here to this room at seven o'clock three nights a week, when we will spend at least two hours together. I have drawn up a schedule of your reading. Here are your first two books, the first Hume Brown's *General History of Scotland*, the second Duncan's *The Border Wars*.' He handed over one of the volumes and turned the pages of the other at random. 'You don't realize what a splendid time you are going to have . . . the amazing people you are going to meet. And to think that I had to drag you to it. Take this Earl of Angus for instance, named Archibald Bell-the-Cat, he was a character, I can tell you. Draw your chair nearer and we'll go over him together.'

We began to investigate the heroic eccentricities of Angus, head of the Red Douglases, how he hanged the King's musicians and earned the nickname of Bell-the-Cat. In spite of myself, I became interested. Whatever Pin might have been in the pulpit he was always a sympathetic and engaging teacher. I was sorry when at nine o'clock he ended the session.

'That's enough for a start. Now apart from the reading I've set you, I'll expect a short written account, say five hundred words, on what we've just been over. Bring it when you come on Friday.'

I stood up, trying to find a proper expression of willingness. How could I have been so obstinate, so timidly averse? But he checked me.

'I know you, Laurence. No raptures, please. Hard work.'

With the books under my arm I took my usual sprint through the Park and then, so eager was I to resume my acquaintance with the Border Reivers, I continued my run all the way to Templar's Hall, choosing the back way by the river, speeding along deserted side streets and ill-lit alleys, hearing my footfalls echo behind me between the dark sheds of the docks, until at last I was in my own room, propped up in bed, with the candle lit and the book open on my knees.

TWENTY-EIGHT

SUNDAY, so eagerly anticipated, came at last. Although I was up and about by seven, I went out as usual to the ten o'clock Mass at St Malachi's with Mrs Tobin. St Malachi's was our neighbourhood church, serving the poorest district in the city, and remains associated in my mind with rows of women in shawls and the perpetual sound of coughing. But Mrs Tobin liked it, she had friends in the congregation, and I always went with her. Actually on this exceptional morning I had thought of going to the nine o'clock, so that I might arrive at Park Crescent about ten, but reflecting on Nora's hint that I should not come too early, I decided that I ought to get there around eleven o'clock. Although this, perhaps, on second thought, seemed rather late.

The University clock was, in fact, booming out eleven strokes as I pressed the bell of No. 9, spruced up in the best I had, and nervous of course, but alive with anticipation. My dedication to the Ellison was now a settled thing, but it was still a long way off, and nothing would have made me miss the chance of a day with my adorable cousin.

Perhaps the bell had not rung. I pressed it again and

waited. There was no response. Once more I had my finger on the button when sounds reached me from within, then the door was opened, partially, but enough to reveal Nora in her nightdress and dressing-gown. She blinked at me, with a vague expression, only half awake. At last, not particularly pleased, something seemed to strike her.

'It's you, Laurence,' she said. 'You'd better come in.'

Tightening the cord of her gown and scuffing along in her feathery mules, she led me into the kitchen, sat down on the edge of a chair, and with difficulty suppressed a yawn.

'Oh, Nora,' I exclaimed grievously, yet fascinated by the picture she made. 'I'm afraid I've disturbed you.'

She looked at me, meditatively rubbing her shoulder under her nightdress, then suddenly began to laugh.

'Don't worry, man. I was a bit late last night, out with the gang. Seeing Miss Donohue off. She's away to Perth with Terry and Martin. But if you'll put on the kettle and make me a cup of tea, I'll be ready in two shakes of a lamb's tail.'

When she had shown me the pantry cupboard and retreated to her bedroom, I decided to make her a proper breakfast. Life with Mother had made me fairly expert at improvising a meal. By the time she came back the tea was infused and I had made a rack of toast and plenty of scrambled eggs.

'Well I never.' She viewed my preparations set out on a chequered tablecloth. 'This is luxury. Beats the Criterion. You'll have to share it with me.'

'I've had my breakfast, Nora.'

'What did you have?'

'Oh, mostly the usual stirabout. That's a kind of porridge, Nora.'

'Then you can stand another. That Leo should be shot. Dead.'

She brought out another cup and poured the tea. We started on the toast and scrambled eggs. I had never imagined that breakfast with anyone could be so agreeable. My cousin, now fresh as a daisy, was prettier than ever. Although still bare-legged and in mules, she was wearing a soft white blouse and a short tartan skirt that had a lot of yellow in it.

'It's the Kerry tartan,' she explained, smoothing it over her knees. 'If you're Irish you've got to be proud of it. Now tell me straight, Laurence, what you'd like to do with me today.'

It was her colouring, I decided, the dark hair and eyes against the creamy skin, that made her so enchanting. I loved to watch her wide soft mouth sipping the tea, and as she crunched the toast, her small even teeth were as white as my father's had been—the good Carroll teeth.

I took a big breath.

'I'd like best . . . that's to say if you'd like it . . . if we could go somewhere into the country.'

'Ah, you're not a city boy.'

She glanced out of the window. The sun was shining on the white wall of the courtyard.

'Still, not a bad idea. Winton's ghastly on Sunday. Suppose we take a run down to the houseboat.'

'The houseboat?'

She was enjoying my surprise. That, I thought suddenly, was Nora's special charm—her capacity for enjoyment.

'Lot's of people have houseboats on Loch Lomond. Martin . . . and Miss Donohue . . .' she added, 'have one, not far from Luss. For holidays and so on. It's fun. We'll take the bikes, you can have Miss D.'s, and we'll be there by one o'clock.'

This prospect, after months in the purlieus of Argyle Street, was a real excitement. I could hardly wait to be off. I jumped up.

'Let's start soon, Nora. I'll hurry up and wash the dishes and make some sandwiches, if you like.'

'No sandwiches, man. They're deadly. And never mind the dishes. If you want to go now, we'll go, but first let me get my stockings on. Hand me them. Over there.'

A pair of lisle stockings had been washed and now hung, dry, two slender filaments, on a rail by the kitchen range. As I brought them to her they were light as gossamer.

Sitting there, she began to draw them on, watching me out of the corner of one eye with sheer mischief and something else, a sort of beguiling inquiry that came from beneath her lashes, meanwhile, as I stared fascinated, affording me fleeting yet generous glimpses of white beneath the Kerry tartan.

'There!' she declared casually, rising and shaking herself down. 'Once I get my shoes on we'll be off.'

'Thank you, Nora,' I stammered. This idiotic remark,

which may have sprung from my subconscious as an appreciation of her performance, sounded so pointless that I flushed. To my relief, she did not appear to notice.

The two bicycles were in the basement cellar. We wheeled them out through the yard and set off.

Miss Donohue's machine, an old model with high handlebars and a fixed low gear that had no free wheel, made me work hard. I had to pedal twice as fast as Nora to keep up with her. Going downhill she would dart ahead and turn round to mock me as, perched on the high saddle with my feet on the front fork and the pedals spinning wildly, I rattled behind her. I felt sure Miss D. hadn't used the machine for ages. But the exercise was just what I wanted, the roads had a Sunday freedom from traffic, and the open country, already tender with the green of spring, was a sheer intoxication. The hawthorn was bursting into bloom, I sniffed the sweet perfume as we swept past. In the meadows lambs were bleating after their mothers. Primroses and cowslips were already showing under the hedges. When we came to the Loch, winding along the lovely curving shore, Nora began to caper on the bike.

'Look, Laurence, no hands.'

Then she started to sing. It was not Hetty King's song but one rather like it, beginning:

> *You called me baby doll a year ago,*
> *You told me I was very nice to know.*

This violation of the Sunday stillness had an unaccountable effect on me. I liked it until suddenly it made me remember that Nora had not been to church that morning and that I was undoubtedly to blame for this omission. I pedalled up to her and exclaimed in consternation:

'Nora, you didn't get out to Mass this morning. And the way I rushed you off, it's all my fault.'

She stopped singing.

'Yes, Laurence,' she said gravely. 'That's a bad sin on your conscience. I didn't want to bring it up on you, but it's been worrying me a lot.'

'Why didn't you stop me, Nora? I'd have gone out with you to the Jesuits, on Craig Street. It's my favourite church.'

'You didn't give me a chance, man. You had me on the bike and out of the city before I rightly knew what day it was or where I was.'

'Oh, dear,' I mourned. 'I'm terribly sorry, Nora.'

'Well, don't upset yourself, my lad. Maybe it's not mortal, and if it is, there's some I've heard of that are a lot worse.'

As she spoke she jumped off her bike. We had reached a quiet cove with a pebbled beach on which a small dinghy lay moored to a stake by a rusty chain. Some fifty yards offshore a curious yet inviting white-painted structure with windows and a door that in miniature exactly fulfilled my conception of Noah's Ark floated gently at anchor. It was the houseboat.

Nora took a key from her bicycle satchel and unlocked the padlock on the dinghy's chain. We pushed off and, each taking an oar, rowed to the houseboat. Inside it was exactly like a little house, with a bedroom, a sort of lounge that was the sitting-room, and a kitchen fitted with a metal stove. It was also in a state of extreme disorder, the bed unmade, newspapers and dishes cluttering the table, an empty bottle lying on the floor.

'A bit of a mess,' Nora said, looking round and wrinkling her nose. 'Well, never mind, that's not our problem. What would you say to a bathe?'

'I'd love it.' I said, longingly, for I was hot and dusty. 'But I've no pants.'

'Who's to see you?' she answered coolly. 'I'll not look and even if I did, aren't I your cousin? Go in off the top deck. But mind you, it'll be cold.'

A ladder staircase led to the top deck, which was flat, surrounded by an ornamental balustrade. Woods enclosed the cove on two sides and, beyond, the lake shimmered in the sun. In the distance the Ben was bluer than the sky. I threw off my clothes and, still dubious of my total nudity, hurriedly dived in.

The shock of the snow-fed water was breathtaking. I came up gasping, but as I struck out my circulation came back to me with an exhilarating rush. I had been swimming for some time when an unexpected splash made me swivel round. My unpredictable cousin had joined me in the lake. Impossible to discern whether or not she had on a bathing-suit. Only her head was visible as, with a fast breast stroke, she bore down upon me. But the thought that, like myself, she might be in a state of nature stung me. I took off like a frightened trout, making instinctively for the shore. But she had anticipated this and cut me off. I turned. She followed, a maddeningly persistent mermaid. Only with an effort that left me gasping did I reach the opposite side of the houseboat and haul myself out to safety.

A towel had been placed beside my clothes. I rubbed myself down and got into them light lightning. Five minutes later she appeared, dripping, shaking water from her hair and, to my immense relief, adequately covered.

'Why didn't you stay and let me duck you? Really, Laurie, you're so shy, it's painful. Don't be so serious, man. Let yourself go. You're far too nice to be a stick. Do you know what? I took a wee peep at you in your birthday suit and, to put it mildly and not to swell your head, you've nothing to be ashamed of.'

'But, Nora, I only thought . . .'

'You think too much. That's just your trouble. Anyhow, I'm too hungry to argue, we both need something to eat.'

'If you've anything to cook . . .' I muttered helpfully. 'I could light the stove . . .'

'When you know me better, and I hope you will, you'll discover I hate cooking . . . about as much as I hate sandwiches. In any case, there's nothing to eat on this tub but tins of sardines and mouldy abernethy biscuits.'

I started to tell her that these would do, but she had already started to go below, saying:

'I'll be ready in a tick. Then I'll tell you what's on the cards.'

She was not long in coming back. Then we got into the dinghy and under her directions I rowed about half a mile up the lake and into another bay where, on the shore road, there was an inn with the sign: *Inchmurren Arms. John Rennie, Proprietor.* We disembarked at a little wooden jetty. Here I hesitated. Truth must be spoken.

'Nora . . . I've no money.'

'What!' She affected an exaggerated surprise. 'Not even a round O for Paddy Murphy? Then we're stuck.'

As I reddened she burst out laughing.

'Don't worry, dear Laurence, this is my treat.'

Nora was apparently a fairly regular customer, the pub-keeper knew her at once and shook hands with her.

'Mr Donohue not with you today, miss?' He then gave me a long stare followed by a dismissive turn of his head, and said: 'There's chicken, roast beef or boiled mutton with apple dumpling or curds and cream to follow. You'll have the Snug to yourselves.' As a kind of afterthought, he added: 'The wife will be sorry to miss you. She's down the village at the daughter's.'

The Snug was not a particularly good room, the table covered with oilcloth, and spittoons on the sanded floor. A sad stuffed pike in a glass case swam over the mantelpiece. But the food, when it came, was the best country fare. We had the roast beef, thick slices pink in the middle and charred at the edges, with floury potatoes and greens. With this Nora ordered a glass of beer. I took lemonade. Then the home-made apple dumpling with lashings of thick fresh cream. I had a second helping. Finally, a round of sound yellow Dunlop cheese was put on the table. Sitting back and finishing her beer while she nibbled a sliver of cheese, my cousin viewed my activities on a much larger wedge with a faint smile.

'We'll do this again, won't we, man?'

'Oh, Nora, if only we could . . . This is all . . . so perfect.'

'There's just one thing we need to top it off. Remember the sup of port I gave you in the bar when we were both kids? We'll each have another sup now.'

She got up and went out of the room to fetch it. After a longish time, she came back with a glass in each hand.

'Rennie tried to keep me talking about horses,' she said. 'Martin usually gives him a tip.'

At the mention of that name the sweetish port tasted slightly bitter. Even so, it was giving me courage.

'Nora . . . Do you come here often with Martin?'

'Well, occasionally. And with Miss D. too.'

'I suppose . . .'—I was developing a way of going round this painful subject—'it's only natural that you're fond of Martin.'

'Sometimes I like him a lot. Other times I hate him. I'm out with him now.'

'I hope you stay out with him.'

'Why?'

'Because, if it won't offend you,' the port was helping me, 'I'm terribly fond of you myself.'

'Why should it offend me?'

'Well,' I muttered deprecatingly, 'I'm not much, you know, Nora.'

'For God's sake, man!' She sat up. 'When will you stop running yourself down? You don't think enough of yourself. If you want to know, I'm liking being with you in a way I never thought I would. Do you hear me? I'm enjoying this every bit as much as you are. You'll see, I mean it. Let's go back to the boat.'

As I got up a delicious euphoria pervaded me, induced by the lunch, the port, and this warm expression of her regard. Decently, under the pretext of discussing horses, Nora had already paid the bill. Outside, as we came through the inn garden, the velvet wallflowers, hot in the sun, distilled their faint delicious fragrance. It was a beautiful still afternoon. We reached the houseboat, tied up the dinghy, and went inside. Nora was looking at me with that faint suggestive smile I had noticed when she drew on her stockings. Yet somehow it had changed. She was no longer mocking me. Instead of mischief in her eyes there was warmth and a strange, sweet, vague allurement. She gave a little laugh.

'After that gorge, I feel like a nap. Don't you? We could stretch out there.'

Following her gaze I saw that the bed had been made up. She must have done this when she was changing after the swim.

'But it's such a lovely day, Nora. Wouldn't it be nicer lying on the top deck?'

'I've tried it.' She gave me a slight endearing grimace. 'It's awfully hard.'

'I could take these cushions off the settee.'

'Well . . . if you like.' She gave in. 'But it's not half as cosy as the bed.'

I gathered all the cushions and carried them up. They were rather knocked about, exuding feathers, but seemed soft enough when I spread them on the deck and we lay down on them. It was blissfully warm. I shut my eyes. Even through my closed lids the sun made a radiance that matched my state of mind.

'Are you comfortable, Nora?'

'Yes,' she said. 'I never thought of the cushions. That was clever, Laurie. But where are you?'

She stretched out an arm. Still with blind eyes I found her small warm hand and held it. She began to tickle my palm with the tip of one finger.

'I'm so happy, Nora. Thank you so much for everything And especially for being with me.'

'You're still too far away. Come nearer.'

As I turned on my side her arm encircled my neck. I opened my eyes. Her face was ravishingly close to mine. I could see the blue specks in her dark eyes, the mole on the angle of her cheekbone, so exactly placed it became a beauty spot. A tiny bead of perspiration glinted on her upper lip. Her skin, usually creamy pale, had a slight suffused flush. A strange and scented warmth came from her nearness. It made my heart flutter and miss a beat.

'Shall I tell you something, Laurie dear?' Then she spoke slowly, with a pause between each word, as though to bring its meaning home to me. 'I like you very, very much.'

'And I like you, Nora dear,' I breathed. 'In fact I absolutely love you with all my heart.'

'Then love me, dearest Laurie.'

She drew me tightly to her and put her open lips against mine. A great wave of sweetness passed through me. In all my life I could not wish for anything more than this. I felt carried away, out of myself, borne on a stream of the purest most powerful emotion, a feeling so utterly detached from my body that it was like a rapture of the soul.

Alas, poor simpleton, I did not dare presume that my cousin was in pressing need of my assistance. My capacity to co-operate was not in question, heaven knew I had trouble enough steering my way through the devious paths of puberty. But Nora was to me mysterious, exceptional, almost angelic. Not only would I have died rather than offend her, my exalted mood restrained me from the earthy fumblings of an act which then seemed a sordid and indecent business. Was I an utter ass, a prig perhaps, or simply a soft, inexperienced, idealistic youth? Do I merit the contempt of the present generation of knowing adolescents who set out on such excursions with bored assurance and a pocketful of contraceptives? And would I, in fact, have sustained my seraphic attitude to the end? Whether or not, at least I am now spared the obligation of providing my history with that most banal of all performances, the loss of a youthful virginity, for as we lay together, blissfully, breathlessly, in each other's arms, there came a loud arresting shout from the shore.

'Miss Nora, I've brought you some flowers to take home.'

'Oh, God,' Nora groaned. 'It's Mrs Rennie from the inn, blast her.'

'Some for you and some for Miss Donohue,' came from the beach again, and turning on my elbow I saw a stout little woman waving masses of daffodils at us.

'I'll go for them,' I said.

'No, stay here. Don't move an inch. I'll get rid of her and be back in no time at all.'

She got up, though with reluctance, shook back her hair, and a moment later I heard the splash of the dinghy's oars. Presently the sound of amicable greetings, of voices in conversation drifted over the lake. Mrs Rennie was a talker and less easy to get rid of than Nora had hoped. How wide the sky was, and how drowsy the slow lapping of the lake. I began to feel that I was floating dreamily through the clouds, floating more and more dreamily until, in the end, the long bicycle run, the stupendous lunch, the port, and the hot sun had their way with me. To my everlasting shame, I fell asleep.

When I awoke it was cooler, the sun was beginning to go down and Nora was not beside me. I sprang up to find that she was below, and had actually made tea. She greeted me not, as one might expect, with reproaches or disdain but tenderly, and with a certain new, and to me puzzling, clinical interest. She kissed me cherishingly on the cheek, uttering words of commendation which I thought strange.

'You're a doat of a lad, Laurie. Such a gorgeous day, and not a thing to reproach ourselves with.'

'Did you have a sleep too?'

'No, lad. I had another swim to cool off, then I put the kettle on, sat down and had a bit of a think to myself.'

'About what, Nora?'

'Ah,' she smiled. 'I'll tell you some day.'

When we had drunk the tea, which I found most refreshing, we locked up the houseboat, rowed ashore and, having padlocked the dinghy, set off unhurriedly on the bikes for home. Nora rode very close to me, often putting a hand on my shoulder so that we could talk. Indeed we talked most of the way to Winton. I told her about the Ellison and she urged me to work hard for it. Other advice she gave me, warning me not to let Terence take advantage of me.

'Terry's a good sort, there's not a bit of harm in him, but he'd wile the bird off the bush. As for Donohue, that fellow would skin his own grandmother.'

It was late when we reached Park Crescent. My lamp had

214

gone out and we had walked our bicycles up the last part of the hill. I took Nora's from her and said I would put both machines in the cellar. As I stood in the darkness she gave me a quick hug and kiss.

'Good night, dear Laurie. And bless you for being yourself.'

Then she ran up the stairs and was gone.

TWENTY-NINE

IT WAS FOUR O'CLOCK on a hot Saturday afternoon in mid-July, and Mrs Tobin had brought a cup of tea to my room. Before going out she shook her head at me as I sat behind a pile of books at the wicker table I had rescued from Leo's junk rooms.

'Education's a wonderful thing. But if I were you, I wouldn't keep at it that hard.'

'But I have to, Annie,' I agonized. 'Time's getting terribly short.'

'Well.' She considered me. 'Don't give yourself brain fever, like Mrs Finnegan's lad when he failed for the Post Office.'

I was too strung up to treat this as a joke. For more than two months I had been grinding steadily under Pin's direction, and had worked myself into a state of nerves. From those early appetizers, Hume Brown's *General History of Scotland*, and *The Border Wars*, I had progressed to more solid reading: Barron's *Scottish War of Independence*, Skene's *Celtic Scotland*, Gregory's *The Stuart Kings*, and was now absorbed in *The Thistle and the Rose*. Apart from my real objective, in which I scarcely dared to hope, I had become interested in the subject for its own sake. At night, my best reading time, I would find myself so caught up in such excitements as the feud between Rothesay and Albany, leading up to Rothesay's mysterious death at Falkland, that only the final guttering of my candle—an illumination surely in keeping with the fourteenth century—brought me to a halt. I now went to Pin four evenings a week, a truly heroic devotion, less on my part than on his. Often my thoughts went back to the days when I foolishly pretended to have a tutor. Now I had one: a patient, admirable teacher. His main concern centred on my lack of literary style, a defect which he constantly tried, by correction and advice but with slight success, to improve.

'You write from the heart, Laurence.' He would shrug regretfully. 'Not from the head. We'll have to leave it that way.'

I turned to Mrs Tobin's kindly offering. As I drank the tea, which had begun to get cold, my gaze returned, not for the first time that afternoon, to the postcard. It had come yesterday and now lay, too conspicuously, on the table beside my notes on the regencies of Murray and Lennox. Frowning, I took it up and, as if to deduce some meaning that had hitherto escaped me, read it through once again.

Meet me under the clock at Central Station 5 o'clock Saturday without fail. It will be very definitely to your advantage.

Terence

Of course, I would not go. I had made up my mind not to go. Time was too precious now to waste on futile meetings. Above all, had not Nora, my dear Nora, distinctly advised me to be wary of the elegant Terry? Yet that final sentence had an alluring ring. *Very definitely to your advantage—* soundlessly my lips formed the words. If, indeed, this should be a real opportunity, and my thoughts went back to my conversation with Terence in the kitchens of the Criterion when he had spoken of his influence at Blackrock, then how badly I should feel if I missed it. While I finished my tea I debated the problem first one way then the other. In the end, I jumped up, seized my cap, and set out for the Central Station.

When I arrived it was ten to five. This was a favourite meeting-place, and others were waiting beneath the big clock. I joined them. At five minutes past the hour, striking a note of unusual punctuality, Terence appeared, carrying a small Gladstone bag. He was not alone. Donohue was with him.

'Good, man, you're there. And looking great.' Terence greeted me warmly. 'I hope we haven't kept you.'

Donohue was smiling too, at least his contained, morose face was fixed into an expression of unusual affability, all the more surprising, since until now he had practically ignored me.

216

'We can't talk here,' Terence said. 'Let's go into the buffet.'

We went into the first-class buffet.

'What'll you have?' Donohue asked hospitably. 'This is on me.'

Commendably turning the offer to my advantage I said I would have a ham sandwich and a glass of milk. They both had Guinness.

Terence waited until we had been served, then, having inquired of me solicitously if everything was all right, he took a pull at his stout and made the following announcement.

'Now, man, you've often heard me say I wanted to clock you on the mile. Well, it's today we're going to do it.'

I ought not to have been surprised since the matter had indeed been brought up before more than once, in Terry's half-serious, half-jocular manner. But the suddenness of the proposal did take me aback.

'Why today?' I asked warily.

'We'll come to that all in good time,' he said, with an intimate, knowing look.

'But I haven't been doing much serious running lately. I'm rather out of form.'

'Ah, a fit young fellow like you is never out of form. Is he, Mart?'

'Shouldn't be,' Donohue replied noncommittally. 'From what I see, there's not an ounce of fat on him. Still, I'm not convinced he can stay.'

'Don't worry. He'll stay all right.'

'But has he the speed?' Donohue looked at me doubtingly. 'He'll need that for a fast finish.'

'I'll guarantee it,' Terry said emphatically. 'Haven't I told you how he sprinted me practically level when he was a kid?'

Donohue waved away the argument.

'That was years ago.'

'Maybe so. But there's his two big wins with the Harriers this year and the year before. Laugh that off, D.'

'Mm, yes,' said Donohue, as if half convinced. 'Well, I suppose we may as well give him his chance.'

'And a real chance it is.' Terence turned to me. 'It's all fixed up, man. The togs are here for you. My own Rockcliff kit, if you please.' He tapped the Gladstone bag with his toe. 'And I've arranged for us to try you out at the Harp ground.'

'But why, Terry?' These preparations, the interest displayed in me, and the manner in which Donohue had been unwillingly won over were extremely flattering, yet I was not to be taken in by them.

'Later, later, man. What's the use of going into it till we see what you can do?'

'No,' I said determinedly. 'I have to know how it'll effect me.'

'Didn't I tell you on my card?' Terence exploded. 'It's definitely going to be a good thing for you. Provided you're all we think you are, which now I'm beginning to doubt.'

That note of scepticism decided me. I agreed to go. Actually, I saw no harm in the expedition. And now I did want to show them what I could do. Because I disliked him and resented his association with Nora, Donohue especially I wished to convince. We left the buffet and got into a taxi from the rank outside the station. Trust Terry, I thought comfortably, to do things in style. My cousin had again impressed himself upon me with his charm and self-sufficiency.

Our objective lay quite far out in an eastern suburb of the city. After a drive of some twenty minutes it was revealed as a football ground belonging to the Harp Juniors Club. The neighbourhood, dominated by two huge gasometers and the contiguous gasworks, was poor and stank, not unnaturally, of gas. I had never heard of the Harp Juniors, and their domain, surrounded by a rusty corrugated iron fence in the process of falling down, enclosed an extremely worn football pitch and a small wooden pavilion. Surrounding the pitch there was, however, a cinder running-track.

'Here we are then,' Terence exclaimed enthusiastically, telling the taxi driver in an aside to wait. 'You stop by the track, Mart, and I'll go in with Laurence.'

We entered the pavilion, which was even less impressive than the ground. The floor-boards were bare and broken, a few old striped jerseys hung on pegs, dust was everywhere, also a strong odour of stale sweat, beer and urine.

The bag, when snapped open, revealed shorts, singlet and spiked running-shoes. Solicitously aided by Terence, who had constituted himself my valet, I began to change. Everything fitted well except the shoes which were too long, leaving an inch of soft leather beyond my toes. I pointed this out to Terence.

'It's not a bad thing,' he said, with an expert's judiciousness. 'It'll give you more spring.'

We went outside. Donohue was strolling up and down, with his hands in his pockets and an air of expectancy. He had lit up a sporty-looking cheroot.

'There he is,' Terence exclaimed, pushing me forward. 'And doesn't he look a runner, every inch of him.'

'By God, he does. He has the height. And look at those legs.'

Donohue's tone, in which I sensed a grudging respect, was highly gratifying. Actually in this lightweight kit with the Rockcliff colours I felt that I should not disappoint them. I took a few preliminary paces.

'That's right, limber up, man.'

'Only don't weaken yourself,' Donohue said, momentarily choking over his cheroot.

'Now, Laurie.' Terence, with a glance that seemed to repress D.'s enthusiasm, put one hand on my shoulder. In the other he held his watch. 'Four times round this track is exactly one mile. Are you ready?'

'Yes.'

'Then get set.' He stood back, eyes on the watch. 'Go!'

I made a good start and, doing my level best, went round the track four times. The sandwich I had just eaten troubled me somewhat on the final two circuits and Terry's shoes, while bending freely on the hard cinders, had less spring in them than he had promised. When I drew up, pale and panting, I felt dissatisfied with my performance. Apparently I was mistaken. Bent over the watch Terence gave out a whoop of delight.

'Well run, man. I knew you'd be right for us, and you are.'

Not a whit behind, Donohue slapped me heartily on the back. Still gasping, I flushed with pleasure.

'What was my time?'

Terence put a finger to his lips.

'Not a word about that at the moment. You'll see why. Now away and change. The water seems cut off in the pavilion but give yourself a good rub down, there's a towel in the bag.'

Ten minutes later we were in the taxi on our way back to the city. As we rolled along Terence turned to me in an extremely confidential way.

'Now listen to me, man.' He spoke in a guarded tone, as though he feared the driver might overhear. 'There's a sports meeting coming up the beginning of August at Berwick-on-Tweed. It's a small country affair and it's mostly no-account clodhoppers who enter for it. But,' he eyed me keenly, 'there's a lot of betting goes on and Martin, as you know, is in just that line of business. Our idea is to enter you for the mile. We've studied the local form and from what you've shown us today we're convinced you can do it.'

'Win?' I exclaimed.

'The cup.' Seriously, he inclined his head, adding even more impressively, 'And win a packet as well. We'll take care of the money angle. Martin'll handle the bets. And you'll be ten quid to the good.'

'Ten pounds!' It was more than tempting—a dazzling amount. 'But, Terry, I'm taking my examination the first week in August. On the seventh.'

'The sports are on the fifth. Two whole days before. It's no more than a three-hour run from Winton and we'll get you there and back the same day. What's your worry?'

I bit my lip in agonized indecision. I wanted to win that cup, and I particularly wanted the ten pounds. My mother, in a recent letter, mentioning the flat she would take on her return, had bitterly regretted having sold our furniture when we left Ardfillan. Ten pounds would buy furniture, might even furnish a whole room. But how would Pin regard such an expedition, practically on the eve of the Ellison?

'Why, it'll do you a world of good to have a bit of a break before your exam.' Donohue must have read my thoughts. 'Of course, if you want to throw good money away I've another fellow in mind who'd jump at the chance.'

The thought of being supplanted was too much for me.

'I'll do it.'

'Good, man.' Terence shook my hand in congratulation. 'You'll find you won't regret it. All you have to do is keep your mind easy and do a little light running of an evening. Don't overtrain. And if you look in at the back of the hotel occasionally I'll see you get a few good steaks.'

Familiar thoroughfares were being traversed. I saw that we had passed the North British Station and were entering Mortonhall Street. Donohue lowered the window and dispensed with his cheroot. He glanced at me.

'Where would you like us to drop you?'

I judged it must be well past six o'clock, almost time for me to be starting for my session with Pin.

'Anywhere near Hillside Street.'

Obligingly, Terence told the driver to make a sweep round the Park. The taxi stopped at the foot of Gilmore Hill, not far from the University, and I got out.

'I'll be keeping in touch with you, man,' he shouted, as they drove off.

I walked towards Pin's lodging, still rather excited and with a pleasant feeling of importance. It was flattering to have been sought out by Terence, and to have confirmed my innate belief in my own exceptional fleetness of foot. This awareness of my own speed, first implanted in my consciousness when I ran for the doctor for my father, and fostered by my own efforts to maintain myself in condition, was well supported by material evidence, since when I trained with the Ardencaple Harriers I had twice won the race for boys under fourteen at the end of the season Annual Sports. Yes, this was unquestionably a special gift, comparable almost to the capacity for levitation bestowed by heaven on some of the rarer saints. Indeed, when I ran, in the rush of air occasioned by my transit, I not infrequently had the impression that I had temporarily lost contact with terra firma. In view of all this it seemed only just that I should capitalize on my advantages. Terry's handsome proposal was perfectly legitimate, and if Donohue wanted to bet on me that, too, while entirely his affair, was a permissible proceeding. Nevertheless, in its bearing on the Ellison my conscience was not altogether clear, and as I arrived at Hillside Street and climbed the stairs to Pin's room I decided I must let him have the final word. He was already seated at the table waiting for me, and turning over a sheaf of papers with every appearance of interest.

'Laurence,' he began immediately, motioning me to the other chair. 'I've been fortunate enough to get hold of the Ellison exam papers for the last ten years. They make advantageous reading.'

'Do they, sir?'

'In the first place, in six out of ten occasions the essay set was devoted exclusively to a Scottish historical character of the sixteenth century. In the second place, I observe that it is exactly ten years since the character selected was Mary, Queen of Scots.'

'What does that mean?'

'Nothing probably.' He smiled, tugging at his beard. 'Still, as a guess, I've an idea it would do us no harm to pay special heed to the fifteen hundreds with a little extra attention to that unfortunate young woman and her immediate circle. Andrew Lang would help us there. I got his biography from the Library today. And how he favours the poor creature!'

He was opening the book when, anxious to clear my mind, I spoke up.

'Just one thing before we begin, sir.'

I told him that my cousin had asked me to take part in a sports meeting in Berwick two days before the Ellison and that while I had provisionally accepted, if he thought this in any way likely to impair my chances I would immediately withdraw.

He considered, gazing at me with kindness. His face at that moment had a simple dignity that outweighed his absurd deformity, prosy sentimentality and old-maidish ways, and all at once I felt how much I liked him.

'Why, Laurence, I believe it would be the very thing for you. I always advise a break just before an exam. And a day in the open air would be perfect.'

This reasoned approval was a great relief. With renewed ardour I joined Pin in a fresh and more intensive examination of the character of Queen Elizabeth's cousin.

THIRTY

THAT SAME EVENING, when I finished my session with Pin and came out of the house into the street, Nora was not there. Quite often, when the weather was fine, she would walk across the Park to meet me and I would find her waiting under the lamp outside No. 212. Then, arm-in-arm, we would stroll back to the Crescent where Miss Donohue, who fancied her talent in this direction, and enjoyed a tasty bite, made welsh rarebit on toast, to which we drank cocoa. The concentrated application demanded of me by Pin had prevented further excursions to the country, nor had Nora herself proposed them. Although I sensed it only vaguely, never having grasped the full significance of these abandoned moments on the houseboat deck, Nora's attitude towards me had undergone a subtle yet material change. I felt that she was fonder of me than before, not quite in the same casual and mischievous way, but always encouraging me, and telling me how she hoped I might win the Ellison. She seemed suddenly to be older, more restrained, and while we kissed with tenderness, something I could not define was missing—solicitude had taken its place. Lately, indeed, I had begun to imagine that something was worrying Nora. Although she denied this and brushed aside my inquiries she often had an absent look and at times appeared thoroughly depressed. As it was more than a week—an unusually long interval—since I had seen her I decided to call in at Park Crescent on my way back.

Here, however, I was unlucky. There was no answer to the bell and though I took trouble to go round to the back court no light was showing in any of the windows. I hung about for a quarter of an hour vainly hoping that Nora or Miss Donohue would turn up. Then I set off along the Crescent towards Craig Hill. This was by no means my shortest route to Argyle Street, yet Craig Hill held a special attraction for me in the shape of a Jesuit church which, contrasting with the many conventional Pugin chapels of the city, was outstandingly attractive, at least to my mind, in a grim Romanesque style. Partly this was due to lack of funds, since the original design to marble the interior had been shelved, leaving stark arches and pillars of brickwork that cast medieval shadows across the nave. Moreover, in the late evening the church was usually empty, darkish and very silent, all of which I liked, and I will confess that I had the habit after leaving Park Crescent—it was in any case the nearest church—to enter this sanctuary not from pure religious fervour, which I could never claim, but, with a trusting heart, in order to solicit heavenly aid for success in the Ellison, without which I felt I would not have a chance.

This evening when I entered, I proceeded to my favourite side altar where there was a replica of Simone Martini's Madonna that I enjoyed looking at, which usually put me in a proper petitioning mood and induced me to part with a penny, if I had one, for a candle. Tonight, however, I could barely see it; all but one of the surrounding votive lights had gone out. A woman, opposite me, was presumably responsible for the single candle, since it was newly lit. Most holy women who lit candles were invariably discovered on their knees with beads between their fingers. But this woman, who was young, merely sat, staring straight ahead, as though hypnotized by the tiny flickering flame she had herself created. Surprise, rather than curiosity, caused me to concentrate my vision through the intervening gloom, then, all at once, with a start of pleasure and surprise, I saw that it was Nora.

I could scarcely believe it. Nora was not devout. I had now discovered that she was careless about such things as not eating meat on Fridays and her Easter duties. Indeed, she was apt to make jokes about holy water and holy smoke that worried me. Yet what happiness it gave me that, aware of my evening habit to light a candle, she should tonight actually have forestalled me and herself made the votive offering for my intention. My heart swelled with love and gratitude. Still unseen, I contemplated her with a rapture that here I usually reserved for heaven. Yet she too, against the background of the altar, her pale, pure profile, softened and made serious by her mood, was like a little madonna. I could wait no longer. Tiptoeing forward, I bent towards her and whispered.

'Thank you, Nora. Thank you for the candle . . . and everything.'

'Laurence,' she said, turning sharply.

'It's the nicest thing you could ever have done. I'll always remember it.'

She looked at me.

'Will you?'

'Yes, I will, Nora. Even if I don't get the Ellison. What made you think of it?'

She looked away.

'It seems I just did. I was sort of in that kind of mood. Strange, isn't it?'

'No, Nora. I believe it will help.'

'I hope you're right,' she said.

There was a silence.

'Do you want to stay longer?' I asked.

She shook her head. I smiled at her.

'Then let's go together.'

Outside, as we came down the steps of the church, I took her arm.

'What a lucky meeting, Nora. I called at the flat but there

was no answer. And it's ages since I've seen you. Shall I walk
back with you now?'

She stopped at the foot of the steps.

'I'm not going back yet. I've a message to do . . . for Miss
Donohue.'

'Where, Nora?'

'Why . . . down by Mortonhall Street.'

'I'll come with you.'

I spoke eagerly, prepared to step out. But she seemed to
hesitate and I wondered if my inadvertent discovery of her
offering for me had annoyed her, until a moment later she
said:

'Aren't you tired? You must be. After all that study and
everything.'

'I'd never be too tired to walk with you, Nora.'

'Oh, very well, then,' she said, after the slightest pause.
'Come along.'

We set off. Had there been the faintest note of impatience
in her tone? Impossible. Yet, glancing at her sideways, I
had the impression that she was not quite herself. The city
was enduring a midsummer heat wave and the evening was
still and stifling. Under the street lamps she was pale, with
a distant expression and darkish patches under her eyes. She
was also unusually silent. But I was dying to tell her about
my eventful day.

'I don't suppose you know that I've been running. And
that I'm entered for the Berwick Sports.'

'Yes, I did hear that was coming off. Apparently we're all
supposed to be going in the Gilhooleys' car.'

'You too?' I cried.

'It depends. To tell you the truth, dear Laurie,' she turned
to me, 'I've been a little off colour lately.'

'I'm terribly sorry. What is it?'

'Oh, just a bit out of sorts. I'm sure I'll be all right soon.'

'Then do come, Nora. The trip would be good for you.'

'Well, then, we'll see.'

We were at the end of Craig Hill and had turned into
Mortonhall Street, crowded, as usual, and thick with traffic.
Not far from Market Cross, near the Market Arcade, she
disengaged her arm.

'This is as far as I'm going.'

We stood on the pavement opposite the Arcade, a covered
passageway occupied by odd little interesting establish-

ments: a herbalist's, a queer sort of chemist's, even a fortune-teller and a naturalist's shop with live tortoises in the window. It was here that Mrs Tobin bought the ants' eggs for her goldfish.

'Before you go, Nora.' It was difficult, I didn't want to keep harping on the subject, but I simply had to get this out. 'Thanks again for your candle.'

Again I thought I had offended her. But no, as she stepped off the pavement she gave me a faint, wry smile.

'Well, Laurie, as you probably know, I'm not all that religious, but when you want a thing badly enough you'll try anything.'

I could not speak for an overflowing gratitude. Her manner, the very words she used, told me how much she was behind me in my effort. I waited till she had crossed the street, then, still uplifted, took my own short cut to Argyle Street and the Templar's Hall.

THIRTY-ONE

AT HALF PAST EIGHT on the morning of Saturday, August 5th, I set out for the Criterion Hotel. Although the sky was still grey, the softness in the air was refreshing after the recent heat. I had said nothing to Uncle Leo of my plans. The good news from my mother made me hope that, if all went well, I should not be with him long. Her appointment in the Department of Health was now assured and she expected to be back in Winton within the next few weeks. She would then surely terminate my stop-gap arrangement with Leo.

Although Terence had insisted on an early start I expected that I should have to wait, but when I approached the hotel I saw that the red car was already drawn up outside the entrance with Terence in the driver's seat and Miss Gilhooley beside him.

As I hurried forward Terence waved his arm in greeting.

'Glad to see you, man. How do you feel?'

'Fine, thank you, Terry.'

'Hop in the back then. The others won't be a minute, Nora's just gone in for a coffee.'

As I stepped into the rear seat Miss Gilhooley half turned

226

and exposed her gold teeth in a welcoming smile. She had on
a showy check coat and a flat saucer hat secured with her
favourite pink tulle. She might be Miss Donohue's best
customer, and undoubtedly her expenditure in Earle's was
lavish, yet I had never known anyone who contrived to look
so garish, an effect which she intensified by a variety of
vulgar affectations. She was always fluttering about, primp-
ing herself, touching up her hair, powdering her nose, looking in her handbag, patting herself in unexpected places,
examining her finger-nails, straining her neck, gesturing
with genteel flicks of her wrists or demanding unnecessary
attentions from Terence with an air of languishing feminine
charm. Miss Gilhooley was neither beautiful nor youthful
and her pretensions to these attributes together with her
habit of prefacing every other remark with the words 'I
always say . .' seriously offended me, even though she now
greeted me with gracious condescension.

'Good morning, young man. I hope you're going to make
a nice bit of cash for me today.'

'Are you in need of cash, Miss Gilhooley?'

Terence gave a loud laugh.

'He had you there, Josey. We all know what the name
Gilhooley stands for. But what's keeping Nora?'

'She must have had a rush getting here,' Miss Gilhooley
remarked. 'I always say you should never rush. She looked
quite faint too, the love. Pale as paper.'

A moment later Nora came through the swing doors of
the hotel followed by Donohue. Urged on impatiently by
Terence, who now got out and took up the starting-handle
from its leather strap, they joined me in the back of the car.

'Take the rug, Nora. There . . . on the rail. It may be
chilly. Wrap up well, I always say, before you start.' Miss
Gilhooley offered this advice as Terence, after several swings,
started the engine and, resuming his place at the steering-
wheel, set us in motion.

Nora, who was sitting in the middle between Donohue
and me, spread the rug over our knees. As she did so, she
smiled at me, but did not speak. The car moved off.

Actually this was my first experience of a private motor
and as we rolled through the main streets of Winton towards the Edinburgh road I gave myself up to the smooth
luxury of our progress. Terence was an excellent driver, it
seemed likely that he had driven this car many times, and I

could now surmise why Miss Gilhooley possessed attractions for him beyond her rather meagre physical charms. They were both in a festive mood, laughing and talking with a vivacity that contrasted notably with the almost total silence in the rear.

Now it was impossible not to recognize that the split between Nora and Donohue had widened. While he did, presumably for the sake of appearances, address an occasional perfunctory remark to her, she barely answered, but continued to look ahead with a pale, set face. This did not suit Donohue at all and presently, with a shrug, he abruptly gave up this pretence and, leaning forward in his best manner, began to devote himself to Miss Gilhooley, whispering in her ear, making her laugh, and competing with Terence for her attentions.

Nora gave no sign, her expression did not change, but after a time her hand moved under cover of the rug and sought out mine. Her fingers were so cold I began to chafe them.

'Are you all right, Nora?' She looked at me and nodded.

'I've been a bit off lately, but the fresh air's helping me. I just wish I hadn't taken that coffee.'

The others were so engaged, and Miss Gilhooley's spasms so shrill, there was no danger of our being overheard.

'Do you feel sick?'

'Just a little. It'll pass.'

I gazed at her with concern. She did not look herself at all. Had Donohue's defection upset her to such an extent?

'If you don't feel well you shouldn't have come.'

'I couldn't bear hanging about all day alone. Miss D.'s away buying in Manchester. And don't forget, I want to see you run.'

Did she really mean this? In her present state of mind I doubted if the race was even remotely in her thoughts.

At this point a diversion occurred. Terence had mistaken our route and now discovered, on consulting his map, that a wrong turn beyond Dunbar had taken us about fifteen miles off the direct route. Rather than risk getting lost in country lanes, it became necessary to go back to the coast road, a divergence which raised the question as to whether we should arrive in time for the start of the Sports at two o'clock. Conversation was now reduced as Terence pushed the car to its top speed, and with such effect that at twenty minutes past one we slipped through a narrow stone archway and entered Berwick-on-Tweed.

This was an old grey border borough, straddling the River Tweed where it entered the sea, with cobbled streets and twisting wynds, ringed by a medieval wall, with ramparts that overlooked the harbour. As we passed through the old arched gateway I felt at once that it would be a delightful place in which to wander round and dream. Today, however, it presented a scene of activity that was clearly unusual, the main street alive with people, the central square crowded with cars, wagonettes and farm carts, the entire town in a state of commotion that, from their comments, proved highly gratifying to Terence and Donohue.

'We must get a paper,' Terry said, drawing up beside a newsboy and tossing him a coin. It was a small double sheet —I saw the name: *Berwick Advertiser*—and Terence scanned it quickly.

'Is it in?' Donohue asked, craning forward.

'It is,' Terence answered. 'And it's good.'

They both examined the page with every appearance of satisfaction until Miss Gilhooley, peeved at her temporary desertion, exclaimed:

'Look here, you two, when are we going to get lunch? That looks like some kind of a hotel over there.'

'No, Josey dear,' Terence said. 'The food there would kill you. We'll run down to the sports field, have a drink and a snack in the marquee, and on the way home we'll stop in Edinburgh for a big blow-out at F. & F.'s.'

I experienced a premonitory thrill. F. & F.'s, the smart name for Ferguson and Forrester's, was the most famous restaurant in Edinburgh. Terence was certainly going to treat us well. Before starting off again he turned and, with a smile of approbation, handed me the paper, pointing to the centre of the page.

'Take a look, young fellow-my-lad. That'll show you what they think of you here.'

It was a conspicuous box paragraph in a section devoted entirely to the Sports, giving the times of the races, the names of the runners, and the probable betting odds.

A Dark Horse for the Mile

The general belief that the Open Mile lies between Peter Simms, last year's runner-up, and the present holder, hardy veteran Harry Purves, may be rudely shattered just after 4 p.m. today by a young stripling from the West in the person of Laurence Carroll. This ex-schoolboy, who will be in the Rockcliff colours, was recently timed over the measured distance at the ground of the Harp J.C. and rumour hath it, much to the annoyance of his trainer, that young Carroll showed a clean pair of heels to the record. This will not be a long shot now, but for my money it's the best thing on the card.

Glowing with pride, I lowered the paper. I wanted to show it to Nora, but now, bumping over a rough track, we had joined the crowd already making for the sports field, and she was leaning forward, supporting herself against the handrail on the back of the front seat. I folded the paper carefully and put it in my pocket. I would show it to her later; in any case, it was something I wanted to keep.

Presently we came to the field, an expanse of flat, cropped downland stretching along the cliffs, neatly railed off, marked out with limewash and gay with flags, marquees and a variety of booths that gave the place the air of a county fair. On one side was a small golf course, on the other the open sea. The situation appealed to me and the fresh breeze blowing in from the ocean stirred my blood. I knew that I could do well here. I jumped out of the car and, while Miss Gilhooley and Nora went off to the refreshment marquee, began to help untie the gear from the luggage grid. Terence had not parked the car in the regular enclosure but behind the row where the bookmakers were putting up their stands. And now, as Donohue began to set up his board and a kind of platform made of sections that fitted together, Terence said: 'Mart, don't you want a sandwich first?'

'Later,' Donohue said. 'You go . . . and take him.'

As the principal participant in the great event of our day, this oblique and somewhat slighting reference to myself was not particularly agreeable. When I went off with Terence I said:

'I daresay I should be careful what I eat. And not too much either.'

'All you'll get here won't hurt you.'

The truth of these words was borne out when we joined Nora and Miss Gilhooley at a long crowded bar. Miss Gilhooley had an outraged air.

'This is the giddy limit, Terry. What a low-down mob. And there seems to be nothing but sausage rolls.'

'Just put up with it,' Terence said, placatingly. 'You'll have lobster and champagne tonight.'

'Tonight's a long way off. And here's Nora, sick as a dog, she ought to have a cognac. I always say there's nothing like cognac to settle the stomach.'

'Do you want a brandy, Nora?'

She shook her head. She did look sick and unutterably miserable too.

'If I'm to have something I'd rather try some gin.'

'All right.' He pointed to a table in the corner of the tent. 'Both of you go and sit over there.'

Terry, who was extremely good at that sort of thing, managed to get two plates of assorted food and some drinks. Between us we carried them over to the table. Nora drank the gin but did not eat anything. Miss Gilhooley ate half a sandwich, then, with an air of wounded refinement, discarded the other half. I had a couple of sausage rolls sanctioned by Terence who finished what remained of the sandwiches, even absently consuming the half left by Miss Gilhooley. He then produced a round competitor's tag and handed it to me.

'That'll take you into the changing-tent. I have your togs in the car. Get there in good time.' He got up. 'Come along, Josey dear, we'll go out for a breath of air.'

As they went off together, I tied the tag to the lapel of my jacket. I was glad to be alone with Nora, anxious to discover exactly why she was so upset. Then, raising my head, I saw that Donohue had come into the marquee and was advancing towards us. He sat down, and glancing at me as though he wished I wasn't there, said uncomfortably:

'I'm just going to start work. I thought I'd see how you were first.'

I thought Nora wasn't going to answer, but after a moment she said, stiff-lipped:

'Aren't you a bit late? If you do want to know, I'm feeling awful.'

'Can I get you something? A gin.'

'I'm sick of drinking gin. I seem to have been living on the blasted stuff. And you know I hate it.'

'Now, Nora . . . pull yourself together. Things may not be as bad as all that.'

'I'm glad you think so.'

I wanted to get away from this quarrel but the bench Donohue was sitting on wedged me in. I had to listen as, trying to control his temper, he sad:

'Don't be a bloody wet blanket, Nora. For God's sake make an effort. The party tonight will buck you up.'

'I'm not going to the party,' Nora said.

'What!'

'No, I'm not. I'm going to stay here in this marquee and if I don't feel any better I'm not going back by car. I'm going to take the train home.'

'What train?'

'The ten to six express. Yes, I mean it. I thought I mightn't stick it out all day so I looked up the timetable before we left.'

'You're not coming back with me?'

'No. And don't look at me like that.'

'Not so long ago you were glad enough for me to look at you.'

'That's all finished now. And you are too. Finished and done with.'

Donohue was silent. Then he gave her a long hard stare.

'Well,' he said. 'If that's how you want it, go ahead.' He stood up and pulled at my arm. 'Come on, you. It's time I got you over to the secretary's office. I don't know why the hell everything falls on me. If we don't confirm your entry, that'll be a washout too.'

We left Nora and went to the office, a square tent near the finishing line. Outside, Donohue paused and said, warningly:

'Don't let on who brought you here.'

'Why, aren't you coming in too?'

'I've got my book to make,' he said. As he was turning away he suddenly stopped. 'And listen, if they ask you what your age is, you're sixteen past.'

'But I'm not sixteen till the second of next month.'

'You are now, you stupid young bastard, or you'll be disqualified before the race. And if that happens I'll break your bloody neck.'

I stared after him in angry dismay. What right had he to treat me like that? And what was all this pretence about my age?

Still indignant, I went into the tent. The secretary was

a short, red-faced man, wearing a Hawick tweed knicker-bocker suit and a club tie. He made no disagreeable inquiries, indeed, when I signed my name in the book he looked at me with interest and held out his hand.

'We want more of your sort here.' He smiled, salving my damaged pride. 'Good luck.'

When I came out Donohue had gone to his stand. Terence and Miss Gilhooley were still not in evidence. It was almost two o'clock and all the bookmakers had begun to call the odds. I walked slowly along the line, noting that the prices for the main event, the mile, were already chalked up on the boards. My self-esteem was further restored as I observed that I had been made joint favourite with Purves at evens, with Simms at two to one behind us. Indeed at one board I was quoted at evens with Simms and Purves both at two to one. I had now had quite enough of Donohue, I did not go near his stand, but from the crowd around him he appeared to be doing a roaring trade.

The report of a pistol shot split the air. The first event had begun. Pressing forward to the rails I saw that it was the first heat of the hundred yards. Almost at once the second heat came up. I wanted to go to Nora, she was terribly on my mind, intermingled confusedly with a number of other worries that had begun to trouble me. Yet I felt that she wanted to be left alone and that any interference on my part would only make things worse. A strange passivity had come over me, an indefinable impression that I had been caught up by circumstances in which I could do nothing but submit. I remained at the rails and continued to watch the races.

As time went on and one event succeeded another, my nerves tightened. Restlessly, I moved my feet, and bent my knees, restoring elasticity to my legs. My moment of truth was approaching, I must not be late. Edging out of the crowd I retrieved the Gladstone bag containing my togs from the car, then walked along the bookmakers' row to the changing-tent, encouraged by the fact that I was permanently installed as favourite at evens. More people than ever were gathered round Donohue now, hands reaching out, clamouring to place their bets. Curiosity alone caused me to glance at his board. I could not believe it. With a painful shock I saw that, chalked up in plain figures, he was giving odds of five to one against me. Even as I went by, he rubbed out the five and made it six. At that, the crowd around his board increased.

I entered the tent in a state of absolute incomprehension. The thing was meaningless. Had Donohue gone out of his mind? From the outset, every step taken had been premised on the certainty that I would win and now, if I did, he would pay out six times what he took in. Suddenly, as I stood in a maze of mystification, a hearty grip brought me to myself. A lean elderly man, bald as a coot, with a thin weather-beaten face, wearing a red and blue striped jersey and old washed-out tight trunks that clung like a second skin to his sinewy legs, was shaking me by the hand.

'I'm Purves.' He grinned, nodding towards the bench at the back of the tent. 'And that's Simms. I hear you're going to knock the stuffing out of us old timers.'

Simms, in the process of stripping and practically naked, came forward. He was a much younger man than Purves, about twenty-six or -seven, solidly built, with short muscular limbs and a thick chest covered with a moss of matted black hair. He did not look particularly dangerous, he was altogether too heavy. As for Purves, why, the thing was ridiculous, he was virtually an old man.

'Well, good luck, youngster,' Simms was saying, good-naturedly. 'May the best man win and devil take the hindmost.'

'Better get shifted, lad,' Purves said. 'The bell will be going soon.'

I began to change. Some others were on the benches pulling on singlets or lacing up running-shoes. A lanky youth, addressed as Chuck, whom I guessed to be about seventeen, was the only one near my own age. Most of my rivals seemed on intimate terms and, from their jocular references to past events, regular competitors at all the Border meetings. Beyond that I scarcely noticed them. Out of the turmoil in my mind one clear certainty had emerged. Whatever trickery Donohue was up to would be scotched if I won the race. I took a long deep breath. I had come to win, I had promised to win, and by heaven I would win!

The clanging of a bell summoned us from the tent. When we filed out I counted the runners: we were eight altogether. Outside, we drew lots from a hat for positions. My slip, number 4, was at least moderately good. Then we came through a narrow opening in the railings into the arena. Hitherto I had not realized the full size of the crowd; now, with intimidating force, it struck me as enormous: a great massed ring of watching faces. But strangely, that ring receded as we lined up on the curved white starting line. Leaning slightly forward, my eardrums tense for the starter's pistol, I was conscious only of the sun shining on the grassy track stretching in a wide oval before me, and of the fact that three circuits made the mile.

Crack! I was off with the shot, sprinting across to the inside of the track and, as I had intended, taking the lead from the start. The rapid pad of footsteps behind did not disturb me. I was ahead and meant to stay there. Moving freely in the cool fresh air, I felt I could go on like this for ever. How quickly the first circuit was completed. And now, as from a distance, but deliciously, in a foretaste of triumph, I began to hear my name shouted and repeated. I was halfway round on the second lap when a runner, neither Simms nor Purves, but an unknown and unfavoured contestant, unexpectedly thrust past me by a good three yards. Impossible to submit to such an insult. To the accompaniment of further wildly excited shouts I spurted hard, and with a burst of speed left him again behind.

But now the air was suddenly less cool and the movements of my limbs scarcely so elegant or easy. Nevertheless, the second circuit was achieved, I was still ahead, and only the final lap remained. Head up, heart pumping, I pounded on, conscious that I was flagging but praying that I could hold my lead. Alas, that prayer produced no answer from the celestial powers to whom it was addressed. I was no more than halfway home on the last round when, with a tremendous rush, Purves shot past me, his leathery legs going like pistons, elbows flailing the air. Slogging along closely behind him came Simms and two others. I tried but could not match this mass assault. My own legs, if indeed they now belonged to me, for they were entirely without feeling, would not respond. My lungs were bursting, my throat choked and raw. I knew that I was done. My name, no longer shouted, sunk in obloquy, was lost in the roar, dimly heard through the red haze that swam before me, of 'Purves, Daddy Purves!'

Still going, but blindly now, I had the vague consciousness of more shadowy forms gliding past me. As I staggered across the broken tape, only a single runner, one lone laggard, the youth called Chuck, was behind me. I had finished second last.

Mercifully the changing-tent was near. Beat to the world, humiliated to the verge of tears, I tottered into it and hid myself. As I sat, bowed, with heaving chest, on the bench, Daddy Purves tried to console me.

'The mile's not your distance, boy. You'd have done well in the half. But never mind, you've years ahead of you.'

I felt his kindness but could not respond to it. What a fool I had been, Terence too, to imagine that at my age, untrained, out of condition, I could compete with men, experienced runners, who did the Border Circuit, who were in a sense professionals. At last I pulled myself up, got into my clothes, flung my sodden togs into the bag and went outside.

Immediately, I ran into Terence. He had been waiting for me and before I could utter one word of abject apology he took me by the lapel of my jacket.

'What a time you've been!' he exclaimed, urgently, and before I could speak went on: 'Now listen, Laurence. You're not to come near Donohue or any of us. Don't come to the car. Not on any account.'

'Why not?' I faltered. 'Because I didn't win?'

'No, you idiot!' He hesitated, looked about him, and lowered his voice. 'As a matter of fact, there's been a spot of trouble over the bets. And it's much safer for you to keep out of it. It's all that damned Donohue's fault. What I thought was just going to be a lark has turned nasty. So what you'll do is this . . . you'll walk quietly into the town now and wait for us at the Archway. Remember where we came into the town?'

'Yes.'

'Right, then. We'll pick you up there with the car in less than an hour. Here's a pound note if you want to have a snack or anything while you're waiting.'

'I'm sorry I lost, Terry.' Anguished, I managed to get it out at last.

He stared at me in a curious manner then, without a word, swung round and hurried off.

For a moment I stood watching him disappear in the crowd then, with bent head, carrying the Gladstone bag, I slunk out of the ground by the golf course exit and started to trudge along the field road towards the town.

THIRTY-TWO

THE ROAD AHEAD, to my relief, was almost clear. Since the Sports did not finish until five o'clock and the time now was not more than half past four, only a few spectators had begun to leave the ground. Dead tired, I walked slowly, so sunk in my own gloom that at first I had no consciousness of the figure, walking with equal languor, not far ahead of me. But suddenly, I saw who it was and, hurrying forward, called out:

'Nora.'

'It's you!' She had turned, surprised. 'Have you left the others?'

I nodded miserably.

'Terence told me to keep away from them. I'm to meet them at the Archway in the town.'

'Why to keep away from them?'

'They're having trouble over my bets.'

She considered me palely, but with compressed lips.

'Did you win the race?'

'No, I didn't, Nora. I was practically last. They were all men, far older than me. I didn't have a chance, in spite of all it said in the paper.'

'What paper?'

We were now moving along the road together. I took the *Berwick Advertiser* from my pocket, unfolded it and showed her the box paragraph.

She read it, looked at me, read it again then stared straight ahead. Under her breath she murmured something with such anguished bitterness, I felt relieved not to hear it. After that she was silent for a moment, then she seemed to draw herself together.

'My poor Laurence. You're not going to meet them at the Archway. You're coming home in the train with me.'

This was an unexpected, brightening prospect.

'But won't they . . . keep on waiting for me?'

'They won't. Don't worry about them, for they aren't worrying about us.'

'When is the train, Nora?'

'Ten minutes to six.'

'Won't we have to change at Edinburgh?'

'No. Luckily, it's a through express. Before we leave we'll have time to get you something to eat.'

'You, too, Nora.' When she did not answer, I added anxiously: 'Are you still sick?'

'I'm not altogether at the top of my form, dear Laurie. But I'm doing my best to get over it.' She moistened her lips and made a fair attempt at a smile. 'We've both been messed about a bit lately, but if we stick together we'll come out of it all right.'

Taking it very slowly, for Nora apparently did not wish to hurry, nor for that matter did I, we reached the town. I had thought that all of Berwick had gone to the Sports but here the streets were swarming with people, many of whom appeared to have come in from the surrounding country, and in an open space near the central square a sort of fair, with roundabouts, had been set up.

'It's fearfully busy,' Nora said. 'It must be some kind of holiday.'

Looking around for a place where we could have a meal, she stopped outside a small restaurant with a bill in the window marked: *Tweed Salmon, Boiled or Grilled, 1/6 the cut.*

'You'd like that, wouldn't you?'

'Very much,' I said. 'Especially grilled.' I had not tasted salmon since the days of those affluent lunches, now seemingly so distant, with Miss Greville.

We went inside. It was a simple eating-house, steamy from the kitchen, and so full that we had difficulty in finding places. Nora ordered salmon for me and a pot of tea for herself.

'Eat something, Nora,' I begged her. 'Please do.'

She simply shook her head.

While we were waiting to be served, I said:

'I still can't understand why Terence said they were in trouble.'

'Laurence, dear,' she said. 'We won't go into it now. It was simply a dirty little trick to make some dirty money. They knew all along you had no chance of winning. But don't blame Terence too much—he's soft and selfish, but he's not a bad sort at heart. It was just fun to him. Donohue's the one who's to blame. He thought it all out.' Her voice hardened. 'I hope he gets well beaten by the crowd. But he won't. He'll get away with it, as usual.'

She took out her handkerchief and wiped her forehead. She was breathing quickly.

My salmon came at last. Served with a dish of potatoes boiled in their jackets, and slapped down before me by a man in his shirtsleeves, it was a noble cut from as good a fish as ever came out of the Tweed. I suddenly discovered that I was starving, and for a brief but active interlude my troubles receded. Only when I had practically finished did I observe that Nora had pushed her tea away untasted.

'It's so hot in here,' she said, by way of excuse. 'I think I'll go and wash.'

I watched her with concern. She was so unlike herself, even in her way of walking, that I decided that the sooner we were in the train the better. While she was away I asked the man for the bill. This came to 2/9 and I paid it with the note Terence had given me, adding a threepenny tip from the change.

We started up the main street for the railway station. Unfortunately, this was situated at the summit of the incline on which the town was built. Although she made no remark, I could feel that Nora did not like the climb. But presently we arrived and found the booking office open. I told myself that she would be all right when we were in the train.

Nora took out her purse and asked for two third-class singles for Winton.

'Thirty two and ninepence, please.'

The clerk selected two pasteboard tickets from the rack, twirled the little black stamping machine on the ledge and was about to snap the two tickets into the slot when he looked up.

'You want them dated for Monday? The early train leaves at seven fifteen a.m.'

'Monday!' Nora exclaimed. 'We're going with the ten to six train tonight.'

He shook his head.

'There's no ten to six tonight.'

'But there is,' Nora protested. 'I looked it up specially in Murray's Diary.'

Silently he produced a timetable, leaned forward and, removing the pencil from behind his ear, pointed to the page.

'You see that little star, miss. Except Sundays and bank holidays. And today, Fair Saturday, is the biggest bank holiday of the lot.'

Watching Nora anxiously, I saw what a shock this was to her. She seemed to shrink into herself.

'Surely there's another train?'

'Nothing, miss. And nothing tomorrow either.' Detaching himself from us completely he began to add up figures on a pad.

Nora supported herself against the ledge. I thought she was going to faint. An icy shiver contracted my skin.

'Nora, we'll have to hurry back to the Archway. Terence might still be waiting there.'

'No,' she said, hopelessly. 'They're sure to have gone.'

'We must try. We must.'

The Archway was not far from the station. We were soon there and for nearly an hour we stood waiting, straining our eyes for the red car, never speaking a word, elbowed by the passing crowds, while the holiday traffic of the main street rolled and rattled past. Now it was almost dark.

'It's no use.' Nora spoke at last in a beaten voice. 'They probably had to run for it, and they have.'

'Then what are we to do?' I said, desperately. 'Can we hire a car to Edinburgh? And take a train from there.'

'Even if we could, I couldn't stand the journey.' All at once she broke down and began to cry. 'Laurence, I've kept up all day feeling like death, but I can't, I can't go on any longer. I've got such a bad stitch in my side if I don't lie down soon I'll drop. We must find some place to stay the night.'

A sensation of unutterable consternation left me dumb. All sorts of weird contingencies flashed through my mind. Would that booking clerk allow us to stay in the station waiting-room, or could we perhaps find some sort of shelter in the local park? Then I saw her look of collapse as she stood with one hand pressed against her side. I knew that she must find a room in a hotel.

The hotel in the main square behind the fairground, despite Terry's slighting comment, had seemed altogether reputable. I took Nora by the arm—she now seemed incapable of voluntary movement—and brought her down the street to the square. The hotel had a sign: The Berwick Cockle. Streams of boisterous country folk were moving in and out yet I managed to steer Nora through the crush into the red-carpeted hall. After the street it seemed a blessed sanctuary. But the man in the little glass office scarcely looked at us. The hotel was full, he said, full to the doors, they had been turning people away all day.

We went out. Across the square was a much smaller inn, the Masons' Arms. Leaving Nora outside, with instructions not to move, I squeezed my way into the crowded, smoke-filled lobby. It was packed with groups of men standing with glasses in their hands, laughing and talking at the pitch of their lungs. No one took the least notice of me. I spoke to several men, asking for the office, before one pointed with his pipe to a plump, yellow-haired woman in a black dress whom, from her general air of sociability, I had assumed to be part of this convivial gathering. I pushed my way towards her and with some difficulty succeeded in catching her eye. She had a red, amiable face that encouraged me. But my heart sank as she shook her head.

'You'll not find a room in Berwick tonight, lad. Not one.'

'Is there no place you can think of?' I pleaded. 'Anywhere at all.'

'You might try Spittal, across the river,' she said, doubt-fully. 'There's a pub there, just over the bridge, called the Drovers' Rest. They might give you a bed.'

'How do I get there?'

'Turn second on the right. Down Cooper's Alley. It's just over the old bridge.'

Outside again, I took Nora's arm. She was silent, un-resistant, almost lost, hand still pressed against her side. The town was now in a ferment, crowds milling in the square, the fair in full swing, music from the roundabouts splitting the night air. Twice I took the wrong turning and had to get back to the main street but in the end I found Cooper's Alley. And there at the foot of the hill was the river, dark and smooth, rushing out with the tide. We crossed a narrow humpbacked bridge and came to Spittal village. Here a merciful sense of quiet prevailed, a smell of seaweed and the blessed coolness of salt air. The masts of fishing smacks stood out against the glare of Berwick as I helped Nora along the cobbled quay.

Quite soon we came to the Drovers' Rest. It was an old brick building, poorly lit and with few signs of accommo-dation. With nothing to distinguish it from an ordinary public house it did not give me much hope. Inside we were faced with a narrow stone passage that led to the bar. The sounds of voices, raised in discussion, emerged. I did not want to take Nora there. On the right was a door marked *Private*. I knocked, and presently an old man appeared. He was in his slippers, wearing a long knitted blue spencer and he had in his hand a dog-eared copy of *Chambers' Journal*. So overstrained were my sensibilities, I registered these unessential details as, simultaneously, desperately, I burst out:

'We've been to the Sports and missed our train home. Please give my cousin a room. She's not feeling well. I'll sleep anywhere you like.'

While, with palpitating heart, I held out the Gladstone bag conspicuously as evidence of our respectability, he examined us over his spectacles. He glanced from one to the other of us and I knew in my bones that he was about to refuse. I saw it in his face.

Just then a woman came out of the bar. She was about thirty, plainly dressed in a blouse and skirt, carrying an empty tray under her arm. She had a decent, competent look.

'What's the rub, Father?' she asked.

'This pair want a room.'

'What!' she exclaimed, shocked. 'Together?'

'No, m'am,' I burst out. 'Only for my cousin. I'll walk about outside if you like.'

There was a silence.

'Ye say you've been to the Sports,' the old man said.

'Yes, sir.' To authenticate the fact I martyred myself. 'Harry Purves won the mile.'

The woman had been looking at Nora, then at me.

'They're all right, Father,' she said suddenly. 'She can have Number 3. and the boy'll shake down in the boxroom. But no tricks, mind you, or I'll throw you both out myself.'

My chest heaved, I gave a great gasp of relief. Before I could thank her she had gone back into the bar. The old man shuffled into the room and brought out a key. We followed him upstairs where he opened the door of a small single room. It was a poor room, sparsely furnished, with faded wallpaper, and a cracked ewer, but the floor-boards were scrubbed and the bed-linen fresh and clean. Altogether my survey assured me, with relief and pride, that in our extremity I had done well for Nora.

'You'll sleep well here,' I said, forced to keep my tone impersonal. 'And be all right in the morning.'

'Oh yes, thank you, Laurie.' She managed a faint, pale smile. 'Just to be able to lie down and rest.'

'Don't you want to leave that with her?' The old man was eyeing the bag, which I still clutched in a permanent spasm.

'Yes, of course,' I agreed hurriedly, though it was no use to either of us.

I wanted to say more to Nora, beyond everything I longed to kiss those soft blanched lips, gently, with all the tenderness of my loving heart. But the old man still had his eye on us, though now with less suspicion. I simply said good night, and went out of the room with him. As we moved along the passage, I heard the closing of her door.

THIRTY-THREE

MY FUTILE EXERTIONS in that disastrous race and the struggle to find a lodging had left me almost dead with fatigue. The mattress on which I lay, on the floor of the boxroom, was not uncomfortable. Yet I couldn't sleep. Round and round, inextricably tangled, the events of this most unnatural day kept spinning inside my head. What a fool I had been, what a *soft mark*, so easily, so willingly duped, flattered into the belief that I was a paragon who must win today. And what ironic diversion my idiotic credulity must have afforded Terence and Donohue as, from that first farcical trial at the Harp football ground, they led me on, with serious faces, stuffing me for the slaughter. Why did I lack the common sense to see that while I might run well enough for my age, competition against seasoned professionals who habitually made the rounds of all the Border sports was lunacy? From the beginning it had been a hoax and it ended as a swindle. Donohue had planted the paragraph in the local paper and by offering excessive odds against me, had cashed in heavily on my defeat. If only I had won, and made him pay out five times over, ruined him in fact, what a triumph it would have been, not for me alone but for Nora too, since from her own words, I knew that she must hate him. But that, like most other things I had wanted in my life, was beyond me, an achievement realized only in my dreams, never by accomplishment.

Tortured by my own inadequacy I turned restlessly on the mattress. It was evident that I had been born to fail and to be imposed upon. A sudden recollection, as from a distant world, of the Ellison added to my distress, less on account of the difficulty in getting to the University on Monday—the early train would be in Winton at least by noon—than from the settled conviction that, as I had failed in the race, I would fail there too. Pin had led me on, not like Donohue, but from the best motives, merely to improve the standard of my education.

At this point, I drifted into a troubled sleep, but not for long. Suddenly my brain snapped back to consciousness with the startled impression that someone was calling my name. I raised myself on my elbow, listening in the darkness. Sounds from the bar beneath and the distant hum of the fair in Berwick both had ceased. The faint scratching of a mouse somewhere in the room intensified the stillness. I was about to lie down again, convinced that I was mistaken, when again I fancied I heard someone call.

I jumped up, knocking my shins hard on the sharp edge of an unseen object, and felt my way to the door. Undecided, I stood there, listening with my ear against the panel, but hearing nothing. Yet if someone had called me it could only be Nora. Guardedly I opened my door. The corridor was in darkness, but halfway along a faint sliver of light showed beneath the door of her room.

I had not undressed, having merely taken off my jacket and my boots. Now, moving softly in my socks, I advanced to the lighted door and tapped on it with a finger-nail. There was no response.

'Nora,' I whispered. 'Are you there?'

Her voice came back to me, indistinctly yet with an unmistakable appeal. I turned the handle and went in.

She was lying sideways on the bed with nothing on but her chemise, which had rucked up above her knees. Her eyes were shut and her hands half clenched. The sheets and blankets of the bed, tumbled in a heap, were bunched in disorder on the floor. Worst of all was the strained, sunken greyness of her face. She looked older, almost ugly, scarcely recognizable.

'Nora,' I faltered. 'You called me.'

She half opened her eyes.

'I couldn't stand it alone any longer. I've such a pain.'

'Where, Nora?'

She made a gesture towards her stomach, but lower. She was obviously in severe pain. A fear that had hovered in the back of my mind during the day now took formidable shape. I might be a fool and a failure but, thank God, I had enough sense to know about appendicitis. I went forward to the bed.

'Do you still feel sick?'

'Yes. I feel awful.'

'Nora.' I tried not to alarm her. 'We'll have to get help.'

Still pressing her side, she did not answer. I took her free hand. It was hot, the palm moist with sweat.

'We've got to find out, it's dangerous not to. You must have the doctor.'

'Oh, not yet.' She gasped in another spasm. 'We'll wait for a bit.'

'We must,' I pleaded.

'It's the middle of the night. You'll get no one to come. I'd rather stick it out by myself. Just stay with me.'

'But, Nora . . .' I broke off, aghast that she wouldn't let me go for assistance.

'Please stay. If only you'll get me up to walk about the room, that might get rid of the pain.'

She raised herself on one elbow and put her other arm on my shoulders. While I supported her, I was conscious of a bad, unhealthy smell in the room. Then I noticed that the Gladstone bag was open and empty. My white singlet and shorts were lying, sodden and terribly soiled, a dirty brownish colour, in the corner.

I thought she had been sick on them and that decided me. I put her back on the pillow. Without a word I went out and downstairs to the room marked *Private*. I knocked hard on the door, then, as no one answered, I turned the handle and went into the room, found the switch and put on the light. I was in a small comfortably furnished sitting-room. A clock, ticking on the mantelpiece, caught my eye. The time was half past two oclock in the morning. Another door, almost hidden by a curtain, led me into the kitchen where, starting up from its basket before the red embers of a fire, a small dog began to bark and growl at me. Suddenly a sharp voice called out.

'Who's there?'

I called back, saying who I was, and that I needed help at

once. For some minutes nothing happened, then, to my immense relief, the woman, who was the old man's daughter, entered the kitchen. Still tugging at the cord of her wrapper, she quietened the dog and stared at me angrily, her eyes swollen with sleep, her hair, in a thick plait tied at the end with tape, hanging down her back.

'My cousin's terribly ill and in great pain.' I got it out before she could start on me. 'I'm sure it's appendicitis.'

This silenced her: she was still angry, but could not quite bring herself to abuse me.

'Oh, Lord,' she groaned. 'Why did I ever let you in?'

'It's awful to have to trouble you. But please come and see her. Or phone for the doctor now.'

Another silence, then she said:

'I'll have a look at her. Go on, you clown. Don't keep me standing here all night.'

I led the way upstairs and opened the door of Nora's room. The woman went in, at least she paused, one step beyond the threshold. Her gaze took in Nora, the disordered bed, the tumbled blankets, my soiled singlet in the corner, even the half full chamber-pot and some alarming stains on the sheets, which I had not noticed before. Then, in quite a different manner, a voice that suddenly chilled me, she said:

'Go to your room, you. And don't stir an inch out of it till I send for you.'

She shut the door in my face.

I could not disobey her, yet, back in the boxroom, I sat close to the door, in the darkness, listening, with every sense quivering and alert, afraid, dreadfully afraid for Nora. I shivered as I thought of her chalk-white face, so drained and sunken. I prayed that the doctor would come quickly. The operation for appendicitis was in itself serious and I knew also that if an inflamed appendix was not quickly removed it would burst, with fatal consequences.

The woman was still in the room with Nora; for perhaps ten minutes she had been there. Suddenly I heard her go downstairs. The boxroom was directly above the lower passage and its old floor-boards bare of any covering. Flattened out and straining my ears, I heard her go into what I guessed was the sitting-room. Almost at once she began to talk and although I could not distinguish the words I gave a quick sigh of relief. She was telephoning for the doctor.

This went on for some time and when it ended I heard her come upstairs again.

An interval elapsed, insufferably long, before the doctor arrived. He was not long in Nora's room. Almost at once he went down to the telephone. I knew, with a slight shudder, what that meant. Then I heard him on the stairs again.

Now a few streaks of dawn were beginning to creep into the boxroom, revealing a dusty clutter of boxes, mops, pails, odd pieces of broken furniture and other lumber. I went to the single window to watch for the ambulance. But when it swung into the still, grey street, I could bear it no longer. Retreating from the window I listened to the sounds of Nora's removal. I could not bring myself to look.

At last all was quiet again. I put on my boots and jacket, and half opened the boxroom door. I could hear nothing. Surely I couldn't be expected to go on enduring this suspense. Cautiously I came along the corridor. The woman was in Nora's room, with her sleeves rolled up and her hands on her hips, surveying a scene of appalling disorder.

Only one thought was in my mind. I said:

"Will she be all right?'

She spun round. Her face was a deep red, mottled and distorted with anger.

'I don't know and I don't care. You young blackguard, bringing that slut in here, messing up all my bed-linen, mucking the room so it must be scrubbed, and keeping me up half the night, and all for a two-faced little bitch you pretended was your cousin. I ought to turn you over to the police, that's what I ought. And I will too. Just like they'll be after her.'

I might be scared, yet I had to stand up for Nora.

'She couldn't help it.'

'Couldn't she? I'll swear she brought it on herself.'

What on earth did she mean? She must be mad with rage.

'Brought on what?'

'You young twister, don't pretend you don't know. She's had a filthy miss.'

I did not understand.

'A what?' I said.

'A lowdown dirty abortion from taking pills.' She shouted and caught me a stunning box on the ear that nearly knocked me down. But the brutal force of her words stunned me worse than the blow. Unable to speak, I stared at her dully, so shocked I lost all sense of where I was, or what was making me shake all over. Then something within me gave way. I covered my face with my arm and leaned against the passage wall.

THIRTY-FOUR

THE TRAIN, gathering speed after its stop at Glaisend, was on the last stage of its journey to Winton. Alone in the corner of the end third-class compartment I sat with commendable stillness, my hands on my knees, devoid of all sensation but that of profound apathy. For three hours I had been sitting like this, looking fixedly out of the window, dulled by the swift, confused passage of the landscape which served to block off or at least submerge the sluggish current of my thoughts. I hoped this state of blankness would not leave me. I encouraged it, when the scenery failed me, by staring at the advertisements on the opposite side of the compartment until they merged gradually into a mesmerizing blur. Now I'm looking at nothing, I thought, as though this sensation of visual and mental vacuum represented the summit of achievement.

Yet this stupor, a defence against the state of acute shock that I was in, did not always save me. And from time to time, fragments of fear and horror floated up like foul refuse to the surface of my mind. Then, the experience to which I had been subjected struck at me again. The net of deception that had entangled me was not the hardest to bear. Worse than that, worse even than my interrogation and detention by the police, when everything had come out, even the faking of the race, was the thought of Nora. I shuddered as once again the woman's voice rang through my head: 'Good-for-nothing little slut . . . fetch the police . . . tampering with herself . . . a mucking abortion . . .' Life was sordid and hateful, could I ever believe in anyone or anything again?

The suburbs of Winton were now drifting past, the train had begun to slacken speed, and the ticket inspector, sliding open the corridor door, was again in my compartment. With a start, I surrendered the ticket the police sergeant had given me that morning and which had already been punched three times.

'Winton next stop.' He was disposed to talk, since obviously he did not know that I had spent Sunday in Berwick gaol. 'You've had a long journey, lad. And an early start.'

I had to think a moment before I could find an answer.

'You have too, Inspector,' I said at last.

He laughed.

'That's my job. Are you going on holiday?'

'No,' I said, immediately, as though a button had been pressed, releasing the fixed idea in my mind. 'I'm on my way to the University to sit an examination, at two o'clock.'

'Are you now?' he said, impressed.

'I am. I've been working for it for three months.'

'I thought you looked a bit hard done by. Well, good luck to you, lad.'

I thanked him. He gave me a friendly nod and went out.

It was true, and I felt a strange relief to have openly established my intention. Perhaps, in my present state this was no more than an obsessive compulsion, the reflex to those months of constant preparation. Yet I knew that I had given my word to Pin, and after the shambles of that shameful week-end I must try to keep it. Nevertheless, while I understood what I must do, while my movements were directed almost involuntarily towards that objective, I occasionally had difficulty in identifying myself with the individual who must perform them. This tendency of my personality to fade out into a sort of exterior wasteland was a frightening sort of thing in which I seemed to lose myself completely and to wander alone, all identity gone, in a strange shadowy landscape. Yet it was not persistent, and when it passed, as now, I was again Laurence Carroll, possessed by the necessity of attending the University Hall, Gilmore Hill, W.1, at two o'clock precisely this afternoon.

The engine, with a last hissing expulsion of steam, jerked to a stop in Winton North British Station. Obscurely, I felt relieved that we had not come into the Central. I got out of my compartment and walked along the platform to the Queen Street exit, taking pains, as I did so, to confirm that the train had arrived at 12.40, only five minutes late. I had no need to hurry, everything would be performed in a well-regulated manner. Although my ticket had been given up, I still had some coins in my pocket and, as it seemed correct to sustain myself before taking the examination, it became obligatory for me to have lunch. Not far down, on the other side of the street, I saw a Rombach, one of a chain of modest Winton restaurants. I crossed over and entered.

The menu, in light blue typing, offered a choice of mutton chop, boiled ox tongue, or steak and kidney pie. Unhesitatingly I selected the chop and, when it was served, with peas and mashed potatoes, I ate it as though complying methodically with a fixed routine, quite unconscious of any appetite or sense of taste. Although I could not realize this, all my actions were now controlled by an automatism, certain prelude to nervous disintegration, which, even had I tried, I could not have resisted. A clock on the wall of the restaurant above the entrance kept me informed of the time and at twenty past one I asked for my check, paid it at the cashier's box and went out.

A green tram would take me to the foot of Gilmore Hill. They ran frequently on this route and presently one appeared. Although it was crowded with workers going home for lunch, I boarded it handily. But I had to stand during the journey and when we arrived at Gilmore Hill I was not feeling quite so competent, particularly in the management of my legs. I climbed the hill slowly, from necessity rather than choice. It had apparently turned warmer and I was also experiencing a strange retarding tightness at the top of my head. Even when I reached the coolness of the cloisters this feeling persisted. The clock in the tower struck two o'clock as I entered the University Hall.

'Cutting it a bit fine, aren't you?' the man at the desk said as he ticked my name off on the list. He handed me the test paper, gave me an odd look and pointed to a vacant desk. I sat down and glanced about me, observing that the other competitors, about twenty in number, contorted in assorted attitudes of concentration, were already writing hard. I refused to be hurried. In an orderly manner I opened the exercise book on my desk and took up the test paper to study the question.

The Ellison Essay

Write an apologia of not less than two thousand words exonerating, as best you can, Mary, Queen of Scots, for her

conduct in relation to Lord Darnley and with particular
reference to the night of February 9th, 1567.

I might have smiled—the temptation was almost irresistible—not because, at the back of my mind, something, or
perhaps someone, had suggested that this, or a comparable
subject, might turn up, but solely from the absurdity of
the idea that in my present state I could ever bring myself
to defend that royal adventuress, even if it were to win the
Ellison for me a hundred times over.

Calmly, aware that I was wrecking my chance of success,
I dipped my nib in the inkwell and began to write. I did
not hesitate, words flowed from my pen, and every word
I wrote sprang from the hurt I had received. The period in
Scotland covering the fifteenth and sixteenth centuries had
been my special study, I knew the full history of the unhappy
Queen and now, invested with this urge from my subconscious, almost with malice, I scarified her mercilessly and
with a subtlety of which I could not have believed myself
capable. Under the pretence of defending her, one by one
favourable arguments were advanced then ruthlessly
demolished, extenuating circumstances suggested, only to
be crushed by the hard facts of history.

In this manner I made it obvious that her misguided
marriage to the youthful, foolish Darnley, ostensibly a love
match, had been conceived for no other reason than her
ambitious hatred of her cousin Queen Elizabeth—only one
year later the outlawed Earl of Bothwell was her adulterous
lover. Estranged from her husband—who lay ill and dis-
figured, longing for a reconciliation, in the city of Glasgow
—was it wifely solicitude that caused her to decree, after
a secret meeting with Bothwell, that he might more conveniently recover his health in the lonely, half-ruined house
of Kirk o' Fields? Once Darnley was installed, not with
comfort perhaps, for it was a miserable dwelling for a sick
man, nothing could have been more virtuous than the
assiduous attentions of the young and beautiful Queen who
devotedly sat through the day with him on her red velvet
cushion and at night slept in a bed in the room below.

Unfortunately, on one particular night, the Saturday
night of February 9th, she could not well be there. A promise
to be present at a masque and ball following a wedding had
been given, the royal word could not be broken. She kissed

her husband good night, saw that his candle light was trimmed. One last touching, pious gesture before she went out. She handed him his book of Psalms. Strange that Paris, Bothwell's servant, soiled with gunpowder, should pass her at the gate. Strange the locking of doors, the dismissal of the few attendants. Strange too that tremendous explosion, almost a royal salute, while she danced the night away.

For more than an hour I had not once looked up, while my pen travelled to and fro across the white pages with a robot regularity. Devoid of conscious thought, it was automatic writing, nothing else, and no planchette could have more relentlessly evoked the past. But gradually, as I approached the final description of Mary awakening on the morning following the murder amidst the silken hangings of her great bed and, already contemplating her marriage to Bothwell, sitting up to enjoy her favourite breakfast of a soft-boiled fresh egg, my bitterness seemed to flag and to be replaced by an extraordinary sensation of lassitude which obtruded itself in a manner so peculiar as to compel my attention. The lines were now wavering on the page, patches of shadow floated before my eyes and when, in an attempt to adjust my vision, I raised my head and looked about me the tightness previously experienced at the top of my skull was transformed to an actual vertigo. At the same time, giddily, it dawned upon me that most of the other candidates had handed in their essays, the time allotted must almost have expired. With an effort I completed my final paragraph, blotted the page, and closed the book.

What next? I supposed I should hand it in. But that seemed altogether pointless, and besides, I had a strange disinclination to stand up. Now that I had expelled my venom, rid myself of that fearful sense of outrage against decency, like a devil cast out, I felt weak and limp, altogether spent. The examiner, if that was the term I should apply to him, was leaving his desk and advancing slowly towards me. To my surprise, as he drew near and I could see him better, he appeared to be a clergyman, long, lean and saturnine, complete with dog collar. Had I noticed that when I came in? Surely not.

'You are the last.' He was addressing me mildly, in a speculative way. 'Have you finished?'

'I believe I have.'

'Then may I take your book? It's just after four.'

I gave it to him. He was watching me out of the corner of one clerical eye.

'You've written a lot,' he said rather ironically, turning the pages. 'I trust you've been kind to the poor woman.'

'No, I haven't. As far as I'm concerned she was just a *two-faced little bitch.*'

'Indeed!' He raised his eyebrows, and said nothing more.

Holding on to the desk I stood up. I was reluctant to leave it, but somehow, with a pretence of normality, I got out of the hall. Outside in the cloisters someone was waiting. It looked like Pin. If so, he was in a state of fearful agitation.

'Laurence! I've looked everywhere for you. Where were you?'

I put my hand to the top of my head to see if it was still there.

'I can't exactly remember.'

'Can't remember?' He was weaving in indistinct outlines, as though seen underwater. 'Have you done a good essay?'

'No, a damned bad one. I answered it all the wrong way. And I told the examiner so.'

'The examiner! Oh, heavens, that was the Professor of Divinity himself.'

'Well, I don't care. It was the truth.'

'Laurence, are you ill?'

'I don't think so. It's just that my head aches. I feel not myself any more.'

'Oh, dear, what have you been doing to yourself? Where did you sleep last night?'

'I remember now. In gaol.'

'Good God, boy!'

'Oh, they let me go this morning. Said there was nothing against me. The sergeant even gave me breakfast. But it was all hateful while it lasted. They had thought I was the cause of it all . . . and of Nora. That I was . . . I was . . . I was . . .'

He began to weave more and more, growing larger and larger, like some queer aquatic monster, and finally faded away altogether in the wave of universal darkness that swept down and absorbed me in its black, rushing tide.

THIRTY-FIVE

IT WAS PAST four o'clock in the afternoon some six weeks later. I had been lying down but now I was up and moving about the still unfamiliar flat my mother had rented. At last I was beginning to feel better, dimly to realize myself again, to know that I was making the journey back, out of that dark and spectral country in which my breakdown had so long confined me. It was not easy to forget the fear and horror of that shadowy period wherein my mind, narrowed to a single minute focus, was fixed in tormented apathy. The paths of my return had been tortuous and difficult, yet this morning the doctor had said to me: 'You're out of the woods now, my boy, and soon you'll be clear of the undergrowth.' The most joyful symptom of my escape was my ability to look outwards, away from my imprisoned brooding self, and to see things with an eye in which a spark of interest had begun to glint.

Thus, again, I examined the flat. It was small and very empty, made up of no more than a kitchen and a single front room with a tiny bathroom between, but it pleased me. The front room, which I occupied, was furnished with nothing but an iron bedstead, one chair and a rickety folding bureau, but the wallpaper was new, in colour a warm rich red, and when the evening sun came in, as it did now, the room glowed with a rosy flush that flooded and filled its emptiness. The kitchen, into which I wandered now, had the usual fittings, sink, built-in cupboard and dresser and, in the curtained alcove, that unique Scottish feature, a concealed box-bed.

But the main attraction of the flat was its height. Situated on the top storey of a working-class tenement recently erected by the Winton Corporation on Clarkhill, it afforded a sweeping open view of the rooftops and even, on clear days, of the Ochil Hills away to the west. Later I was to learn that in securing it my mother had been specially favoured by virtue of her new appointment with the city.

The nickel alarm clock on the mantelpiece told me it was not far off the hour of her return and, in the new lightness of my mood, I asked myself if I might not attempt to prepare our evening meal. Although the woolwork tasks I had been set had improved my sense of co-ordination, this had not been fully restored. I was afraid that I might drop things, and our store of crockery was not large. However, I succeeded in nerving myself to begin. Slowly and carefully I filled the kettle and, surprised by its weight, put it on the stove. I then spread the table-cloth and began to set out the tea cups. I found the loaf in the cupboard and the bread knife in the drawer. There was no disguising the fact, however painful the admission, that this big serrated knife frightened me. No one who has not experienced a breakdown can remotely realize the agonizing phobias it may induce. Earlier in my illness, I had been mortally afraid . . . and of what?—the small wooden bureau in my room. Invested with every sinister attribute, it had terrified me. I could not bring myself to look at it. Here, surely, was an indication of what I had gone through, and the abysmal state to which I had been reduced. But now, shame and the will to prove that I was well again forced me to grip the knife and cut some slices of bread. But my heart was still racing as I set them under the gas-ring to toast. All that remained was to cook the sausages, a rare treat in store for us tonight, and the gift of my faithful visitor. Annie Tobin did not bring flowers, she had a practical mind and knew my fondness for 'Annakers'. She brought also news which, while surprising, touched me not at all. Nora and Donohue, constrained perhaps by the ecclesiastical powers, were to be married. It meant nothing to me now.

A sense of accomplishment pervaded me when I had finished grilling the sausages. I felt that Mother would be encouraged by this evidence of my recovery. It was not that I particularly wanted to please her, although in our earlier days together this would certainly have been my motive. Our relationship was not the same. No longer did I feel for her that intimate, all-suffusing, all-encompassing jealous love. The cord was severed. I respected and trusted her, I was fond of her, but whatever the inflictions I had suffered, these had killed the passionate complex of my childhood.

Perhaps my mother's altered attitude, still affectionate, yet restrained, had contributed to the ending of those transports. Although this change had begun, insidiously, after Father's death, her sojourn in the convent had markedly altered her. She had become more serious in manner and disposition, and in a striking way, altogether more religious. In our early days at Ardencaple she would go to church on Sundays uncaringly, with a sort of light-hearted complaisance, and solely to please my father. Now, every morning she rose at six o'clock and before going to work went out to Mass at seven, taking daily Communion with every evidence of sincere devotion. No doubt conventual discipline had imposed its pattern upon her. Yet the change in her nature was deeper and more fundamental in its origin. Estranged from her own family, and with our Carroll associations now irrevocably severed, she must have felt herself a solitary figure, compelled by unhappy circumstances to stand against the world alone. Still, the moods of sadness that later afflicted her, and which eventually settled into a permanent melancholia, had not yet asserted themselves. She knew how fortunate she had been in receiving the Corporation appointment and was especially happy in her new work, which had to do mainly with the inspection and rehabilitation of rickety slum children. In Winton the numbers of undernourished, verminous, deformed children suffering from this disease had become a national scandal.

Although she gave no apparent sign of this, I could not fail to realize that Mother's main anxiety was centred upon me. What on earth was to become of me? Through my mad efforts at the Ellison I had thrown away my one slight chance of attending the University. At the age of sixteen a return to board school seemed equally out of the question and if it were not, how could I expect my mother to support me for another two years with no assured prospects at the end of them? What a mess I had made of my life! My future seemed dim indeed.

A step sounded on the outside staircase and I heard a key turn in the door. Mother came into the kitchen wearing the navy-blue coat and skirt and the neat turned-up blue chip-hat with the Winton Corporation badge, all of which made up her new uniform. She smiled and exclaimed:

'Why, Laurence, you've made the supper.'

'The sausages seem all right. But I've very cleverly burned the toast.'

My reply seemed to please her.

'That's how I like it.'

She went into the bathroom and I heard her shaking herself in the empty bath, an essential routine procedure to rid her garments of the fleas she invariably acquired in her daily pilgrimage amongst her unfortunate children.

While she was changing I went into the front room to straighten my bed. As I folded the coverlet at the window I saw that Pin, who not infrequently came at this hour in an effort to console me, was stumping towards the common entrance to the flats. He had completed his 'Annals of Ardencaple', but alas, no publisher seemed to want the book, and soon he would go back to the village to finish his days on his meagre pension. When I finished folding the bedcover the sharp staccato of Pin's peg on the pavement was still ascending to me and I saw that he was pacing to and fro in a manner manifestly indecisive and disturbed. It puzzled me. Then all at once I understood the reason of his reluctance to come up. This was no surprise at all and caused me no distress. It was part of my recovery that I could feel sorry for Pin in his disappointment with me. I went into the kitchen.

'Mr. Rankin is outside. Shall I call him up?'

'Do, Laurence . . . but first put on more toast.'

I went and put two slices of bread on the stove. When I returned to the window Pin had gone. Apparently he had decided to depart. I just caught sight of him as he turned the corner of the street. And yet, mysteriously, some ten minutes later, when we had begun our meal, the bell of the flat door rang and there, when I answered it, was Pin.

'Laurence,' he said at once, 'I've been waiting for your mother, outside, and at the tram stop, but she seems to be unusually late.'

'She's here,' I said. 'She came back early.'

He appeared somewhat disconcerted by this information. Indeed, when he came into the clearer light of the kitchen, I saw that his general air was disturbed. He seemed obliged to find an excuse for his condition by remarking:

'I'm not so good at the stairs as I was.'

'Be seated then,' Mother said. 'You'll have a bite with us.'

'No, thank you, no.'

'Then let me give you a cup of tea.'

'No, no . . . well, as you're so kind.'

He sat down and accepted the cup that Mother handed him. His hand was slightly unsteady, so that some of the tea spilled into the saucer, but he was becoming more assured. He gave me a sidelong solicitous look.

'How are you today, Laurence?'

'Much better, sir.' I almost added: And quite prepared for your bad news.

'Good . . . good,' he said.

His habit of repeating the word suddenly annoyed me. I knew exactly what he wanted to say and I wished to heaven he would get it out. I said:

'If there's anything on your mind I'm quite able to hear it.'

He gave a sigh of relief.

'In that case I'll go ahead. I did think of speaking first to your mother. To see if it might set you back. But now I may as well admit that I've just come from the University and as you've guessed, the results of the Ellison are out.' He took a slow drink of tea and went on, in a flat voice, not looking at me: 'You probably remember the nature of the question, an apologia for Queen Mary, and I can assure you that most of the candidates fell over themselves to gild the lily. They didn't see the catch in the question, in the words "as best you can", and by heaven I didn't see it myself. They fell into the trap and practically beatified her, and with a panel of judges made up of two Presbyterian ministers and a Divinity professor by the name of Knox, they were dead from the word go.' His voice was rising and becoming so hoarse, he had to gulp down tea. 'By some chance, however, some turn of the unpredictable, there was one candidate who, unable to sustain any favourable evidence, found himself forced to condemn, in the strongest terms. I understand that his essay was an immense satisfaction to the judges, a vindication of their own belief, and the subject of the highest praise. They've given him the Ellison, unanimously.'

I began to feel queer all over. There was a strange, strained expression on Mother's face as Pin went on:

'Laurence, there's supposed to be someone up above who looks after fools, especially if they're young fools with some sort of ability.'

He could contain himself no longer. Jumping up suddenly, knocking over his cup, he flung his arms about my neck hopping with me in a kind of one-legged dance. Half stifled, I scarcely heard his shout of victory. But I knew that by an amazing fluke, a freak of circumstance over which I had no control, I should go to the University after all.

At that exultant moment everything seemed settled. Our future was assured at last. The thought of the long and wearing struggle that must lie ahead never entered my mind. Yet for the next five years we were to fight a battle with circumstances that wore us to the bone. While my mother's position with the Corporation was assured, her weekly wage was pitifully slender, scarcely enough to provide us with the bare essentials of life. Yet somehow by a miracle of economy and self-denial she managed, and all without assistance, except from Simon, who himself had so little, yet who sent an occasional small contribution from Spain. From the other relations nothing was asked or given. Bernard continued to muddle along in great comfort in the condemned Lomond Vaults, somehow evading all orders for their demolition, while Leo silently and implacably went on to amass a stupendous fortune. In that laudable process his meanness and parsimony increased to such a degree that Annie finally left him and sailed from Greenock to join her son in Canada. It was a sad moment for me when I saw her off on the *City of Montreal*. On the rare occasions when I passed Leo in the street he pretended not to see me. Even then I was struck by his look of emaciation, and when he died, years later, completely alone in a miserable room in the Gorbielaw—Templar's Hall having been sold for some fantastic sum—there was more than a suggestion that death was due, at least in part, to starvation. In his holograph will, from which health-food societies were the main beneficiaries, there was a clause specifically dispossessing his nephews and niece from any inheritance whatsoever.

The only one to suffer from this manifestation of family feeling was Nora. By that time my own medical practice was flourishing and Terence, shelving Miss Gilhooley in favour of the proprietress of an old-established Dublin hotel, was then extremely well off. But Nora's marriage, arranged in an atmosphere of reparation—a futile idea on both sides of straightening things out—was a disaster. Donohue could never be anything but Donohue, he was seldom at home, and when he finally disappeared Nora was left stranded in Liverpool with three young children to support.

All this, of course, still lay in the future and meanwhile Mother and I were struggling along on shillings and pence. It is sad how little I then thought of her heroic self-sacrifice, and how often our relationship turned strained and difficult.

As a student of comparative anatomy I was not now devotionally minded, while her religious fervour had become intense. On other matters too our ideas were in conflict and we had periods of estrangement when to me her withdrawn, tight-lipped silences had the semblance of martyrdom.

I am sure I was to blame. Yet amiability and good temper do not come easily when one is hungry, ill clad—for years I remained garbed in Shapiro's camouflaged effort—isolated by an obvious poverty, and worried to death by the constant threat of failure. Although in my first two terms the record shows that I took honours in botany and zoology, every succeeding examination loomed as a terror from the knowledge that if I did not pass I was finished. The lush state assistance of later years did not then exist for impoverished students and my bursary, barely adequate, could never have afforded me a second chance. I can still see myself with my elbows on the desk and my head in my hands poring over Quain's *Anatomy* while Mother went out just before the shops closed on Saturday night to bargain in the cheapest market for a miserable scrag of meat, or on her return suffered the insults of some brute who had called for our overdue rent.

But at last, slowly and wearily, like a storm-beaten ship staggering towards the shore, we came in sight of the promised land. I passed my final examinations, the graduation day arrived, and Pin came from Ardencaple to join my mother at the ceremony. As I pushed my way out of the Bute Hall to meet them at the Union where, to avoid the crowd, I had told them to wait, I drew a long, deep, triumphant breath, conscious of my new personality: strong, reliant, and successful, equal henceforth to any emergency. Now I knew that the ingenuous softness of my youth was gone. Never again would I permit myself to be imposed upon. Never, never would my heart get the better of my head. The Greek ideal of my boyhood had been achieved at last.

At that moment when I had almost reached the doorway, I felt a touch on my arm. Despite the grey hair, which aged her markedly, I knew her at once. Miss O'Riordan. She had seen my name amongst the list of successful candidates and had wanted to see me capped. When we had talked for some minutes—she would not come with me to the Union

—she placed a small, religious-looking leather case in my reluctant palm. Impossible not to know what it contained.

'I'm sure you've broken the one I gave you. Or lost it. So here's another. So you don't forget.'

After she had gone I glanced at the case with mixed sensations, mindful of my soulful performance at the Presbytery so long ago, and only too well aware that when I got home I would drop the beads in a drawer and never give them another thought. Suddenly, under the pressure of my fingers on the soft leather, I felt a faint crackle. I opened the case. Yes, the rosary was there. But Miss O'Riordan had tucked in beside it a neatly folded Bank of Scotland five-pound note.

Oblivious of the press around me, I stood there, quite motionless, so overcome by this opportune kindness which would enable me to get the few instruments I needed to apply for an assistantship, that slowly, inexorably, against all my efforts, my throat tightened, my vision was blurred with moisture.

No, it was no use—I had not changed, and never would. There was a soft spot in my nature, a strain of weakness, a sensitivity that would never harden. All that I longed, and had striven, to be—cool and stoical, detached and aloof, a true Spartan—was beyond me. Marked ineradicably by my singular childhood, by an upbringing in which too many women had participated, I was, and always would be, the victim of every sentient mood, the unwilling slave of my own emotions.

A POCKETFUL
OF RYE

ONE

THE EXPRESS LETTER came late in the afternoon.

I was standing comfortably with Matron Müller on the terrace of the clinic, putting on my usual act of kindly interest as the children packed into the big green departure coach that would take them through the mountains by the Echberg Pass to Basle for the chartered night flight back to Leeds. It hadn't rained much during their six weeks and the little runts looked well and full of themselves, packing the open side windows to shout *auf wiedersehen* and other picked-up bits of Schweizerdeutsch. They were waving the paper Swiss flags that Matron always handed out with sample bars of patriotic milk chocolate. As the coach rolled down the drive they began to sing 'Lili Marlene'. They had picked that up too, endlessly playing the old scratched record in the playroom.

'Well, that's the last batch of summer, Matron,' I remarked on a poetic note, as the coach disappeared behind a frieze of firs. 'They weren't bad brats.'

'Ach, Herr Doktor.' She raised a reproving finger, but fondly. 'Why must you use that wort. Brats. These last were goot children and for me a goot child is the handwerk of Gott.'

'But Matron,' I improvised quickly, 'brat is just an affectionate English idiom. In Britain people of the highest rank will publicly refer to their offspring as brats.'

'Ach, so? You are serious?'

'I assure you.'

'So! A fun affection. An English odium of well-born people.'

'Exactly.'

Her small eyes approved me indulgently. Hulda Müller was a short, thick woman of about sixty, her architecture late Victorian, with a magnificent portico. Thorny grey hair protruded from her white stringed cap, her faint moustache was discreetly powdered. Draped to the heels in the shapeless white gown to which the cantonal nurses were condemned, she was the genuine Schweizer article. Correct, hygienic, humourless, unutterably dull, and while not, in the cheap sense of the word, a snob, imbued with an inherent Germanic reverence for rank. But capable and industrious, a worker fifteen hours a day, coping with shortage of staff in the ward and the kitchen, feeding me as I had never, in my spotty down-at-heel career, been fed before.

'It is highly agreeable to me that you make explanations of such odiums, Herr Doktor Carroll. You, a person knowing and yourself coming from the *Hochgeboren*.'

'A pleasure, Matron. You'll have all the odium I'm capable of.'

Oh, careful, you clown, don't push it too far. I flashed a smile at her, loaded with charm. In any institution it is the first rule of life to be in with the matron. And since my heaven-sent arrival seven months ago I had worked diligently on Hulda, soaping her with some inspired fictions, creating a few noble ancestors to strengthen my image. So now this fire-breathing old dragon, this veteran of the bedpans, this Hippocratic priestess in a white soutane was entirely mine or, rather, I was hers—her bright-eyed *Junge*.

'Now we have the six weeks' pause,' she reflected. 'You will recommence your post-graduates at the Zürich Kantonspital?'

'I'll go down at least once or twice a week,' I agreed thoughtfully. 'Beginning on Tuesday.'

'Ach, it is goot to have the charge of a young, eager, scientific doktor. Our late Herr Doktor was . . .' she shook her head, *'ein Schrinker.'*

'Das war nicht gut für Sie,' I responded, demonstrating my advance in colloquial German.

'Nein, aber das ist ein Problem für seine neue Frau.' The law that married doctors were unacceptable at the clinic thus defined, she examined the watch dangling from her bosom. 'But now I must go to see for your tea.' Moving off she glanced at me archly. 'You like perhaps these ramekins I make special for you.'

'Matron, they're a dream and you . . . you're a regular "dreamboat".'

She giggled, not amused, just pleased.

'Dreambote? That's goot?'

'The best.'

When she had gone I suddenly felt annoyed with myself. In her own way she was kind and decent. And shouldn't

I be thanking my lucky star to be here? On velvet at last after eight years of mucking around in the worst kinds of General Practice.

When I graduated at Winton University I had taken a voyage to Australia as ship's doctor in a cargo boat, then come back all set for the quick trip to Harley Street. It did not take long to demonstrate the financial and professional worth of a low grade Scots degree. Who wants you with that, with the dung of the kail yard on your boots, and the porridge still stuck to your chaps? At first a few locums, one in the highlands with a hard-drinking member of the Macduff clan, then a short assistantship, followed by another locum in the slums of Winton where, half starved, I worked overtime for an obese old sloth who staggered back from his holiday at Glendrum Hydro loaded with the menu cards for every meal, immediately sat down, still drooling all over his paunch, and one by one read them out to me.

Then came a long assistantship in Nottingham with the vague view to a partnership that was never meant to materialize. But why elaborate the sorry record: the long hours in sweaty surgeries, the night calls, the health insurance cards to be faked after hours, the scanty, irregular over-desiccated meals, the unequal division of labour smugly passed off with: 'Oh, by the way, Carroll, my wife and I are going out to dinner and the theatre. You won't mind polishing off these three late calls that have just come in.'

And not every wife was taken out to dinner. 'I often think I am wasting the best years of my life in Sudsbury, Doctor Carroll. Sidney is so wrapped up in his practice; you must see that—for a young man you are so understanding.' Slipping me an extra slice of scraggy mutton under the mashed potatoes, with a lingering look, while Sidney had his mug in the B.M.J. Poor plump, but fading yearner, I helped you with kind words alone. How could one find romance in those droopy drawers strung out every other Monday in the Sudsbury backyard?

My last stretch hit mud bottom when, as obstetric physician—so called—in a Medical Aid practice in the South Wales Rhondda Valley, knocked up by the midwife most nights of the week, staggering out into the shadow world of endless miners' rows half dressed and still half asleep to grope up the ladder to the attic, clash on the forceps and pull, I seemed to be a robot performer, perhaps the cymbalist, in a bizarre symphony of sweat, tears, filth and blood.

It was in the murky dawn after such a night, as I stood on the concrete floor of the central surgery, still in my professional rig of pyjamas, old overcoat and pit clogs, wrapping a bottle of ergot—that panacea for the reluctant placenta—in a disembowelled page from the *Lancet*, that my blood-shot eye was caught by a small strip advertisement on the half-torn page.

Wanted: For the Maybelle Children's Clinic and Holiday Home, Schlewald, Switzerland, as Medical Superintendent, British doctor, single and preferably under 30. Knowledge of German and pulmonary lesions a recommendation. Full board and comfortable quarters provided. Salary £500 per annum, payable in Sterling or Swiss francs. Further particulars and application forms from J. Scrygemour & Co. Solicitors, Halifax, Yorks.

I stood there, hypnotized, with a kind of prevision that this was precisely what I needed, wanted, and must have. And yet, as I stared through the dirty dispensary window, hung over by the gallows outline of mine headstocks against the coal tips, I did not fail to comprehend that normally I hadn't an earthly. Nevertheless, a strang feeling had begun to form at the back of my mind that this was no fortuitous intervention in my life, that here was an opportunity specially designed for Laurence Carroll and one which I must take. Compulsively, I sat down and wrote to J. Scrygemour & Co.

The reply came within three days.

The clinic was a foundation from the estate of Mrs. Bella Keighley, widow of a wealthy North of England cotton spinner, who had settled in Schlewald with her daughter Maybelle in the year 1896. The daughter was delicate, a consumptive case, consigned for the short span of her life to an Alpine existence. When she died some years later the mother, for sentimental reasons, or from a genuine attachment to Switzerland, had continued her Schlewald domicile, and on her death, under the terms of the will, the large chalet had been extended, a ward of twelve beds and a number of small out chalets constructed and the establishment set up for the benefit of under-privileged British children, 'particularly those suffering from weakness or disorders of the lungs'. The staff consisted of the resident doctor, matron, and probationer nurse.

Six times a year batches of children were received for convalescence or holidays. Those requiring further treatment were retained in the ward.

Two weeks later I went to Halifax for the interview, which took place at the Scrygemour office in Market Street. Naturally I was nervous, yet in view of the preparations I had made, and for which I trust no one will misjudge me, not altogether lacking in hope. Four other candidates were in the waiting-room, not a bad-looking lot, in fact two had London degrees considerably better than mine, but when I sounded them it appeared that, of the four, none could speak German. So far so good. Before I went in, last, I took a final glance at the old tourists' phonetic phrase book I had found second hand in Cardiff and been mugging up for the past ten days, then tapped respectfully on the frosted panel of the door.

The committee had three members: Scrygemour, who was small, benevolent and shiningly bald, and two solid Yorkshire businessmen of the stand-no-nonsense school. When they had looked me over, the interrogation began. I was in my best form: quiet, alert, convincing, modestly forthcoming yet personally reserved: not pressing the advantages I had thought up, letting them winkle all the good points out of me as though it embarrassed me mildly to acknowledge them. Yes, I admitted I liked children, had always got on well with them, not only as one of a large family but in my extensive practice. At a mention of the excellence of my testimonials I betrayed no surprise — naturally enough, since I had composed two of the better ones myself. Yes, I agreed calmly, a South Wales colliery town was not perhaps socially the most desirable field of action for an ambitious young man. Yet, oddly enough, it *was*: I had purposely chosen that location to study pneumoconiosis, adding a moment later when this floored them: 'Which, as you obviously know, gentlemen, comprises the pulmonary diseases — anthracosis, silicosis, and tuberculosis — specially affecting workers in the mining industry.'

An impressive silence followed this well-thought-out

gambit; after glancing at the other two, Scrygemour remarked: 'That is a point of considerable interest to us Dr Carroll.' Then, diffidently as though scarcely hoping, he cleared his throat:

'I don't suppose you would happen to know German, doctor?'

I smiled, staking my entire position on the clincher. Either I was in, or out flat on my ear.

'Aber, mein Herr, Ich kann das Deutsch gut sprechen.'

It knocked them cold—they hadn't one word of German amongst them. And before they could recover I let them have a few more fluent, though not particularly appropriate, cuttings from my little green book.

'Entschuldigen Sie, mein Herr, können Sie mir zeigen wo der nächste Abort ist?' (Excuse me, sir, can you direct me to the nearest lavatory?)

'Zimmermädchen, ich glaube unter meinem Bett ist eine Maus.' (Chambermaid, I think there is a mouse under my bed.)

'Very satisfactory, doctor. Very.' This actually from one of the hard types. 'May we ask how you acquired such proficiency in the language?'

'Mainly from my study of pulmonary diseases in the original German text books,' I murmured, knowing that I was home, even before they had me in again, after a short wait outside, to congratulate me and shake me warmly by the hand.

Of course, it was a thoroughly discreditable performance. It was cheap, contemptible, despicable, downright dishonest. But when you have been on the verge of the bread line and been kicked around for seven years, your sense of ethics becomes somewhat blunted. And although next morning I was prepared to cry *'mea culpa, mea maxima culpa,'* I was happy, that same afternoon, to be packing my bag for Schlewald. After all, in my usual fashion, I could try to exonerate myself. The Jesuits, who were partly responsible for my schooling, had, in the brief term of our relationship which occurred when I was extremely young, imbued me with their most practical principle, that the end justifies the means. And in utilizing my only means of persuasion upon these worthy Yorkshiremen I was no more than accomplishing a necessary act to achieve a necessary end.

So at least, for the moment, let us admit that I was safely

here in Schlewald, happily anchored in the Maybelle Clinic, breathing the delicious mountain air and gazing about me with a mildly proprietary air. It was one of these perfect Alpine afternoons that lit the landscape with a pale translucent blue. In the pasture before the clinic, which stood high on the southern slope, autumn crocuses, still unfolded, stained the vivid green where rivulets of cold clear water tumbled over each other downhill to the river. In the pinewoods across the valley the toy train that ran to Davos had begun its slow vertiginous climb, turning on its own tail, stopping now on a loop of the higher grade as though to recover steam, but actually to allow the Davos down train to pass. Above, on the scar of the Gotschna Grat, a faint dusting of early snow was already anticipating the sunset, turning from gold to a rich rose madder. Distantly, and far below, dwarfed by the mountain, the roofs of Schlewald Dorf looked cosy, *gemütlich* was the word. Lush descriptions apart, it was a sweet spot, and when you thought of those miners' rows, the slag heaps without a blade of grass, the surgery bell going day and night and Tonypandy Blodwen croaking in your half awakened ear: 'Eh, doctor bach, I'm mortal sorry to 'ave you out again but it's a britch and I canna' get the 'ead away:'—well, it was peaceful as a bottle of tranquillizers. I liked it here, in fact I was completely sold on it.

A young moon, pale as a sliver of Emmentaler in the persistent light, was beginning to slide over the ridge and suddenly from across and far away came the sound of an Alpine horn. A herdsman sitting by his lonely hut on the upper pastures with that ridiculous six-foot wooden tube which, like the Scottish bagpipes, is hideous near the eardrums but which, floating down from the hills, has a magic all its own. Again it came, vibrating in the still air. It hits you, that prolonged deep sadness, losing itself in the distance, silenced by the peaks. It cuts the cord, and suddenly you too are lost. You sink into yourself, and given a chance, some secret misery sneaks up from your subconscious.

With me it is always the same—a torment and a mystery —I am in that dark empty street of an unknown city and in the dead silence of the night I hear footfalls behind me, slow, persistent, menacing. I cannot turn round and must sweat out the agony of that unknown pursuit until suddenly a dog barks and all is still again.

Oh, come off it, Carroll, and stay happy. No one is interested in your private little phobia, at least not yet. It was time for me to get back to my tea and ramekins.

Then, as I turned, I saw someone come through the lodge gates—Hans, the postmaster's son, hurrying up the drive, now waving to me with something in his hand. A letter.

'*Express, Rekommandiert, Herr Doktor*.' It was probably my monthly cheque and for this the Swiss post never keeps you waiting.

He was pretending to be out of breath, but as I was in a soft mood, when I signed the receipt, I told him to hold on, went into my sitting-room which opened off the terrace. This was a snug little room with a warm red carpet, solid, well-polished, comfortable furniture upholstered in brown velveteen, while on the table Matron very thoughtfully kept me supplied with a bowl of the Valais fruits, apricots, pears, apples and cherries, which were so plentiful at this season.

'Catch, Hans.' I threw him a big Golden Delicious apple from the open window.

He wouldn't eat it now, I felt sure, but as a true little Swiss, to whom possession is ten points of the law, take it home, polish it, and keep it—at least until Sunday. I watched him go off with a *vielen Dank, Herr Doktor*.

Then I examined the letter, and was suddenly set back on my heels. It wasn't possible! The envelope was post-marked Levenford, that most distasteful, almost fatal word from which in all its connotations I hoped I had finally cut myself adrift. Reluctantly, I opened the envelope. Yes, from my old playmate, Francis Ennis.

My dear Laurence,

I must ask pardon for failing to write congratulating you on your appointment last summer. There was a very pleasing little paragraph in the 'Winton Herald'. May I now, belatedly, wish you every success in your new and most worthy endeavour.

And now I hesitate to proceed. For I am constrained to ask a special favour of you.

You remember Cathy Considine, I'm sure, that very sweet companion of our boyhood days who married Daniel Davigan, and was so recently and tragically widowed. Yes, Laurence, theirs was a model marriage, a

*shining example of marital unity. It was a fearful blow
when Dan was taken. You must have seen the account and
obituary notice two months ago in the public press,
locally, at least, it created quite a stir. And lately, alas,
another affliction for the sorrowing widow. The only
child, Daniel, just seven years of age, and without question
a most remarkable and exceptionally clever little boy, has
turned quite poorly. Very pale, glands in the neck and,
not to put too fine a point on it, a suspicion of T.B. Canon
Dingwall, though in retirement and still in his wheel
chair following another slight stroke, has shown a great
interest in the boy, has brought him along in every way
—actually Daniel is two classes ahead of his age—and
he has taken the matter up strongly with Dr Moore who
at once suggested a spell, brief we hope, in a sanatorium.
All very well to suggest, but here, with the waiting under
the new Health Scheme it would be a good six months
before a place could be found for Daniel. And then only
in the Grampians, which I dare say bear no comparison
with your sunny Swiss Alps.*

*So it has been decided that Cathy must take the boy to
Switzerland and devote herself to his cure. The two dear
pilgrims propose leaving here on Tuesday of next week,
October 7th, arriving Zürich Airport at 5.30 p.m., and
as they have no contacts in that city and must feel quite
lost, I am relying on you at least to meet them. If you can
do nothing further, please see them on their way to Davos
where they have an address from Dr Moore. But Laurence,
if it is at all humanly possible, won't you take charge of
them yourself, find a place for Daniel in your clinic, get
him well again? Please! For the boy's sake. God will bless
you for it, Laurence, and we, all your good friends in
Winton, will never cease to thank you.*

I read it again, slowly, shuddering slightly over 'the dear
pilgrims', then instinctively I crushed the letter, tight and
hard. What a rocket! What a blasted imposition. Coming
after me 'for old times' sake', thanking me in advance, handing me the good old heaven will bless you. And spoiling my
Tuesday in Zürich, the one day of the week when Svenska
Ornflyg were normally free of regular flights.

Yet, how could I give Ennis the brush off. My name would
stink at home. I would have to do something about it and,

after all, it was only on a short-term basis. I supposed I must handle it but, as always, I would do so with calm detachment and mature consideration.

TWO

THE PROBATIONER brought the tea-tray into my sitting-room, that snug little carpeted den with the easy chair before the blue and white tiled wood stove. She was a fresh country girl from the Valais, smelling pleasantly of the dairy and with well-formed milk-bars, who, as she went out, before closing the door always gave me a look over her shoulder not altogether bovine. But today I failed to respond, nor did the fragrant cheesy odour of the fresh baked ramekins break through my moodiness. Yes, the letter was a nuisance, a confounded nuisance, it had upset me, taking me back to a period in my early life that I was never unduly eager to recall.

Personally, I cannot endure throwbacks, they interrupt the action which is dying to burst forth, but to put the picture in perspective it must be related that at the age of fifteen I had gone to live with my grandparents in Levenford. One month before with that touch of the absurd apparent to those familiar with the beginnings of my erratic career, I had precociously won the Ellison Bursary to Winton University, an achievement somewhat dulled when it became apparent that to enter the University I must attend Levenford Academy for one year to take the Higher Leaving Certificate examination of the Scottish School Board.

My welcome by the Bruces at their semi-detached villa in Woodside Avenue was not effusive. In running off with my Catholic father, their favourite daughter had deeply distressed them. And now, fifteen years later, fulfilling their worst forebodings, they were landed with the sole surviving evidence of that ill-fated union.

My grandfather, Robert Bruce, was an upstanding, dignified burgher of the town, retired on a pension from his position as head of the timber department in the local shipyard of Dennison Brothers, whose staid existence was transfigured by the belief, generally regarded as fictitious, that he was the lineal descendant of the Scottish hero who, after cracking de Bohun's skull with his battle-axe in single combat, led the Scots to victory over the English at Bannockburn in 1314—a date I was never permitted to forget.

Do not imagine that my grandfather was either a fool or a laughing stock. He had documents, genealogical trees, extracts from meetings of the local Historical Society, and had traced his family in Levenford as far back as the fifteenth century, a record in which the name Robert was generic. Moreover, Cardross Castle where King Robert I died in 1329 stood by the river Leven on the outskirts of the town and it was from here that Sir James Douglas had set out to take the heart of Bruce to the Holy Land, only to fall, fighting the Moors in Spain. Without digressing further, it is enough to say that my grandfather's obsession or, if you prefer it, delusion was honest, and so deeply felt, that he made every year a pilgrimage to Melrose Abbey where the casket containing the heart of King Robert was now enshrined.

Some of this genealogy rubbed on to me and, suitably embroidered, was often socially opportune, but this apart, Bruce treated me always with decent toleration and a fine sense of justice, while my grandmother, a small bowed wisp of a woman, devoted yet quietly resigned, her head carried patiently to one side—she was slightly deaf—addicted to the Bible, strong tea and the works of Annie S. Swan, and to the habit—to me endearing—of talking soundlessly to herself, her lips moving to the accompaniment of little nods, grimaces and other subtle sympathetic changes of expression, decidedly was, despite the worn-out look of Scottish wives who have served strong men hand and foot, a sweet person.

Levenford Academy which, under the terms of the Bursary I was compelled to attend, was a solid, old-established institution situated in the heart of the Borough, with the excellence and all the prejudice of the true blue Scots Grammar School. My advent here was even less welcome, and it was with some relief that I discovered a co-religionist already in my form—Francis Ennis, son of Dr Ennis. As the only two Papists in the Academy we inevitably drew together, not at first from any natural affinity, but simply because we were in the same uncomfortable boat, objects of suspicion and derision to our fellow scholars.

Frank was the only son of a painfully pious mother, a devotee who haunted the church, not merely to wear out her knees before the Stations of the Cross, but as a kind of female sacristan who dressed, adorned, and tended the altar with a holy solicitude that defied the repressive hints, discouraging looks, and even downright prohibitions from the rector of St Patrick's, the fabulous Canon Dingwall. Unhappily for Frank, his father was a cock of less downy feather. Dr Ennis, perhaps the best and the hardest-worked doctor in town, was a big untidy man with a rough, ribald tongue, a strong addiction to neat whisky and a fondness for squeezing the dairymaids at the outlying farms he visited. Careless of public opinion, he did as he pleased, and while nominally Catholic, his views of religion were unorthodox, often spectacularly unpredictable. For that matter, using the pretext of his busy practice, he was rarely seen inside the doors of St Patrick's. It was he who had sent his son to the Academy, preparatory to entering him at Edinburgh University where he would take a medical degree and join his father in practice.

Frank was a most prepossessing boy, open and friendly in manner, and quite exceptionally good looking. Tall, slightly built, with a delicate girlish complexion, and thick chestnut hair, he had the bluest, long-lashed eyes I had ever seen. In school he was not noticeably clever, rather the reverse, and in his physical contacts with the rougher boys he was inclined to timidity. Although he never complained of this bullying. he had obviously suffered until I was able to take his part. But his one outstanding quality which set him apart was simply this: in the strict sense of the word he was *good*.

One morning during our first week together he was late coming to school and was given an imposition.

'What happened, Frank?' I asked him. 'Did you sleep in?'

'Oh, no.' He smiled. 'Canon Dingwall was held up by a sick call. You see, I serve his seven o'clock Mass every morning.'

'What! You do . . . get up so early!'

'It's quite easy once you have the habit.'

'I suppose Dingwall's forced you into it. He puts the wind up me.'

'You're quite wrong, Laurence. He just seems terribly stern and severe. Once you know him he's the sweetest person.'

I glanced at him doubtfully. The Canon, a black, forbidding, hatchet-featured Highlander, six feet two tall and thin as a ramrod, an emaciated Scots Savonarola, towering in the pulpit, scourging his groundling Irish immigrant congregation with an intellectual sardonic wit that bit deeper than mere crude blastings of hell-fire, flagellations interposed with sudden ritual snuff takings during which a pin might be heard to drop in a church packed to suffocation, scarcely struck me as a fount of sweetness and light. He invariably stood at the church door before the eleven o'clock Mass, had already spotted me, and was undoubtedly aware of my dubious antecedents.

'Every time I pass him he gives me the excommunication stare.'

'He just has to put on that kind of act, Laurence. To get results. And he has. All the top Prots, the Dennison Brothers especially, think the world of him, the way he's stamped out drunkenness in the town. It was mostly in our lot. But beyond that he's terribly interesting, well read and cultured, a real scholar. He spent five years teaching philosophy at the Scots College in Rome. You'd love him.' As I shook my head he smiled and took my arm. 'I'll give you a knock down to him after Mass next Sunday.'

'Some hope,' I said, scornfully. 'I'll skip him by going in the side door.'

Nevertheless, rather averse myself to morning rising, I respected Frank for this unexpectedly revealed asceticism as I did progressively for other comparable aspects of his character. He never, for example, took the slightest notice of the usual school smut, the lavatory scrawlings, the dirty jokes. And if anyone told a doubtful story in his presence his starry eyes remained fixed on the horizon, the actual meaning of the thing seemed to pass over his head.

All this struck me as commendable, more perhaps as the indication of an original refined and superior turn of mind than from considerations of morality—since I was probably as venal as the boys he despised. One day, however, a peculiar incident occurred.

I still had a bicycle, from my better days, an old Rudge Whitworth, and as Francis, whose mother denied him nothing, had a brand new Humber, we began on Saturdays to take rides together into the surrounding country, then quite unspoiled, still wild with the freedom of Scottish hills and heaths. Summer was coming in and as the days got warmer we went farther afield, to Malloch and along the winding shore of Loch Lomond to Luss where we bathed. It seemed slightly odd that when we undressed on the warm pebbled beach Frank always moved off a few paces to the shelter of a rock, emerging well covered by a full bathing suit. I did not remark on it, imagining that perhaps he had a mole or some kind of birthmark and was sensitive about it. One day I forgot to bring my pants and, thinking nothing of it, tore off my clothes and dashed into the Loch in a state of nature.

'Come on in,' I shouted. 'It's wonderful.'

There was a pause, then he called back:

'I'm not bathing today.'

'Don't you feel well?' He did not answer.

I took a long swim out to the island. The water was warmer than usual and the sense of being completely naked and unhampered made it even more delicious. When I came back and had dressed Frank came out from behind the rock. He was deeply flushed, his lips set in a firm line.

'You know, of course,' he said accusingly, his voice stony, 'that it's a sin, almost a mortal one, to expose yourself.'

I stared at him in amazement.

'And that you make me sin too if I look at you.'

I burst out laughing.

'Oh, come off it, Frank. Don't be such a sissy. None of the other boys wear pants, let alone complete bathing suits, and it's far nicer without. You must try it.'

'I won't,' he shouted, beginning to tremble. 'Never.'

'Oh, for heaven's sake . . .'

'Stop it,' he said, in a low intense voice. 'It is for heaven's sake. I don't care what the others do. And I'm not a sissy. I simply want to remain pure. And you must too, Laurence. So if you don't cover yourself decently in future I won't bathe with you at all.'

I saw that he was in dead earnest and was wise enough to let the matter drop. We were both rather silent on the way home and I caught myself glancing oddly at him from time to time, but when we got back he stopped, straddled his bicycle, and seemed to want to talk.

'We are still friends, aren't we, Laurie?'

'Of course.'

'More than ever in fact. I do wish I was coming with you to Winton instead of being shoved off to Edinburgh.'

'Then talk your father into it.'

'Oh no.' His face clouded as it usually did at the mention of Dr Ennis. 'I've tried it before. In fact I've often tried, and had no luck, talking him out of shoving me in for medicine. You know, I'd far rather take an arts degree.'

I was silent, wondering if some unrecognized or at least undeclared aversion to his father had put Frank off the idea of medical practice, and with the incident of that afternoon still in mind I said suddenly:

'What surprises me, Frank, is that you haven't plumped for the priesthood. It's so . . . so obvious. Not only would it delight your mother, you're the one person in the world who ought to have a vocation.'

He looked at me for a moment then, to my amazement, he burst into a fit of laughter, very boyish and natural.

'You won't have to wait long for the answer to that one, my boy. Next week I want you to meet someone *very* special.' Before I could question him he smiled over his shoulder and started to pedal off. 'Come on, let's hurry, or we'll miss our half hour with your friend the Canon.'

Yes, the impossible had happened, and to Frank's amusement, tinged perhaps with a little chagrin, Dingwall had practically adopted me. One day on the way from school I had come upon a depressing tableau. Frank, frightfully pale, on his knees in the gutter with two of our chief tormentors, the Buchanan brothers, bending over him, the younger of the two holding a can of liquid mud.

'Confess your sins, Ennis, or we'll baptize you with this. Come on, begin: holy father I killed a cat . . .'

Intervention, however unpleasant, was the only possible course of action. I snatched the mud can, put the younger Buchanan out of action with a direct hit, then sailed into his big brother. Heavy damage was done on both sides but I had the worst of it and was undoubtedly due for a bad beating when a sudden apparition obscured the daylight: Dingwall himself, dressed 'for the town' with his invariable priestly precision in long black overcoat, black umbrella held upright, and his famous tall top hat, that made him look a mile high. A terrifying spectacle, a veritable spectre of Popery, before which, to my gasping relief, even before the umbrella went into action, the Buchanans wilted, and took to their heels.

For a moment the Canon did not speak, then turning to Frank, who, still pale, had collapsed against a convenient wall, he said, sadly:

'Go home, my boy, and lie down till you recover.'

Then, taking me by the arm, he led me to the presbytery and upstairs to his study. Still in silence he set about repairing me. I had a badly cut lip, a fat ear, and the inevitable black eye, not to speak of skinned knuckles and a fearful hack on the shin where the younger Buchanan, free of mud, had weighed in towards the end.

'Stout lads, these Buchanans,' the Canon murmured, engaged with cotton wool and iodine, and still wearing the hat. 'Thank God you have some of that same good Scottish blood in you.'

When he had finished with me I had to sit down. He gave me a look, went to a cupboard, brought out a thistle-shaped wine glass and a bottle.

'A tablespoonful of this won't hurt you. It is the genuine Glenlivet.'

It tasted extremely genuine.

'Well, Carroll,' he went on, 'you've been dodging me rather skilfully for some weeks but I'm happy to have made your acquaintance. And in such not unfavourable circumstances, too.' He turned on me his smile of infinite charm. 'Since we are no longer strangers I invite you to come here, to my study, with your friend Ennis, on every Friday afternoon, after school, to discuss the affairs of the day, literature, even theology. You accept?'

My head was still ringing with that bash on the ear. I accepted.

'Good.' He took out his watch. 'As I must go to a School Board meeting, for which I am already late, may I ask how you intend explaining your present appearance to your grandparents?'

This, indeed, was a problem already worrying me.

'I could tell them I was sticking up for King Robert the first.'

'A subtle thought, Carroll. Emerging from the disgraceful Irish in you. But no, we will not demean a noble action with a lie, for which I perceive you have a natural aptitude. I will telephone your grandfather from the Board offices.'

So that, exactly, was the beginning of my association with a remarkable personality. His objective was not then apparent to me and became only so when it had failed. But for many months I was to enjoy the benefit of his wit, learning, and kindly charm. They left their impact upon me.

Today, however, I was less attentive at our usual session, I kept wondering what Frank had up his sleeve and who might be this someone special.

School was on the point of breaking up and on the following Thursday Frank and I set off for home together. He lived at Craig Crescent not far from my grandfather's house, and we took the same road across Levenford Common. This afternoon, however, with an offhand yet mysterious air, he said:

'Let's go by the station tonight. I've someone to meet there.'

'Who?'

'Cathy Considine.'

'And who's she?'

'She's my girl, Laurence.'

I must have shown my amazement. He laughed delightedly.

'We've known each other since we were kids. Brought up together in our prams so to speak. It's not surprising we're in love with one another.'

Now I was staggered. All that gush about holy purity and now this . . . this early commitment to Venus. God, you're a queer one, Frank, I thought. And I was suddenly extremely curious to see Cathy Considine.

'She's at the S.H. Convent at Dalcair. Home for the holidays. We'll have a ripping time.' Frank ran on excitedly as we climbed the station steps to the upper level. Having exploded his news he was eager to talk. 'I'm sure you'll like her . . .'

But the train had just arrived and almost at once Frank cried:

'Cathy! Look, Laurence, there she is!'

A stunningly pretty girl was coming towards us, smiling, and with an answering wave of her arm. She was not wearing her school uniform but, probably as one of the older convent girls, had on a natty little navy blue reefer jacket with brass buttons, a swinging kilted skirt and a fetching blue beret tilted slightly to one side. Never could I forget that first view of Cathy Considine. She was of medium height, her figure supple and free moving, her expression full of vivacity and life. Her eyes were dark, almost black, and sparkling with animation against her warmly coloured skin. She had a short rather flat undistinguished nose but her mouth was delicious, large, beautifully shaped with very red lips, parted now in a wide smile which exposed perfect teeth. Her dark brown hair, hanging loose from her beret, framed one cheek on which, high over the cheek bone, was a tiny dark mole. I felt my heart turn over as she drew near and, barely seeing me, took both of Frank's hands.

'Cathy.'

'Frank.'

They stood like this, looking at each other for a long moment, then she gave me a cool examining look.

'Who is the long-legged Borstal boy disguised in an Academy Blazer?'

'Just A. N. Other standing in the background of this lovesick tableau,' I said coldly. 'Sorry I haven't a camera. It's so touching.'

Her eyes narrowed.

'I'm glad you like it, because we do.'

'Well, while you're drooling over each other, have you any luggage? If so, I'll get it.'

'A suitcase. In the guard's van.'

I left them together, found her case, then we set out for Craig Crescent. Frank offered to carry the case, which was no light weight, tried to bring me into the conversation, but without much luck. She was too busy with him, and apparently bent on excluding me. This vacation was going to be the greatest fun. They'd been set a competition at Cathy's school to see who could bring back the best album of pressed wild flowers. A silver cup was the prize.

'Naturally I'm not wild about botany, Frank. But I'd like to win that cup. Just to put Sister Philomena's eye out, the old hag, she always has her knife in me. And it'll be terrific fun scouring the Overton woods, and the Long-crags too.'

Frank agreed with enthusiasm, half turning to me.

'You'll join us, Laurie.'

'Well . . . possibly,' I said, distantly. 'If I have time.'

'Of course you will. Now, here we are. You'll come in and have tea. Joint invitation from Cathy and me.'

'No thanks. I'm expected at Davigan's,' I lied calmly

and atrociously. I loathed the Davigans, and Daniel the son
I particularly despised.

'Well . . .' Frank said doubtfully. 'If that's so . . .'

The Considine house was next door to Ennis's property,
a villa of the same size, with an adjoining unfenced garden
which suggested intimate communications. I put the suitcase down at the front gate. Cathy was inspecting me with
a critical, not quite comprehending yet definitely unfriendly
eye.

'I'm obliged to you, porter. Was it too heavy for your
delicate constitution?'

'A mere trifle. What have you inside? Coals or steel
corsets?'

'Both, naturally. And a hair shirt. How much is the tip?'

'Pay Frank,' I said. 'I usually stand in for him when any
physical effort is required.'

As I took off I saw colour flood Frank's face at this underhand reference to the few engagements I had undertaken
on his behalf and I felt badly about it. I blamed her, of
course, and swore I would have nothing more to do with
her. Yet, walking home in a rage, my mind was exasperat-
ingly full of her. When I'd had my tea I put a few
deliberately offhand inquiries to my grandmother. Yes,
she knew of the girl's mother in a general sort of way. Mrs.
Considine was the widow of the late head draughtsman at
Dennisons, comfortably off on a life pension from the shipyard, a stout, lethargic woman whom I now vaguely recollected moving slowly, bedizened in beaded black, to a
front seat in St Patrick's.

'So you've met her daughter?'

'For the first and last time.'

'They say she's rather spoiled.'

'She's the giddy limit.'

Nevertheless, while I hated this little trollop in the brass-
buttoned reefer jacket, I had fallen for her, stricken with
the ridiculous anguish of an adolescent first love. When
Frank came to the Bruce house next morning, without the
slightest reference to my ill humour of the day before, my
resolutions broke down, I agreed to go botanizing that
afternoon.

Nothing could have been more mistaken, more fatally
damaging to my self-esteem. Never before, even in the
worst discomfitures of a penurious youth, had I been made

to feel so unwanted, not of course by Frank, but by her. Our few verbal exchanges, at first deliberately offensive, became towards the end of the expedition, heatedly hurtful, and I swore by my favourite saint—Augustine before his conversion—that I would never go out with them again.

To assist them in their idiotic floral hunt they had roped in and were occasionally accompanied by that other youth, Daniel Davigan, a despicable hanger on, a clod who, though he had outgrown it by two years, was still at St Patrick's parochial school, and whose obsequious attempts at friendship I had stiffly discouraged.

This co-optation of Davigan in my place was a bitter pill and since it has point later on he must merit a more accurate portrayal. In appearance he was not prepossessing: a flattish face with ill-assorted features, rusty red hair and the blanched skin and pale greenish eyes that often go with such colouring, as if all his pigmentation had been expended on his scrubby brush. Yet it was his manner that offended me, a blend of truculence and ingratiating intimacy with which he sought to advance himself. Doubtless I was prejudiced. Frank, who disliked nobody, was at least prepared to tolerate Dan who, after all, had his social difficulties as the eldest son of a small jobbing builder, a short, hairy red gorilla of a man lampooned in the town for his feat of propagating sixteen children, eleven of which survived. Once on a rare visit to the Davigan home I had caught a shuddering glimpse of the marital chamber with its huge brassbound bed on which such incessant procreation and parturition had been enacted and which seemed to justify the lines dedicated to Mrs Davigan, whose maiden name was O'Shane, and generally attributed to Dr Ennis.

'Oh, a terrible life has Bridget O'Shane,
Three minutes' boredom and nine months' pain
A fortnight's rest then at it again.
Oh, a terrible life has Bridget O'Shane.'

This admittedly was a hard thing for Dan to live down and although I grudged him the privilege of accompanying Frank and Cathy he at least served as a kind of watch-dog. Indeed I began to want him to be with them, since when he was not, and they went alone, I suffered most cruelly, broodingly picturing them, not only in the most tender intimacies, but hotly and falsely endowing them with every act of sexual abandonment. Indeed, on many of these summer afternoons I hung about the vicinity of Craig Crescent, behind a convenient wall, in the vain hope of observing some evidence of misconduct and throwing it in their faces. Once, unable to restrain myself as they came down from the wood, I stepped out and brazenly accosted them, peering for signs of guilt. Alas, they only looked happy. Cathy certainly was bright-eyed and moistly flushed, diffusing a heady perfume, entirely her own, and gaily excited, full of life and undulant movement, but Frank, calm and undisturbed as ever, wore unmistakably that confounding expression of happy, guileless innocence. I was on the point of turning away when he called out.

'Look what we found today. An absolute rarity. A bee orchis. And by the way, Laurie, I have to go to the Rectory tomorrow afternoon. Why don't you take Cathy up the wood.'

It seemed the chance of a lifetime to get even with her. While she watched me with a queer expression, half derisive, half expectant, I said,

'Sorry, Frank, I wouldn't be found dead with your Cathy, in or out of the wood.' And I walked off.

From the first I had not meant to go, equally convinced that she had not the least intention of keeping the appointment. Nevertheless, at two o'clock on the following afternoon I was drawn irresistibly to that now detested end of Craig Crescent. And as I came round the final bend there she was, perched on the gate leading to Longcrags Wood. Surprise rooted me.

'So you decided to turn up,' she said.

I found my breath. 'I wanted to see if you would.'

'Well, I did. Disappointed?'

'Not particularly.'

She laughed. 'That's a strange admission from the Bruce heir apparent. I thought you hated me.'

'Isn't it the other way round?'

'I ought to be pretty sick of you. Frank's been feeding me your good points until I almost threw up. Did you know it, he thinks you're quite marvellous?'

'Strange delusion, isn't it?'

'I'm beginning to wonder. It does look as if you'd done some remarkably odd sort of things. I mean for instance, writing that essay just after you came out of gaol and winning the bursary . . .'

There was nothing I could say to this, and a silence fell during which she seemed to study me with a scrutiny so unsettling that I said:

'Shall we get a move on with your collecting?'

'Let's just take a walk.' She jumped down from the gate. 'The truth is I'm sick of all these ghastly ragged robins and bladderworts. And thanks to Frank I have enough to knock out Sister Philomena's false teeth.'

'You want to?'

'Frequently.'

'What's wrong with her?'

'Oh, just being herself.' As we took the path into the wood, she went on: 'Always nagging on propriety and that sort of stuff, making us wear shifts when we take a bath and looking me over as if I was going to have a baby.' She broke off. 'But let's forget her. I get enough of her at school.'

For a few moments we walked on in silence under the tall beech trees that fretted the sunlight on the winding green path. The wood was warm and deeply still. I could not believe that I was physically here with her, in this quiet secret place. Perhaps she felt this too, for she moved restlessly and suddenly laughed.

'Funny we're doing this! And getting along quite nicely.' She gave me a quick side-glance. 'I really owe you an apology for being so beastly.'

'We didn't get off to a very good start, did we?'

'It was my fault being so chippie at the station. I suppose I wanted to impress you.'

'You did,' I said, with a sudden constriction of my heart. 'I thought you were the prettiest girl I'd ever seen in my life.'

She actually flushed and kept her eyes down.

'You see, Laurence,' she paused awkwardly, unaware of the commotion aroused in me by her use of my first name. 'It's just that I'm so bound up in Frank that I sort of resented his being fond of anyone else. But I don't now. If it means anything to you, and I don't suppose it does, I really like you very much.' She hesitated, still not looking at me. 'I only hope you'll like me.'

Now my heart seemed to expand and fill my chest so

that I could scarcely breath. With all the anguish of un-sullied adolescence I managed to say:

'If you want to know, I fell in love with you the minute I set eyes on you.'

She gave a shaky little laugh. 'You can't possibly mean that. But it's nice of you, Laurence. And a relief. I've been upset and sort of jumpy over our misunderstanding. I suppose,' she added hurriedly, 'because I felt it was up-setting. Frank. He's so . . . so scrupulous about everything.'

'Yes, he is.'

'Do you think . . . perhaps he's a little too much that way?'

'What way?'

'Well . . . sort of strict about little things. Straitlaced. Just think, if you can believe it, all the time he and I have been up here by ourselves in this lovely wood he's never once kissed me. He says we should wait till we're properly engaged.'

'If only I'd had his chance.'

Had I spoken these words and if so why had she not protested? Now my heart was thudding like a trip hammer. She was so close to me our arms touched as we moved slowly up the hill, a sudden contact that ran through every nerve in my body. Yet she made no effort to with-draw. Most disturbing of all there was the strange sensa-tion of an answering emotion, an emanation that made my senses swim, an outreaching that sought with a nervous excitement for some long-frustrated fulfilment.

'Oh, dear,' she almost sighed. 'It's so warm. Let's rest a bit. It's dry and lovely here.'

She sank down on the grass by some wild azalea bushes. Her face, sunflushed, was turned towards me, her eyes dark and startled. Beside her, I took her hand, the small palm hot and moist. Her fingers closed on mine tightly, so tightly.

My head was swimming, yet some sense of loyalty re-mained. This was Frank's girl, how could I poach on his preserves? And more: under his influence and the many sessions we had spent in Dingwall's study, I had achieved a commendable state of virtue, even to the point of serving the Canon's Mass when timed for eleven o'clock. Alas, in this recreation of the original Garden, the serpent was hissing in my ears and at any moment the apple might fall from nowhere into my companion's lap. Indeed, as though in acceptance of this phenomenon, her eyelids slowly drooped. Then, as I bent blindly towards her, there came from below a shout, a series of shouts, almost a hullabaloo, and as we scrambled to our feet, shocked and shaken, a figure appeared threshing through the undergrowth, Davigan, sweating, panting, propitiating, yet somehow suspicious.

'I thought I'd lost you. Met Frank on Chapel Street. Thought I'd come after you and give you a hand.'

He stood there, grinning, the oaf, clutching a tuft of something earthy.

'And look what I got for you. I don't know what it is but it looks good to me.'

Cathy, her eyes downcast and averted, was fearfully pale. My breastbone was thrumming like a drum. I looked at Davigan and his trophy.

'It's a stinking fennel root, you clod. Why don't you eat it?'

But nothing would ever get Davigan down. He hung on to us all afternoon and when I could stand it no longer and took off he was still there.

My state of mind may be imagined as I swung across Craig Crescent on the way home. Suddenly at the corner Dr. Ennis came out of the side surgery door, carrying a cased salmon rod and a gaff. He called out.

'How's the gooseberry today?'

Although I couldn't trust myself to speak I forced a sickly smile.

He looked at me keenly.

'Want to come fishing?'

I knew that the good-natured old rip was sorry for me, apparently mooning around at a loose end. To preserve my self-esteem I should have refused his invitation. But I needed companionship and I liked to go fishing. Often I'd gone out with my father before he became ill.

We got into the old black Ford. Dr Ennis drove in silence and, as could be expected, at a wild, erratic speed. We were soon at Malloch on the far side of the Loch where he had a boat, and until late afternoon I sculled hard for him, sweating desire out of me, while he cast across all the likely bays. It looked like being a blank day, but just as we were coming in he changed his fly to a big Zulu and at the first throw was into a fish. Ten minutes later I struck with the gaff and had it in the boat, a fine fresh-run salmon.

'A good twelve pounds.' He chuckled. 'You did well for me, lad. And with the oaring too. This deserves a drink.'

We beached and padlocked the boat, went up the shingle to the bar of the Blairmore Arms where the doctor, after displaying our catch with a good deal of profane boasting, ordered a double John Dewar.

'And what's yours, Laurence?'

'Beer,' I said, hardily. I would have died sooner than ask for lemonade.

He laughed. 'You'll make a good medical student. Give him a mild and bitter, barman.'

About an hour and three double whiskies later, Ennis nosed his way into the soft dark night, racked the gears, and we set off for Levenford. I felt cosy after that second order of not so mild ale and the doctor was in high good humour. He liked an audience and in the bar he had unloaded his repertoire of broad Scots stories on the locals. He kept chuckling, coughing and grunting to himself. Suddenly he said:

'Carroll, you're a lad after my own heart. What's your opinion of this damn business between my son and that Considine girl? It's been going on since they were in their blasted hippins.'

'Well, sir,' I said carefully. 'I think they're extremely fond of one another.'

'You mean to tell me they're in love? At their age?'

'They certainly mean to get married when they're a bit older.'

'Heavens almighty! But what goes on the now, up in the woods, the two of them, thegither?' He always lapsed into broad Scots when excited.

'Nothing, sir. Absolutely nothing.'

'My arse and Jeannie Deans!' he exploded. 'They must do something.'

'They pick flowers, sir.'

'Almighty Heavens!' He was silenced. Then: 'Listen, lad. That girl drips sex like one of McKay's Ayrshire cows leaks milk. Do you mean to tell me that up in these Long-crags with not a soul to watch them, Frank isn't . . .you know what?'

'I swear to you he isn't. I know Frank. He's good. Absolutely good.' With two pints of Tennant's best inside me I felt noble, rising in defence of my best friend. 'Why, his influence has even kept me good. He's incapable of anything like that!'

'Oh, Lord.' He gave out a kind of groan. 'You mean he's not even trying for a tickle?'

'Positively not, sir. I'd swear to it.'

Again he was silent, then he murmured to himself:

'But picking flowers. What a daisy.'

We were approaching the lights of Levenford and had reached Craig Crescent before he spoke again.

'Come ben the house and I'll give you your half of the salmon.'

'Oh I couldn't, doctor . . .'

Despite my protests he insisted, giving me the better tail half which sent my grandmother into such transports she didn't even ask to smell my breath. I refrained from telling her the doctor's final remark.

'I daresay ye'll get it served with Bannockburn sauce.'

Before I went to bed I said some extra prayers, celebrating my deliverance from the curse of Adam. But all of that night I scarcely slept one hour.

THREE

DAWN COMES EARLY in the Swiss uplands and on the morning of October 7th, although it went against the grain, I was up with the lark to make a quick round of the ward. We had only five cases, none of them serious: two simply retained for observation after pleurisy, a mesenteric adenitis and a synovitis of the knee, the so-called 'white swelling', both certainly due to bovine T.B., and finally an early Pott's curvature that I had already put in plaster. By half past eight I had finished and after breakfasting and checking with Matron, whom I had already skilfully briefed and who, to my surprise, seemed quite intrigued at the prospect of the new arrivals, I set out for Zürich in the Clinic's Opel station wagon. Why so early, Carroll? Why such indecent haste? You are not duty bound to meet and greet the dear pilgrims until half past five. Could it be that there was purpose in that telephone call last night when the good matron had retired and that once again you are putting pleasure before business?

At first the mountain road is steep, winding and narrow but beyond Jenaz it opens out into the Coire valley. At this hour, except for a few farm wagons, there was no delaying traffic. I made good time and was in Zürich, cruising along the Tielstrasse, looking for an unmetered parking place, just after eleven o'clock.

Zürich has been decried as a city of underground bankers. I have nothing against bankers, since I never meet them, and I liked this fine, rich city, presiding over its broad river and the Züricher See with the dignity of an elder statesman, and never cluttered with gaping tourists, since most foreigners came quite simply to visit their money. A stroll down the Bahnolstrasse, where I stopped at Grieder's to buy a couple of ties, brought me to the Baur-au-Lac just before noon. I went into the garden and ordered a dry martini. It came at once, substantial and really dry, with a thin curl of well-pared lemon peel, confirming my unbiased award of five stars to this superb hotel. Naturally it is expensive, but now that I had some sort of income I enjoyed blowing it, moreover my visits were infrequent and as Lotte enjoyed everything de luxe it paid off to indulge her here.

She arrived at that moment, bareheaded and smiling, very smartly turned out in a plain but attractive tan suit that exactly matched her corn straw hair. I should explain that Lotte is Swedish with the colouring of her race, not the conventional slinky fictional blonde, but a big, easy-going, solidly beautiful girl with the athletic body of a champion discus thrower and careless honey-coloured eyes that usually seem full of laughter. Of course she doesn't throw the discus. She is an ex-air hostess promoted to receptionist at Zürich for a big Scandinavian Charter Line . . . the AKTIEBOLA-GET SVENSKA ORNFLYG and, both being practised in the art, we had picked each other up in the airport bar about four months ago when I was dispatching a consignment of boys to Birmingham. I had become fond of Lotte since then and except for one thing I would have been mad about her. As it was, I warmed all over as she sat down and crossed her legs under her short skirt. But the waiter was already at my elbow.

'I'm one ahead of you,' I said in German. As part of her

job she spoke five languages and, teaching it the best way, had brought my German to what might justly be termed top form—we often laughed together over the way I'd had on the Committee with my *'Entschuldigen Sie, mein Herr, können Sie mir zeigen, wo der nächste Abort ist?'* 'Can you cope with a double?'

'If you'll have one.'

I leaned forward when the waiter had gone.

'You're looking most unbearably attractive, darling.'

'Thank you, sir.'

'Been meeting many V.I.P.'s lately?'

'Lots and lots. Dark handsome men.'

'Hmm. African or Burmese?'

'No, no, one Italian, one French.'

'Ah! A mixed Vermouth.'

She laughed shortly, narrowing her cat's eyes.

'Really, I'm serious, Laurence. Two gorgeous men.'

'Liar. Only don't start sleeping with them or I'll break your Swedish neck. Incidentally,' I said, with a momentary anxiety, 'you *are* free this afternoon? You weren't quite sure last night when I called you.'

'What about those medical researches?'

'We'll work on them together.'

She kept me on edge for a moment then nodded, companionably.

'Not on duty till five o'clock.'

'That's perfect. I have to be at the airport myself then.' And I told her briefly I was meeting a patient and his mother.

The waiter had brought two menu cards with the drinks. We studied them in silence, ordered, and half an hour later we went into the restaurant, a glassed addition built out into the garden with the river on one side.

I remember so well that delicious luncheon, the last before my troubles began. We both had the iced canteloupe as a starter, so golden, so sweetly ripe, and dead ice cold. Lotte, who never seemed to look ahead, or perhaps had no need to supercharge her vitality, chose for her main course poached turbot with hollandaise sauce and little new potatoes *vapeur*. I had a thick *filet mignon* cooked *au point* with spinach and *pommes pont neuf*. We drank two of the best, yet relatively inexpensive, Swiss wines, she the light Döle Johannesburger, I the red Pinot Noir, and just enjoying the food and looking at each other, we didn't talk much. Coffee was all we wanted afterwards, and we put it down suspiciously fast.

Lotte's apartment was in a new block in Kloten, quite near the airport. I drove there, parked the car at the rear of the building and was beside her as she turned the key in the door. I knew it all: living-room with small kitchen off, bedroom and nicely tiled bathroom, all furnished simply and functionally in modern Scandinavian style and excessively clean. Whenever we entered she drew the curtains in the bedroom, gave me her big warm smile and began with complete naturalness, keeping her eyes on me, to take off her clothes. Soon she was stretched out flat on the bed.

'Come quick, Laurence. It is too long since the last time. . . . I want lots and lots of loving.'

Stark naked, lit by the filtered daylight, she invited the physical act openly, naturally and with undisguised desire.

Afterwards, she studied my face, so intense, it seemed to amuse her.

'We must have a cigarette.' She rolled over, like a big languid cream-fed yellow cat, reaching to the bedside table, speaking in English which she knew moderately well. 'Then again we have much more fun-fun.'

That, exactly, was the trouble with Lotte. Bliss when we made love, and afterwards nothing. No tenderness, no persistent sense of belonging, nothing of that yearning which springs not from the body but from the spirit. Of course, an excess of yearning could be dangerous: to my cost I had learned how difficult it could be getting rid of a yearner, particularly the soulful type. But surely, I told myself, there should be *something*, a communication of the heart rather than the adrenals, that endures after the intensity of such a union. Was I asking for the moon? In this case, perhaps. The Swedes, I reflected sadly, were known as prolific copulators, they took it all in their athletic stride. A hygienic exercise.

Lotte drew on her cigarette, her mind already diverted to the mundane.

'Who are these people you are meeting?'

'I told you, darling. A small boy and his mother. It's odd . . . years ago I fancied I was in love with her. Yet in a queer sort of way I almost hated her.'

'See you go on hating. No more of the other thing.'

'You can bet on that. . . . But Lotte, you don't really love me.'

'So you want to be loved? Heart to heart. And pink roses round the door.'

'Don't jeer, Lotte. I mean something deeper . . . that you can hold on to when you need it . . . when you're not on top of the world.'

She burst out laughing.

'When the dog barks at you in your dark street.'

Once, misguidedly, I had tried to confide in her. I was silent. Perhaps she had sensed that she had hurt me. She said quickly:

'Ah! Love, what is that but meeting trouble? I like you much. We give each other much satisfaction. And I'm not a gold brick.'

'Gold digger,' I corrected.

She repeated the words, laughed, then put her arm round me.

'Come. We forget love and enjoy each other.'

It was a quarter to five when she got up and dressed.

With my hands behind my head I watched her out of one eye. In the comedy of life nothing is nicer than a pretty girl stepping out of short, clean white pants—you can keep all your tiddy pastel shades. The reverse process, the stepping in, now being enacted, strikes a bourgeois note. Drawing the curtains, shutting up shop. But in her perfectly fitting saxe uniform, the cockaded bonnet not the common saucy touch but elegant, she looked distressingly smart. The afternoon, which had slightly tarnished me, had put a bloom on her.

'We must hurry, or I'll be late.'

I sighed and heaved out of bed. My knees creaked. I was no longer young and healthy.

'I do hate leaving you so soon, Lotte. After being so close to you . . . it's a wrench.'

She shook her head.

'You are a nice man, Laurence, of whom I am so fond. I never thought for an Englisher I could feel so much. Don't spoil it all with such sentimism.'

'Sentiment,' I amended sadly. 'And I'm Scottish.'

I brought the car round to the front entrance and we drove to Kloten. You may accuse me of being oversold on Zürich when I commend Kloten Airport as the best in

Europe—meticulously efficient, immaculately clean, with a first-class restaurant and a snack-bar serving the best coffee I ever drank. We each had a quick cup, standing up. Typically, there was no one at the B.E.A. counter, but from the long range of bustling Swiss desks on the other side Lotte came back with some bad news.

'Your flight is seventy minutes late.'

'Oh, blast.'

She showed all her lovely teeth in an irritating smile. 'You must sit and dream of me, liebling. With your so tender heart. And I tell you. When your friends arrive I bring them quickly through customs to you.'

I went through to the lower bar, found a quiet corner and ordered a Kirsch. Suddenly I felt tired and unaccountably depressed. No, not unaccountably—it was the old post-copulative *triste* The Augustine tag came to my mind: *Post coitum omne animal triste est*. How true, how everlastingly true! Usually I can ignore it but today I failed to shake it off. Her crack at my secret hallucination had upset me. And what a fool I was, wasting my time, and substance, in fact wasting my life with these frivolous fringe benefits. Lotte wasn't a bad sort, but what did I really mean to her. A partner in fun-fun. And although she wasn't promiscuous, I had a dismal notion that I was not the only one to share her suspiciously broad and springy bed. But this was the least of my sudden dejection. That mood was coming on, that familiar cursed mood, the epigastric syndrome, or if you prefer it, that psychological punch in the guts. For me there was no escape. Never. Even as a back-slider I could not escape that sense of guilt. I had been brought up on sin, both varieties, venial and mortal, the latter, if unforgiven, a prelude to damnation. Ah, goodness, that comprehensive word, that ever elusive, state of good!

Oh, cut it out, Carroll. Be your age. You gave up all that truck years ago. And nowadays who gives it a thought? And if you want to argue, hasn't the recent Commission of Christian Churches practically sanctified all forms of pre-marital sex, throwing in a few self-service practices as extra jam, with three hearty Christian cheers for *Lady Chatterley's Lover*!

With an effort I turned my thoughts towards the approaching meeting, which disagreeable though it might be, was not without a certain mild expectation. Interesting, in a minor way, to see Cathy again and to know if anything of that juvenile regard for me remained. The probability stirred faint memories and, encouraged by another Kirsch and a sustaining club sandwich, I drifted back to Levenford, to that eventful day, and the events leading to it, when I had last seen Cathy Considine and Francis Ennis, the day of Frank's ordination.

FOUR

THE SUMMER that year had been exceptionally fine, and on that late August morning as I set out from Winton station the sun beamed benignly in a cloudless sky.

The train was a 'local' and as the slow journey wore on with stops at several stations, I had ample time to reflect on the event that was bringing me to Levenford. Actually it was an inconvenience for me to make the trip since, having graduated M.B. at the University during the month before, I had signed on as ship's surgeon in the s.s *Tasman*, a cargo-cum-passenger liner plying between Liverpool and Sydney, due to sail on the evening of the day after the ceremony. But I had promised Frank to be there on his big day, although since leaving Levenford to attend the University, my communications with him, to say nothing of my visits, had been infrequent. Frank's sudden decision to enter the priesthood, so logical in one sense, had taken me by surprise. He had never spoken to me of a vocation although I had long suspected it. I had already surmised that a subconscious aversion to his father's way of life, while never admitted, perhaps never recognized, had deterred him from continuing the Ennis general practice. But he had meant to be a teacher, and had set out to take his M.A. degree at Edinburgh. And beyond all other considerations his future had been centred on Cathy, their marriage was an understood thing, practically preordained. What could have upset the apple cart? A sudden call to give himself to God? Perhaps there had been pressure from the everlasting Dingwall. This I was inclined to doubt, recollecting an incident when the Canon, detaining me after one of our Friday sessions, had caught me by the collar and shaken me till my teeth rattled.

'It's you I want, with your good Protestant blood. What use would Frank be on the parish milk round? Put a rosary in one hand and a lily in the other and you're done with him.'

Had some deeper psychological reason inclined him towards celibacy? There was the occasion when, during one of our conversations—I was then a three-year medical student—Frank suddenly exclaimed:

'Isn't it disgusting, Laurence, that the organ of procreation should be the very sewer through which half the impurities of the body are discharged?' And how his expression had frozen when I laughed.

'You'll have to blame that one on the Creator, Frank.'

'Not blame, Laurie,' he said severely. 'It was meant. By omniscient design.'

He was an interesting conundrum, still open to speculation! For reasons that were unrevealed, and remained inexplicable, Frank had suddenly slipped out of his commitment to Cathy and taken off for the seminary.

The train was late in arriving and although I put on speed from the railway station to St Patrick's, the service had already begun as I slid into an inconspicuous seat beside a pillar. From this retreat I had a clear view of the altar and of the two front rows, where I made out amongst a number of others, Mrs Ennis, Cathy, and what looked like the entire extensive range of the Davigan family.

This ceremony is always impressive and I admit it gave me a bit of a turn. The sight of Frank, all in white, prostrate in an attitude of supreme subjection, made me feel a bit of a sickening character. Since I'd cut loose from Levenford I had not infrequently been in the same position for altogether different reasons.

After the final blessing I waited outside, the emerging congregation, which was large, milling round me. Aware that I should not immediately see Frank, I hoped that Mrs Ennis or Cathy might give me some idea of his arrangements for the day. However, it was Dan Davigan who found me, pumping my hand and patting me on the back with the insufferable presumption of a lifelong boon companion.

'Well met, man. I saw you, had my eye on you, as you slipped in. Why didn't you come forward, proper like, to the place I'd reserved for you? I'm a St Pat's sidesman now, y'understand, and I throw my weight around. Anyhow, here we are, and I've an invite for you. Celebration repast at the Ennis's home for six o'clock. You'll be there?'

'I'll try.'

'Oh, but you must, or Frank'll never forgive you. Sure, your name's never off his lips.'

Restively, I looked about me. I still hoped to have a word with Cathy, but she was lost in the crowd or had already gone. I had begun to move away when Davigan exclaimed:

'And now I've a message from the Canon. He wants to see you. In the sacristy. Poor suffering soul, he's a done man, due for retirement to the sisters next month. In you go, I'll wait for you.'

There was nothing else for it. I had to go. The old autocrat was in a wheeled chair, but still erect, with a book on his knee. His eyes, sunken but still burning in their sockets, unmistakably alive, took me all in.

'So,' he said, when he'd finished looking me over. 'I'd a notion to see you before they sent me to the scrap heap.' Without taking his eyes off me, he felt for his snuff box from under his soutane, using his good left hand and, still adeptly, inhaled a pinch. 'I perceive that you have slipped, Carroll. Badly. It's written all over you.'

I felt the blood rush into my face and neck.

'At least you've still the grace to be ashamed of yourself. I needn't remind you it was you I wanted in there. I worked hard on you too. All those Friday afternoons.' He nodded sideways. 'But, with that slippery Irish side to you, you got away. However, don't think you'll ever escape. The seed is in you and you'll never get rid of it.'

There was a pause. I was grateful that he spared me a cross-examination of my faults, and somehow sad and shamed that I had disappointed him.

'I hope you're feeling better, Canon,' I mumbled.

'I'm as well as ever I was, except for the use of one flipper, and good for another ten years. I'll have my eye on you, Carroll.'

'I've always appreciated your interest in me, Canon, and all that you did for me.'

'Drop the blarney, Carroll. Just let some of our Fridays stick.'

Another pause. He took up the book. 'As a quasi literary character, notably an essayist, do you ever read poems?'

298

I shook my head.

'Well, take this. It's a prize they gave me at Blairs many a year ago. I've marked one poem. It might have been written specially for you.'

When I took the book he snapped the snuff box shut.

'Kneel down, sinner.' I had to obey. 'I'm going to bless you, Carroll, and it's not only the Lord's will, but mighty appropriate in your case that I have to do so with the wrong hand. For before God, if ever you achieve salvation it'll be the wrong way—by falling in backwards through the side door.'

As I left the sacristy, horribly discomposed, I realized I had barely uttered a single coherent word. To recover myself I sat down in the now empty church and opened the book he had given me. 'The Poems of Francis Thompson'. I had never heard of him. His photograph was the frontispiece, an emaciated, self-tortured face with a faint straggle of moustache.

A bookmark indicated the poem towards which my attention had been directed. I looked at the opening lines. I began to read. My mind, full of the recent interview, and the puzzle of Frank and Cathy, was not on the words, but I wanted to get rid of Davigan, so I sat there reading on, without real comprehension, until I came to the end. Absently, I put the book in my pocket, got up slowly, and left the church. And there outside, still waiting for me, was Davigan.

'I never thought you'd be that long. But maybe he wanted to *hear* you. Where are you off to?'

'To visit my grandparents.'

'That's my way also. I'll give you a butty along Renton Road.'

In subsequent encounters since that memorable interruption in the Longcrags Wood, my dislike for Davigan had not been mitigated, a feeling which, under his habitual ingratiating effusiveness, I sensed he returned with interest. And now, armed with a greater confidence, an exudation of affluence, and cherishing some secret satisfaction that imparted a smirk to his heavy, pallid features, he struck me as even more objectionable. He was got up in a stiff white choker, spongebag trousers and a cut-away coat, the sidesman's outfit, in which he showed people to their places and shovelled up the two collections, but this sartorial elegance was now brought to the verge of the ridiculous by a bowler hat which sat down on his ears, causing them to protrude. Prejudice, no doubt, made me liken him to a stage butler in a second-rate farce. I avoided the gesture with which he attempted to take my arm as we set off towards Renton Road.

'A heavenly affair,' he began. 'And what a fine turn out. You were a shade late in getting in, Laurence.'

Being first named by Davigan did not lessen my resentment, but I made no protest, except to maintain silence.

'I noticed you didn't join us all at the altar rails. You'd see we all took Communion. Oh, I don't doubt you're in a state of grace all right. I daresay you weren't fasting. Of course, Dr Ennis was an absentee. No use to pretend he was out on a case. He's not really one of us now, Laurence. No, no, sadly fallen away. Ah, what a sorrow for the young priest. But the mother, ah, there was a joyful face, even though the tears were running down her cheeks. A saint. That's where Francis, I beg his pardon, Father Francis, gets it. His holiness I mean. They say the Canon hasn't bespoke him for St Pat's, but the mother will press for it, I'll be bound. Though they tell me the young Father's not too glib with the sermons.'

A further silence followed, then with a sly side glance he said:

'And what did you think of Miss Considine, Laurence?'

'Cathy? I thought she looked extremely sad.'

'Ah, didn't we all now, more or less. A fine young man giving up the world for God. But she looked well, you thought? She's come on, like, in her looks?'

During the Mass I had found myself watching Cathy, thinking that she had altered in some way but that the change, whatever it might be, had given her something that was not there before.

'She's an extremely attractive young woman,' I said shortly. 'And an interesting one.'

'She's all that, and more,' he agreed fervently. 'Of course, being all in the black for her mother's decease hardly gives her a chance.'

'What!' I exclaimed. 'Is Mrs. Considine dead?'

'She is that, none the less. This couple of months past. And after a long and painful illness, God help the poor soul. May she rest in Peace.' He tipped the bowler and made the sign of the Cross. 'It's hard on Cathy, for you understand . . .' he gave me a look, 'the pension died with her, the mother I mean. Still anon, the dear girl has friends, that fine Spanish lace mantilla she had on came from my own mother, just to show you an example.'

He had my attention now.

'But what'll Cathy do with herself? Has she a job? She'll have to give up that big house.'

'Well, no.' He assumed a considering manner which widened his smirk. 'She'll not be given notice to quit. You see, Laurence, being in the building trade like, my old man has bought the house. It's a desirable property and may come in handy in the not too distant future.'

'Why so?' I asked sharply.

He let the smirk go. Instead he faced me with a defiant yet triumphant grin.

'As a matter of fact, Carroll, you may as well hear it now, sooner nor later. It's not out yet because of the other attraction, the ordination. But when you speak of Miss Considine you're speaking of the future Mrs Davigan. Cathy and yours truly are engaged to wed.'

I stopped short.

'You're joking, Davigan.'

'Devil the joke, Carroll.' The grin had become a sneer. 'We've come up in the world since you and your stuck-up Prot relations looked down your long noses at us. Take a peep up there.'

We had reached the end of Renton Road where it branched to Craig Crescent and Woodside Drive. He was pointing to the lower slope of the Longcrags, visible now beyond the Crescent, that wooded hill where the thrushes nested and wild flowers grew, the choice beauty spot of the town, that same wood where Cathy and I had almost found our Eden. Now the wood was razed, and amidst the stumps a rash of jerry bungalows was in process of eruption.

'Oh, God, what a bloody mess!'

'That's what you think! Let me tell you, it's the Davigan Building Estate. Our own financial empire! And it's going to make our pile. Put that in your pipe and smoke it, you half-baked snob!'

He left me with that parting shot and after a long speechless inspection of that shameful, hideous vista I made my way slowly to my grandparents' at Woodside Avenue.

Here was a different atmosphere. They were quietly pleased to see me, finally qualified as a doctor, a result atoning in their eyes for my indifferent start in life. They gave me a simple lunch, a kindness I was able to repay by prescribing for the old lady's rheumatoid arthritis. Bruce himself had slowed down but, still haunting the field of Bannockburn in spirit, spent a good hour showing me marked passages in an old Parish Register he had recently uncovered from a barrow in the Levenford Vennel. My present mood was tolerant of his obsession—it seemed less a prideful mania than an old man's pathetic delusion—yet while I bore with him my mind kept grappling with that incredible situation not half a mile away, in Craig Crescent. Cathy and Davigan . . . it simply couldn't be! I had to get to the bottom of it. Although I was not due at Frank's until six, towards five o'clock I said goodbye to the Bruces and started off by the back road towards the Crescent.

No sign of life was visible in the curtained windows of the Considine house as I came through the front garden, and when I rang the bell there was a longish pause before Cathy appeared, still wearing the black dress that Davigan had deplored. It made her look older, but to my mind, lovelier. How to approach her?—it was difficult. I smiled in a friendly manner.

'May I come in? I'm too early for the banquet next door.'

She held out her hand without surprise.

'Hello, Laurence. I sort of thought you'd look in.'

The parlour was exactly as I had known it during my rare visits in the past, the same formally placed furniture, stiff, polished, and lifeless as the vase of dried-up honesty on the chiffonier. And there was little animation in Cathy as we sat down on hard chairs on opposite sides of that dead room. Her eyes were dull, she looked only half awake. Perhaps she read my mind.

'I was trying for a bit of a nap after one of the tablets Dr Ennis has been giving me. I don't sleep too well these nights, alone in the house.'

'I was sorry to hear about your mother.'

'She's better gone. Cancer isn't much fun.'

'It must have been hard for her, and for you.'

A silence fell between us, stressed by the slow beat of the longcase clock in the hall.

'And now, Cathy,' I said, trying to speak lightly, 'what's all this I hear about your engagement to Davigan?'

'It's no hearsay.' She answered at once, as though prepared for the question. 'While nothing's settled, Dan wants to marry me.'

'And you?'

'I'd be better off married.' She said it quite flatly, then after a pause: 'Dan's no prize packet but he's been helpful and kind. His parents too. Since Mother died I've been sort of sunk, Laurence. And of course with the pension gone there's nothing but debts. I wouldn't be in this house now if it weren't for the Davigans.'

'Cathy, you're not the one to give up. You'll get over this . . . this upset, and find a decent job.'

'Such as? I'm not really qualified for anything.'

'At least you could try . . . to make a go of your life by yourself.'

'By myself?' She gave me a sudden direct glance, then looked away. 'You don't really know me, Laurence. Or do you?'

I did, of course, but how could I speak of it. Dimly outlined against the darkening window, her head slightly drooping on her neck, a sad Rosetti profile, there was in her attitude a softness, a sense of mystery and longing, that touched me to the heart. All I could find to say was:

'Things haven't worked out too well for you, Cathy?'

She did not evade the question, yet the readiness of her answer made it sound forced, unreal. A prepared statement.

'You know I'd been saving myself for Frank for years, looking forward . . . waiting, even thinking he'd chuck the seminary. You're a doctor, Laurie. It can't go on, all that repression . . . it's against my nature.' She gave me a wan smile. 'If I'm to stay respectable it has to be marriage.'

I was silent, unconvinced by her apparent frankness, and with a sudden sense of pain and loss, envy too, as I had a distressing vision of her married, and unrestrainedly possessed by the sidesman of St Pat's. Instinctively, I wanted to comfort her. I came forward and took her hand. I daren't speak of Frank. Yet my sympathy was tainted with a strong carnal curiosity.

'It must have been a great shock when . . .' I broke off.

'When he preferred the Lord to me. Don't deceive yourself, Laurence.' She shook her head slowly. 'It would never have worked. How can I dress it up nicely for you, my tender young medico? Frank wasn't made for marriage.'

She must have seen disbelief in my face. All the straining humiliation of the past came through in her short, pained laugh.

'The very idea of making love was enough to turn his stomach.'

'A psychological block. You could have broken it down.'

'Useless to try. Why, I'd realized it years ago when we . . .' She caught herself up suddenly, avoiding my eyes. Then she said: 'No, no. Frank's better off in the dog collar. So why shouldn't I make do with Davigan?' She gave me a strange inquiring glance. 'He's not such a bad sort, he's come up in the world, and at least he'll warm the blanket.'

There was a long silence. What did she mean? She had realized years ago? Even half spoken it contradicted and falsified all that laboured explanation. She had not released my hand. Her fingers were limp and unresistant. That old beating had started under my ribs again.

'I suppose you know I was wild about you, Cathy? But I always thought you had a down on me.'

She looked away, seeming to pick her words carefully.

'Yes, in a way I resented you, Laurie. But it was because you had what I couldn't take from you. Anyhow, isn't that all water under the bridge now?' She paused, with a shadow of her old provoking smile. 'We'll not want to start it flowing again?' There was another longer pause, as of waiting, then, as I struggled to find the proper words, she suddenly stood up and switched on the light. 'Time's getting on. I'd better be off to tidy up and change my dress. I can't join the celebrations like death at the feast. I'll be with you in a minute.'

When she had gone I got up, paced the room, went into the hall, came back to the room, hearing her movements on the floor above only too acutely. All the feeling I'd had for her had risen again, intensified by a most unusual compassion, I longed to go upstairs to console her, but had not the heart or the nerve to chance making a ghastly mistake or to impose myself unwanted upon her, in her present state of mind. And a sense of decency, again unconscious and induced, perhaps, by my encounter with Dingwall that morning, was holding me back. Why should

I further complicate her life when already it had become so sadly tangled.

Before I could decide, a step on the stairs made me look up. She was coming down, wearing a white chiffon dress with a red velvet bandeau in her hair. She had put some colour on her cheeks and she looked fragile and unlike herself. She took my arm lightly, and with a trace of her natural spirit said:

'Come on. You can lead in the bride. They'll be waiting.'

We went next door and into the Ennis living-room. Here, in a well-heated, unventilated atmosphere, the Davigans were already in possession and our appearance together made Dan start suspiciously. He darted a meaning look at his parents: the mother, a big-boned angular woman, her features indelibly seamed with sixteen successive resignations to the laws of nature; the father, short, thick and bandy, with a stupid brick-red face and the look of a sanctimonious ram. Mrs Ennis, delirious with happiness, was serving drinks, Powers whisky for the men, a sherry for Mrs Davigan.

'A great day it is for yourself, Katie,' the latter was remarking with an air of repetition, as she accepted her glass. 'A great . . . a holy day!'

'The Lord knows it. What'll you have, Laurence, seeing it's an occasion? We're just waiting on Francis. He'll be pleased to see you.'

'Is the young Father at his orisons?' old Davigan inquired. I thought at first it was a joke, but he was dead serious, although he'd probably had a few.

'He's at an interview with the Canon.'

'Ah . . . the Dingwall himself. It'll be for the curacy.'

'You're hoping he'll be lucky, Katie?'

'Oh, yes, dear, I've prayed for it. I would dread a separation.'

'Come over and sit by me here, Cathy,' said Davigan the younger, after a brief silence.

'I'm all right where I am.' She was half seated, half standing by the window ledge. 'Is nobody giving me a drink?'

'Of course, dear,' Mrs Ennis said coldly. 'You'll have a drop of sherry?'

'If you don't mind I'll take the malt. Dr Ennis prescribed it as a night-cap.

Mrs Davigan raised her eyebrows.

'Well, well!' she said, in the tone of a future mother-in-law.

'Is the doctor himself likely to be detained at his case?' asked old Davigan meaningly, after a silence.

'He's at his surgery now. And I know he's due on a confinement. But in between he promised to look in.'

At that moment there were brisk sounds outside and Frank came in as though he'd been hurrying—smiling, cheerful, radiating such an air of heaven only knows what one could call it, simple, natural or supernatural goodness perhaps, or if one were cynical, priestliness. Yes, Francis was now the ecclesiastic, neatly habited in rows of black buttons, walking on the balls of his feet, smoothly shaved, ready of smile, an idol for the aged parish spinsters. He came directly towards me and took both my hands warmly.

'It's so good to see you, Laurence. Thank you for coming.'

Then, to the others: 'Sorry I'm late,' he apologized, 'I had a long session . . . quite a lecture in fact. But I'm to stay, Mother.'

Congratulations drowned Mrs Ennis's ecstatic sigh, and after Frank self-consciously said grace, we sat down to a lavish spread of all that is worst in that destructive Scottish meal which combines tea and supper and is normally served at six o'clock. Mrs Ennis, a parsimonious housekeeper, had thrown caution to the winds, producing such extremes as boiled silverside and black bun, sausages and trifle, ham, tongue and cherry cake. But for all this variety and the pervading air of pious gaiety which accompanied its dispatch, it was a strained and difficult repast, with undercurrents springing from the circumstances that had brought us together. Of Frank himself there could be no question. Whatever his physical composition, his behaviour was perfect: quiet and unassuming, gentle towards his mother, tolerant of the frequent Davigan lapses into bad taste and, beyond an occasional moment in which I detected strain, considerate and affectionate towards Cathy. And suddenly I saw him for what he was: a made-to-order celibate who from his first glimmerings of understanding had been taught, brought up and conditioned to regard chastity, that cardinal virtue of the Church, as the essential objective of his being, whose heart responded fervently to that final dramatic peroration of Canon Dingwall's mission sermon: 'Show me a pure man or woman, and I will show you a saint.' A belief so self-exaggerated that the mere thought of physical union was gross, repugnant, a defilement to be rejected instantly from his thoughts. Of course he had loved Cathy, but with a total sublimation of sex, an idealized conception of marriage so impractical, if it had not been pathetic, it would have been a joke.

Conscious of my own earthy bondage, I could not help admiring, even half envying, this built-in continence. Yet I felt sorry for Cathy. Her glands had not been presanctified. She had been let down and humiliated and she was hating it, probably hating Frank too, since she remained moodily and unresponsively silent. Had she thought to hurt him by taking Davigan on the rebound? It was a possibility, yet I wondered if she really could go through with it —marry that vulgarian who, lit by a few double Powers and a final Guinness, which he drank to the trifle, was becoming increasingly possessive. I wanted to tell her: 'for your own sake, don't, Cathy,' but as she moved restively in her chair, not eating but defiantly pouring herself another drink, I did not have a chance, time was getting on, and having asked myself uncomfortably throughout the meal what the devil I was doing in this galley, I now felt like a fish out of water. I looked at my watch: almost a quarter to eight: I must leave soon for my train.

I had hoped to see Dr Ennis and just as I got up to go his shaggy head came round the door. He was cold sober. He must have made a considerable effort since at this hour he was usually the best part of a bottle to the good. Knowing how he had wanted Frank in the practice, I dreaded a scene. But he was completely in charge of himself, talked civilly and pleasantly, made a few innocuous jokes welcoming me to the profession, then as he went out to his case, he caught Cathy by the arm.

'Come along, dear lass. Time for you to turn in for your good night's rest. I'll see you home. You'll never dance at your own wedding or raise a fine brood of altar boys for Frank if we don't make you a big strong girl.'

At the doorway I stepped into the hall to let her pass.

She held out her hand.

'Well, goodbye, Laurie, it'll be long enough before I see you again . . . if ever.'

'Goodbye, Cathy.'

How acutely, painfully conscious of her I was as she stood there, close to me, looking me straight in the eyes. It was a look that lasted longer than it should, filled with a strained anxiety and something else that went direct into my heart. Then she turned away and I watched her go out with the old doctor. After that I had to get away and, despite Frank's pressing me to wait for a later train, I hurriedly said goodbye.

Outside, in the clear dry night I stood, motionless, hearing the vanishing sound of Ennis's Ford, looking at the dark Considine house. A light went on in an upper window, then a blind was drawn. That brought a sigh out of me, not ecstatic like Mrs Ennis's, just sad, the lament for a lost happiness now gone for ever. What was I anyway? An eager Romeo or a jilted lover? Neither. I was a substitute ship's doctor on my way to Australia. With an exclamation that Frank would not have liked, I turned up the collar of my coat, stuck out my chin and set off at a hard pace down the road towards the railway station.

FIVE

A HAND ON MY SHOULDER was shaking me with unnecessary vigour. That, and the roar of a jet taking off, returned me to Zürich Flughafen. I started, turned sharply, and there was Lotte in the airport bar, standing over me with a woman and a small boy beside her.

'You went to sleep . . . again?' With an embarrassing emphasis on the last word, Lotte laughed, put down the suitcase she had been carrying, then said to the others: 'You are all right now I have delivered you. But do not trust this man too much, Mrs Davigan. He is not so simple as he looks.'

Cathy muttered some words of thanks. I kept staring at her, in total unbelief, like an idiot. At first sight I had barely recognized her. My mental picture was not more than eight years out of date, but here was a woman who seemed much older, with a strained, almost broken-down look. Her expression was harder, her mouth, though full, was no longer tender, and her eyes, those wonderful dark eyes, had an edgy, questioning look, as though she would find it difficult to smile. She had on a felt hat without much shape and a brown suit, cheap-looking and shabby, but neat enough to do justice to the one thing that was unchanged. Her supple, fluid figure and the natural grace with which she stood and moved had the same appeal that had once made my heart turn over with desire. But now I had no more than a strange and painful awkwardness, pity perhaps.

'I'm afraid you had a bumpy flight,' I said, when Lotte had gone. 'Can I get you something before we start?'

'I couldn't eat a thing. But,' she hesitated, not looking at me, 'I'd not say no to a drink.'

'Coffee?'

'I'd rather a brandy, if you don't mind.'

'What about the boy? A sandwich?'

'He ate some of his dinner on the plane. He's probably too tired to eat.'

I bought her a cognac, with a ham sandwich and a Coca-Cola for the boy. He thanked me. Until now he had not spoken, although he had been studying me with observant eyes. He was extremely pale, too slightly built by far, with a reserved, examining expression—a delicate, even gentle look, if it had not been so composed. His brow was the best part of his face, which thinned towards the chin, a feature reminiscent of his father who, I recollected, had had a receding jaw. He was wearing grey shorts and stockings and a hand-knitted grey jersey. What was his name again? Of course . . . awful but inevitable . . . it would be Danny boy. Dislike rose up in me, at the memory of Davigan, but I checked it with a false kindness.

'Don't finish your sandwich, Daniel, if you don't want it.'

'I'll keep this piece for later.' He wrapped half in the waxed paper it had come in.

His mother's silence was so awkward, so restrictive indeed, I had to keep talking to him.

'Your first flight I suppose? It didn't upset you?'

'Oh, no, thank you. I played a game part of the time.'

'A game?'

'Yes, Chess.'

I smiled, in an effort to lighten the situation.

'Who did you take on? The pilot?'

'He plays games against himself.' His mother broke in almost sharply, as though my facetiousness had offended her. 'He has a pocket set.' After a moment, still in that unnatural and distant manner, she said: 'Are we going to Davos or not?'

'Decidedly not. We have everything ready for you at the Maybelle.'

'The Maybelle?'

Was there the vague inflection of a gibe?

'Ridiculous name, isn't it? But I think you'll like it.'

'Is it far?'

'A longish drive, I'm afraid. We'll leave as soon as you're ready.'

When she put down her empty glass we went out to the parking lot. As before, I carried her suitcase. On this occasion it was light. I sat the boy in the back seat of the car.

'He can stretch out there and perhaps get a sleep.'

After a momentary hesitation she got in beside me.

For some time I drove without speaking, taking the by-pass to avoid central Zürich, striking the shore of the See beyond, hoping that silence and the darkness might relax her nerves. Any anticipation I had entertained of our meeting, a reunion one might say, born of nostalgic recollection of the past, had been flattened by the stiffness of her attitude. And I had not failed to notice that she kept herself apart, well over to her own side of the car. Had Lotte's remark upset her, as it had me? I made another effort to start the conversation.

'I owe you an apology for not being at the barrier to meet you, Cathy.'

'Yes,' she said. 'If it hadn't been for your girl-friend we'd have lost ourselves completely.'

My girl-friend. So that had nettled her. I smiled in the darkness.

'My only excuse is . . . believe it or not . . . that I was thinking of you. Yes, hanging on in the bar, I got into a day dream of the old days, with Frank and you, lost all sense of the present in the past.'

'I've had more to think of than that lately.'

'Oh, of course,' I said appeasingly. 'I didn't know you'd lost Dan until I had Frank's letter. I'm sorry. Was he taken suddenly?'

'Yes, very sudden.'

'Too bad,' I said, trying to sound sympathetic.

Obviously she didn't want to talk of it, so I curbed my curiosity and said:

'Then you've been worried about your boy. How long has he been . . . let's say . . . off-colour?'

'About five weeks. We first noticed the T.B. gland then.'

'Well, don't worry, Cathy. We ought to be able to get him right for you. It's not an uncommon condition in children of his age. Just a bovine T.B. infection. Not the pulmonary type. We'll not worry him by putting him in the ward. I've arranged with Matron for you both to have the guest chalet. It's very cosy . . . usually reserved for visiting committee members.'

'The Matron? Is she nice?'

'Not bad at all, if you take her the right way. Oh, by the by,' I hesitated, 'I had to work a bit of an angle with her . . . to get you and Daniel in together, and with all the fancy trimmings. You see, normally we're not allowed to take parents. So I established a sort of family relationship, told her you were my cousin. You can disown me if you like.'

She did not speak for some time, then she said:

'Still playing about with the truth, Carroll. You were always good at it.'

After that, I let it rest. Damn it all, I had only put on the act for her sake, to give her a good start with Matron and to get her the privilege of the committee chalet. I drove on in silence, and at speed, climbing now as we left Zürcher See behind, flashing through the villages of Landquart and Jenaz, almost deserted at this hour. The night darkness was deepened by the overhanging mountains. There was no mist but a fine rain had begun to fall. I switched on the radio to get the late news and weather report. Another level-crossing accident. Two killed in Grisons. Disarmament Conference reconvened in Geneva. More trouble in the Yemen. Servette had beaten Lucerne in the Cup two goals to one. Brighter weather lay ahead.

From the swift occasional glare as we passed an illuminated sign I saw that she was sitting erect with closed eyes. Daniel, in the back seat, had fallen asleep, his audible breathing synchronized with the regular beat of the windscreen wipers. I switched on the heater. Out of sheer decency and good-heartedness I had tried to make it a cosy threesome in the snug little Opel, but something had gone sour and it was making the journey twice as long.

However, towards eleven o'clock we were there at last, and as we came up the drive it was a relief to see lights in

311

the guest chalet. I had been a trifle uncertain of Matron, but she had actually stayed up, well beyond her usual hour of retiring, to make a welcoming party of one.

'Ach, so! You are tired. So late. and so much journeyings.' With an arm round Cathy she helped her from the car. 'And the leetle boy? Sleeping. That is goot. But so pale. Can you take him, Herr Doktor? We are all prepared.'

Inside, the chalet glowed, a bright fire in the little sitting-room warmly burnishing the freshly polished furniture, gilding the pot of white cyclamen that since morning had undoubtedly found its way from the village *Blumengeschäft* to the centre table. Nearby, on a tray, was a Thermos jug flanked by a plate of pretzels. A clean warm smell of burning pinewood seeped from the burning logs. Shaded lights were on in the large and adjoining small bedrooms, both beds were turned down, and on each, light as swansdown, lay that unique provider of nocturnal comfort, a Swiss *Steppdecke*.

What a tribute to myself that Matron had put herself to such trouble to achieve so warm and convincing a welcome. Cathy, tired and exhausted to the point, almost, of an estrangement from me, looking about her with an expression of dazed surprise, had clearly expected nothing so attractive, so heartwarming.

'You like, ja?' Matron said, in a pleased tone, studying her.

'It's perfect . . . so lovely . . . and comfortable. I . . . I don't know how to thank you.'

'Goot! Now you must take your hot trink, while I put to bed the cheild. And for you, Herr Doktor, there is also hot milk and pretzels already in your room. So, *gute Nacht.*'

She bustled through the main bedroom into the little room where I had taken Daniel. As Cathy stood motionless and silent, her eyes lowered, I unstoppered the Thermos and poured a glass of milk which I slid along the table towards her. I scarcely knew what to say, exactly what note to strike, how in fact to break the ice which seemed to have congealed between us. But it was she who spoke first. Apparently still thinking of Matron she said, almost to herself:

'That's a kind-hearted woman.'

'She is, Cathy,' I endorsed heartily, then with some justification, feeling that I might take my fair share of the credit, I added: 'We both felt, she and I, that you deserved the best.'

'Because I was your cousin?'

'Well,' I shrugged, 'that was just to help things along.'

She did not answer but remained, with head averted, not looking at me. At the sight of that drooping figure, still slender, even youthful, another touch of pity came at me. Not the journey alone, trying though that might have been, but some other, harrowing experience, anxiety for the brat, perhaps, I couldn't yet discover the hidden cause, but whatever it might be, had worn her down.

'Don't worry, Cathy. We'll get the boy right, and you too. I'll examine him first thing tomorrow, and do everything I can to help you.'

I came towards her and took her gently, soothingly, by the arm.

Instantly she froze. In a low but intense voice, looking me dead in the eyes, she said:

'Keep your dirty fingers off me. You . . . you lying woman chaser.'

I was staggered. After all I had done; inviting her to stay; meeting her; driving her in the pitch dark for hours over those damn dangerous mountain roads; to be blasted like some bloody sex maniac. Then I saw that she was more upset than I, and at once everything became clear. Not just her seeing Lotte, of course, the big Swede had given me away, yes, all the way—I might have known she couldn't be trusted to keep her mouth shut—and Cathy, eagerly looking forward to meeting me again, had been hurt. Well, it would pass. I would soon put things right. Meantime, take no offence, remain calm and sympathetic, time would heal the breach. I said gently, but in a slightly injured voice:

'I can see you're tired, Cathy. So I'll say good night. I hope you sleep well.'

I went out on the balls of my feet, just like Frank, and quietly closed the door.

SIX

NEXT MORNING, after my exertions on the previous day, I slept late. After I'd had my croissants and coffee, which was always kept hot in a Thermos jug in the sitting-room, I ambled into the office. Matron, at her desk, looked meaningfully at the clock as I gave her *'Guten Morgen'*, but she was in a smashing good mood.

'Ach, Herr Doktor,' she beamed all over her face, 'I like much your cousin Caterina. Ja, already she asks me to call her so. And she is risen so early, all dressed, and knowing my absence of staff, is helping much with my verk.'

'I'm so glad, Matron.' Slightly bewildered, I managed to get this out.

'I, also. That is a most goot, nice voman.'

These superlatives caught me unawares, but I kept on my smile.

'Where is she now?'

'In the *Küche*, so do not disturb.' She raised a minatory finger then nodded with an approving chuckle. 'She makes for *Mittagessen* a Scotsmann's food . . . the meence.'

Hell mend the old battle-axe, she killed me with her mangled double jargon and whatever might lie behind it. But I was still a bit slack-headed myself—I usually felt that way after an outing, or should I say an innings, with Lotte, and besides I'd had all the fag of that late night drive—so I could only beam back.

'I'll leave her to it then. I'm terribly pleased you're friends already. Now I'll go over before my ward round and see the boy.'

I walked slowly to the guest chalet wondering what the devil this Caterina was up to. Making a play for Hulda's good will? Could be: to prolong her stay. Or, after years of Davigan, was she just the thoroughly browbeaten domesticated little housewife? *The meence!* It would make a horse laugh.

I opened the chalet door expecting to find the kid in bed, but like his nice goot ma he was up, dressed in his shorts and jersey, bent over an absurd little chequered board on the living-room table.

'Good morning.' I put into it the usual affability I use for all the kids. 'Are you receiving visitors, Daniel?'

He looked up and smiled. 'Come into the lion's den.'

It seemed a neat sort of remark for his age, but probably someone had at one time tagged it on to him.

'What are you doing?'

'Oh, just working out something.'

'You like chess?' I asked curiously.

'Yes.'

'Do you always play with yourself?'

'Oh, no. Only when I'm thinking out a problem. At home I play with the Canon.'

'Dingwall?'

He nodded.

'Are his old bones still hanging together?'

'Very much so, though he's with the Sisters now at the Convent and doesn't get about much. He likes a game . . . usually after Benediction. He was the one first put me on to it.'

'I expect he licked the pants off you.'

He looked up at me sideways.

'When Greek meets Greek,' he said.

The remark silenced me. Frank's letter had not erred. This little runt really had something rather out of the ordinary, but I fancied he knew it, which made me want to take him down.

'I'll give you a game some time. There's a decent full-sized board in the playroom.'

'Oh, good. Do you play much?'

'Well, off and on, so to speak,' I temporized. 'As a matter of fact, there's a café in the village where you can always get a first-class game.'

'How splendid. I'd like that. Can we now?'

'Later, young fellow. We've got to have a proper look at you first.'

He got up at once and I took him round the main house to the small dispensary that adjoined the ward. He was nervous and tried not to show it, but kept stealing glances at the instrument cabinet and the rows of reagents on the test bench. I felt that Matron had been wise putting him with his mother in the chalet and not in the ward. Stripped to the waist there wasn't much of him. Precious little, in fact, no credit to his late departed sire. Still, most of the kids that came to us were like that, pinched little city sparrows, so almost automatically. or perhaps because I wanted no reproaches from the Caterina, I went over him with extra care: lungs, heart, joints: I gave him a good half hour. In fact, as I put away my stethoscope, he said:

'You took longer than Dr Moore.'

'He's your doctor?'

'He's Dr Ennis's assistant. At present anyway. He's leaving for Canada.'

Another one, I thought, trying to escape from that damned nationalised medicine.

'How is Dr Ennis?'

'Quite well . . . I think.' He looked away. 'At least, some-times.'

'I see.'

He was still lying on the couch and I bent over and took another look at the slightly swollen cervical gland. Apart from that fairly common manifestation of T.B. in children, I had not found anything, certainly nothing in the least degree serious. But I wanted to make sure. A well-equipped radiography room opened off the dispensary. Ample funds at the disposition of the Maybelle Trust had ensured that this essential diagnostic unit was completely up to date. Of course, as a rule most of the kids were scared to death of it, so I prepared him as casually as I could.

'You don't mind if we go next door and take a picture of your ribs?'

'X-ray?' he said quickly.

'Nothing to alarm you.'

'Oh, I'm not alarmed, Dr Laurence.' He added quickly: 'May I call you that?'

Trying to play it brave, I thought, and making a play with first names. I gave no answer.

We went in, and after drawing the heavy curtains I screened him thoroughly. He blinked and turned pale as the current sparked on but beyond that kept perfectly still, and when it was over he said:

'That was a very interesting experience.'

I gave him a hard look: I didn't at all go for this pre-cocious, Little Lord Fauntleroy line of talk.

'What should interest you is that there isn't a single spot on either of your lungs. They're absolutely clear.'

'I'm not surprised,' he said mildly. 'I understand that what I'm suffering from is the King's evil. You know,' he added: 'Scrofula.'

'Who put you on to that medieval rot?' I said sharply.

'My friend the Canon. We discussed it during a chess session. And I suppose it is rot. We were inclined to doubt the efficacy of the royal touch . . . as a cure.'

What could you do with that, except give him another hard look. He was beginning to annoy me.

'Your cure will be to obey my orders. And for pity's sake

stop sounding off as if you'd just swallowed the Children's Encyclopedia, or I'll begin to think you're just a little toad.'

His face fell. I had hurt him, but he tried to smile.

'Couldn't you make it a tadpole . . . that sounds nicer? And I haven't *swallowed* the Children's Encyclopedia, I've only read it once. I'm sorry, Dr Laurence, I can't help being brainy, it's a bit of a curse, but in spite of it I hope you can put up with me. You see, although I didn't like you at first, I'm rather inclined to like you now.'

Good Lord, what was he giving me? But I had to know.

'Why didn't you like me at first?'

'When I saw that the rude Swedish hostess was your girl-friend.'

That seemed to me enough for one session,

'Get dressed,' I said, and began to write up his case history. He was cathetic and underweight, but that would be taken care of, and the gland was not painful or in any way adherent. No point in keeping him in bed. I would do a von Pirquet and watch his temperature.

'Just a minute. Roll up your sleeve. I'm going to make a little scratch on your arm.'

'Is that the treatment?' he inquired anxiously.

'No, a test. Your treatment is lots of fresh air, gallons of milk, plenty to eat, and obligatory rest periods after lunch.

When I had finished with him it was almost noon, and I had just time to do my routine ward visit before lunch. The Swiss take *Mittagessen* early, and as this is the main meal of the day, Matron and I always had it together. Today, laid for four, with a big pot of African violets, that speciality of Swiss florists, as a centre piece, the table had an unusually festive air. Cathy, dressed in a plain blouse and skirt was already there and after I had said a pleasant word to her I did not fail to compliment the old dragon.

'Ja, it is goot to have *Gäste*. She smiled at the female guest, who sat with a quiet humility on her right. 'Ven we are without the child-ern we are so much alone.'

Hmm! She hadn't objected to being alone with me before.

As we began on the thick, vegetable, deliciously-cheesy soup, I said:

'You'll be relieved, I'm not too unhappy about your boy, Cathy. We'll get him right for you.'

'Ach, that is goot, Herr Doktor. But your cousin also

317

needs your care. She tells me this morning of much suffering from her husband's loss and other bad chances. She must surely stay, also with Dan-iel, till she is better, yes?'

'Oh, of course,' I agreed, choking on a spoonful. 'Most welcome.'

Cathy raised her eyes towards Matron, then lowered them.

'Only if you'll let me help you.'

'*Jawohl, meine* Caterina.' She leaned over to execute a little arm patting. '*Aber nur ein wenig.*'

Well, well, I thought, there's certainly been some fast work by Caterina in the kitchen this morning—a deduction fully endorsed when the next course appeared, borne in by Rosa the maid, as though it were a flaming boar's head. After some quite professional tasting, rolling a large spoonful around her double dentures and smacking her lips, Matron leaned back in her chair and clapped her hands.

'*Wunderbar,* Caterina! It is so goot, your meence.'

'I'll make it any time you wish,' Cathy said modestly. 'It's very nourishing, and inexpensive.'

'It is like,' Matron rolled another full forkful down the hatch, '. . . like a goulash, a ragout.'

'My Dan was very fond of it.'

'Ach, so, the poor husband.'

'You like it, Cousin Laurence?' For the first time since her arrival she gave me a direct look, blank, yet just possibly one quarter satirical.

'Best Scotsman's meence I ever tasted.'

After a short silence, encouraged by that glance, though I did not at all care for the cousinly appellation, I said:

'Perhaps you'd like a short run in the station wagon this afternoon. Get the hang of the countryside.'

'No thank you.' She refused instantly. 'Matron thinks I ought to rest this afternoon.'

'Ja, is besser to rest,' Matron agreed. 'After the journeyings.'

'But why don't you take Daniel? You'd like that wouldn't you, Danny?'

'Oh, enormously.'

'Daniel must lie down too,' I said firmly. 'I'm going to stretch him out on the balcony, all wrapped up like an Egyptian mummy.'

'But ven he arises?' Matron persisted.

I was on the point of saying 'no' when I realized that I must for the moment swim with the tide.

'Well, we'll see,' I grunted.

SEVEN

IF THE FACT is not already evident I wish firmly to establish that I have no addiction whatsoever towards children. During our 'health walks' when two by two the little blighters make a dismal procession struggling up the hills in the rain, their thin transparent plastic capes flapping around their bare skinny knees, peering into the cow barns, grabbing an occasional common wild sorrel and shouting 'Idlewise', stopping to piddle or have their noses blown, or to show me blisters on their heels, then bursting into shrill sporadic song, well, I'll admit to a shade of what might be called compunction. For the sake of my job, too, I have to make a show of interest and sympathy, even a heartiness so foreign to my nature that it almost makes me puke. So do not accuse me of more than a grudging effort to fulfil an obligation when I state that at three o'clock, after I had written my monthly report for the committee, I went up to the balcony where I had planked the Davigan offspring, quite prepared to take him for a drive. He was awake.

'Have you come to unwrap the mummy?' He smiled.

'You didn't sleep?'

He shook his head. 'After your remark at lunch I've been pretending I was one of the Pharaohs and that you'd have to dig me out of the tomb.'

'What did it feel like?'

'Very cold.' He broke into a fit of laughter and gave me his hand. It was half frozen. The *bise* had risen and I hadn't covered him well enough.

'Why didn't you call out for more blankets?'

'I can't speak Egyptian.'

This was going to kill me.

'Never mind,' I said. 'We'll walk to the village and I'll buy you a hot drink.'

On the way down, having been landed with this chore, I felt I might legitimately turn it to advantage.

'Daniel,' I said chummily. 'It's so long since I've been in

Levenford. Is the Davigan Housing Estate still going strong?'

'Oh, yes. Extremely strong.' He gave me his upward sideways look. 'But not for the Davigans.'

'Why not?' I asked quickly.

'Didn't you know? It's ancient history. Grandpa Davigan failed and went bankrupt.'

'I can't believe it.'

'Only too true, unfortunately. The bank called in the big lot of money he'd borrowed. Before the houses were finished. It was a fearful mess. Everything was lost.'

'Good heavens, Daniel!' I exclaimed, masking my satisfaction, drawing him out more. 'But surely your father . . . before he got ill . . . I mean, wasn't he connected with the Estate?'

'He was employed there by the new owners. But only as a working mason.'

I had no need to pretend surprise. I was astounded. Admittedly old Davigan was bone stupid, but he was crafty and he had known his job. Obviously he had got out of his depth and been swallowed by some bigger fish.

'Hard luck, Daniel.'

'Hard up, you mean.' He spoke philosophically. 'That's what the boys shout after me at school. But at least there'll be no more chewing the fat over it at home now Father isn't there. That was never ending.'

'Was your father's a sudden illness, Daniel?' I inquired tactfully.

He seemed to shrink under the question, but glanced up again, this time sharply.

'It wasn't an illness. He was killed. . . . An accident. But would you mind, Dr Laurence, if we don't talk any more about this . . . it upsets me even to think of it.'

I scarcely knew where to look, suddenly feeling guilty and ashamed. What a mean, underhand, dirty hound, sneaking information out of him. Although I was eaten up with curiosity, I said hurriedly:

'We'll say no more about it, Daniel.' Adding, although I did not mean it: 'Never again.'

By this time we were approaching Schlewald Platz and, picking up, he began to look about him as we came along the river bank below the telepheric, crossed the bridge and came into the lower part of the village, which is mostly seventeenth-century Swiss and decidedly attractive. I could see that he liked it.

Outside Edelmann's I took his arm. It was thin as a chicken bone. 'This is where we go in.'

As we entered he asked:

'Is this the chess café?'

'No. But it's one where the cakes are a lot better.'

Edelmann's, in fact, was known all over Switzerland.

His expression had cleared further at the sight of the superb display of patisserie in the long glass case beside the counter, and when I said: 'We each pick up one of these plates by the window, go over and stand at the counter and choose,' he actually laughed.

'We're a couple of Mad Hatters.'

'We're *what* . . . ?'

'Don't you remember, in Alice? He always carried an empty plate about with him in case someone offered him a cake.'

When we were seated he ate his cream sponge slowly, as if it were a new experience, savouring each small bite, and washing it down with the hot chocolate I had ordered for us both. When he had finished he remarked thoughtfully:

'That is the best cake I have ever tasted in my entire life. Perfect ambrosia.'

'It's the best I've ever tasted, and I've lived considerably longer than you. Have another go of ambrosia?'

'I should imagine they're very expensive.'

'We can stand it, this once.'

'No, I think not. But perhaps you'll ask me another time, if you feel like it.'

Where had the kid got them, amongst the Davigan ruins —good manners? Cathy, perhaps, if so one good mark to her. Yet more probably they came from the old man in the wheel chair.

When we left I picked up my *Daily Telegraph* at the station bookstall where Gina, the girl there, regularly kept it for me. She was a dark-haired Italian, rather short in the gams but, with her black eyes and white teeth sporting a dazzling smile, chock full of brio. Although she wore a wedding ring there were no signs of a husband, which made her an interesting prospect. We had made quite a bit of progress already and, while the kid stood waiting, we traded a few repartees.

On the way home I took the main road to make easier walking for him. Suddenly he drew up.

'That's a very striking little church, Dr Laurence. Is it ours?'

I nodded.

It was one of those small ultra-modern R.C. churches that had begun to sprout in Switzerland, part of the new movement to be with it. All lopsided angles of wood, glass and concrete, half imitation Frank Lloyd Wright and half pure Disneyland, it stuck up in the old village like a sore thumb. Outside, on something like a gibbet, a peal of bells hung off centre. Inside it was naked stone, cold enough in winter to freeze the knackers off you.

You'll gather I could not stand the place. In fact, I hated it. Since I had to take the Catholic children there on Sundays, on more than one occasion it had for various reasons really got me down. Usually when I had parked them, I'd go out for a smoke, or amble down to the station kiosk to pass the time of day with Gina, who was always open on Sundays, selling soft drinks and cigarettes to the peasants who invaded Schlewald on their one free day.

'It grows on you. I like it.' He had completed his survey. 'Let's go in.'

This was too much—I shut him up.

'You've had enough for one afternoon. We'd better get back.'

He was short of breath coming up the hill, stopping now and then to, as he put it, 'catch his puff', and to say: 'I have enjoyed myself, thank you, Dr Laurence.'

'Good,' I said shortly. I didn't want slop of any kind. 'I'm going to take your temperature when we get in.'

I saw that I would have to keep a stricter eye on him. And at least further excursions of this nature were out. He was all brains and bumph, and not much else.

EIGHT

EVER SINCE that opening luncheon a vague premonition of impending trouble had existed at the back of my mind, but I could never have believed it would hit me so soon. The profound observation of Confucius, that after three days guests and fish stink, was working in reverse at the Maybelle Clinic. By the end of the week it was I, apparently, who seemed slightly tainted while Caterina, as the Matron had re-christened her, was presumably smelling like the rose.

Pondering the matter, in an effort to get to the roots of it as I sat at breakfast in my room, I assembled the evidence, tenuous perhaps and circumstantial, but none the less disturbing. My coffee, for instance, was not entirely hot this morning, and on my tray lay not the usual three fresh, tender croissants, but instead a single one, unfresh, and two of those unmentionable *ballons*, the lowest and most debased form of Swiss rolls, guaranteed tooth-breakers, regular hockey balls. Perhaps the baker's girl, a red-checked fräulein who delivered before school, had failed to materialize. I doubted it—she was regular as a Swiss clock, not the cuckoo variety sold to tourists, but a reliable Patek Philippe. No, as other kindred deprivations came to mind, I found it impossible to evade the suspicion that Hulda had cooled towards me. Definitely tempered was her lush and overflowing affection. A critical glint had invaded her eye, a short laugh now replaced the beaming 'ach so' assent that had hitherto welcomed my most speculative observations. At our midday dinner an optical collusion had developed between her new protégée and herself, meaning glances that passed over my head but which I suspected were derogatory to myself, followed usually by remarks exchanged in undertones. On several occasions these had touched with unpleasant significance on my Levenford antecedents in a manner scarcely in accordance with my previous elaborations on this theme. How otherwise regard this little tit-bit of a tête-à-tête, which took place in Matron's room just loud enough for me to overhear in the test room next door:

'Of this Scots town of your birth, dear Caterina, you speak seriously? Is it not nice?'

'Far from nice.'

'But before I am believing it is fine, historique, eine noble *Stadt*?'

'Who could have told you such an untruth? It's a small, ugly, working-class, shipyard town. All day you hear nothing but hammering of rivets.'

'But surely . . . I am confuse . . . surely there is a fine castle, on the river?'

'That's just a tumbledown old ruin by a dirty stream.'

'No one still lives therein?'

'Only the rats.'

'Ach, so! And the peoples are not *Hochgeboren*?'

'No. Of course, some think they are.'

Hulda's voice, which had risen in tone, octave by octave, in a crescendo of forced amazement, now dissolved in a fit of laughter. Then, wiping her eyes:

'Here, in Schweitz, if some silly Scotsman believes he is *ein König*, he must be put straight away in *Krankenhaus*.'

Equally disturbing was the Matron's remark on the following morning when Lotte, disregarding my injunction never to telephone me, had rung up to say she had an unexpected free day. I couldn't blame the big stupid Swede since at another time I would gladly have joined her in Zürich. But it was Hulda who took the call and afterwards, in a tone impossible to mistake, she had inquired:

'Your professor from the Zürich Katonspital, Herr Doktor?'

Well, what of it! I was still the boss. Yet when I thought on the instigator of all these scheming little tricks, these dropped hints and innuendos, I felt like wringing her neck or better still, setting up a good rough bedroom scene with her. What the devil was she after? Beyond the recognition of that strain of antagonism which had always existed in our complex relationship, especially in our early days when she had tried to get the better of me, I could not even guess. Seeing her every day, in the same house, made it worse. Recovered from the journey, refreshed by the mountain air, she had shed a few years, lost that beaten look, and in the words of that murky ballad, begun to bloom again.

There was a knock at the door.

'Come in!' I shouted.

Daniel's head appeared inquiringly round the lintel. He smiled. 'Are you busy, Dr Laurence?'

'I'm busy trying to get enough calories out of this bloody bad breakfast.'

'It doesn't look too bad.'

He advanced and sat down. He was still in his Maybelle dressing-gown and pyjamas, holding his infernal pocket chess board.

'It's just that Mother and Matron have gone shopping in the car. I was wondering if, since we are alone . . . we might try a few moves.'

So they had paired off again. I glared at him.

'I believe I told you to stay in bed until I came to examine you.'

'Well . . I had to get up.'

'What for? To piss?'

'No,' he said, adopting my vocabulary. 'To puke.'

'You were sick?'

'I only threw up a little. It's a bit of a habit I seem to have developed.'

'Since when?'

'Just the last few days. I think it's the codliver oil. What comes up all tastes of it.'

I looked at him and nodded.

'That's probable. It's pretty foul stuff. We'll knock you off it and put you on extra milk. Now back to your room.'

'Won't you? I'm rather tired of playing against myself.'

I finished my tepid coffee and pushed the tray aside leaving the *ballons* conspicuously untouched.

'Come on then. I'll give you a game. Then you must come to the dispensary and have your injection.'

'Good,' he said. 'It's a deal,' and began to set out the board.

Although I was no Capablanca I played chess off and on with the kids during wet recreation hours, and I meant to knock him off quickly, partly to take him down, but also to eliminate the nuisance of further games.

We began calmly. I had the first move. But why make a song about it. There is no disguising the sordid facts. This unnatural little upstart mated me in exactly six moves.

'That's extraordinary.' He smiled. 'I never knew the Giuoco Piano opening succeed so easily. I fully expected you to use Petroff's defence.'

'You did?' I said sourly. 'Well, I don't go for Petroff. Suppose you play me another without your queen.'

'Certainly. In that case you'll probably open with the Ruy Lopez.'

'Not on your life. I'm anti-Portuguese.'

'Oh, Lopez was a Spaniard, in the sixteenth century, Dr Laurence. He invented his attack—where caution and safety are essential for the defenders. And I'm sure you'll remember to respond with P to K4.'

'That impertinent remark costs you another three pieces,'

I said, removing his two bishops and a castle. 'Now I'll give you and Petroff a damn good licking.'

Even so it was no use. I was cautious but not safe. When he looked at me reproachfully, sparing my feelings by not saying 'checkmate', I scattered the pieces back into the box and stood up.

'I'm used to playing with experts: when I'm up against a beginner it throws me off balance.'

He laughed dutifully.

'You're just a little out of practice, Dr Laurence,' he said apologetically, following me into the dispensary.

'Don't hand me that eyewash.'

I gave him his injection—I had put him on a course of colossal iron—then told him to go and get dressed. In the office I had some paper work to get through but I could not settle to it. My thoughts were depressingly clouded by the campaign that almost certainly had come into being against me. Before this went further, counter action, I clearly perceived, was demanded of me.

The ladies, if I may use the word, returned in excellent spirits and a continued sense of intimacy which persisted during the midday meal. Once or twice I caught Matron's button eyes upon me with an admixture of inquiry and that sly glint of jocular malice which, in the Swiss, passes for humour. But as I had wisely decided to say nothing, the expectation that I would complain about the breakfast was frustrated. This at least afforded me a minor satisfaction and for the rest I maintained an attitude of quiet dignity, reserve and, let me add, determination. I had fully made up my mind to have things out with the soi-distant Caterina.

She had the habit now of walking after the *Mittagessen*, taking the uphill path beside the little stream that tore down through the pasture with picturesque abandon, between banks of meadow sweet and celandine. Today she did not disappoint me. After she set off, I established Daniel on the terrace and followed her with such discretion that she remained unaware of me until she had actually seated herself on the grassy hillock that marked the end of the lower slopes before the mountain took over in a steep glissade of scree. Beyond, the massed pines climbed darkly into a rarefied world of their own.

'You've discovered a favourite spot of mine,' I said, companionably.

She looked up, without surprise or any sign of welcome.

'I suppose you've noticed the heather . . .' I had to keep talking, 'not the usual Swiss erica, real Scottish moorland heath. And there's lots of harebells among the bracken.'

'Quite like home sweet home for you,' she said. 'Should it remind me of our happy days together?'

'Well, it ought to arouse your botanical instincts.'

'I've lost all my instincts.'

Her response wasn't encouraging but I maintained my air of sweetness and light.

'May I join you?'

'Why not? I half expected you.'

I parked myself on the short heathery turf. Glancing sideways surreptitiously I had a sudden warm appreciation of the change wrought in her by alpine air and the Maybelle cuisine. Bareheaded, in a simple Swiss blouse and dirndl skirt which I strongly suspected Matron had bought her that morning, she looked younger and, this came to me with a start, definitely bedworthy. But enough! After a pause of recollection, in a tone which combined both conciliation and reproach, I began:

'It's true. I've been hoping for an opportunity to talk with you. I've had the strangest and most unnatural feeling that in spite of all I've done and intend doing for you and your boy you've . . . well . . . turned dead set against me.'

'I have. And I am.'

The brief reply, delivered without emotion, shook me.

'For heaven's sake why?'

She turned slowly and examined me.

'Quite apart from your character, Carroll, which is unspeakably and sickeningly detestable, you've always been a sort of evil genius for me. Yes, from the day I first saw you on that railway platform. If you want it in a few sloppy words, I'd say you have botched up my life.'

Speechless, I could do no more than gape at her. She went on.

'I never thought I'd have the chance to even the score. Now I have.'

Was she out of her mind? I struggled to find words.

'But Cathy . . . how can you . . . it's inconceivable that I should want to injure you. I've always been fond of you and I have every reason to believe that you . . .'

'Yes, at first sight, on Levenford Station, I had the misfortune to fall for you, head over heels. And I couldn't shake it off. It was you broke up my attachment to Frank. I might have had him if I had tried. I didn't try. You were always on my mind. I wanted you. I was sure you would come back when you graduated. Well, you did. And then . . .'

'You were engaged to Davigan.'

'Never. That was just a phase of weakness. I would never have married him,' she paused to achieve a more deadly effect, 'if you hadn't sneaked off like a rat at six that morning before I was awake.'

So it was out, as I had feared. She had hit the nail on the head. There was a long and for me an uneasy silence. I pulled myself together, cleared my throat. I meant to speak soulfully and in the circumstances the throb in my voice came almost naturally.

'Cathy,' I said, trying to make it ring true, 'I hope we're not going to desecrate what was, at least for me, the most wonderful memorable experience of my life. When we said goodbye after that ghastly celebration for Frank's ordination you must have sensed how much I needed you and how much, thinking of your attachment to Davigan, I was fighting it. As you know, I set out for my train but had, simply had, to turn back to you. I won't embarrass you, now, by dwelling on the warmth with which you welcomed me. A night we could never, never forget. But when morning came, what a position I was in. On the one hand your engagement to Davigan, on the other my commitment as ship's surgeon. I had signed ship's articles, I must report to the *Tasman* or be posted as a deserter. I simply had to go. The least hurtful way was to slip out without disturbing you. I thought of you continually during my enforced absence. But when I got back . . . you were married to Davigan.'

Incredulity had almost supplanted the bitterness in her expression. She gave me a short laugh.

'My God, Carroll, I wouldn't have believed it possible! That you could hand me that line. You're more of a twister than ever. I'll swear you even succeed in deceiving yourself. Yes, I married Davigan.'

'Then why blame me? He made you a good Catholic husband.'

'You've said it, Carroll. He was the best Catholic husband the Pope ever invented.'

328

'Meaning what?'

She took a cigarette from the pack in the pocket of her blouse and lit it.

'Since we're letting our hair down let's not spare our blushes. You've got to hear it sooner or later.' She drew on her cigarette, eyes looking back in time. 'You know what I'm like, how I'm made. At least you ought to.'

'Yes, indeed I'll never forget how exciting . . .'

'Cut it, Carroll. You gave me the first taste of honey. And it was the last. Daniel Davigan! That man! Well, because he'd been part of the town joke for the sixteen births in his own family he was compelled by a single monstrous obsession . . . to prevent me becoming pregnant. Not by means that would help me or meet my needs, but within the permitted canon law.'

'But surely, there was little Dan.'

'The fact that he came early made everything worse. Nothing ever took place at the natural times when you wanted it. Only at the mid term when I was flat out. Timing it by the calendar! Have you counted the days? I wonder if it's safe? Then the quick get rid of it, followed immediately by the "get up and make your water, squeeze hard, that's not a douche, it's permitted and it'll help". God, what a sacrifice of all fundamental decencies and dignity, and the wants of a woman's unsatisfied nature. Love according to the Catechism! Am I shocking your delicate feelings, Carroll, you're such a sweet man? Then for days after, the waiting and pestering, "have you not come on yet?" And his sickening look of relief when I had. No expression could be lower, more hideously hyprocritical than that which greeted me when I was out of action. Actually he always knew, for the deprivation I suffered intensified the distress of my periods, especially when forced at such times to listen to the Reverend Francis in the pulpit extolling the sacred bonds of matrimony. Even when I went to him in Confession all I got was some soulful advice at no cost to himself—prayer, proper feelings, and submission to the will of God. When I pointed out that desire cannot be summoned up by the calendar I didn't get an ounce of sympathy.'

These revelations, delivered with no sense of propriety, would have made tasty hearing as a demonstration of the farce of unsatisfactory conjugal performances had they not been so shamelessly bitter or so relevant to my present situation. Any temptation to laugh was stifled by my need to placate. I also already had in distant view the future possibilities in this damned-up flood of desire. And when, after a decent pause, I thought fit to make a murmur of medical sympathy, suggesting that her tribulations were over and could be redressed, she fixed me with a look that would have chilled a polar bear.

'None of that, doctor. After what I've been through I'm a different woman. The very mention of sex sickens me now.'

'Well,' I sighed, 'you must blame Davigan for that, poor fellow.'

'Poor fellow! A low, sickly, priest-ridden coward. I came to regard him with as much disgust as the sediment in his own chamber pot.'

This was plain speaking. I felt myself justified in exploiting the situation.

'It must,' I said tactfully, 'have been a relief to find yourself free.'

'A God-given relief.' She turned and faced me. 'I bless that gust of wind that blew him over.'

Blew him over, what *was* this? I had to know more. I said, thoughtfully:

'Thinking it might distress you . . I've been reluctant to press you as to how . . . ?'

'He fell off the top of the new tenement . . . just when they were finishing the upper storey. He was proud of it in a stupid sort of way, the tallest block of flats in Levenford with a view, God help it, of Ben Lomond. He'd had to do with the erecting of it and of course it was on land the Davigans once owned. So that Sunday afternoon he took the boy and me up to show us. I didn't want to go, it was so windy, but he insisted, was out cat-walking on the parapet, gassing away, when . . .' She shrugged indifferently.

So that was it. I felt like saying: a sort of Ibsen-ish ending, the Levenford Master Builder, but this was no moment to be smart.

'He was killed?' I spoke with becoming seriousness.

'On the spot.'

'Well, he's gone beyond recriminations. What good did they ever do? For that matter, if I've offended you in any way . . .' I paused significantly.

'Why don't I let you off too? No, no, Carroll. I have no malice towards you. Nevertheless . . .'

'Yes?'

'I have a use for you.'

My imagination jumped ahead of me. I smiled engagingly, with just a touch of disbelief.

'After what you just said? You're kidding.'

'Far from it.' She glanced at me in a manner that augured ill for my future. 'If you want to keep your soft, cushy, useless, no-job here, to hold on to it by the skin of your teeth, you'll have to go along with me.'

What was she after? Obviously she hated me and wanted her own back. But what else? She went on:

'I'm just as sick of Levenford as you ever were, Carroll. The only offer I got there was to keep the house for old Dr Ennis when his wife died last month. Cook, clean, scrub out the surgery. And he's so far gone on the bottle now he's hardly ever sober. No, no, I don't want to go back to that stinking, scandal-ridden hole, not ever. I like it here, I like it a lot, it's heaven after what I've been through. The Matron has taken to me and she's so short of help she needs me. To cut it short, I see a chance that I never expected, to remake my life. And you're going to help me to it.'

Suddenly it struck me. Could it be that after all these years she finally wanted to snaffle me. If so, what a hope.

'That's impossible. They won't have a married doctor here. It's in the charter.'

She gave me a lethal stare.

'Don't flatter yourself, Romeo. I'd sooner go to bed with a rattlesnake than you. All I need from you is your unwilling co-operation, a kind word to the committee, acceptance of the fact that I'm here for good. Otherwise,' she paused, 'you're out on your ear.'

I glared at her.

'You're crazy. I like it here too and I'm going to stay. You'll never get me out of the Maybelle.'

She looked me dead in the eye.

'I knew there must be something fishy about your appointment, which is more than you were ever worth. And there is. Matron has copies of your testimonials. I've seen them and they're . . .'

'That's enough!'

'Yes, it would be a nasty word, wouldn't it? False pretences. Might even be forgery. And what a bother it might get you into with the General Medical Council.' While I listened with growing, deep-seated uneasiness, she went on. 'Doctors have been struck off for less. I hope that won't be necessary. For you'd need your miserable little medical degree if I sent you back to general practice in Levenford. That's where you belong and that's where you will go if you don't toe the line. You're the one that'll go back to old Dr Ennis. He's losing his assistant and he'd take you, on my recommendation.' She gave me a thin, bitter smile. 'I'm going to get a lot of pleasure watching you sweat it out here with that hanging over you.'

NINE

I BARGED DOWN the hill in a state of mind in which rage, resentment and apprehension prevailed over the suspicion that I was dealing with an unbalanced character. Naturally I had left her without a word. I had found it unprofitable at any time to argue with a woman; still less so now with one thrown off the beam by a prolonged stretch of marital frustration. Did she actually imagine I could be yanked out of the best, yes, if you prefer her word, the softest crib I had ever hoped to drop into? I was established at the May-belle, I now spoke German fluently—there was no need to fake it—and on the two occasions when the committee had visited the clinic they had expressed themselves as fully satisfied with their choice. If the validity of the testimonials were questioned I could explain that I had lost the originals. And hadn't I been foreseeing enough to protect myself against just such a contingency, this threat to my security? The bold Caterina hadn't thought of that one. I was safe. No need to worry, Carroll, my boy. And yet I was worried. There remained with me a sense of something in the background, unspoken, unrevealed, retained, so to speak for the *Meisterstück*. Curse that German, I meant the *coup de grâce*. No, that was nonsense, yes, rot in any language. Get me back to Levenford? That noxious hole in Clyde-side mud? Back to another G.P. Assistantship, stuffed with night calls and surgery grinds, with an old boozer as principal, who was more or less tight half the time. She was right —it would be hell. But, never. No, not on your bleeding life, Carroll. I would fight it to the last ditch.

Suddenly, as I approached the clinic, I heard someone calling me, the voice immediately recognizable as Matron's. Perched on the rear balcony like a moulting hen, she was flapping me in with a towel. Refusing to be hurried, I slowed to a walk, so that she had ample time to come down to the terrace to meet me.

'Ver haf you been, Herr Doktor?' She was practically foaming at the mouth. 'Eine Stunde almost I am seeking you.'

I permitted myself the liberty of a really dirty look, the first I had ever directed towards her.

'Where the devil do you think I've been? I'm surely entitled to a little time off. I've been taking my exercise.'

I perceived with satisfaction that she was taken aback. In a modified tone, though still complaining, she declared:

'Your patient is not so good. Much sickness. All his good *Mittagessen* thrown back.'

'What! Sick again?'

'Much.'

'You did stop his codliver oil?'

She reddened uncomfortably.

'But it is so goot for him . . .'

'Damn it all, I told you, instructed you, to stop it.'

She was silent, giving me best.

'Very well,' I said shortly. 'I'll have a look at him.'

'*Jetzt?* Immediately?'

'When I've had a wash. He won't harm just because he's had a vomit.'

This was merely to keep Hulda in her place. When she was out of sight I went across to the guest chalet.

He was lying fully dressed, on his bed, with his eyes on the ceiling. Beside him an enamel basin seemed to contain most of his lunch, but it gave out no stink of fish oil. One hand was placed protectively on his stomach. He removed it quickly as I came in, an action I did not fail to observe.

'So you've been at it again, you little rat?'

As may be imagined my mood was not attuned to sympathy and loving kindness.

'Sorry,' he said.

'You may well be. Damned little nuisance. You knew I'd put you off the oil.'

'Of course. And I didn't take it. When Matron wasn't looking I poured it down the wash basin.'

'You did?' This shook my preconceived opinion. 'Come on then, pull up your shirt and let's have a look at you.'

'It's all better now, Dr Laurence.' He half smiled. 'Let's let sleeping dogs lie.'

'None of that smart guff, strip to the waist.'

I didn't altogether like the look of him and while he got ready I reassembled the evidence. His von Pirquet had proved negative, his temperature varied no more than a fraction of a point and beyond that cervical swelling I had found nothing specific to confirm the presence of T.B., or, indeed, to account for his obvious pallor, shortness of breath, palpitation and general asthenia. I began to suspect that the good Dr Moore before leaving for the wide open spaces had landed me with a stumer of a diagnosis. With this in mind I took a new look, considering that recurrent sickness, giving particular attention to the abdomen. As I had previously observed, his was somewhat distended, but this 'big belly' was a not uncommon feature in the rundown children who came to the Maybelle, and I had rather taken it for granted. Now, however, I began carefully to palpate. Once again everything seemed in order, but suddenly there it was: I no more than caught the edge of it: a tender and slightly swollen spleen.

'That hurts you?'

'Somewhat . . . yes, a little,' he admitted, wincing despite the understatement.

'Does it pain you when I don't press? I mean when you're up and around.'

'Not really . . . just a sort of dragging feeling sometimes.'

So now what? A palpable, tender spleen, at that age, and instinctively my eyes went back to the inner surface of his arms on which I could just make out a faint purpuric staining of the skin. It had me puzzled.

'Nothing bad I hope, Dr Laurence?'

My silence had worried him.

'Don't be a toad. This probably means you don't have T.B. at all. Coming here with a false tag on you and all that rot about scrofula.'

He looked at me doubtfully.

'That's a relief. Or isn't it?'

I ignored this and said: 'What else have you been hiding, you little coward? You've had these sick attacks for some time?'

'For a little while. But when they pass off I'm quite hungry and can eat anything.'

'What about these red blotches on your skin?'

'Well, yes, I've had them off and on. But they fade very quickly. I thought they might be just an irritation.'

'Naturally.'

Then I took a shot in the dark. 'Have you had bleeding recently from the inside of your mouth, I mean from your gums?'

His eyes widened with surprise and, actually, admiration.

'That's remarkably clever of you, Dr Laurence. Yes, as a matter of fact I have. But I think, I mean, I thought it was my hard toothbrush.'

I was silent, staring at him with ill-concealed misgiving intensified by this sudden and unanticipated prospect of further trouble. What had I let myself in for? Wasn't it enough to be saddled with his bitch of a mother? There wasn't a trace of T.B. in this obnoxious little smartie. At a guess I was faced by one of the obscure idiopathic blood syndromes, of which there were probably a score of different varieties, conditions that never properly clear up, run on for years, and break the back of the average G.P. with the need for repeated tests, to say nothing of probable haemorrhages and transfusions. I would not stand for it. In this instance my own modification of the Hippocratic oath was never more applicable: when stuck with a difficult and prolonged case, get rid of it. Yes, I would put through a couple of basic tests and if the results spelled trouble he would have to go to hospital. The Winton Victoria would take him if he proved pathologically interesting. With a brightening of my mood, I reflected that if he were sent home his mother could have no excuse for remaining at the clinic. I would be rid of them both, kill two birds with one stone, and be free again.

Naturally I could not fling any of this at him. He had been watching me intently as if trying to discover what was going on in my head. Assuming an air of cheerful camaraderie, a useful aspect of my best bedside manner, I picked up the enamel basin.

'Can't have you wasting good food like this, young fellow. We'll have to do something about it.'

'You can?'

'Why not? There's nothing wrong with your stomach.

335

You're anaemic. I'll just take a sample of your blood to make sure.'

'Bleed me? Like the old apothecaries?'

'Oh, cut out that nonsense! This is simple, and scientific. It won't hurt you a bit.'

I had some difficulty in finding and puncturing his saphenous vein, which was almost threadlike, but he was quite good about it, almost too passive. I drew off 5 c.c., stoppered the test tube after I had smeared several slides, and exclaimed cheerfully:

'There we are. When these slides are dry we'll stain them. By tomorrow we'll know all about your red corpuscles. You can even take a peep at them under the microscope yourself.'

That perked him up slightly.

'What an interesting situation. A boy examining his own blood. What about that little tube?'

'We'll use that for your blood haemoglobin, and,' I added indefinitely, 'other things.' He was obviously admiring me a lot and I scarcely liked to admit I would send it to the Kantonspital in Zürich. 'Now relax for a bit. I must let them know in the kitchen about your diet.'

'Bread and water?' He gave me a wan smile.

'You deserve it. Still, what would you like?'

'I'm rather hungry now after that emptying.' He thought for a moment. 'Mashed potatoes and,' with another smile, 'the meence.'

Impossible not to smile back at him.

'We'll consider it. At least you can have the mash and some of that good gravy. Now cheer up. I'll do what I can for you.'

I went out of the room with my own words ringing derisively in my ears. 'I'll do what I can for you.' Well, damn it, I would—at least I'd do as much as I reasonably could.

Naturally I avoided the office where I knew that both of my enemies would be expecting me. Instead I lit a cigarette and went into the test room. It wouldn't hurt the kid to wait for his supper and although I had told him I would leave the slides till the morning—since I did not want him cliff-hanging on my neck all evening—I was rather curious to have a look at them.

Still smoking, I stained them, a quick simple job, and

336

put one on the stage of the excellent Leitz. Rather than waste my cigarette, one of the oval Abdullas Lotte got me duty free through her airline, I sat down comfortably and finished it before rising to take a look.

At first I thought my oil immersion lens was maladjusted, but as I focused and refocused the same picture came up. It made me catch my breath. Although I am no virtuoso as a biologist there was no mistaking this—it hit me full in the eye. Fascinating, actually, in its own morbid manner, the sort of thing you might never see once in a G.P.'s lifetime. This was it: the field crammed with lymphocytes, white corpuscles multiplied five or six times over. I could even make out immature forms, myelocytes, large immature corpuscles from the bone marrow never present in healthy blood. Obvious, of course, what was taking place. A hyperplasia of white cell precursors in the bone marrow, progressive and uncontrolled, crowding out the progenitors of red cells and platelets, probably even eroding the bone itself. I clipped on the second slide with the measuring scale, dropped on fresh oil, and made a rough count on one square and multiplied. That settled it.

I could scarcely unlatch myself from the eyepiece. It was one of those moments, so rare in my dreary run of the mill experience, when you strike the exceptional. have been good enough to uncover it, then see the whole sequence of events, past, present and future, laid out before you. The future? I had to stop patting myself on the back. This was bad news for young Capablanca—in fact the worst. Oddly enough, at the airport, the first time I sighted his sad little pan, I felt he was unlucky, marked out in some queer way for disaster. Born for trouble, out of that impossible failure of a marriage, the mark of the Davigans upon him. And now he'd had it. Still, though God knew it was the last thing I would have wanted, there was no denying that it solved my problem. I thought this over thoroughly for several minutes, then took up both slides and went into the office.

They were both waiting for me, one on either side of my desk, and brave Hulda actually occupying my chair. She looked at me uncomfortably, but with a glint of defiance, which told me they had been putting in more overtime on my character.

'We attend to ask what is for Daniel's supper.'

'Later.' I brushed it aside. 'If I can have my desk, Matron?'

I stood there waiting for her to get up, which she did, though with reluctance. When I had seated myself I faced up to the widow Davigan. That was how I meant to think of her now, or simply as Davigan, she had joined the tribe of her own free will, and after all she never called me anything but Carroll, and I would let her have it straight. She could expect no mercy from this throne.

'It's like this,' I said. 'For some time I've suspected that we've been misled by a false diagnosis. We're not dealing with a tubercular infection. Your boy has never had T.B.'

'Then what . . . ?' She broke off suspiciously.

'I've just made a blood smear. Here are the slides. They show a massive increase in the white cells. Instead of the normal five to ten thousand lymphocytes per cubic millimetre there's not far short of sixty thousand . . . plus an abnormal proliferation of myelocytes.'

This meant nothing to her, but it chilled the Matron.

'You are not serious, Herr Doktor?'

I liked that Herr Doktor, the first in several days.

'Only too serious, unfortunately.'

Davigan was looking confusedly from me to the Matron. 'This is something bad?'

'It coot be . . . but natürlich we are not sure.'

I cut in firmly.

'I regret having to tell you that I'm only too sure. It's an open and shut case. The boy has Myelocytic Leukocythemia.'

Did Davigan really get the message of these two words? I think not. At least, not entirely, for she didn't wilt. She flushed up and her suspicions of me, never absent, deepened.

'I don't understand this sudden change and I don't like it.'

'Are you suggesting that I like it, or that I'm in any way responsible for the sudden change?'

'It's all very peculiar . . . I don't understand . . .'

'We have been trying to make you understand.'

The Matron, recovering herself, suddenly cut in.

'Who is we? Caterina *hat recht*. There must come more advice. *Ein zweiter* opinion, *und der beste*. You must bring specialist Herr Professor Lamotte from Zürich.

'You'd only be wasting his time. And he has none to waste. Anyhow, he'd never come this far . . .'

'Then you must take the boy to him at the Kantonspital,' Hulda persisted.

On the point of refusing, I suddenly changed my mind. A second opinion, particularly Lamotte's, would take the pressure off me. They could never get round his diagnosis. It must stick. And that was all I needed. I was calm, quite sure of myself.

'Very well. I agree. I'll ring up and make an appointment for the earliest possible day. Meantime,' I turned to Matron, 'as you were so anxious about Daniel's supper, perhaps you'll see that he gets some *consommé* and *Kartoffel püree* with meat gravy.'

She had something to say, but thought better of it. When she had gone I stood up, and made for the door. But Cathy caught me on the way out. Her flush had left her. She looked drawn, tight-lipped.

'I know you're up to something, Carroll, so I'm warning you. Don't try any of your dirty tricks on me or it'll be the worse for you.'

I stared her out, in chilly silence. What else could you do with such a troll?

TEN

THE ZURICH KANTONSPITAL is agreeably situated on the Zürichberg, in a residential district high up on the left bank of the Limmat. An excellent site typically ill chosen, since approaching from the river by the interminable line of steep steps, you are half way to a coronary by the time you get there. The hospital is a massive structure, lamentably in the Swiss taste, with modern additions, offset by some tall and beautiful old trees, and to such patients as may be interested, it affords a striking view of three ancient churches; the Predigerkirche, the Grossmünster and the Fraumünster which, with the innumerable banks, suggest the split of personality of this city—a devotion to both Mammon and the Lord.

On Saturday afternoon, of the following week, I came through the swing doors and out of the Medical Department with Daniel. It was a beautiful day and as the late autumn sunshine and crisp cool air greeted us he let out a long breath of relief.

'Well, Dr Laurence, I'm glad that's over.'

He gave a bit of a laugh and took my hand, an action which I need not add, embarrassed me acutely, gave me what in Scotland is called the *grue*. I was not in the best of moods. After all my trouble in making the appointment I had been hung up for most of the afternoon with only two quick chances to telephone Lotte, trying to explain why I was in Zürich without seeing her, and getting pretty well told off for my pains. Still, in the circumstances, I could not do other than let him drag on to me.

'Surely it wasn't too bad?' I said.

'Oh, no. I liked Dr Lamotte. Very serious, with that way he has of reading right through you. But he gave me such a nice smile as I was leaving. He's clever, isn't he?'

'He's the tops,' I said shortly. 'French-Swiss. They're the best . . . intellectually.'

'But I never thought he would send me in to all those young ladies, doing all sorts of things to me.'

'Those girls are technicians . . . each trained to do a special test.'

'Such as?'

'Well, more or less everything, for example, find out all about your corpuscles, and of course your blood group.'

'But couldn't you have done that, Dr Laurence?'

'Naturally, if I had their equipment. You're a group A.B. if you want to know.'

'Is that quite regular?'

'Perfectly. It's the least common of the blood groups.'

'What group are you?'

'I'm group O.'

'They did seem rather interested in my blood.' He reflected. 'Perhaps it isn't blue enough.' He looked up as if expecting me to smile. 'I hope Dr Lamotte gave you a good account of me.'

'Of course he did,' I said, freeing myself from his sweaty little clutch to give him a reassuring pat on the back. 'We'll have a chat about it presently.'

We walked through the avenue of plane trees, the dry fallen leaves crackling under our feet. I'd had nothing but a cold beef sandwich for lunch so I said:

'We'll have something to eat before we start back.'

'Good!' he said cheerfully. 'As a matter of fact, now it's all over, I'm quite peckish, and ready for anything.'

This silenced me for the moment.

We got into the Opel station wagon, which I had parked in the Hospital lot, and I took him to Sprüngli's which at this hour between lunch and five o'clock was not over-crowded. Upstairs at a window table I ordered poached eggs on toast, hot milk for him, café crème for myself.

'None of these lovely cakes?' he hinted. 'Remember, we had a sort of agreement . . .'

'You'll have a couple after your eggs.'

What the hell did it matter anyway. Let him have some fun while it lasted.

As I watched his pale-skinned, tight face brighten, I looked quickly out of the window, barely seeing the heavy traffic moving in the Bahnhofstrasse or the long low blue trams swinging round the island with the newspaper kiosk in the Parade Platz.

Classic Leucocythaemia. Malignant Myelocytic type: cause still unknown. Lamotte had flattered me by confirm-ing my diagnosis, putting a few knobs on by way of orna-ment. Relentlessly progressive. The multiplying abnormal cells colonizing the various organs of the body—choking liver, spleen, kidneys, lungs, proliferating in the bone marrow, pouring out more and more from the bone marrow. Symptoms: acute weakness and wasting, big belly, haemorrhage from the stomach and bowels, oedema of the feet and legs from obstruction of the lymphatic vessels. Treatment: specific medication unknown: radiations in small doses inadequate, larger doses destroy the few healthy cells: in emergencies, blood transfusions. Prognosis: inde-terminate yet inevitably fatal. Minimum, six months; at the most, three years.

Too bad, naturally. But he was not the first kid to get his marching orders. I had a sudden recollection of the epidemic of cerebro-spinal meningitis I had come up against in the Rhondda. How many dirty blankets had I pulled over those poor little stiffs? No wonder you get tough. The groundwork had to be laid and better now than later. When he was well into his second egg I leaned forward.

'How is the grub?'

'First rate.'

'Good. That's part of your treatment—no more cod-liver oil but lots of protein. I think I did mention that you are anaemic.'

'Oh, you did. You were the one who really spotted it. Did. . . . did Dr Lamotte agree?'

I nodded.

'And your treatment's all worked out for you.' I paused, then added cheerfully: 'It's just a pity that we can't work on the important part of it at the Maybelle.'

His mouth opened like a hooked trout's, and a piece of egg dropped off his fork.

'Why not?'

'We haven't got the facilities.'

He digested that slowly.

'Couldn't I go to the Kantonspital. Like today?'

'I'm afraid not, Daniel. It's too far from Schlewald. You need regular treatment. And the natural place for you to get it is the Victoria Hospital at home.'

His chin really dropped, down into his thin chicken's neck.

'You mean, go back to Levenford?'

'Why not, boy?' I laughed. 'You live there, don't you?'

'Yes,' he said slowly. 'I did live there. But I . . . Mother said . . . we were hoping we might spend a longer time in Switzerland.'

'I was hoping so too, but needs must . . . and what's wrong with dear old Levenford?'

He was silent, his eyes on his plate.

'I've not been particularly happy there since my father died.'

'You miss him?'

'I suppose I do. But it's not . . . not quite that.'

'What then?'

He had gone white round the lips and suddenly I wanted to rise, get the bill, and clear out to the car. But something held me there, bending towards him, waiting for the answer. And it came. Speaking slowly, not looking at me, he said:

'When my father died, or was killed falling off the roof, there was a lot of unpleasant talk.' He paused, and the thought hit me like an electric shock: no wonder Mama doesn't want to go back to Levenford.

'Yes, Danny?' I prompted.

'Boys shouted things after me. And at the inquest, after Canon Dingwall told me . . .'

He broke off, raising his head pitifully to look at me, and I saw the tears running down his cheeks. How low can you get, Carroll? Cut it out, for God's sake. You've heard more than enough.

'Come, Danny boy. Not a word more. You know we wouldn't upset you for the world. Here, take my handkerchief and I'll pop over to the counter for your cakes.'

In five minutes, playing it good and hearty, I had him dried off and polished up, eating a meringue with no more than an occasional sniffle.

On the way to the car, which I had parked in Tielstrasse, I hoped it wouldn't happen, but it did. First the hand, then the usual:

'Thank you for being so decent to me, Dr Laurence.'

But when you are Carroll you can brush off compunction after no more than a brief, bad moment. Self preservation is the first law of nature. Anything by the name of Davigan had always spelled poison for me. I positively had to get rid of them. I had nothing against this little semi-animated bit of grey matter, but the mother would kill me. Always she would have her knife in me and one day, so help me, she would out me from the Maybelle.

As we got into the car the sky had turned to a livid grey and a few soft flakes came fluttering down.

'You see, Daniel,' I reasoned. 'It's beginning to snow. Soon we'll be into winter and that's not very suitable for you.'

'I like snow,' he said, and looking up at the lovely feathery drift he muttered, half to himself as if explaining it away: 'It's just the angels having a pillow fight.'

'They must be knocking the hell out of themselves,' I said—it was getting thicker. I left it at that, revved the engine and set off.

It was not an easy drive, the de-icer wasn't working too well and at one point, near Coire, I thought I might have to stop and fit chains. But at the back of ten o'clock we reached the Maybelle.

I dropped the boy at the chalet where his mother was waiting to put him to bed, and went on to the main building.

Matron, alerted by the headlights of the car—for the snow muffled all sound—was at the door to meet me, and her manner, while restrained and formal was, to my surprise, not hostile.

'*Schlechte Nacht*, Herr Doktor. You have managed well

343

to come safely.' Then, as I shed my coat and scarf: '*Haben Sie Hunger?*'

'I've had practically nothing to eat all day.'

She nodded and turned away. Further surprises lay ahead. In my room the stove had been freshly stoked, the table was set for supper, and almost at once the old battle-axe came in with a tray on which I made out a tureen of steaming soup and something I had not seen in years—a big ashet holding the good remaining half of a steak and kidney pie.

I couldn't wait to get into it but, softened, not sitting down, I said:

'I suppose you want to hear everything?'

'*Nein, Herr Doktor.*' As I stared at her she went on: 'You must forgive. Caterina becomes so anxious and I alzo, that I did telephone the ward sister of Dr Lamotte. We know all, alas. Alzo that everything you have said of this bad illness is absolute and correct.'

This from Hulda was a very handsome amende—if I hadn't been so chilled I might have glowed. But as I eased into my chair and began to ladle out the soup, she went on:

'So now, without question it is settled that Caterina and the boy must remain. This afternoon I wrote express to Herr Scrygemour telling how undispensable she becomes to me, so long without proper assistance. He will consent. It is sure. And so, Herr Doktor, I wish you *gute Nacht.*'

With that she bobbed me that recently developed formal little bow and went out.

After the soup I ate the steak and kidney pie, slowly and thoughtfully, savouring the flavour of good Scottish food. I ate all of it, and it couldn't have been tastier. The brave Caterina had certainly been putting in more good work on Hulda, than whom no one liked better to feed well. So be it, let them have it their way for the present. I held the card that was the clincher. At the moment it was not up my sleeve, but it would be, for I knew where to find it.

After I had finished, though I was full to the ears and all in with tiredness, I sat down determinedly and wrote to the Circulation Department of the Levenford *Herald* requesting their report on the Davigan inquest by return of post.

ELEVEN

I HAD A FOUL NIGHT. So far I have refrained from elaborating on the extrordinary fantasy that afflicts me. It is a personal matter. It worries me. And as it is patently an hallucination, both auditory and visual, I prefer to keep it to myself. Nevertheless, lately the attacks have been more frequent and last night I suffered one of unprecedented severity. In fact, a shattering nightmare.

It began as usual. Darkness and desolation in the strange silent city. A sense of heartbreaking loneliness and the need immediate and terrible, to seek help, to escape. Then, after that moment of fearful anticipation, the slow footsteps beginning, following, deliberate and insistent, echoing from behind me in the empty street.

I began to run. Usually I ran with speed. But tonight my feet were weighted and by the greatest effort I achieved only a dragging trot. The sounds behind me increased, drew gradually nearer. I must be overtaken. Almost, I could feel the touch of that unseen hand upon my shoulder. I swerved into an alley. Immediately I was in a network of narrow streets lined with low windows, each curtained red, and open, offering some hope of refuge and escape. But as, one by one, I stretched towards them a wind arose and blew in gusts along the narrow alleys, slamming the windows shut. Now I had reached an empty square, enclosed by tall half-ruined buildings, through which I toiled in a breathless sweat, and still relentlessly pursued.

The syndrome was lasting longer, much longer than before, the more so since this final enclosure appeared to offer no possible exit. To be trapped so abjectly was more than I could bear. I would not endure it and at last, flinging myself into the doorway of a deserted warehouse, I forced myself to face about and at the pitch of my lungs to shout towards that invisible approach.

'Keep away. Don't come near me!'

Instantly I heard the signal of release, the low, distant baying of a hound, and in the same second the rush of footsteps ceased. The pursuit was over, once again, though by the skin of my teeth, I had escaped.

In the morning when I half awoke with a ringing head, it took an effort to pull myself together. Yet it was some relief to realize that it was Sunday and I could drowse on until ten o'clock. When the holiday groups were here Sunday could be a trial but lately it had treated me handsomely since Matron, who regularly attended the eight o'clock Mass, had taken both the Davigans with her. So although I always set out, book in hand, before eleven-thirty to keep in good standing with Hulda, I rarely lingered near the church but, by a convenient detour, reached the station kiosk for a chat with Gina or, more profitably, the Pfeffermühle where they kept an admirable light beer.

I got up at half past ten and after breakfast which, although served without *ballons*, I did not want, I hoofed through the usual routine ward visit, where I decided to mark one of the boys for an early discharge. His pleurisy had cleared up nicely and his parents had written, wanting him home. Then, before taking off for the town, I crossed to the chalet to have a quick look at young Davigan. He met me, fully dressed, at the door.

'They let me sleep in, Dr Laurence. So I'm going with you this morning.'

This was an unexpected snag. Critically, I looked him over—he was smiling, seemed better and well rested after the Soneryl I had given him. It was not altogether unexpected. I saw that he was on the uplift, surely one of the most pitiful manifestations of the myelocytic brand of leukaemia, a sudden inexplicable improvement which arouses false hopes only to be followed invariably by a relapse.

'You're an invalid,' I said. 'You're not obliged to . . . to come to church.'

'Oh, I wouldn't miss it for anything. Especially with you.'

Could anything be more sickening than this unwanted and too open devotion? This morning especially. If he had not been so ill I would have given him a flat 'No.' Instead, I tried to think up an excuse. No luck. Nothing else for it then, I was stuck with him, otherwise there would be a shindy. I had a feeling in the small of my back that eyes were watching from windows.

'Let's go then,' I said, with false optimism, putting my hands carefully in my pockets to avoid the clutch.

It was the kind of morning that follows a snowfall in the Grisons—a sky blue as a mandril's behind, a sparkling sun making false diamonds of the snow crystals and a crisp air that tingled and made you want to lose your headache and live for ever. In Switzerland they know how to deal with

346

snow, and the village council, well disposed towards the Maybelle, had swept and banked our drive all the way down to the main well-scoured highway. We walked between walls of a dazzling blue whiteness that stung the eyes, mine, at least. The village roofs were heavily blanketed and as we moved along the bells began, the waves of sound showering us with icy particles from the projecting eaves.

'An avalanche.' The encumbrance laughed. 'Let's pretend we're crossing the Alps. Three cheers for Hannibal and us.'

We went into the church. After the exterior brightness it seemed darker, gloomier than ever, the congregation scanty and scattered—on a day like this most people came to the earlier service. He had made, of course, for the front row.

I have already reported my allergy to churches. They give me a low feeling, a sinking nostalgia, plus an angry 'let's get the hell out of it' sensation, in all, a complex especially aggravated by this particular church. Outside it was fantastic, inside so like a tomb it struck me with the chill of the anatomy room where I had dissected my first cadaver, and on the reredos, a raw red granite wall, there was a great flat carving, a sort of impressionist bas-relief in the same red granite that always got me down. It was the Man, of course, not on the Cross, nothing conventional or agonized, just the profile and an outline, the suggestion of a figure, bent forward, and half turned towards you, with one arm stretched forward. It killed me, that Figure. Your eyes kept going back to it, not only because it was a damn fine original piece of work, totally at variance with the tiddy design of the church, but because if you didn't disconnect the contact and tell yourself, as I did: Forget it: you were liable to start going back over things best forgotten.

I had scarcely knelt down and gone through the usual sketchy motions, to save my face, when the local Father appeared, not yet robed. He was a thin little man who looked ill, a Pole, with a name like Zobronski, if that is how he spelled it—Swiss clergy were scarce in this remote end of the valley, they had to make do with political refugees. He was conning the congregation with an upturned forefinger.

'He wants a server?' The words were hissed in my ear. 'I'll go.'

And before I could grip him he was up and away. The

moment I came in I'd had a premonition that things would go ill for me. When he reappeared, in a natty red cassock and white surplice, looking like the boy Pope, and began to light the candles with an expertise he could only have acquired from Dingwall, I began to sweat down the back of my neck. It was worse when the Mass began. You never saw such a show-off. This little upstart knew all the tricks. I kept hoping he would trip on the hassock or drop the book, but he never put a hand or a foot wrong, and all with such an air of presanctified devotion he might have been performing before a bevy of Cardinals in the Sistine Chapel. Zobronski, if that was his name, seemed to go along with the act. Other times he had been a fairly scrubby performer and you kept noticing how much he coughed, or that he'd cut himself shaving, or that the cuffs of his pants were frayed and his boots practically worn out. Now, however, you would have thought he had money in the bank, he was putting a few flourishes in on his own.

When it came to the Communion I bet myself the little pain in the neck wouldn't take it, he had been too long away from Confession. But he did, and the way he shut his eyes turned me over. Most of the congregation went up and as he passed up and down the rails with the paten I felt the corner of his eyes slanted towards me. What a hope! How long was it now since they caught me? Must be more than five years, since that Mission at Nottingham. I went in for a lark, to hear that Franciscan, Father Aloysius —they said he was dramatic, as good as Charles Laughton —and came out reconverted. I had kept it up, too, for a couple of months until I met that red-head North of Ireland nurse from the local hospital. She was a dandy too, except for that Belfast accent. For a bet she could crack glasses with it in the Sherwood Bar.

After the blessing I went out to the clean fresh air and waited for him. He did not keep me long, and came out spry and cheerful. I did not respond.

'The Father was so anxious to meet you, Dr Laurence. D'you know he speaks four languages?'

'Don't mix me up with that Pole. He needs money.'

'Oh, yes, he's terribly poor. A big debt was made building the church. And now he's running things on practically nothing. That's why there's so little oil for the heating. I don't think he even gets enough to eat.'

'That's his problem,' I said. 'Mine is to get the *Sunday Telegraph*. We're going to the station.'

As we set off he said:

'Did you see that wonderful carving on the wall?'

'Only when I looked at it, which is something I avoid.'

'Apparently it was done by a young sculptor who was ill in Davos.'

'Then he died.' I shot at him. 'The masterpiece was his last act.'

'Oh, no. He got cured and is quite famous now. He has an exhibition in Vienna this year.'

'Let's go,' I said. 'I can't wait. Now come on and don't be so full of yourself.'

You couldn't shake him. He had about him a kind of glow. Was it due to these few extra red corpuscles he had managed to manufacture overnight? I doubted it.

We were at the kiosk and the Sunday papers were in, which gave me a slight lift. It made a dull day for me when they missed the connection at Zürich. I bought my *Telegraph*, without much palaver, and was turning away when he said:

'Could you change me a half-crown into Swiss money, Dr Laurence?'

'You have a half-crown?'

'Naturally.' He smiled. 'The old Canon gave it me before I left. And now we have snow I'd very much like to send him one of these pictures.' He pointed to a colour postcard of a big St Bernard and a pup, both with brandy flasks around their necks.

"I'll give you fifty centimes for the card,' I said, thinking how often this old bag of bones came up between us. 'You can bore a hole in the half-crown and wear it round your neck.'

I regretted that immediately I had said it. But he did not seem to mind.

'It wouldn't be very spendable there. Besides, I already have a medal that he gave me.'

I bought the card and lent him my ballpoint. Although I was curious, I avoided looking at what he wrote since I felt he would show me the effusion, and he did.

Dear Very Reverend Canon,
Your pupil and esteemed chess enemy sends you greetings from the Alps where in company of (scored out) with his

349

*pysician he has just passed through an avalansh, small but
troublesome. These two St. Bernards, the large with
brandy for Dr Laurence, the small with lemonade for me,
were fortunately not needed. I am very well today, but
may be coming back soon. So beware of P to K4 with the
Ruy Lopez opening.*

'Two mistakes in spelling,' was all I could say.

'Yes, I'm an awful speller,' he agreed. 'It's my Achilles'
heel.'

Yet the effort was commendably neat, so I softened and
bought him a stamp from Gina, who, all through, had
watched the proceedings with particular interest. I knew she
would rib me mercilessly later.

'You're quite attached to old Dingwall?' I said, as we
walked off.

'Oh, yes . . . closely,' he said seriously. 'He's always been
so kind to us, lately especially.'

'After the . . . the accident?'

He nodded, expansively. 'You know, Dr Laurence, it's
something for a boy of my age to be, well, trusted by someone like Canon Dingwall.'

'Who wouldn't be?' I said encouragingly. 'Still . . .' I
smiled. 'I don't quite see how he'd need to trust a little
nipper like you.'

'But he does.'

'In what way?' I laughed.

'To keep a secret.' This came out proudly, then his face
closed down as though he had said too much.

'I can't believe it.'

'But it's true,' he persisted.

'Then won't you let me into it?'

He kept silent, still with that shut expression, then he
looked up at me.

'I couldn't,' he said slowly, 'although I would like to very
much. You see . . . you can't break the seal of confession.'

This was one out of the bag that I would never have
dreamed of. But I couldn't push it too far. I had to drop it
for the time being. I must wait for that report from the
Levenford *Herald*. But I was not at all discouraged. Something queer, decidedly queer and more than decidedly
suspicious lay beneath all this, well below the surface, deep
down in fact, but sooner or later if I kept digging I would

strike pay dirt. These, I reflected, not without satisfaction, might prove to be appropriate words.

We had reached the end of the platform before he spoke again.

'I hope you're not offended?'

'Oh, no,' I said, on just the right note of hurt reluctance. 'I'd never want to come between Dingwall and you.'

Nothing more was said until we were outside the station, then he made an obvious effort to change the subject.

'There's nothing else we can do, now we're in the village? I'm feeling so . . . sort of well. No chance of that game of chess?'

'They'll all be out on a day like this,' I said. 'But if you like we'll stop in at the Pfeffermühle for a drink.'

We did just that, stepping off the side road into the snug little dark-beamed Stube. As I had expected, it was empty. I gave him an apfelsaft and had an Eichberger. The place seemed to thrill him and when he saw the cups of the Chess Club, most of which had been won by Bemmel, the former schoolmaster, he made me promise to bring him back again. When he saw on the notice-board the name Schachklub, he gave out that brainy little yelp, prelude to the exposition of some special tit-bit of knowledge.

'Schach! How very interesting, Dr Laurence. Don't you see, deriving directly from Shah. Of course chess too is a corruption of that word, though less obvious.'

'What are you drivelling about?'

'Chess was the Shah's special game and is believed to have originated in ancient Persia.'

'You're kidding. It's as old as that?'

'Terribly old, and royal. A favourite of ever so many kings, like Charlemagne and Harun-al-Raschid. Even King Canute played it.'

'Wasn't he too busy with the waves?'

'Far from it. There's a historical record of a game he played with a courtier named Earl Ulf, which he lost and got up in a rage knocking over the board. Oddly enough, two days later Earl Ulf was mysteriously murdered.'

He looked so serious I burst out laughing and, after a shocked moment, he joined me. We both laughed our heads off over the end of Ulf.

Strangely enough, my mood had mellowed, not entirely due to the good beer. Things were beginning to work well for me. And I did not mind young Davigan showing off in this sort of atmosphere, I was getting used to him, in fact I almost liked him. All the way home he talked his head off. Even when we got back after one o'clock he couldn't keep his trap shut. They were both waiting for us, Davigan and the Matron, and the soup tureen was on the table.

'You are late, Herr Doktor.' Hulda made meaningful play with the watch that was always pinned on to her left protuberance.

'You must forgive us, Matron,' the kid yodelled. 'We've had such a nice time and we stopped for a drink at the Pfeffermühle.'

You could almost see Hulda's hair rise. The widow was giving me a nasty look.

'Ach so, the Pfeffermühle. That is *kein Platz* for Sonntag. And to take the leetle boy.'

'What is it?' said Davigan.

'A low drink place for low peoples.'

All the rungs I had made on the ladder slipped away from me. I was down, with a bump.

The *Mittagessen* began and ended in silence. They had ganged up on me again. Never mind, Carroll, your time will come. And soon.

TWELVE

THE BRITISH postal services have neither the speed nor the accuracy of the Swiss, and the response to my letter to the Levenford *Herald* did not arrive until Thursday morning of the following week. But it was more than worth the delay. The *Herald* had splashed the inquiry on the front page and besides a full report of the proceedings had added a special article on the legal aspects of the case which I found particularly illuminating.

Naturally, I devoured that worthy paper, even letting my coffee cool, in my haste to get to the meat of the news. Then I read everything with extreme care, and with a growing interest and satisfaction. This was all I needed, had hoped for, had indeed expected. I lit up an Abdulla and took a long, deep aromatic breath. What a beautiful day!—the sun shone into my little sitting-room, a mavis was whistling outside my window, all was well with the world of the Hon. L. Carroll.

During the forenoon I was bright, cheerful, and in no hurry. The Davigan had been so beastly to me lately, anticipation became a greater pleasure. I chose the appropriate moment with due care and circumspection. I waited until after the *Mittagessen* when Matron, always a heavy eater, took her usual cat-nap in her room. The brains trust, well wrapped, was stowed away on the far, sunny side of the terrace. From my window I saw Davigan cross to the chalet. I gave her ten minutes then took a leisurely stroll over.

There had been heavy rain during the week, clearing away much of the snow, and the lower pastures were green again, sappy with verdure. The cows, turned out for a brief spell, were jangling around nosing each other skittishly and cropping the succulent grass like mad. From the rain-swollen valley below came the soothing hum of the distant waterfall. In the Spring there would be trout in that deep pool. I liked it all better than before, and soon it would safely be mine again.

I tapped on the chalet door, waited. There was no answer. I stepped in and at once, as she had not heard me, I had a fair uncensored view of her.

She was in the little kitchen behind the living-room, with the sleeves of her blouse rolled up, ironing some of Daniel's shirts and, if you can believe it, singing. I had never heard her sing before and she hadn't a bad voice either. Ninety-nine per cent of Scottish songs are sad, filled with broken trysts, absconded lovers, drowned miller's daughters, or downright laments choked up with sentimental longings for the isles, lochs, hills and heather that make up most of that poor bleeding neglected orphan of a country. But this was one of the happy songs and she sang it happily. Yes, I could see that she was happy, fancying herself nicely dug in, and with no real idea of the boy's illness. From the first she had never believed a word I had told her, and the ever-loving Hulda had considerately kept back the worst of the bad news.

'Speed bonny boat like a bird on the wing.'

She paused for a minute to change the iron. In that kitchen we had no electric iron switch and she was heating them on the stove. Once it was in the shield she put out a neat little spit and saw it sizzle off. I liked that neat little spit—it was human, but it wouldn't get her off the hook. Satisfied, she resumed the ironing and the song.

'Over the sea to Skye.
Carry the lad that is born to be king.'

Believe it or not, although I have just panned them, I am a sucker for these old Scots ballads, perhaps it is my Bruce blood responding. They soften me up. It was time for me to go in, before I started to hum an accompaniment.

The instant I appeared she gave a slight start and stopped the song, but went on with the ironing. After a moment, not looking up, she said:

'Well, Carroll, what are you selling today? A cheap line in smutty postcards?'

'No,' I said. 'But I'll see what I can do for you if you're interested.'

'I'm not. And I'm busy. So let's have it.'

'It's nothing of importance,' I said easily. 'But somebody seems to have sent me this.'

And I handed her the Levenford Herald.

Now she did stop. She put the iron on the stand and, as she saw the date, her face changed. The colour drained out of it.

'Sent you?' she said. 'The Davigans . . . they'll never let me be . . . but they don't know I'm here.' Her brows suddenly drew together. 'No, of course. . . . You . . . you wrote for it.'

'I will admit to a little natural curiosity,' I said, shrugging it off. 'I was naturally interested in my old friend's accident, and you were so reticent I thought I'd go to the fountain head.'

'The fountain head! And your old friend! Carroll, you'll make me die laughing.'

'I hope not. At least not until we've had a little chat. Now I'm no expert on Scots law, but from this worthy paper I learn that it was the Procurator Fiscal, instructed by the police, who petitioned the Sheriff to hold the Public Inquiry.'

She pushed back a strand of hair from her forehead, disconcerted by this approach. I parked on a convenient chair and went on.

354

'The Sheriff then granted the petition, witnesses were cited at the notice of the Procurator Fiscal and the Inquiry was held by the Sheriff and a Jury of seven, relatives of the deceased being entitled to be represented by a solicitor.'

'Why are you giving me this!' she said angrily. 'Don't I know it?'

'Because, in the first place, the solicitor for the Davigan family did not represent you.'

'Thank God, he did not.'

'And in everything he said, he expressed the general feeling of doubt as to how your late husband managed to slip off that parapet. Of course you told me it was a very windy day.'

I thought she would deny it but, no, she said, in a hard voice:

'Yes, I did tell you.'

'But at the Inquiry, the Fiscal made it a big point that it was a completely windless day.'

She was silent, then she said:

'I was unconsciously defending myself when I invented that wind for you, Carroll. I knew what was in your mind then, and what is in it now. You think I shoved Dan over.'

'No.' I half shook my head. 'Still, the Davigans seemed to have that in mind. Dan's father came out with some rough stuff in the witness box.'

'He's always had his knife in me, that old ram. And since he went bankrupt he's practically half witted.'

'But the Fiscal,' I reasoned, 'even he expressed his doubts, you might even say his suspicions . . . at a man, shown by the evidence of the pathologist who did the post-mortem, to be in perfect health, with no evidence of heart trouble or cerebral condition that might cause collapse, a man who was, in addition, a seasoned builder, well trained to heights should, on a dead calm day, suddenly . . .'

'I know all that, Carroll,' she cut in. 'I heard him say it.'

'Then the piece of your dress, torn from your sleeve, still clenched in Dan's hand when they got to him.'

'That was highly inconvenient for me. Naturally, it was his grab to save himself as I pushed. Almost damning, wasn't it, Carroll? But the police did not think so, or they would have prosecuted me.'

'Yes, on criminal charges,' I murmured. 'It was fortunate

you got the verdict. Though it was not unanimous. A split four to three, wasn't it?'

'It was enough. And afterwards I was congratulated by both the solicitor for the employers and the Inspector of Factories — who was officially present. They said my behaviour was above reproach.'

I had to admire her, controlling her nerves under that dead-pan calm. She was tough. But no more than me.

'I'm well aware of your saintly disposition. And of course, by the split verdict you were technically exonerated. However,' I paused, and went on mildly, 'there's just one or two other points I'd like to clear up. Was Daniel called to give evidence?'

'Certainly not. A mere child. He was excused on grounds of his youth.'

'And the good Canon Dingwall? Did he have any part in this affair? His name has never been mentioned, no, not once, and yet . . . somehow . . . I have an idea, one might say a suspicion, that his master mind . . . directed, shall we say, the strategy of your defence.'

She had flushed angrily.

'The old Canon has always been a good friend to Danny and me, and he was a perfect godsend to us all through this ghastly misery . . . it's so like you, Carroll, to try to soil that relationship. Now get this straight. I've been persecuted enough. I'll take no more interrogations or cross examinations from you. You can't do a thing about the case, it's closed, finished and done with.'

'Naturally,' I said. 'But as you've been kind enough to supply the Matron with my past history I might well return the compliment with some of yours. She's a strict, straitlaced character. And while you didn't create that miraculous wind for her, I think you did imply, shall we say, natural causes. There was no mention of this strange fatality, the subsequent Inquiry, the split Jury. Indeed, I think I recollect hearing you sadly breathe those useful words, heart failure.'

'Don't, Carroll. Don't do it. For if you try, I have the drop on you. I'll go to that professor of yours with your fake testimonials and have him accuse you before the Medical Council.'

'You'll have to dig him up first.'

It did not get through to her at first. Then she sat down

suddenly, on the enamel kitchen chair. She was as white as the chair, even before I said:

'You don't think I'm a complete moron. To run such a risk. He had been dead a full year before I wrote them.'

I saw her breast fill up with a slow, painful breath which came out as a long, soundless sigh. A silence followed, during which an extraordinary feeling seeped through me. I felt sorry for her, an emotion evoked, or at least intensified, by her attitude. Where had I seen it before: the head slightly drooping, face half averted, her profile clearly lined against the window—the dark eyes deep set against a high cheekbone, the nose with the faintest upturn that had once struck a note of high audacity, the mouth drooping now, but still beautiful, the clear cut defiant chin? Yes, she was still, or had again become, an attractive woman.

'Carroll.' Speaking slowly she went on. 'Let's make a deal . . . a non-aggression pact.'

For a moment I was tempted. But no, Carroll, no. You're too wise a bird to be caught with chaff.

'It would never work,' I said. 'I'm sorry for you, Cathy. But you and I are natural antagonists. You've already been undermining my authority. All the time you'd get in my hair. You would interfere with my . . . my way of life.'

'You mean the Swede?'

'Since you mention it, among other things, yes. Let's face it. You started this thing. I was ready and willing to welcome you, to be the best of friends. But from the minute you laid eyes on me at the airport you set out to wreck me.'

'Not really, Carroll,' she said, seriously. 'Please believe me.'

I ignored that and continued logically.

'Now I don't want to hurt you, although you've tried to hurt me. I just want you to realize this is no place for you, and go quietly home.'

'Home?' The way she said it was enough.

'You must think of your boy. He's more ill than you imagine. But perhaps you don't trust me.'

'I know you're a good liar, when it suits you.'

I let that pass and went on:

'He'll soon need hospital treatment. But you don't seem to show much feeling for him.'

'I never show what I feel now, it's safer.'

I had said it all, yet she had a secret quality that baffled me. Without moving, her eyes still fixed and sad, she said:

'I can still wreck you, Carroll. I can have the last word. You're such a smartie I'm surprised you haven't tumbled to it sooner. But you will, Carroll, and that's why I've held it back. It's staring you in the face.'

I did stare at her. What was she getting at? Nothing. I shook it off.

'Don't try on that old cliff-hanger. I know you.'

'Do you? It's surprising, Carroll. You've chased women and slept with them most of your life, yet you don't in the least understand them.' Her voice broke. 'And, dear God, you've never understood me. Never. No, not ever.'

There was a deeper silence. The sky had clouded and all at once a heavy spatter of hail hit the window. That is the way of it in the high Alps . . . weather changes so dramatic they shake you, fascinate you, half drown you. Suddenly I remembered the brat parked on the open terrace. I got up and moved towards the door. I would not say another word. I had settled the whole blasted business.

But as I went out, butting against a blast of hail, she said:

'I'm not going, Carroll. Never.'

THIRTEEN

THAT SAME EVENING in my room I poured myself a soothing Kirsch and settled down to work things out. I had just made my routine visit to the ward with particular thoroughness, giving Garvey, the older of the ex-pleurisy cases, who was due to go home tomorrow, a going over. He was completely recovered, but from her little side room Matron's eye had been on me, and it was my policy now to recover lost ground and work in with her again. I had already washed out that first idea of dropping the *Herald* on her desk. She read English badly, Davigan would talk herself out of it in a dozen different ways—such a shock, the accident, could not bear to think, even to speak of it! No, it would not be conclusive, not the real clincher.

A hard case, that Davigan, she had ruffled me, put my back up. While giving nothing away, she had set me worrying, with her: 'I can still wreck you, Carroll.' What could she be getting at, not bluffing I was sure, she had something important in reserve, still held back from me. I was now convinced that she had delivered the fatal nudge. Up there, on the parapet, already sick to death of him and with the big drop below, almost waiting one might say, she had been struck by that sudden irresistible impulse which induced in the same second the reflex shove. In self-preservation he had grabbed at her, caught the sleeve of her dress which had torn away, then toppled. It was a simple positive equation. But I needed proof.

To stimulate cerebration. I took a slow sip of the Kirsch, which is made from the best Swiss cherries with admirable results. Yes, the answer must lie in what might be named the Dingwall-Daniel alliance. Impossible though it seemed, an understanding appeared to exist between these two, or to be more specific, a secret, unrevealed or purposely suppressed, perhaps even a shred of vital evidence, bearing on the case. On the face of it, an absurd situation, an inconceivable hypothesis—involving two opposites—an aged Canon of the Church, steeped in virtue, desiccated by holiness, and a small boy, the son of the victim, no more than seven years old. Yet these two were intimates, the one as teacher, the other as pupil, a strong sense of interest and affection bound them closely. And more, from the boy's manner, his reticence to all my tentative approaches, there was evidence of a pledge, at least a given promise, not to reveal the secret.

The longer I brooded over this the more my curiosity grew, the more I realized I would never get the bare un-varnished truth until I had it from Daniel. And I wanted it badly. I couldn't force the boy in any way, but there were subtler ways of getting round him. And on this decision I finished the Kirsch.

I knew I would not sleep easily with this on my mind so I went to my desk and dashed off a letter to Lotte explaining how busy I had been and I hoped, and wanted, to see her, but for the time being must continue to toe the line of duty. I'd had two from her since she phoned, the second had been more than impatient. It was late when I sealed the envelope. I yawned, undressed, took a warm shower, and turned in. Even then I could not sleep. For once my phobia was not the trouble. Apart from the Davigan muddle, it was too long since I had been in Lotte's bed.

But next morning I was up, bright and early, consorting

with Matron in the office and winning a brief nod of approval for my punctuality.

'You know that we send Garvey home today?' I said, after I had greeted her.

'*Jawohl.*' She gave me a queer look, charged with suspicion. 'So you go once again to the airport?'

'No, Matron,' I said, confidingly, almost endearingly. 'I've had rather too much of that place lately. Garvey's a big boy, I'll put him on the train at Davos with his air ticket in his pocket and a tag in his button hole. All he has to do is walk across Zürich station to the air terminal. They know all about our Maybelle lot there.'

'Ach so.' She looked pleased, even gave me a half smile. 'That I like besser for him . . .' adding significantly, 'and for you, Herr Doktor.' It was the second Herr Doktor I had that week.

'And if it's all right with you, Matron—you know I always consult you—I thought I would take Daniel along. It would be a nice change for him.'

'So! You think him well enough for such?'

'You know what his future is, Matron.' I presented her with my most humane expression. 'Don't you feel he ought to have a little enjoyment in his short life, while he's having this good spell?"

'Ja, it is well said. I agree.' She nodded, and gave me that look again, the Hulda version of whimsy. 'At least he keeps you from mischief, which is goot.'

As might be expected, Davigan was busy in the kitchen, producing savoury smells from a range of pots. Without disturbing her, I managed to get hold of Daniel who jumped at the unexpected prospect of the trip. We got into the Opel, Daniel and I in front, Garvey behind. He was a lumpy boy of fifteen from Edmonton, who never had much to say for himself. Since his pleural effusion had dried up he had put on weight, he looked well, and although incapable of expressing his thanks he was, I imagined, grateful for what we had done for him.

'Glad to be going home, Garvey?' I said, making conversation over my shoulder.

'So, so, sir.' He almost whistled that one.

'You've missed your folks?'

'Well, I've missed the Spurs.'

'Your what?'

'He means his football team. Tottenham Hotspurs,' said the little know-all at my elbow.

We were at Davos in half an hour and after I had put Garvey, well labelled, on the Zürich train, we had a hot chocolate at Zemmer's in the High Street, after which, as I'd planned, I took him to the big covered ice stadium. The hockey match between Villars and Davos had just begun.

I had thought he would enjoy it, but not all that much. He lapped it up, cheering the home team like the oldest inhabitant. After the fourth quarter, when we went out, he said:

'I wish I could skate like that, Dr Laurence.'

'Why not?'

He smiled and shook his head.

'I'm afraid chess will have to be my game.'

'It is your game,' I said heartily. 'If you're still keen on that match at the Pfeffermühle I might put it on for you.'

'Ah, yes,' he said eagerly. 'I would love that, absolutely.'

'Let's make a date then,' I said. 'How about next Saturday?'

He began to laugh, in great spirits.

'May I look up my little book to see if I'm free . . . ?' Then broke off the joke. 'No seriously, that would be wonderful.'

There's a restaurant in Davos called the Fluehgass, which is quiet and good. I took him there. Although the Grisons is a German-speaking canton the menu was promisingly typed in French, and after an amicable show of consulting my companion I decided on *filet mignons aux bolets* with *pommes frites* and a cup of clear strong oxtail soup as a starter. You get tired of the eternal veal in Switzerland and that tender pink steak would be good for him. And I ordered a half bottle of the Val d'Or Johannesburger, a light delicious wine from Sion. One glass wouldn't hurt him.

'This is very cosy.' He rubbed his hands. It was a good corner booth, near the pine log that was smouldering on the field-stone hearth.

We were getting chummier than ever, as I had planned. It was too easy and I didn't dislike it. Although he might be a little toad, he was well mannered, never bored or nagged you and knew when to be silent.

361

He lapped up the soup and on the first chew of the *filet*, rolled his eyes at me.

'Try a sip of the wine.'

He did.

'That's delicious too. Like nippy honey. Good job Matron isn't looking, Dr Laurence.'

'Why don't you drop the doctor,' I suggested. 'Just make it Laurence.'

He stopped eating.

'What a compliment.'

'To me or you?'

'To me, of course.' And looking up, he gave me a warm, diffident smile.

It hit me, that smile, right smack between the eyes. Where had I seen it before? In some old cracked snap-shot, or mirrored faintly in a long forgotten past. Smile now, dear, and look at the camera. Or, as I grinned in the looking glass, admiring my new school cap. My smile, before the early gloss had worn off me.

I felt void, sick and shaken. God, it was the moment of truth all right. Why hadn't I rumbled it before? She had told me it was staring me in the face—the AB blood group should have warned me—almost a natural follow on from a group O father. But I had got out of so many beds scot free, I never dreamed that I had balled up the issue in that one.

And Davigan had waited, ready to spring it on me when the time came, holding it, nursing it alone for the knock-out. That rattled me. Did she expect me to fall on her bosom and weep? Soft music and the young lovers reunited at last. If so, what a hope. I wasn't the type to swoon and melt. I would work something out. I would . . .

'Are you feeling all right, Laurence?'

I pulled myself together. He was looking at me with concern.

'I'm fine.' After all, he wasn't to blame. 'Just something . . . something that went the wrong way.'

No words of mine were ever more truly spoken.

With the help of black coffee and a brandy I got through the rest of the meal. Then it was time to take off.

As on the night of our meeting I made him lie down on the back seat of the car. I wanted no chatter, and he needed the rest. The meal had made him sleepy. I drove slowly, scarcely aware of the twists and turns of that difficult road, staring straight ahead.

The thought that I was co-proprietor of this derelict little property in the back seat, this sad little freak, of frail physique and precocious intellect, the bright brain in the dim body, was a crusher, all right. Take it from me—a crusher.

Yet as I drove on, blind reason began to assert itself. A crusher? But why, Carroll? Why? Don't be so hasty, counting yourself out, when you're not even in the ring. All this is past history. Long past. I swerved instinctively on a bend, missing the other car by an inch, barely seeing it. Yes, the book is closed and can't be reopened. Who saw you turn back that night of the ordination and go skulking . . . well, let's be polite and say speeding, towards the Considine house? Only the Almighty, and He is unlikely to broadcast it from the heavens. And were you not welcomed? You were, Carroll. Warmly welcomed. And afterwards, while you remained in total ignorance, she accepted her responsibility, married Davigan, covered up the situation, lived with it. Who is to believe her at this late stage of the game if she tries to pin the blame on you? Can you see her going to Hulda: 'Excuse me, Matron, there's something I forgot to tell you, just escaped my memory, so to speak . . . the truth is that . . .' She's wearing a shawl and it's snowing outside. What a B picture! She couldn't do it ever, she is too . . . too tough. She would know it must get the horse's laugh. No, Carroll, don't rush in where angels fear to tread. I liked that touch—it made me smile. Yes, say nothing, play it sostenuto, and await developments, if any. Meanwhile, on your side of the fence, keep after the kid for further revelations.

I felt somewhat better, relieved in fact, after this self-communion, and by the time we'd reached the Maybelle I was able to face the Matron, who had been waiting on us, with my usual self-possession.

'So, you are safe home again, Daniel. Was it a goot time?'

'Splendid, thank you, Matron . . .' I stood by while he sketched our programme for her.

'Ach, so.'

She turned to me, looking pleased. 'And he seems not too tired?'

'I was extremely careful,' I said soberly, encouraged by

363

her manner which was mild, even remotely kindly—perhaps Davigan had been laying off me at last.

'Well, now it is for you the bed,' said Hulda, taking his ever ready hand. 'Come. Your mother shops in the village so I will put you.' Looking over her shoulder as they went out: 'Hot coffee in your flask, Herr Doktor?'

It wouldn't last of course, I felt in all my bones there must be stormy weather ahead, but for the present I almost felt a member of the family.

FOURTEEN

TOWARDS THE END of the week the thermometer had risen and on Saturday, under a grey and humid sky, the *Foehn* was stirring, that soft damp neurotic wind detested by the Swiss. There are two winds in Switzerland, the *bise* which blasts down Lac Leman to Geneva and chills you to the bone, and the *Foehn* which on occasion blows everywhere and is worse than the *bise*, reducing you to a wet sweat rag, wrung out and limp. Around the Maybelle patches of soiled snow despoiled the landscape, slush glued up the streets and a steady drip came from the suffering pines. In short, a horrible day, but one well suited to our purpose. Without a doubt, this Saturday afternoon all the habitués would be parked round the stove drying themselves out at the Pfeffer-mühle.

Looking him over that morning I was less inclined now to go through with my promise; indeed, if I had known the living hell that would be let loose on me that same evening I would have cut out the entire affair. But Daniel had not allowed me to forget it, and in fact I had my own purpose behind the expedition. This afternoon when I had indulged the kid with his chess I meant to coax out of him the one last bit of information I needed. So when he'd had his rest after the *Mittagessen* I smuggled him into the station wagon and took off quietly. At the worst I could tell Matron we had gone for a drive. As for Davigan, we were now barely on speaking terms. He'd had a sleep and was in his usual chatty mood, grateful that I was taking him and a bit excited.

He was not on the uplift now, though still bearing up, just a trifle shimmery—his red cells rather better than when I first made the count, but these infernal whites creeping up on him again. By exerting myself I had become even more chummy with him.

'I hope I don't let you down, Laurence,' he said, as the car slushed through the village.

'Don't give it a thought. Just enjoy your game.'

'Oh, I will. I love a good stiff contest.'

'I'm sorry I'm so little use to you. One of the advantages of going home, you'll resume your games with Dingwall.'

'Yes . . . I suppose so,' he said, rather doubtfully.

I drew up and parked at the Pfeffermühle where an array of old bicycles, the form of transport favoured by the locals, indicated a full house. We went in, greeted by a waft of odorous steamy air and a general exhalation of '*Grüssgotts*'. The Maybelle, as I have mentioned, not without pride, was in good standing with the village, an esteem which, perhaps because their knowledge of me was slight, I appeared to share. I took the table at the window, farthest from the stove, which was red hot, and ordered a beer and an Apfelsaft. Yes, as far as I could judge, they were all there; Bemmel, the man we were after, ex-teacher and leader of the troupe, Scwhartz the water bailiff, Minder the undertaker, not busy today, a couple of near-by peasant farmers, and of course Bachmann, owner of the tavern, together with a fair congregation of the usual village hangers-on.

Bemmel, though a man of some learning, which explained his prestige with the group, was a weird piece of work. Extremely short and thick, uncouth, untidy and unbelievably hairy, with an all-enveloping yellow stained beard that left only his two small sharp eyes exposed, he might have passed for the original beatnik or the oldest of the Seven Dwarfs. He wore a soiled knitted brown cardigan and a skull-cap, a half-smoked unlit cigar end protruding from its hairy nest. This half burned-out stub, well masticated, held for hours between the jaws, is, in the rural cantons, the prestige symbol of the Swiss male. Thus equipped, and with the coloured Cantonal skull-cap set well back on his head, he may undertake the most menial tasks, shovel snow or muck, spread liquid manure with the hose between his legs, disembowel the dung heap or handle the *Glockenspiel*, yet remain a free man, a voter, which the women are not, a true upstanding Swiss, consciously aware of himself as the lineal descendant of the mythical Wilhelm Tell.

A marked silence had followed our arrival, they had their eyes on us, inclined to welcome our intrusion as a diversion on a dull day. I waited until our drinks were brought then casually asked for chess men and the board, a request which seemed to stir them up. Once we had set up the men and begun to play, beyond a few desultory remarks made simply as a cover for their self-esteem, they were watching us closely.

For reasons of strategy, since I wished to avoid the obvious, I did my best but, as usual, our game ended in short order, which gave me the opportunity to make a public exhibition of myself.

'Verflixt! Gopfriedstutz! Every time he wins.' I threw it at them in loud, angry Schweizerdeutsch.

This caught their fancy and Bemmel, who was stuck on his French and liked to show it off, said indulgently:

'Il est bon, le petit?'

'Bon! C'est un geni. En Ecosse il est champion de sa ville.'

'Et vous dites qu'il gagne toujours?' The cigar end looked amused.

I thought it time to bring in the others.

'Niemand kann gegen diesen Kerl gewinnen,' I said it in Schweizerdeutsch, and continued in the same crude lingo. 'And I prove it. For a round of drinks I back him against the best man here.' It would be worth the money just to drag in Bemmel.

There was silence followed by a sudden cackle. In a minute they were all bursting themselves.

'You can laugh,' I said. 'But will you play? You, Herr Bemmel? You accept my bet?'

This dried up the laughter but not the grins. They were all looking at Bemmel.

'Ach, Herr Doktor, we can not refuse your so generous hospitality. Perhaps I give your leetle friend a short lesson.'

He got up, stretched, still grinning, then waddled over and took my place. The gang grouped themselves back of him while, after a preliminary of setting up the pieces, he made a condescending gesture.

'Pegin then, leetle poy.'

'Oh, no. We must be fair. You are the challenger. You have the honour and may have the white.'

Although I did not know this, apparently white always starts first.

With a hand like a ham the schoolmaster made the initial move, a Knight. Daniel replied with a pawn. I was wishing by now, wishing like mad, that I had a real knowledge of the game beyond my usual incentive of trying to knock off my opponent's queen. I knew that Daniel must lose, banked on it in fact, to soften him up. But with the thing begun, I wanted him to put up a good show and the devil of it was, I couldn't follow the technique of the game. All I could do was watch the faces of the players.

Daniel was pale but calm, the schoolmaster still wearing his cigar end jauntily, making his moves quite fast and, after the fourth, sounding a helpful confidential warning.

367

'Achtung, leetle poy!' He was worse than Hulda.

Whatever happened in the next few moves was beyond me but it seemed that, after two pawns were exchanged for a bishop that Daniel calmly sacrificed, the butt came in for some harsh mastication and instead of the Achtung we had an *'Ach so'* followed by a measurable pause. Something had gone wrong with that quick and sudden *coup*.

After that the pace was slower. Bemmel in particular took his time, punctuating his moves with aggressive grunts in different keys. Background noises from the spectators accompanied the various moves. Unlike me, they knew the game, and were watching it, waiting for the kill. Daniel remained silent, paler than before, but gradually a few beads of moisture began to break on his brow. This sign of concentration, or of stress, had me worried, and I blamed myself for letting him in for it. Worse followed when the schoolmaster moved his queen, gave out a thick chuckle, and lay back in his seat, supported by a chorus of approval from the rear.

'*Czechk.*'

I thought: It's the beginning of the end. But no, not yet. Daniel moved out of check then sacrificed a rook that had been threatened by the queen. Bemmel removed it with a grin. Daniel moved his remaining bishop. Then came a hollow pause. A hint of surprise had crept into the assembly, they were muttering.

'*Achtung; der Bauer,* Bemmel!'

The bishop moved again, two further moves, then Daniel slid forward an inconspicuous but nasty little pawn. At least Bemmel did not appear to love it. And there was yet more noise from the background, but differently attuned.

'*Grossartig, mit dem Bauer spielt er den Ruy Lopez. Die Dame ist bedroht.*'

I was watching Bemmel now. He moved restlessly, shifting his position to lean forward, peering hard at the board. Finally he lay back and with a forced grin and an attempt at bonhomie exclaimed:

'You defend yourself well. I think we agree it is null.'

A low rumble of dissent came from the followers which seemed to indicate an honest note of warning.

'*Nein, nein, mein Lieber.*'

It was unnecessary.

'You want me to concede a draw? I'm afraid I must refuse. But if you wish I will permit you to resign.'

'Ach, nein, nein!' Bemmel grunted.

After a long, long pause which would never have been permitted by a time clock, the schoolmaster, his brow furrowed by confused concentration and the beginnings of anguish, moved a defensive pawn. It was taken by the same bishop.

'Ach, so . . Wieder der Bauer.' Bachmann had left his counter and was craning his neck in the background.

Two other moves followed, slow, extremely slow, from Bemmel, who was sweating now all down the back of his neck, very fast and confident from Daniel. And that was it.

'Check mate.'

A stupefied silence; it had happened so quickly. Then a burst of genuine applause. I thought Bemmel had swallowed the cigar, but he tore it out of its nest and flung it at the stove where it stuck and started to hiss at him. Thus disarmed, he was no longer a free and virile Swiss but a poor stuttering fool. Impossible to see his face, but the beard seemed definitely bloodshot.

'Ach so, ach so,' he kept repeating. 'Ein glückliches Stück.'

'Yes,' said Daniel, picking up the meaning. 'I was very lucky. You played splendidly.' And he held out his hand.

I didn't like the kid for that—he was back in his Lord Fauntleroy role, you'd think I had just entered him for Eton, but I must admit it went over big with the gang. It seemed appropriate to celebrate. I called for the drinks.

For the next ten minutes we had a regular party. I did not let it go on any longer. When the excitement began to subside I got up and, to promote good feeling, paid the score. This seemed to help Bemmel, who managed a dim smile. I hoped it might lower his blood pressure. Still brooding, he was feeling around for the stub, wondering where it had got to, and beginning to think up excuses. But we had wrecked him, he would never be the same again. Le petit Ecossais would become a legend at the Pfeffermühle.

When we left they saw us to the car, and every good Schweitzer one of them, even Bemmel, shook hands with the kid before they waved us off. I drove slowly, taking the long way home.

'You put on a good show,' I said.

'Not really, Laurence.' He laughed. He was brimming over. 'You see he tried to fool's mate me straight away. It put him at such a disadvantage. I went straight into a reverse Ruy Lopez and against that, the Sicilian defence that he put on was no use. You noticed those last moves, didn't you, P to B5, P to B6, B to Kt2?'

I nodded. to please him.

'Poor man, I'm afraid he was very upset.' •

'It'll do him good. He's always been a bit of a blow hard. They don't really go for him back there.'

'He's quite good, really, and could beat me the next time. I don't always win you know, Laurence, in spite of what you said, but I did want to, for your sake.' He looked up at me. 'Not to let you down, you know.'

Now he was at his worst again. He had just won The Wall Game with the first goal in twenty years. But I put up with it.

'How do you make out against the old Canon?' I asked, working towards my objective.

'He's beaten me several times, especially at the beginning.'

'He taught you?'

'Yes, and lots of other things.'

'You like him?'

'Well, naturally.'

'You know, Daniel,' I manufactured a sigh, 'I'm rather jealous of that old bag of bones. You're so very close to him. I keep thinking of that private understanding you share with him. In a way it worries me.'

'Oh, it needn't,' he said quickly. 'If anyone, I should worry.'

'Then why don't you let me in on it?' It griped me to say this, but I had to get what I wanted. 'I might be able to help.'

There was a silence. The warmth had gone out of his face. He looked deflated. At last he said, slowly:

'I have become very attached to you, Laurence. In fact if I didn't know how much you hate sissy stuff, I could put it much stronger. But I've absolutely given my word not to speak of a certain thing.'

The nudge that sent Davigan over! He could mean nothing else. He was there: he had seen it. I wanted almost unbearably to know the truth.

'Come on, Danny boy. We're such pals now. No one would ever know.'

'I can't.' He shook his head sadly yet firmly. A sober pause followed, then his expression cleared as though he saw a way out. 'However, if you guessed it by yourself there would be no harm. It would let me out, for I still wouldn't have told you.' He added: 'I might even be allowed to give you a little hint. You're so clever it might help you.'

'Let's have it then.' I couldn't bear this. We were almost at the Maybelle, turning into the drive.

'That same afternoon, when the Canon came out with me to the Convent door, he sat up in his wheeled chair, tapped me on the shoulder, and said: "Silence is golden."'

I stared at him, stupefied. Was he having me on? Impossible. Yet what a let down. I could have clipped him on his aggravating little pan.

'Out,' I said, drawing up with a jerk at the front porch, 'and for God's sake don't give the women any hints we were in the pub.'

When I had dropped him off I garaged the car with a violence that reflected my mood. After all my careful planning, my staging of the chess match, all this build up, I was left with nothing but a three-word prissy proverb from the kindergarten copy book: 'Silence is golden!' The sleet was coming down again.

FIFTEEN

THAT EVENING, after I had locked up, I sat up late in my room tippling Kirsch, going over that blasted riddle: *Silence is golden*. What a cliché! Was it merely an injunction from Dingwall, meaning keep your trap shut? Yet the phrase was the last to be expected from a man of such incisive mind. It belonged with such lollypops as: a stitch in time saves nine, or: don't count your chickens before they're hatched. Of course, he was using it towards a child. No, no, that wouldn't work, not with that juvenile brains trust. Certainly the *command* existed: silence, don't talk! Yet there must be another, and a hidden implication, possibly in the word: golden. An idea occurred to me: could this be a reference, jocular, no doubt, to the half-crown tip given by Dingwall at that precise moment, to ensure co-operation? Nonsense. I dismissed it as totally out of key with either character. Yet golden suggested money, wealth, some precious thing. But nothing could be more apparent than that Davigan had no money. I knew for a certainty that the widow hadn't a stiver. I had seen Matron slipping a few francs into her purse before she came back with that new pair of snow boots.

I gave up at last, locked the bottle in its cupboard, undressed, and as an afterthought, washed out the glass so that no incriminating evidence should go back to Hulda. Shortly after midnight I fell asleep.

It seemed less than an hour before I woke with a start. Someone was banging on my window. I stumbled up and opened it to be met by a blast of sleet through which I dimly saw Davigan, in her dressing-gown, bareheaded, hair blown by the wind, with a wild look about her.

'Come, quickly. Daniel's taken ill.'

'What's the matter?' I had to shout. 'Stomach upset?'

'No. A bleeding. Hurry. Please hurry. He looks dreadfully ill.'

Make no bones about it, she seemed half out of her mind. I waved her away, banged the casement shut. I could never find that light switch in the dark, but I did at last, buttoned on my pants, pulled a sweater over my pyjama jacket, shoved my feet into slippers, picked up the emergency case that always stood in the hall, and unbolted the front door.

It was a hell of a night, gale force wind and heavy sleet.

372

I cursed myself for forgetting my raincoat. I was well soaked before I reached the chalet.

All the lights were on. She had left the door open. I went in. He was lying on his bunk, flat on his back, collapsed, shrunk into himself, totally blanched. No palpable pulse. He didn't know I was there.

'How did this come on?' I was opening my bag in a hurry. 'He had diarrhoea, went to the bathroom.' She was shivering all over. 'I left it for you to see.'

I put my head round the bathroom door. One look was enough—the curse of myelocytic leukaemia is the liability to massive haemorrhages. He must be practically exsanguine. As I broke an ampule of camphor in oil and charged the hypodermic, I said:

'Get some clothes on, or a coat, for God's sake, and run round and knock up Matron. The side door's unlocked.'

He didn't apparently respond to the injection but now there was just the hint of a carotid pulse. I took the extra blanket from the end of the bed, spread it, and rolled him in it. Double wrapped, he was practically weightless as I carried him across the courtyard into the little side room off the ward. Davigan had pulled on a coat and the new snow boots and gone ahead of me.

So now what? Ever since that first glance at him I had been cursing myself. I knew I should have laid in at least a temporary blood bank for him. Apart from my own knowledge Lamotte had stressed this precaution. Being what I am, I had put it off, passed it up, or plain forgotten. An immediate transfusion was what he must have and the only way was for me both to perform it and act as donor.

Though stinkingly sentimental, this was a plain necessity. It sounds simple. Perhaps you have lain at ease, feeling praiseworthy and benevolent, while the nurse drew off and bottled your 350 c.c.s before you knew it, then ushered you in sweetly to coffee and biscuits in the cafeteria. This was going to be a double act, and quite different. I had only the barest equipment, nothing prepared, and the patient, with practically no penetrable veins, was in extremis.

'He still is bleeding?'

Hulda had appeared, in silence for once, and unbelievably in full uniform. Never had I been so glad to see her.

'He's about lost it all,' I said. 'We must let him have it back at once.'

373

'But how?'

'I'm universal type O and he's group AB. Let's make the shift quick as we can. There's a vacuum transfusion flask in the surgery emergency cupboard. Bring it now.'

'I already look.' She did not move. 'Someone is taking things from that cupboard. It is perhaps broken, at least no longer there.'

I was too shaken even to swear.

This was the final crusher. These vacuum flasks, treated with an anticoagulant, sodium citrate, or better, heparin, and capped with thin rubber to take the needle puncture, are essential intermediate receptacles in standard practice. I had meant to fill it from my own brachial vein, suspend it high on the stand and transfuse. Now, if at all, it had to be direct and I knew the full meaning of that word. Useless to attempt direct transfusion from my vein to his—the venous pressure was insufficient. He needed arterial pressure and arterial blood.

All this passed through my mind in a flash, and Hulda must have read it in my face. Why ever had I tried to make a cod of her? The old battle-axe was a regular stand-by, calm, efficient, experienced. In four minutes, while I took his blood pressure—it was less than fifteen—she had collected, sterilized and assembled tubing, canula and needles —such primitive equipment by Kantonspital standards, but it would work. She put her hand on a chair, even got a towel to dry the worst of the rain off me, then said:

'You wish to sit?'

I shook my head. We'd get a better flow if I stood.

'Just tighten the tourniquet on his upper arm.'

Now we were off. I bent forward to insert the needle. The tourniquet should have brought up the brachial vein by interrupting the venous flow, but there was no flow and no vein. I felt, and felt again. Nothing. I began to sweat. Over the years in practice there are some skills you acquire and some that will always be beyond you. Ignoring my deficiencies, I had at least this ability: for a sad six months, running a V.D. clinic in Plymouth, taking Wasserman specimens and giving intravenous Salvarsan, I must have pierced hundreds of veins, until I could do it, first time, clean as a whistle, in my sleep. And now, when I needed it, I was stuck.

'I'll have to incise and go into the jugular.'

She already had the lancet. He was too far gone to feel

374

the incision I made in his neck. His eyes, glazed like the eyes of a dead fish, stared glassily towards the ceiling. And finally there it was, thin as a bird's windpipe. I inserted the canula, then with my one free hand I simply broke the cord of my pyjama pants and let them drop with my trousers. Holding the other needle tight between my thumb and second finger I felt with my free forefinger for the big throb, just below the inguinal canal. I had it. Finally, with the unspoken thought: this is it! I plunged the needle deep and laterally into my right femoral artery. I knew at once I had hit the big artery of the leg, the shock ran all through me.

I kept it going, controlling the tube between my finger and thumb. I didn't want to choke him up at the start. After a long moment the Matron said:

'It does well, Herr Doktor.' She had a finger on his left carotid. 'The pulse begins.'

The change, if you had not seen it before, or perhaps you would not wish to, was spectacular. He began to lose that shrunken look, to fill out and gain colour like an inflated breath test balloon. The pulse in his neck was quite visible now and his lungs were making up for lost time. Then his eyes flickered and he looked straight at me.

It gave me the damnedest, silliest feeling I had ever had in my entire life. I wanted to burst, laughing at myself. Carroll, the sob-sister's dream. What a squirt, standing there, completely debagged, leaning against the table for support, pants tangled around the ankles, the personal article dangling visible and loose. How in the name of everything correct and proper had I ever landed myself in such a clownish situation? Only because it was my fate to be wrong-way Carroll. My unlucky star, with a devilish sense of humour, had arranged it for me. I could not escape it. That was my one alibi that saved me from being a creep. I hated it worse when Hulda said:

'Oh, it is so goot, *fuhlt sich viel besser.*'

As I didn't answer, she asked, hurriedly:

'But he will bleed again?'

'He's getting enough healthy platelets to clot everything for weeks.'

Actually, I was beginning to feel slack at the knees, but to punish myself and because I wanted no repeat of this performance, I would give him the full quota.

'I think now he goes straight asleep.' Hulda breathed it into my left earhole.

Probably the alcohol still in my blood from the Kirsch was sending him over. Do him good too, the little rat. Better ease this over with Matron.

'I took a simple hypnotic before turning in, he's probably got a trace of it.'

'Goot.'

It had to end some time. He'd had more than enough now and was fast asleep. I disconnected, at the cost of another femoral spasm, put two fine stitches in his neck incision. He barely moved. Matron had everything ready and without blinking an eye at my private possessions, carefully and firmly taped the puncture on my leg. Then she settled him in the bed and covered him up. I didn't want to see him again for years.

'Now I go tell the poor mother all is well.'

'Do that,' I said. 'But don't let her disturb him.'

'I return quickly.'

Now I was glad to sit down. I shut my eyes and rested my head on one hand. I felt light on top, as though I had emptied my brains into him. Not that he needed them. Matron was back.

'Ach, she has such relief, poor woman. But you must take her also a sleeping pill, or surely she vill not rest.'

'Okay,' I said, giving the stupidest affirmative in Christendom. It shows how low I felt.

'Now I make you some coffee.'

I refused it.

'I want to sleep too.'

I stood up. She was between me and the door. I couldn't avoid it when she took my hand. What's the matter with you Carroll, everyone wants to hold your hand?

'Herr Doktor.' She drew a deep breath. 'I think . . . I know I misjudge you. That was a most fine action.'

There it comes again. Green lights and soft music. Carroll, the bloodgiving hero, pride of the comic strip.

The old battle-axe was killing me. She kept watching me like a mother hen as I got a couple of sodium amytal capsules out of my bag—those red and green knockouts.

'Good night,' I said.

'*Gute Nacht, mein lieber Herr Doktor.*'

SIXTEEN

AS I STRUGGLED across the courtyard against the wind the village clock struck two, the sound muffled by the driving sleet. In the chalet a single window showed a narrow rectangle of light. I went in, without knocking, in a hurry. I needed sleep, and meant to make this short.

She was seated on the edge of her bed, in her thin, cheap dressing-gown, bent forward, half supporting herself with an elbow on her knee. Although she had shed the coat and the wet nightdress, she still had on the snow boots.

'I've brought you a couple of sleeping pills.'

She came out of her thoughts with a start. Beyond that she did not move or speak. I went over and gave them to her. At least she let me put them in her free hand. A bottle was standing on the dressing-table. I saw the special clinic mark on it, the big copying ink: M.B.

'Stolen from the store cupboard,' I said.

'How else would I get it?' she said dully, adding an after thought. 'You know I'm broke. And God knows I'm not a drunk, but just like yourself, Carroll, I need a drink occasionally. I did tonight.'

I could agree with her there. She had that broken-down look about her I had noticed when she first arrived, but now there was no fight in her. It bothered me.

'Don't take the pills then. Brandy and the barbiturates don't mix.'

'Who cares?' She sipped the brandy, it was neat.

There was a silence.

'I suppose I ought to thank you.'

'Save it. I'm going to bed.'

'Couldn't you do with a drink? On the house.'

I hesitated. I felt all in, the walls of the room had begun to tilt, and the label on the bottle said Martell Three Stars.

'In your own interests,' I said, when I had fetched a tumbler from the bathroom, 'don't let your pal the Matron see this bottle. She already has strong suspicions in your direction. By the way, did you knock over a glass flask when you were pilfering?'

'Yes. I heard someone coming. It broke.'

So what? I merely said: 'I'd forget that, if I were you.'

The cognac was good. The only chair was occupied by her wet coat, hung over the back to dry. I sat down on the bed. She was so unnaturally silent and depressed I had to know why.

'What's biting you, Davigan?'

'She did not answer for a minute.

'For one thing I've just realized how ill Daniel is.'

'You care?'

'You think I don't?'

'On the evidence, I think you're a pretty well-seasoned character, Davigan.'

'What evidence, Carroll?'

'Circumstantial.'

'Because I don't whimper and weep? I've stoppered up my feelings so long it's become a habit not to show them.'

Was it the brandy? We were mugging it like a couple of cross-talk comedians. It had to stop.

'Let's just say: You've had a rough passage, Davigan, and it shows.'

There was a pause, then she said:

'Have it your way, Carroll. Your trouble is you only think the worst of people.'

'I've only seen the worst.'

'That's all you've ever looked for.' And she gave me a long sad look that made me drop my eyes. Naturally I lamped her big ridiculous boots.

'Why don't you take off those blasted snow boots? You look so damn pathetic in them,' I shouted, and pushing her back, I made a double swoop, unzippered them, and tore them off.

Upended like this, lying back, with her knees up and apart and her thin wrapper flung open, she gazed up at me with such a look of silent pleading and half frightened appeal, it hit me like a bomb. Everything seemed to happen instinctively and at once, and we were in bed under the blanket, her arms were locked around me, and her terribly wet tears running down my cheek.

'You said you never wept, Cathy,' I whispered.

'This is my one big chance.'

No one will ever get the record of those next long moments. Why should I pander to dirty minds like mine, and foul up what was certainly to that date the sweetest, and, in the aftermath, the most revealing experience of my slightly soiled life? The more so, since it might induce the false and pernicious hope that all was now set for a happy and sentimental reunion. Yet it is permissible to state that afterwards her arms still held me, as mine held her. She had no desire to free herself, roll over, and light a cigarette, until lust promoted another essay. Nor had I. Restful and at peace we still belonged to each other, united by the act, and grateful to one another. All frustration, all antagonism dissolved, there was in her a softness I would never have believed existed, nothing kept back in her response, a total surrender. Let's be cynical and use Lotte's jeering phrase: it was heart to heart, and roses round the door.

She sighed at last, not releasing me.

'Why didn't we make a go of it, Laurie? It's all been such a misery and a mess.' I couldn't stop her, she went on. 'Davigan knew Daniel wasn't his. Did he ever let me forget it? Poor man, I suppose it was hard for him too. He knew why I took him. Oh, if only you'd answered my letter.'

'What letter?'

'The one I wrote to the ship.'

'I never had that letter,' I said slowly, and it was the God's truth.

'How can I believe you, Laurie? You're such a terrible liar, darling. But I love you, I always have, and heaven help me I always will. You know what, darling?'

'No,' I said.

'Everything stems from that afternoon when we were kids in the woods. I've thought of it so often. Have you?' Had I not? 'That frustration . . . at the very moment . . . it set us against one another, made us fight each other.'

'Hark at the little Krafft Ebing!'

'It's true. Let's not quarrel any more, Laurence. You're so sweet when you try.'

'Shall I try again?'

'Don't desecrate it, Laurie. This isn't just sex. I love you from my heart.'

And she did, with all the rest too, snuggling to me afterwards and saying sleepily:

'Don't make me get up, love. That was always the worst. Creeping into that cold toilet like a drab.'

How warm and comfortable and soft she was, her arms still round me. As she began to breathe deeply and quietly I felt myself sinking down, down into a sound and blissful sleep.

SEVENTEEN

ABOUT A HUNDRED YEARS LATER I woke with a start. It must have been at least a hundred years for I felt that old. I was on my left side and a soft arm lay across my chest. With an effort I dismembered my wrist from the blankets and squinted at my watch. Ten minutes after nine. Not possible. But it was, and bright daylight glared in the room. Bright daylight and a cold indraught of air. Had that awakened me?

I turned, with an effort, and there with the open door behind her, unbelieving horror spread across her face, was the Matron.

No, not a vision of the night, but sordid reality. The ultimate humiliating discovery on the morning after, the joke of the music-hall comedian, the lowest form of bedroom farce. What the butler saw! You could churn it out for a copper, turning the handle of the antique slot machine on some half-rotting pier.

I did not find it amusing. My start had roused the third member of the party and for a long, long moment a painful silence bore down on the room.

'You will come to my office in one hour.' Hulda finally let this command go at me.

Moving to the dressing-table, she picked up the brandy bottle, turned, and went out, holding it away from her like a hand grenade. The bang of the door shook the chalet, like an explosion.

'Oh, God. I'm sorry, Carroll.'

'Yes,' I said. 'We can't laugh this one off.'

I got out of bed slowly. She was before me. 'Just give me a few minutes and I'll make your breakfast. Do let me, Carroll, I want to so much. There's Nescafé and eggs and fresh bread in the kitchen. You need it, Carroll.'

'I'd better not stay.'

She saw that I meant it.

While she watched me with concern, I began to drag on my garments. My joints creaked. The puncture in my leg was a permanent stitch. I felt myself a fully qualified candidate for the A.H.V., which if you're unfamiliar with these symbols, is the Swiss Old Age Pension.

'What'll happen?'

'The worst.'

'I'm sorry, dear,' she said again, her hands still pressed together. 'I love you and bring you nothing but harm.'

I went across to my room.

No coffee, no croissants, no fresh fruit on the sideboard. Deprived of these reviving elements, my spirits sagged lower, I would have given a lot for a sup of that cognac. I only had the Kirsch and the thought of that sugary draught was enough. I could have done with a good hot shower but I was already dressed. I brushed my teeth, not looking at myself in the glass, then shaved by the sense of touch. Naturally I nicked my chin. Now I had to look. More blood, I thought—it was watery and thin. When I'd finally made the cotton wool stick, I went out.

First I had to see the *fons et origo*, the cause of all my trouble. He was sitting up in bed, washed, brushed and looking better than new. What else could you expect? All those rotten deceased white cells drained out of him and all that healthy blood pumped in. He was bursting with my red blood corpuscles. Just for the moment he was a brand new little bastard. I could have killed him.

'Good morning, Laurence. I've been longing for you to come. How are you?'

'*Wunderbar*. How are you?'

'*Wunderbar* also. I'm feeling terribly fit. And I've just had a lovely breakfast from Matron.'

'Tell me.'

'Cereal and cream, soft poached egg and a glass of lovely pear juice.'

'You're making me hungry.'

The pocket chess was there, on the side table by the bed.

'How is the game going?'

'Matron wouldn't let me set it out on my knees. Not yet. So visually I'm replaying the one with Herr Bemmel. I see now where I could have used a better fifth move: Kt to Q7.'

'Careful,' I said. 'Don't let Bemmel win this one.'

'Oh, this time I'm going to let him, just for fun.'

'How's the little scratch on your neck?'

'Oh, fine.' He looked at me archly. 'Perhaps I cut myself shaving?'

'Yes,' I said sourly. 'Let's say you've had a close shave.' This was moderately witty for me, on such a morning, but he missed the point. He had no idea of what he had been through. I took his pulse.

'Have your insides moved this morning?'

'Yes. Matron said it was quite normal.'

Matron was well in on this act now.

'Well, take it easy. I'll see you later.'

'Please, Laurence. And . . . I know how you hate what you call slop . . . but thank you for everything.'

While I was at it, I dragged myself round the ward. Sheer cowardice, of course, putting off the evil moment. Young Higgins, the synovitis case, had completely healed and could go home with the ex-pleurisy, the Jamieson girl, any day now, which would leave more room for the Christmas holiday lot. But why make Christmas arrangements, Carroll? You'll not be here then, dear boy. I summoned up the blood, what was left of it, knocked at Matron's door.

'*Herein.*'

I went in.

She was at her desk, sitting up straight, waiting on me.

This office was smaller than mine and furnished with her own things, surprisingly feminine—strange, I never thought of her as a woman; to me, despite the milk bars, she was sexless. Two finely worked samplers hung on the wall—how had she ever found time to stitch them?—and between them an old group photograph, row upon row of young nurses, already shapelessly garbed in white, novices of the night vigil—was she among them? She liked flowers and at the window, today, a fine pot of yellow chrysanthemums caught my gaze as, instinctively, it swivelled away from her.

'*Sitzen,*' she said, pointing to a chair. I sat. She looked me over. Already I had lost control of the interview.

'Never,' she went on, 'never in all my life, have I had such shock, such horror. To behave so, while that dear chile, so ill, was sleeping.'

I studied the chrysanthemums in silence. They were the fine feathery variety that cost money.

'And with the mother, too, which makes it most hateful of all.'

Even though she slaughtered the syntax, she did make it sound pretty low. And for an instant I thought of coming clean and throwing the whole works at her. But no, that would not help. She would never believe me. That's the worst of trifling with the truth. When you recite the Lord's prayer they think you're kidding them.

'To spoil such fine work of that evening with such bad morality,' she went on feelingly. 'Are you not ashamed?'

'I might be, Matron,' I said humbly, 'if I wasn't so hungry.'

She gave me another long look, then banged the little hand bell on her desk. The probationer came in, big-eyed, too scared to look at me. Had she been listening at the door?

'Bring *café crème* and a *croissant.*'

I could scarcely believe my ears. Was there, could there be, a gleam of hope, or was this merely the last wish of the condemned man?

'*Ja,*' she said, reading my surprise. 'You do not deserve. And at first I am zo angry I begin a letter to the committee.'

She broke off. The coffee and the crescent had arrived on a tray. They must have been ready and waiting by the stove. I balanced it on the arm of the chair and dunked the crescent.

'But presently I think better. Perhaps it is not all blame for you. For a man such a thing is perhaps necessary, even forgivable. You see, although I am *alte und grosse,* I understand well the men and their neets.' With one eye half closed she gave me a knowing look with just the suggestion of a leer, as if she had just read through the Kinsey Report. It would have been comic if it had not been so fortunate for me. Yet perhaps she did know. Perhaps some dirty old Swiss doctor had seduced her when she was a probationer. No, impossible, she was completely, inviolably virginal.

She took a sharp breath between her teeth and continued:

'But for her, that woman, with all her pretending to goodness and the husband so soon dead, it is a great sin, a crime, a falseness.'

'But surely, Matron . . .'

'Do not speak. Now I see clearly. She tries from the beginning to make me against you, while at the same time to get you to bed. And to steal the cognac from my stores. All *drei* bottles is gone.'

'She needs a drink. At night, Matron. To make her sleep.'

'Ach, it is not that she needs for sleep! No, it is not forgivable. Especially since in her haste to snatch I think she break the vacuum *Flasche.*'

Put like that, the picture looked black. Undeniably there was some justification for this point of view. One way or another, with all these complex motives, Davigan had tied herself up in a nasty tangle. I put down the tray and studied the chrysanthemums, wondering how, or if, I could unravel it.

'All was in order with us before that woman came. I managed you well. And it will return when she is gone, which must be at once. Yes, she must go, and with the boy—now especially that, for your thanks, he is besser.'

'But what's going to happen to her? She hasn't got a bean.'

'At the beginning, to show she is good Hausfrau, she tells me she has the offer to keep the home of some doctor.'

'Dr Ennis?'

'That is the name.'

So in every way I was off the hook. I ought to feel relieved.

'I appreciate your . . . your kindness to me, Matron,' I said. 'Still . . . don't you think you should be equally generous to her?'

'Why do you ask? For weeks you try to send her home.'

'I was thinking of the hospital . . . treatment, for Daniel,' I said weakly.

'Then he shall be at home there to have it, at the Spital you already recommended, which is goot. As for her, no matter, since all the blame is for her. She must go.'

What could I say? I was getting exactly what I wanted. I was in the clear. At one stroke I was rid of that nasty blot on my copybook. Somehow it did not feel so good. But I was in the hole, over the barrel, there was no way out.

'You must tell her,' I said finally. *That* I couldn't face.

'I go to her directly. And you will telephone the Flughafen for places. For the same day that we are sending Higgins and the Jamieson girl. It makes one journey for all.'

She stood up and came towards me with an almost maternal yet somehow patronizing smile.

'So now, Herr Doktor, we shall have good conduct. If so, I wish to keep you. You have skill and are clever. So?'

God help me, she actually patted me on the back. She *was* beginning to mother me.

I had to do it. I went into my office and rang the airport, having first thoroughly shut myself in. I wanted no part of what might take place in the chalet although, as it turned out, there was no shindy, everything passed off in a dead calm. Zürich came through at once, and presently I was on to Schwartz, the Swissair clerk who usually handled the Maybelle. He knew me well, and after I'd made the reservations for the 2.10 DC-6 flight on Friday, four to Heathrow and two on to Winton by the Vanguard 4.30 connection, he held on for the usual chat.

'How is your weather?'

'Bad,' I said. That's the standard opening. The Swiss enjoy themselves as the world's weather pessimists, they couldn't do without the *Foehn* in summer or the *bise* in winter.

'It will be worse. More snow coming.'

'You're probably right,' I said.

'By the way, doctor,' his voice took on the sissy giggle of Swiss masculine confidences. 'A friend of yours keeps inquiring for you with us.'

'Oh?' I said warily.

'Yes, always asking when next you are coming to Zürich.' He gave his neighing laugh. 'I think she misses you, that very pretty Fräulein Andersen of the Aktiebolaget Svenska Ornflyg.'

Lotte, asking for and missing me. It brightened me somewhat, gave me a lift, put some salve upon my ego.

'Tell her I'll be down soon. Don't say actually when. Just say in the next few days.'

'Ah!' He neighed again. 'You wish, *naturlich*, to surprise her.'

I replaced the receiver. Lotte would take my mind off things. She would do me good. Carroll, I told myself, you'll soon be yourself again. You are, and always will be, a no-good heel. It suits you, and you're dead out of character when you try to tread the straight and narrow path that leads uphill all the way.

EIGHTEEN

WE WERE IN THE TRAIN, passing through Kilchberg, and rapidly approaching Zürich Central. Schwartz's forecast on the weather had been amply justified. Heavy and persistent snow had blocked the valley road above Coire, making it impossible to use the station wagon. It had been a fortunate impasse. Not only had the journey been accomplished with that ease, speed and warm comfort which marks the best railway service in the world, the SBB; beyond all this, by judicious arrangement of our seats, I had escaped the embarrassing intimacies of the small closed car. Here, Davigan occupied one of the three seaters in front with Jamieson and Higgins, while Daniel and I faced each other on single seats at the other end of the long coach. What a relief to be spared the forced formality of those last two days—the strained attempt to put a normal face on a situation that might well have gone off like a land mine. I had to hand it to Davigan. If she had feelings she had clamped down on them hard. No signs of distress, never a word or a look that might give her away. She even had a brightly polished smile for Matron when she thanked her for all her kindness and said goodbye. Yes, she was tough, for the past forty-eight hours she had saved the Maybelle from exploding in a battlefield of recriminations, accusations and abuse.

My headache had been the brains trust, who hung on to me like a leech. Without the faintest suspicion as to why they were leaving, he still seemed to have something on his mind. Even now, crouched in his seat, he kept stealing glances at me when he thought I wasn't looking at him, and when caught at this game he sat up like a startled rabbit. His conversation, too, lacked all its usual zip. During the trip he had piped out a series of platitudes, obvious cover for some inner turmoil.

'I must say I have enjoyed my visit to Switzerland, Laurence. It's such a lovely country. The snow is wonderful.' And, twice repeated: 'Perhaps I'll have the chance to see it again, and you, one of these days?'

It bothered me finding appropriate answers to his various speculations without stretching reality too far. But my difficulties would soon be over. You can bring yourself to a sensible state of mind if you look hard at the basic facts, among which I rated highly the acknowledged truth that you cannot relive the past. Yet what mainly buttressed me was the certainty that the late unhappy Davigan had been the victim of a wifely shove. Yes, she had certainly done him in. What could you make of such a woman? Sympathize with her? Feel sorry for her? The answer was a double negative that really hardened me. Admittedly she had her good points. She had guts and in bedworthiness she was the ultimate. But who was to know whether one of these mornings you'd wake up, full of dreamy love, and find arsenic in your coffee?

We were slowing down, sliding gently into the station. I stood up and took our coats off the hooks above the seats. Davigan was helping the other two. There had been no need for me to exchange a word with her during the entire journey. I lowered the window and signalled a porter to take the suitcases, then we were out on the platform following the trolley down Quai 7 to the Swissair terminal, which stands conveniently in the station. Another ten minutes of efficient service and we were in the airport bus, rolling along Stampfenbach-Strasse towards Kloten. I had checked on flying conditions: the airport was swept clear of snow and flights were on schedule. Everything was going smoothly, everyone behaving according to the book. In less than an hour I would be rid of them. And free.

While I was on the way to congratulating myself I had, more and more, the strange and worrying suspicion that something queer seemed to be working to a head in Daniel. Still hanging on to me, though now less talkative, he was shifting restlessly on his seat, wiping the damp palms of his hands on his knees, looking up at me inquiringly from time to time. These signs of increased agitation began to worry me. Impossible for him to start another haemorrhage so soon. He was full of my platelets,. Yet if that odd chance came up, it would kill my whole programme.

'Are you all right? I asked him sharply.

'Yes, thank you . . . Are we nearly at the airport?'

The bus was now on the new bypass beyond Glattbrugg.

'Only another ten minutes. Why?'

'I was just hoping we still had a little time together.'

This silenced me. So far, although we seemed to get along on good terms, I had made no attempt to analyse his feelings towards me, beyond the fact that he apparently did not dislike me. I hoped he would not get emotional and make an exhibition of himself at this late stage. A quick glance across the aisle reassured me that Davigan at least was in full control of herself.

We made a circular sweep, drew up at the airport. While the others went ahead I waited to check the baggage. The head porter took our lot.

'Small party, this time, Herr Carroll.'

'We'll have a larger one coming in before Christmas. At least thirty.'

'That's good. I like always these Maybelle children.'

I gave him a two-franc piece. You are not supposed to tip but they like you a lot better if you do.

I went in through the automatic glass doors. The main hall of the airport stretches a good fifty metres towards a glass frontage overlooking the runways. On the right, a row of Swissair counters, on the left a bank, shops, coffee bar and the offices of foreign airways. Large as it is, this section is always crowded and I seemed to have lost my party. Then, as I pushed forward I half stopped and gave out a rude word. They were standing at the Swedish counter with Lotte.

'Well, here is our good friend, the doctor. How are you, dear Laurence?'

'Still living . . . I think.'

She laughed, yet studying me closely.

'Always he makes a bad joke. Did he make them with you, Mrs Davigan, when you were together at the Maybelle?'

'Not so you'd notice.' She had to answer and she was bearing up, but with a struggle.

'At least I warned you against him. I hope he did not spoil your nice holiday. I know him so well, don't I, Laurence? Well, never mind. He will tell me all when you are gone.'

Damn it, even in her bad English, she was hitting at me. And she was looking stunning, smart, better than ever, a regular Dior model, putting five years on Davigan's age. And knowing it. Davigan knew it too, in her baggy old suit, with that forced expression stuck on her face. And, so help me, I hadn't noticed before, she had on the snow boots. Suddenly I felt sorry for her.

'And now, would you like coffee? Lotte had assumed full charge of the party. 'No. Then if I may have your passports and boarding cards I will show you specially to the plane.'

At least she was taking them off my hands.

'You see,' she went on, 'since I was here to welcome your arrival I think it is only polite to send you away.'

They had begun to move towards passport control when I felt the tug on my arm. I bent down, he was pulling hard.

'I want you to take me to the wash room.'

It shook me. At the last gasp, was he going to have another haemorrhage?

'Come quickly then.'

I took him down the short flight of stairs beyond the coffee bar into the Men's Room.

'In there.'

He still had my arm and he pulled me into one of the cabinets with him and shut the door. He was trembling all over.

'Hurry,' I said. 'Get your shorts down.'

'I don't need to go, Laurence. But I had to tell you. I couldn't bear to leave you and perhaps never see you again and have you feel that I didn't like you enough to tell you my secret.'

In sheer surprise I sat down on the pedestal. He came close to me, his quick breath on my cheek.

'This is exactly how it happened with my father. For weeks, as the big building was being finished, he became very upset. He always took some whisky but now he drank much more, and at home he would get angry, even shouting, that by rights the building and all the new development should have belonged to him.'

He took a quick sobbing breath.

'On the Saturday afternoon when he took us up to show us, Mother didn't want to go. He'd had a lot to drink at dinner time. But we went. At the top he began again, about how it had all been lost. Then he shouted "I can't stand it, and I won't. I'll show them." Mother saw what was coming and tried to hold him, but he broke away, that's how her dress was torn, and jumped. Oh, it was horrible to see him turning over in the air.'

Again that sharp, pained sob. Riveted, I could scarcely breathe myself.

'Of course everyone thought he had slipped, at least at first. Canon Dingwall has always been our friend, we went to him at once, to ask if we should speak. He heard it all, and said the best thing was to be silent, not to make Father a suicide, which would be a big scandal in the church, but to give him what he called the benefit of the doubt. And for another reason too. There was no money left, absolutely nothing. But there was an insurance policy taken in his name by Grandfather Davigan for two thousand pounds, and meant for my education . . .' he faltered, 'and with a suicide it would have been no good at all.'

A prohibitive suicide clause in the insurance policy and Davigan, absolutely blameless, had taken all that suspicion and blame to get the money for Daniel's education. He would never need it now. How did I feel? It is worth a guess.

He was crying now as he put out his hand. I took it and held it. I think he wanted to kiss me but that I couldn't bear. I would have felt like Judas in reverse. Suddenly from the grille in the ceiling the loud-speaker of the public address system screamed at us:

'All passengers for Swissair Flight 419 to London will now leave by Gate 8.'

'Hurry,' I said.

He was still holding on to me as I rushed him upstairs. Lotte had left his passport at the Control. I picked it up, hurried him down, and through the lower lounge. They were waiting for us at Gate 8.

'You want to miss the flight?' Lotte said.

I shook hands with Higgins and Jamieson, then I had to face up to Davigan. Now that expression had become terribly thin, I was afraid she couldn't hold it. Yet she did; the effort, though, was wearing her out, yes, it was killing her. God, she did look old, pale, drawn and sick. We shook hands, just for the look of it. She had it all ready for me.

'Thank you for all you've done for Daniel, Dr Carroll.' She fumbled in her Swissair overnight bag. 'It's been quite an experience knowing you. As we'll not be meeting again I'll give you this. I've been keeping it for you for quite a long time.' She handed me a brown-paper-wrapped package. 'That morning you left me to go to your ship, you left this in my room as well.'

I accepted it, stupidly, having no idea what it might be. Then they went through the Gate. I stood there watching them go.

'Wait for me,' Lotte called over her shoulder.

I sat down in the lounge and looked at the parcel. What was it? A time bomb? It didn't tick. I was not ticking too well myself. Anyway, what did I care? I opened it. Anticlimax. It was a book, the book Dingwall had pressed on me the day of Frank's ordination. I had walked off without it early that morning when I took off for the boat. I put it in my pocket, Lotte was coming back through the Gate.

'Now, Laurence, what have you to say for yourself? You've been up to some tricks. I want big explanations before we come together again.'

'I've nothing to explain . . .'

'That poor woman is breaking her heart to leave you. The moment she was in the plane the tears began. And terrible tears . . .'

'Not for me. The little boy is ill.'

'Still?'

'Yes.'

'There is more. I think you sleep with her.'

'I told you, that's ancient history. You think I sleep with anybody. And what about you?'

'Could you blame me if I do? When you leave me so long. But I do not. That is the difference between us. Well, never mind. I still like you much and now we are together for a nice cosy time. I must be on duty till six o'clock—a charter coming in from Helsingfors. But here, take the key of the flat, go there and wait for me.'

I took the key.

'Mix the cocktails for six-thirty.' She gave me that wide seductive smile.

When she had gone I had a sudden feverish longing to go out on the open terrace to watch the plane take off, to see the last of them, but I shoved it down to that strange pain under my ribs and stifled it, swung round, made for the exit, cadged a lift from one of the Swissair bus drivers, and in twenty minutes was set down at Lotte's flat.

NINETEEN

FOR FIVE MINUTES I hesitated, although I cannot explain why, walking up and down outside the entrance, then I let myself in and switched on the lights. It was at least a relief to be off the cold damp street with the dirty banked snow on either side. The apartment was as neat, warm, and hygienic as ever. She had said to mix cocktails at six-thirty. I needed one now. I went to the trolley where a handful of left-over ice cubes were still stuck together in the Thermos container, broke them up and put the gin and vermouth in. If I try to describe my state of mind you may not believe me for now that my troubles were over and I was free as air, I was sunk in the worst depression that had ever blighted me. The way I had built up the case against Davigan, totally misjudged her, and packed her off like a crate of damaged goods, would be hard to live down. For the first time in many a year I felt compunction, made worse by the thought that here, straight away, I had come up to go to bed with that honey-eyed Swedish troll. No, no, that was pushing remorse too far. Pull yourself together, Carroll, you need relaxation, a bit of fun, a taste of good living. No point in worrying over what has now slid away into past history. You are well out of a particularly nasty situation. And what could you do? You want to charter one of Lotte's jets and overtake them in mid-air, to say, please, I'm sorry, let's kiss and be friends? Forget it.

As I sat down and sipped my drink, I felt the bulge in my side pocket. Dingwall's book: Collected Poems of Francis Thompson. I vaguely remembered it: a nice volume, in a green leather binding, the pages slightly fogged from age, the typical prize they dish out to seminarians. I glanced at my watch. Almost an hour to wait and, in an effort to ease my mind, I looked for the poem Machiavelli had marked for me. That is how I thought of him now, beating the suicide class, because the end justified the means. I found it with the help of the holy picture he used as a bookmark—the Simone Martini favourite of my early years, he must have chosen it specially—and the title, which I had forgotten, was *The Hound of Heaven*.

I took a quick look at the first few lines.

> *I fled Him, down the nights and down the days;*
> *I fled Him, down the arches of the years;*

> *I fled Him, down the labyrinthine ways*
> *Of my own mind; and in the mist of tears*
> *I hid from Him, and under running laughter.*
> *Up vistaed hopes I sped;*
> *and shot, precipitated,*
> *Adown Titanic glooms of chasmèd fears,*
> *From those strong Feet that followed, followed after.*

I stopped abruptly as it all came back to me: the empty church after Frank's ordination where I sat and read the poem through. The incident had passed completely from my mind and now I took up the book and began to read again more slowly. The more I went into it, the more I tried to stop. This was not my line in literature and not, especially, at the present time. If I had been low before, now I was sinking deeper. But I had to go on, and when I had finished it I sat there, absolutely still, stricken and bound by its beauty and mystery.

Now it was clear to me, the genesis of that phobia, my intermittent torment, that mysterious unremitting pursuit from which there was no escape. In the empty church the day of the ordination, in a highly receptive state, I had run through the poem simply to kill time, barely conscious of its meaning, and without obvious effect. My mind was filled with other problems but my subconscious had seized it, buried deeply the theme of the sinner endlessly pursued through the labyrinthine ways of life by the Man. The symbol of the Hound had stuck too, to become the signal of release. Yes, I could rationalize it all. Somehow, that did not help. It did not seem fully to be the answer, since I, too, now felt myself *defenceless utterly, grimed with smears, standing amid the dust of years, my mangled youth dead beneath the heap.*

I had left my drink half finished. Mixed hurriedly, it had done nothing for me. You can never improve a bad cocktail by adding gin. I needed another, fresh and strong. I got up slowly, passed through the bedroom to the bathroom and emptied the glass. As I came back, wholly absorbed, still feeling myself *of all man's clotted clay the dingiest clot,* my eye caught the fly end of necktie showing over the edge of a shut drawer in Lotte's neat little Swedish chest. Absently, I fancied it must be mine. One of the pair I had bought not so long ago at Grieder's. I pulled the drawer.

It was not my tie. Despite my aspirations towards the higher life, I cannot afford Countess Mara ties and both ties now visible were thus handsomely marked with the distinctive coronet and the initials C.M. Also in the drawer were two superfine silk shirts, with fresh laundry bows, very chic and hand made, with the embroidered monogram C.deV. and the neat little tab back of the collar: *Brioni. Roma*. I stood examining these de luxe accessories like a kleptomaniac in a department store. Maybe that 'de' intrigued me. Of course I had occasionally been a trifle suspicious of Lotte, yet at the same time always flattered myself I was the only current bed-fellow. I closed the drawer and took a step towards the built-in wardrobe. It was full of her lovely clothes, possibly, I now reflected, from C.deV., and also her lovely smell. However, one hanger at the end provided a svelte if jarring note: a grey pinstripe suit of the finest quality. Vulgar curiosity made me hurt myself more. I looked at the tab in the inside pocket: *D. Caraceni. Via Boncompagni*, 21. *Roma*: the best tailor in Italy, probably in Europe. C.deV. must be a prince, or some dirty profiteer. I had always promised myself that if ever I had real money and went to Rome to call on the Pope I would have Caraceni make a suit. Now I saw the exact suit. Alas, it was not mine.

I pushed the door to and went back to the living-room. Now I made myself a real hard drink, merely breathing the martini across the gin, and put it straight away down the hatch. When I had mixed another of the same I took it with me and sat down. I had taken no more than a sip when I heard the turn of a key in the Yale lock. How many keys has she? I asked myself, as Lotte breezed in.

'Well, that is pretty.' She stopped short, displeased. 'The guest is drinking before the hostess arrives.'

'You're not a hostess now. You're a V.I.P. receptionist.'

'Don't be so smart or I shall be more cross with you. Then you will be less easily forgiven.'

'Forgiven for what?'

'You will hear.' She came forward, threw her shoulder bag and uniform kepi on the couch, and sat down showing, as usual, that beautiful extent of beautiful leg. But tonight it did not bother me. 'Now give me a quick one before I bathe and change.'

I poured her the slightly watery remains in the glass mixer.

'Yes.' She sipped and made a face. 'I must know about your woman Davigan. Although I cannot believe it, you were sleeping with her.'

'Why can't you believe it?' I didn't want to know, only to irritate her.

'Because, although it is clear she is badly in love with you, she is so unattractive. Such a little bag of woman.'

'She's not in love with anyone. And she's not a bag.'

'You are wrong. She is gone upon you. As for looks, she is quite worn down. Don't you notice these lines under the eyes?'

'That poor woman has had a rough life.' Illogically, but for some unaccountable reason, I was beginning to get angry at this denigration of Davigan. 'Especially lately. Yet it may interest you to know that at your age she was a damn sight better fitted out than you are.'

'Thank you for the compliment, my Scottish gentleman.' Her face and neck reddened deeply. That's the worst of these total blondes, when they flush they look coarse, like the butcher's daughter with the peroxide hair. 'But let us keep to the point. Did you let me down with that woman?'

'Are you jealous?' It gave me a morbid satisfaction to lead her on.

'If you wish to understand me.' She compressed her lips and faced me directly. 'While I would not be so common as to have jealousy, I am fond of you and would painfully resent you making love outside the privilege of my bed.'

'So you value me there . . . in that sanctuary?'

'Should I not?' She was losing control now or she would not have spoken so openly, 'It is something you are very good at, the best I ever knew. Then, when you are not as you are tonight, you are nice really, and amusing with all these lies I can laugh at. Now, however, I wish the truth. Why did you sleep with Mrs Davigan?'

I looked her in the eye.

'Why did you sleep with C.deV.?'

All the colour seeped out of her skin. Now she was no longer a blonde. An albino. A long pause followed. She moistened her lips.

'Who spoke of him, Schwartz?'

I shook my head.

She tried again, bitterly.

'Someone else of my good friends at the airport?' As I made no answer she went on. 'He is simply a friend. A very distinguished, elderly, quite old in fact, Italian gentleman.'

'Not so old he changes his shirts in your bedroom?'

'So? You are a mean, low spy.'

'Yes, I'm low. And tonight I'm not pretending to be anything else.'

She made an effort to be calm.

'Come, let's forget it, Laurence. You did wrong. I did wrong. So two wrongs make a right.'

'Only in Sweden,' I said and stood up. 'I'm going now, and I'll not be back.'

'Don't . . . I'll make a little supper . . . we'll be together, just as always.' She put out her arm. Trying to smile, she was offering herself. 'What is the matter with you? Always you tell me you have two of everything for me.'

'Well now I've one of nothing.' I knew I was cutting my own throat, that I would regret it, but it had to come out.

She was silent with anger and, I think, shame. As I went through the door she said:

'Don't dare ever come back.'

I skipped the lift and barged down the stairs, just in time to pick up a taxi that was discharging its passenger—I would have liked him to be C.deV., but he was not. I flung myself into the back and said: 'Zürich Bahnhof.' I was as mad at myself as she was with me, fully conscious that I had botched everything during the day, and was now swinging wild punches from the floor, yet somehow trying to compensate, to get the whole mess out of my system, and above all, dying for another desperately needful drink.

TWENTY

AT THE STATION I paid off the taxi and went direct to the *Auskunft* board. I had a vague idea that a Coire train was due to leave around seven. Hurriedly, I checked the red figures of the *rapides,* only to find that this particular evening express ran only on Saturdays. But, in the black *Abfahrt* column of slow, secondary trains, a departure was scheduled for 7.15. A glance at the clock showed 7.19. Support of some kind was essential, and I knew what would give me the lift I needed. I had barely two minutes to spring to the buffet, buy a bottle of vodka and beat the gate on Quai 9 before it slammed shut.

The train, strictly non de luxe, was an *omnibus,* the cheapest and slowest form of Swiss travel, with, of course, no possibility of a *Speisewagen.* It was practically empty. Who wanted to go to Coire at this season of the year and this time of night? As we crawled through the outskirts of Zürich, snow began to fall, the large drifting flakes jaundiced by the neon lights of dirty, deserted streets. With a shiver, I shot down the blinds in the bare compartment and, without hope and strictly against regulations, turned the heating switch a couple of notches. It did not click. This would be a long, sad, chilly journey, yet with commendable Carroll foresight I had the means to anaesthetize myself against the sick, despondent sense of botchery, failure and personal disgust let loose in me this afternoon. I settled in a corner of the hard wooden bench, pulled up the collar of my overcoat, and examined the bottle.

The label was in German.

> *Superior Slovene Vodka.*
> *Specially for Export.*
> *This pure vodka is made by the original Slovene*
> *recipe entirely from rye and green rye malt and not,*
> *as with inferior brands, from potatoes and maize.*

Trust the Swiss to import the best. But a couple of peasants were passing me on the way to the forward coach; I shoved the bottle back into my overcoat pocket. So now, Carroll, I thought sourly, you have a pocketful of rye, it follows naturally, after your juvenile maunderings, and I hope it nourishes you. It was time to try, for now I was quite alone.

As a temperate, or at least a cautious drinker, I was more or less unaccustomed to excess. This is the alibi I create, like Davigan's miracle wind, to exonerate myself from the subsequent events of this inconceivable Walpurgis night. I took out my pocketful of rye. I had no glass, it was necessary to drink from the bottle, a difficult technique, with the short squat neck and one which, badly accomplished, made me choke and cough. Nevertheless, I managed a good slug that warmed my insides, but for the moment afforded me no alleviation of my misery which, rather, was intensified by the discovery that the Slovenes had really gone to town not on purity alone, but on strength. This stuff must be two hundred over proof and would probably rot my liver.

Yet, did I not deserve to suffer? What an S.O.B. I had been, what a Gadarene swine, what a putrefying bastard. And what a B.F. I had been to top it off by reading that bloody, beautiful poem. All Dingwall's doing of course, he had probably made a Novena to have the action delayed, so it would score a bull's eye on me at the psychological moment, when I was most vulnerable.

I felt like throwing a healthy curse at the old schemer, but no, that I could never do, particularly since, after a second slug, I had begun to feel more hopeful. Carroll, I told myself, do not despair, it is always darkest before the dawn.

Thus encouraged, I took a third slug, more skilfully accomplished and with more positive results—this vodka might be unhealthy, but it had an Iron Curtain kick. The old Carroll morale began to assert itself, the blood began to pulse, the spirits rose. Yes, I could bring myself, decently, to forget it, wipe out the entire complex mess, and get myself set for the future. Life was full of mistakes, everyone made them, why should I be the exception to the rule? We were all sinners, humanity was frail. Why mourn, why shed crocodile tears? No use crying over spilled milk, the only reasonable attitude was to wipe the slate clean and start afresh.

As the train jogged through the snowy darkness, leaving the valley behind, climbing higher towards the mountains, halting at interminable wayside stations, I continued my application to the rye, achieving not personal exoneration alone, but a state of physical and mental euphoria in which all my faculties, while somewhat blurred, seemed fired up to a point of abnormal activity. In this expansive mood my present situation in the empty coach offered neither scope nor opportunity. Conversation with the conductor, who gave me a strange look and my ticket a quick punch, proved unproductive. Song, in the circumstances, would have been an infringement of good taste. Instead, with shut eyes, rolling slightly with the movement of the train, I created a series of brilliant situations justifying my position, the most diverting set in a court specially convened at my request at the Vatican wherein, with the Pontiff's blessing, I successfully brought charges of malfeasance against Dingwall, who appeared, much to the amusement of His Holiness, in a full dress kilt. What, I asked myself, with a grin, *is* malfeasance? Anyway, I really loved that old Highlander.

Two hours later, when I tumbled out on the deserted platform of Schlewald Dorf, leaving the empty bottle on the hat rack as a testimonial to its country of origin, I was virtually airborne, yet with a calculating and elevated perception of myself, my surroundings and my condition. This last convinced me, after a careful study of the station clock which on closer examination showed nineteen minutes past eleven, that it would be unwise to present myself to the good Matron immediately. A cooling off period was indicated and, indeed, the Arctic blast loaded with icy flakes that tore down the deserted platform caused me a preliminary shiver. In my absence a blizzard had apparently taken over. Where should I find sustenance and shelter? As I floated off through the village, a sensation to which the deep wet snow contributed, thinking in terms of coffee, I had to admit that Edelmann's was closed. Yes, confound it, everything must now be shut and, in the wise Swiss fashion, shuttered, except the Pfeffermühle. This was an establishment that, unofficially, never closed. But there I should indubitably drink more and, rather disconcerting, be flailed with recollections of the chess match. That match, the young participant therein and his maternal relative were henceforth to be eradicated from the tablets of my memory.

I would have to chance the possibility of Hulda staying up to wait for me. Even so, everything would be arranged to her entire satisfaction. With this in mind I set off up the hill towards the main street of the town.

It was a steep hill, ankle deep in soggy slush and where the snow, earlier, had drifted, an unwary step frequently took me in up to the knees. The wind, too, was hitting me in the teeth in an effort to knock them down my throat. Altogether, to my immense surprise, when I reached an intermediate level, I found myself gasping for breath and actually hanging on to a convenient railing. That the railing belonged to the church was ridiculous enough, but not more so than the realization that this very edifice would provide me with the respite I must have before taking off again on the higher slope to the Maybelle. As usual, it was open and received me in darkness and silence when I staggered in, animated by the feeling that I was participating in the joke of the century.

Naturally I treated myself to the front pew, sat down, and shook the wet snow off myself. Not that I minded the wet, it gave me a soft, steamy feeling, as good as a sauna— that further tickled my fancy, having a steam bath in this dark, crummy church. Yet it was not all dark, for suddenly I saw a little red light flickering like an eye. They kept it at the side underneath the bas-relief on the wall. No more than a rushlight in a red glass holding oil, it still diffused a glow and I knew that, as usual, He was watching me. But tonight nothing could worry me, I had the answer to that idiotic phobia, in fact I had the answers to everything, and the situation suddenly seemed to me so amusing I broke into a loud laugh and exclaimed:

'You didn't expect to see me in here, did You?'

Naturally, there was no reply, and that put my back up. So I threw my voice over and answered for Him.

'Certainly I did not expect you, Dr Carroll.' It came back perfectly with a slight echo from the hard, granite wall. 'As you are now aware, I've been following you around without much success for years. But I am only too pleased to see you.'

Off I went again into a fit of laughter. This was going to be good, so I slewed round, put my feet on the seat and returned the compliment.

'You don't mean that, You're just being polite. I'm afraid I'm disturbing You.'

I threw the voice again.

'It's quite agreeable to be disturbed. It's a long night here, all by Myself.'

I was enjoying this, I wanted it to go on, and it did.

Me: 'You mean no one looks near You all night?'

The Man: 'Yes, Father Zobronski looks in occasionally. He has T.B., you know, and the cough keeps him awake, so he pops in to have a word with Me.'

Me: 'That cheers You up?'

The Man: 'Naturally. But of course I'll not have him much longer, he's booked to go next year.'

Me: 'He's being transferred?'

The man: 'No, buried. On the 9th of October.'

I had another good laugh at this, but not quite so hearty. Why the date? This thing seemed to be getting a little out of hand.

Me: 'That could be a pretty good guess, since he probably has a large cavity in one lung.'

The Man: 'In both lungs, doctor.'

Now He was going too far, I had to slow Him down.

Me: 'Please don't let us have any of that know-all stuff. While I have no wish to offend, You are ... well ... just a bit of stucco on that wall.'

The Man: 'How right you are, dear Carroll, and how I wish they hadn't stuck Me up in this half empty little chapel. Naturally I enjoy the children, and your good self, on the rare occasions when you are here, but as you surmised, it is often extremely lonely and, indeed, unrewarding.'

Me: 'You'd have preferred one of the larger city churches?'

The Man: 'Yes, a church where I would come across some of the bigger sinners, not just run-of-the-mill transgressors like you, Dr Carroll.'

Had I said that? Like the date, it had slipped out so easily, quite unpremeditated, and it jarred me. I could barely see Him but I threw a hurt look in His direction.

Me: 'Forgive me, but need we be so personal. Of course, I know You've always had a down on me.'

The Man: 'How wrong you are, my dear Carroll. When you were young I was quite devoted to you. And I believe you had some slight regard for Me.'

Me: 'I suppose so.' He forced it out of me.

The Man: 'You weren't afraid to look Me in the eye. You didn't try to avoid Me as you do now.'

I said nothing. When I started the joke I hadn't expected

it to sour off into a dissection of my character. But as such it continued.

The Man: 'Indeed, on several occasions I was rather proud of you. You recollect perhaps your admirable behaviour when they put you in gaol for helping that unfortunate girl?'

Had Carroll said that? Of course, you fool. Don't fancy you've started any of that miraculous stuff. You're lit up with rye vodka and answering yourself back. Nevertheless, it was pretty damn queer and I felt an uncomfortable pricking of my scalp as He went on:

'But when you started slacking around in your worthy profession instead of practising it with patience and humanity, I began to lose faith in you.'

Me: 'You kept after me though?' I had to keep my end up.

The Man: 'Yes, I seldom give up even with the most hardened cases, and of course, on account of your birth and upbringing, you are a split personality.'

He caught me there—I had to admit it.

Me: 'Yes.'

The Man: 'So there was always the chance that your better side might prevail over your worse.'

Me: 'My worse!' I sat up. I was beginning to get angry.

The Man: 'Oh, I don't mind your lies, so much, they are often quite amusing. I could even overlook your amorous exploits since, unfortunately, although you are not particularly goodlooking, you have strong sex appeal which makes many women want to sleep with you and those who don't, like your good Matron, to mother you.'

This was taking me down with a vengeance—when I thought of all my techniques, my efforts to create atmosphere, the records I had bought and played. He was giving me credit for nothing. I was about to bring this up when He interposed suddenly, in a cutting voice.

The Man: 'The Brahms No. 4 was the most effective, was it not? Softening and soothing. Followed by the Sabre Dance. Wild and exciting! What a clever little sinner you have become, Carroll.'

He was taking my breath away. Was it possible? He . . . no, it could only be one side of my personality fighting the other. Yet I tried to defend myself against Him.

'Can't You give me credit for being in love?'

'You have not the faintest glimmering of the meaning of that word.'

And He kept pouring it on.

The Man: 'No, Carroll. What I cannot forgive is your almost total irresponsibility, your lack of charity and pity, your casual indifference towards those whom you have seriously injured.'

The voice—whether His, or mine, I was now too troubled to discern—had lost its calm reasonableness and hardened.

'It is this, Carroll, that has brought you to the end of your tether, and unless you amend, I warn you, in all gravity, you will be irretrievably lost.'

'Lost?'

Was it my faint voice, or merely an echo? The terrible conviction had grown in me that if I was, indeed, still the speaker, He was putting the words into my mouth.

'Yes, lost, Carroll. I will spare you the spiritual implications of that word. But even in its material sense you will be lost. So far, with a good spirit, your natural gaiety, and the remnants of your early training, you have, in your own phrase, got away with it. That won't continue. Unchecked, with everything permissive, you will inevitably deteriorate. You will become a selfish, indolent, useless drifter, and later, a middle-aged, run-to-seed, used-up Lothario, bored and satiated with your own vices, tortured by memories of wasted opportunities and the knowledge that you are a failure.'

I wanted to answer Him. I tried. I could not. And in the silence that followed, all at once I was afraid. For some time now the Slovene potion had not been holding me up so well and, instead, its more sinister elements were taking their toll of my insides, I felt weak, sick, and helpless. And suddenly I was conscious of the terrible stillness, cut off by the snow outside, and within an isolation, chill and morbid as the tomb. We were totally alone. We? Was I out of my mind? A fresh wave of fear swept over me when the voice said:

'Are you still listening, Carroll? Have I convinced you? Or shall I go on?'

I had to end this, or it would be the end of me. I forced myself to look towards the Man, and shouted:

'For God's sake, stop, if it's really You. And if it's me, then shut me up.'

Even before the echoes died, there was a sound, as of the

opening of a door, followed by a sharp current of air, and all at once the rushlight went out. The darkness that followed gripped and held me, trapped beyond time and space, in a dimension wholly unearthly and untouchable. I wanted to rise and run in the frantic effort to escape. I could not. My limbs refused to move. Then in that abysmal dark, the silence was broken by slow footsteps, advancing towards me. Frozen with terror, I was back in that nameless street. Nearer, nearer. It was the end of the chase. I tried to cry out but no sound emerged. Deathly sick, I waited for what must come.

A small circle of light shone on my face. Zobronski was bending over me with a little pencil torch.

'Dr Carroll . . . you . . . you are ill.'

'Watch out,' I croaked. 'I'm going to be.'

Violently, I parted company with Slovenia—there was nothing else, I had not eaten since breakfast.

'I'm sorry,' I managed to gasp at last. 'All over your church. I'll clean it up.'

'No, no. I'll do it in the morning. I'm always up long before Mass. But . . . you must come now and I'll make you some coffee.

Coffee—he couldn't miss the smell of that pure alcohol. I let him take my arm and lead me through the sacristy. I had to be led, my legs seemed not to belong to me. In slow motion we got to his room. As I had been informed, he was poor: a cheap day bed, a wooden table, two hard chairs and a crucifix.

'Would you like to lie down?'

I shook my head and sat on one of the chairs.

He was still looking at me with inquiring solicitude.

'You came to shelter.'

I had to tell someone, I was still far from being myself. I gave him it all and ended with a double reiteration.

'We talked in there, one to the other, like I'm talking to you.'

He simply put his hand on my shoulder and said:

'First . . . your coffee.'

He went out. I still felt as if I had just been picked up from the canvas and that I was not yet out of the ring. Zobronski was somewhere next door. I heard a long bout of deep, patient coughing—that's the big single cavity, I thought: no, from that cough it must be a double. Presently he came back with a bowl of coffee. I thought: they must drink it that way in the Polish seminaries, and it will be the same ersatz coffee. But it surprised me, it was good, and I mumbled this with my thanks.

'My great luxury,' he said. 'A gift from the good Edelmann's.'

A pause. What would happen to me next?

'You feel better?'

'Yes . . . thank you.' I even said, 'Father.'

Another pause. He sat down on the other chair.

'My son,' he said, and went on, slowly, speaking correct, scholarly English. 'I am not one to decry the miraculous. But the answer to your . . . your painful experience is very simple. You have just had a dialogue with your own conscience.' He paused to suppress a cough. 'It is a fearful and wonderful thing, the Catholic conscience, especially when engendered in us at an early age. You can never escape it. Even the apostates cannot quite lose it, that is why an apostate is always a creature of misery. And tonight when you were . . .' he hesitated, 'over-stimulated, liberated from your usual controls, your conscience took over. Normally it is we who examine our conscience. Tonight it was your conscience that examined you. And judged you.'

I was silent. His explanation seemed logical but he was taking all the drama away from me. No, not quite. I could not bring up the question of that fatal date, the 9th of October, but it helped me to cling to my own view.

'And now, my son,' he said with meaning, 'it is evident that you are troubled. Please do me the honour to tell me.'

I was altogether softened up. I was no longer Carroll, I was a dish rag that had been put through the wringer and hung up, still wet, to dry. Leaning forward with my arms on the table, I told him. There was a lot of it and he heard me in complete silence.

'Now,' he said, 'I will give you absolution.'

'You want me to kneel?'

'No, you are still not well, I will kneel beside you.'

I couldn't stop him. I shut my eyes as he murmured words. I could not laugh this one off and, if it interests you, I did not want to.

He got up, turned away from me and coughed for a couple of minutes—he had been holding it back.

'Now I am going to telephone your good Matron to bring the car.'

'She's no sort of driver,' I warned him. 'Even if she gets down she'll never get back.'

'Then I will drive you back.'

He went to telephone. It took some time, perhaps the lines were down. No, now he was talking to the Matron and, although I had lost count of time, she seemed to arrive with surprising promptitude. No words passed between us until we were in the rear seat of the Opel. I wanted to drive, but knew it to be hopeless, I had a splitting headache and was still all over the place. Zobronski insisted on taking the wheel.

'Oh, how I misjudge you,' Hulda was crooning down the back of my neck. 'For so long I sit up awaiting, thinking you are in some bad place in Zürich. And all the time you, so ill, make shelter in the church, and with prayers alzo I hear.' She put an arm round my shoulders. 'Now all is besser between us, *mein lieber Herr Doktor,* and wen I make you soon well, we work always *mit grosser Freundschaft.*'

Zobronski made it at last although twice he nearly had us in the ditch. Hulda insisted he take the car back to the church. Then, her arm still mothering me, she took me to my room.

'Some gute hot suppe, *lieber* Herr Doktor, and then to your warm bed . . .'

Everything had worked out well for me in the end. She had the maternal instinct, and I could use it. Happy days were here again at the Maybelle.

TWENTY-ONE

I GOT OUT of the weary train, out of the dirty compartment, still stuffed with tunnel smoke from the Central Low Level, and went down the station steps to the sound of music.

Had the town brass band turned out for the occasion? Nothing is so welcoming, or reviving as a rollicking Sousa march. But it was Moody and Sankey that swelled towards me, the Salvation Army lassics with tambourines and a harmonium on wheels making a circle under the damp railway arches while a stray dog, its nose stretched towards heaven, set up a sostenuto accompaniment. The Hallelujahs, I recollected, started early on Saturday afternoons and worked their way down the Vennel, arriving at Market Square around the time the pubs opened. Beyond this group there was no one under the dripping arches but a solitary porter, and no sign of a cab. I eased down my bag and addressed him.

'Any chance of a taxi?'

Supporting his back against a pillar, he was busy with a fag end, pinched between forefinger and thumb, to extract the last of the nicotine. He expectorated before replying:

'They're a' at the fitba'.'

'No chance of ringing up Henderson's?'

'They're shut the Setterday afternoon.'

I plucked again at the chords of memory.

'What about MacLauchlan's?'

'It's a funeral parlor noo.'

'So, I'll have to walk.'

'Ye've said it, brother.'

This fraternal greeting, though owing something to percolations from Hollywood, delivered to a sudden tambourine crescendo and lingering canine howl, was at least encouraging. I thanked him politely, picked up my bag and set off. He watched my departure with ill-concealed distrust.

Out in the open it was raining, but by local standards not more than a Scots mist. I had books in the bag which, in consequence, was of no light weight, and I was tired after a long night flight.

Why, I asked myself, was it my beastly destiny to be dragging my luggage into this drab little town where already

I observed signs of hideous new construction that must destroy any native character it had once possessed. The old Academy with its fine twin baronial towers of Aberdeen granite had been replaced by an office complex of glass and steel in which a few overtime clerks stirred slowly, like sad sea monsters trapped in an aquarium. And the Georgian pillared Philosophical Club to which my grandfather had belonged no longer graced the dingy street. Instead, rival chain stores displayed glaring signboards that hurt the eye.

If only some kind heart had had the thought to erect one triumphal arch, festooned with streamers and artificial roses, how different would have been my re-entry to this dismal scene. But who was to know of my return? My grandparents, the Bruces, were both gone, decently interred beneath a Celtic cross in the local cemetery. True, there remained Father Francis, and the indestructible Dingwall, but when you have made up your mind to make a crashing fool of yourself, it is wise to delay all disturbing communications. Sufficient unto the day is the evil thereof, and today the evil was of my own making.

I walked a short way farther up the High Street then turned sharp left into the quieter Burnside Road, which at least still seemed unchanged. The Carnegie Library remained wrapped in its mantle of Victorian repose and beside it was the same little shop where on a Saturday night, forgetting my allegiance to the royal Bruces, I bought myself a pennyworth of hot chip potatoes. Going this way I must pass the church, but at this hour it would certainly be deserted. Shifting the suitcase to my other arm I followed the curve of the road.

Wrong again, Carroll! As I came into view of St Patrick's a long line of cars stood in front of the entrance, a large crowd swarming round them. A funeral, probably—perhaps the old Canon had finally disproved the local myth that he was eternal. No, it was a wedding, I could spot the white ribbons on the cars, some already beginning to move away. I hesitated. Turn again Whittington Carroll? Never. Dignity and the right of way forbade it, moreover it was a good bet that I could sneak past unnoticed in the general commotion.

I hastened my steps, but the cars were beating me, taking the turn towards the restaurant we used to call The Swank. The big one, a landaulette, trailing tin cans and the motto

Just Married pulled away as I came directly opposite the portico and there, through the gap, so help me, speeding the departing guest, was the Reverend Francis. Out of the corner of my eye I saw him as, with averted head, disguising myself with a crouching attitude, a slight limp, and the used-up air of a travelling bagman selling cheap toiletries to unsuspecting housewives, I tried to get by unobserved.

Useless. He saw me and with a bound, left the balls of his feet and flew, soared across the street.

'Laurence!' He embraced me, for a bad moment I feared he might kiss me. He had put on weight, he was plump, and rosy, with a beatific smile, garbed in an immaculate soutane of the best material on which someone had pinned a small rosebud. I used it to ease off his ecstatic greeting.

'Isn't that contrary to canon law, Father?'

He blushed. 'One of the bridesmaids insisted, Laurence.'

'The pretty one?'

'They were all pretty. And of course I'll take it off before we go in.'

'Go in?'

'Naturally, my dear Laurence. Ever since we heard from Father Zobronski that you were coming, the Canon has been parked in the Sister's garden, a timetable on his knees, with strict instructions that you are to be brought to him.'

Well, it had to come. Better now than later. I let Frank lead me down the side walk of the church towards the convent. He was already removing the rose and transferring it to his side pocket. He would put it in his toothbrush glass in his room.

As we approached the statue of the Virgin above the grotto that marked the entrance to the garden, he murmured:

'I'll leave you here, dear Laurence. But we'll be seeing lots and lots of you now, thank God.' Then in a stage whisper he hissed: 'He is blind in one eye and the other is failing. He has to use a high power magnifying glass, but don't, on any account, mention it. It makes him very angry.'

I waited till he had gone then went towards the old, the very old, nearly blind man in the wheeled chair placed in the shelter of an open, cross-latticed summer house. Now I stood before him. Did he see me or merely sense that I was there?

'Your plane must have arrived on time. You caught the
12.15 Caledonian from the Central Low Level.'

'Yes, Canon.'

'My calculations were correct. Always a bad train that.
A workman's, isn't it?'

'Yes, Canon.'

'What induced you to take that bad midnight flight from
Berne? On a DC-3 too?'

Have you ever noticed how old men love to work out
journeys they will never take?

'I took it because it is a dirt-cheap flight.'

'So you are broke, Carroll.'

'Stoney, Canon,' and I added: 'Since you wish to insult
me.'

Was there a flicker of a smile over that old, that very old
gaunt face? It passed.

'Well, at all events, you are back, Carroll.'

'Yes, they'd had enough of me and threw me out.'

'That is one of your good lies, Carroll. Your strange
Polish friend wrote me that you were pressed and pressed
again to stay, both by the Matron and the Committee.'

I said nothing.

'By the way, how is that good father with the strange
name?'

'Ill,' I said, and added, watching him closely. 'Very.
Cavities in both lungs. In fact I'm expecting bad news
about him on October 9th.'

No, it meant nothing to him. He merely said:

'A pity. I should have liked to meet him. Still . . . that
bad night flight . . .'

He was wandering slightly and seemed to sink into himself for a moment. I tried to lighten the interview.

'Have you had anything in the way of chess lately?'
Adding more loudly to wake him up: 'Chess . . . your
reverence.'

He came back.

'No, my young opponent has not been getting about
much lately. By the way, Carroll, they have no idea
whatsoever that you are coming and I did not enlighten
them.'

I felt good about that and was on the point of thanking
him when he added:

'Not that I wished to save for you the joyful surprise of

the returned prodigal. I feared, you see, that at the last minute you might not turn up.'

A pause. I made no comment. He was probably right.

'Apparently it took you some time to make up your mind. Of course, I gather you yourself were ill. A slight chill?'

I nodded—his 'slight' was typical and good. He obviously knew I'd had a virus pneumonia, but I went along with him.

'Due to a sauna I took in the local chapel.'

'Ah! he said, but with infinite relish. 'Doubly cleansing in such an edifice. Then you had to wait for your replacement. Three months, was it not?'

'Yes,' I said, reflecting that it had also given the good Zobronski lots of time to work on me, dying on his feet, too, without even a whimper.

'Well, now that you are here, Carroll, now that through the mysterious workings of the Almighty the back door is open for you—forgive me if I bore you by recalling a remark I once thought to be appropriate—now you are going to stay. For presently you will see how much, and by whom, how terribly much you are needed. And if you fail them, and me, you are a lost soul. When I am up there, and may it be soon, I will personally arrange for your non-admission.' He paused, watching me out of the corner of one good eye. 'Say something, Carroll. Are you with me?'

'Yes,' I said. What else could I say to this Highland Machiavelli?

'Good. Then I want you to come here quietly on Friday afternoon, just as before. However, on this occasion you will bring with you that poor troubled woman who will soon be the mother of your second child.'

What a crusher! The roof of the summer house seemed to fall on my head. Yet at the back of my mind I had feared it. Carroll the potent! Carroll the propagator of the faith. I was hooked now, bait, line and sinker. He went on:

'Father Francis does all the marriages, he loves weddings, and is a great favourite of the ladies, but this one I will do. Are you with me, Carroll? Speak, or for ever be silent and damned.'

'Yes,' I said.

'Good. I rejoice that you are, for once, in a notably affirmative mood.' He held out his hand, vaguely in my direction. I took it, full of bones and blue veins.

'Now leave me. That fat Irish sister whom I detest and

who hides my snuff will be coming shortly and I need my lunch. If that's what I may call the pap they give me. God bless you, my very dear Laurence. And remember Friday.'

My suitcase was at the gate. I picked it up and set off. At first my steps were slow and pensive. The recent interview had not, to say the least, exhilarated me. Yet in that affectionate penultimate phrase I found a strange comfort. A group of men passed me hurrying to the football match. Walking with my head down, the bag dragging at my ankles, the ring of their footsteps, on the hard paving ahead, came back to me. With supreme lack of logic I thought, I have become the follower, I am no longer pursued.

Now I was at the corner of Renton Road and as I turned into that familiar by-way my pace insensibly increased. Obscurely, too, my heart was beating faster. In no time at all I was there, in Craig Crescent, opposite the Ennis house, which looked seedier than of old, paint flaking off the shutters, a cracked window in the surgery annex, where a few patients had collected outside. I took it all in, and using that most obnoxious Swiss word, said to myself: 'Carroll, you've made the *Rundfarhrt*.'

I drew a deep breath, crossed the road, went up the gravelled weedy path, pushed open the front door and walked straight in.

The sitting-room was on the left, and Dr Ennis was lying there, stretched out on the sofa, asleep, with his mouth open, snoring gently through his nose, his mid-wifery bag on the floor beside him. Despite the empty glass of his usual reviver he looked all in, his face raddled, unshaven, a little gob of mucus on his bushy moustache. Not a pretty picture, but a human one. At least it was a face I knew I could live with, and with which perhaps, on a slack afternoon, I might go fishing in the Loch.

I turned without disturbing him and went out of the room. At the end of the hall, narrowed by an enormous mahogany hat and coat stand, on which the doctor's hats, of all varieties, sprouted like cabbages, the kitchen door was open. Still holding the suitcase I advanced and stood in the doorway. Neither of them saw me.

She was seated at the low kitchen table, wearing a slate-blue working wrapper, slewed a little sideways to ease the palpable, visible bulge in her middle, one elbow on the table, supporting the palm that lay against her slanted cheek, while with the other hand, which held a spoon, she was feeding Daniel from a bowl of broth. He sat close, leaning against her, with a grey shawl round his shoulders. That he'd had another bleeding was evident from his general air of apathy, a lassitude which indeed seemed to encompass and bind them. It was pure Picasso, his best blue period, and it went through me like a knife.

I put down the suitcase, my heart beating heavy in my side. They looked up and saw me. Not a sound came from either but on the child's face there dawned a look of wonder and surprise, and a pale delight. And on hers, unbelieving shock, melting slowly into a slow, single trickling tear.

I let it last for a long silent moment, a moment for which it seemed I had been waiting all my life. Just for that one silent moment, all the sickening personality that was Carroll dropped off me and I lived a million years of pure, undefiled joy. Then I was Carroll again.

'I'm back,' I said. A stupid statement of the obvious, but that is what I said.

They had begun to bang on the surgery door—presumably Ennis had been out all night at a case and had skipped the forenoon surgery altogether.

'I'd like some of that broth later,' I said, adding humbly, over my shoulder, as I turned into the side passage, 'if there's any left.' After all, I'd had nothing but a rock-hard bun at the Central buffet.

I went down the ten worn steps into the little cubicle that was the consulting room. I put on the not altogether clean white coat that hung on the back of the door, took up Ennis's stethoscope which lay on the small falldown desk, and clipped it behind my ears. Outside, they were now using their boots on the lower panels. I took six paces through the small waiting room and threw the door open.

'What the devil do you think you're doing, making all that bloody racket? I'm the new doctor here and I won't have it. Come in quietly or I'll throw your cards back at you.' Dead silence.

They came in quietly.

'Now, who's first?' I said, sitting down at the desk.

An old gammer of about seventy struggled in—black mutch, tartan plaid, worn but genteel black gloves. As she settled herself, wheezing away, I looked at her in silence, waiting for what must come, knowing her for what she was, a seasoned veteran of the welfare medical service, bursting with arthritis, neurtitis and bronchitis, with bunions and a probable varicose ulcer and, from the way she sat, constipation and piles. Could I stand it—the bitter medicine as before? Yes, with Dingwall sitting on my neck, Frank hanging round it, and that little package in the kitchen to be looked after, I would have to stick it out. At least, I would have to try.